No Regrets

MICHÈLE ANN YOUNG

SOURCEBOOKS CASABLANCA™
AN IMPRINT OF SOURCEBOOKS, INC.®
NAPERVILLE, ILLINOIS

Copyright © 2007 by Michèle Ann Young
Cover and internal design © 2007 by Sourcebooks, Inc.
Cover photo © Bridgeman Art Library

Published by Sourcebooks Casablanca, an imprint of Sourcebooks, Inc.
P.O. Box 4410, Naperville, Illinois 60567–4410
(630) 961–3900
Fax: (630) 961–2168
www.sourcebooks.com
ISBN-13: 978–1–4022–1016–7
ISBN-10: 1–4022–1016–7

Library of Congress Cataloging-in-Publication Data

Young, Michele (Michele Ann)
  No regrets / Michele Ann Young.
    p. cm.
  ISBN 978-1-4022-1016-7
  I. Title.

PR9199.4.Y69N6 2007
813'.6--dc22

                              2007018375

Printed and bound in United States of America.
QW 10 9 8 7 6 5 4 3 2 1

DEDICATION

This book is dedicated to my husband Keith,
who is my real life hero, and to my darling
daughters, Angela and Fiona, as well as to my
mother Joyce and my mother-in-law Kit, who are
always so proud of what I do.

One

THE FUTURE HAD NEVER LOOKED SO BLEAK. Carolyn Torrington gazed at the soapy plate she clutched in fingers raw from hot water. The white, shiny surface offered no hint of a change for the better. The gold-rimmed dish merely reflected a pair of worried brown eyes and a moon face framed by strands of damp hair. She had no one to blame but herself. She pushed her misted spectacles up her nose, trying not to choke on the strong smell of lye.

Setting the plate to drain beside the old stone sink, she hummed along with the to the sound of a lively Roger de Coverley wafting down the passage. Last year she had been a guest at the Grantham's annual hunt ball. No doubt this year she was simply a source for local gossip. They all knew about the plump Vicar's daughter who had rejected Norwich's most eligible bachelor only to find herself destitute. She winced and plunged her hands back into the suds. Bleak indeed. If she didn't find a paying position soon, she and her sisters would find themselves seeking asylum in the local workhouse.

She shuddered. Perish that thought. She'd pay any price to avoid that fate. Almost any price, she amended. Tomorrow she would visit every business in Norwich. Surely one of them required the help of a refined, well-read female. After that, she would seek rooms with a reasonable rent. Somehow, she must find a way to keep her family together.

Jaw clenched, she heaved the next stack of greasy plates into the sink, blinking as a sharp drop of water splashed up to join the moisture suddenly blurring her vision.

There was always the other way out, a small voice whispered in her head, tempting and wily. After staying away for a twelvemonth, he had presented himself at her door every day for a week. To agree to his demand would be like selling her soul to the devil, and after he'd caused all her troubles in the first place.

Perhaps not caused, she admitted with a sigh; she had his father and her own stubborn pride to shoulder that blame. But he wasn't helping matters by plaguing her daily.

And that was the reason the Granthams' medieval scullery offered the perfect hiding place. He'd never think to seek her here among the dirty dishes while the gentry danced the night away in the Tudor great hall. At midnight, the huntsmen would ride in for their trophy as ancient tradition demanded. Horses in a ballroom, for goodness' sake, and in this day and age. Did men never grow out of such nonsense?

Suddenly, the outside door crashed back against the stone wall. The antiquated flambeaux quivered in the iron wall sconces. Shadows danced wildly across the walls. The rush of cold air sent a shiver down Caro's back.

Heart pounding, a hot, wet plate pressed to her chest, she swung around to face the ebony horse and black-coated rider clattering beneath the great stone arch and into the vaulted chamber.

Think of the devil and he was sure to appear. Lucas Rivers, Viscount Foxhaven, her erstwhile best friend and rejected suitor, certainly fit the bill. Long jet hair scraped back in a queue, the flickering light chiselled his face into planes and sharp angles. A slash of black brow winged up to match the wry twist on his lips.

Her foolish heart tumbled over. By dint of will, she curbed a smile of welcome. The ton might find his antics amusing, but he'd get no encouragement from her, not any more.

How on earth had he managed to run her to earth? Or was he foxed and had simply lost his way? "If you are here for the trophy ride, you need to enter through the front door. Otherwise you will find the stables across the courtyard." She sounded remarkably calm given the stallion's size and the way it replaced good fresh air with the smell of leather and horse.

He cracked a familiar short laugh. "I know where the stables are." His deep voice resonated off the ancient stone walls and strummed every nerve in her body.

She quelled the flutter of awareness. "What do you want, Foxhaven?"

"You. Your sisters said I would find you here." He ran a disparaging glance around the cavernous room.

"I didn't think you'd sunk this low."

Not low enough, if his presence meant anything. A spurt of anger stiffened her shoulders. "There is nothing wrong with honest toil."

He glowered. "It won't wash, Caro. I'm not leaving until you agree to marry me."

"Then you stay and I will leave."

Metal-clad hooves striking sparks on the flagstone floor, the stallion moved deeper into the kitchen, blocking her exit. "I mean it," Foxhaven said.

She glared at him. "You had your answer a year ago. I see no reason to change my mind."

His sardonic gaze swept over the shapeless black gown and the mobcap she'd borrowed from Lizzie, her maid. "Really? I suppose you would sooner wash dishes than marry me?"

She shrugged. "You've had your little joke. Now, take yourself off, before something breaks and I get the blame."

"I'm leaving, all right."

Then why did it sound like a threat?

He clicked his tongue. The horse picked its way between her and the table, trapping her against the sink's hard edge at her back and a well-muscled thigh on a level with her nose.

She sucked in a breath. "Be careful, you idiot."

He lunged down and caught her around the waist. One swift jerk and she swooped off her feet. She screeched as the ground fell away in a sickening rush. For a moment, she dangled in his strong arm, then he settled her sideways across his lap with a grunt.

"Did you strain your back?" she asked with sugary sympathy.

"I expected you to be heavier."

Heavier? Wasn't it enough that she was larger than a Norfolk ewe before shearing, according to one local wit? And he was being kind.

The sight of the handsome face so close to hers froze any words she might have dredged up. The feel of his arm in the hollow under her ribs, his warm breath fanning her cheek, caused an unexpected flutter in the pit of her stomach. How could she respond in this shocking way to his touch when she ought to be angry?

Blast it, she was angry. She slammed her fist against his shoulder. A shock wave jolted up her arm as if she'd struck an oak tree. "Ouch. Foxhaven, put me down." To her disgust, she sounded utterly feeble.

"Not until you say yes." With a delicate touch he brought Maestro around the table and headed down the passage toward the assembled company.

A horrid premonition entered her mind. Her stomach dropped. "You can't mean to take me in there."

"Can I not?"

She grabbed the front of his coat and gave him a shake. "No." She kicked his booted calf.

He winced. The horse sidled, causing her to slip. She gasped and snatched at the reins. "I will not let you do this."

He encircled her wrists in a large gloved hand, trapping them against her chest.

Searing heat flooded her skin at the pressure of his knuckles against her breasts. She forced herself to ignore the casual intimacy. "I will be recognized."

"Then you should not have refused to speak to me each time I called this week. I tried to be civil.

You left me no choice." His square jaw set hard, he urged the horse along the gloomy hallway.

Music and talk and laughter from beyond the ornate wooden screen grew louder. Her stomach sank to the far distant flagstones. "Please don't shame me like this."

"Give me your promise to wed and I'll turn around right now. No one will ever know we were here."

"That is blackmail."

He shrugged and the stallion pranced forward. As they rounded the screen, her captor flung the tail of his full-skirted greatcoat over her head. "One last chance, Caro," he growled.

She ducked beneath his coat, clutching it close.

In the warm dark, her cheek rubbed against the rough wool of his jacket. The scent of sandalwood and male filled her senses, while his heart drummed a steady rhythm in her ear. If the whole thing weren't so dreadful, she might be tempted to cuddle closer.

The hum of conversation ceased. The music trailed off into squeaks and then silence. A raucous male laugh rang out.

"You're too early, Foxhaven," a deep voice yelled. "And whoever you have there, she has a neatly-turned ankle."

She inwardly groaned. Her skirts must be at her knees. Heat scalded her face as ripple of titters washed up against her. She wished it would float her out of the door, like flotsam. Or should it be jetsam? She never remembered which was which. And besides, she was more likely to sink than to float.

She peeped through the gap between Foxhaven's coat and his shoulder at a thin sliver of brightly lit world, at the crowd of avid faces eager for blood. If she jumped clear and ran with her head down, she might make it into the passageway behind the screen unrecognized. She started a downward slide.

Foxhaven tightened his grip. She pried at steely fingers, then bashed his knuckles with her fist. His sharp intake of breath gave her a moment of satisfaction, until the dratted horse lurched and she realized they were ascending the wide stone staircase alongside the dais. She clutched Foxhaven's coat sleeve with a frantic moan. If Maestro slipped, they would both be crushed. "You are mad," she muttered.

A chorus of complaints broke out around them.

"Now see here, Foxhaven," Lord Grantham howled from behind them. "Get that blasted animal out of here."

Foxhaven's thighs flexed beneath her bottom. "Easy, old fellow." He leaned forward for balance, his chin grazing the top of her head. She stilled, afraid a sudden movement might startle the nervous beast beneath them despite his master's iron control.

Awareness of male strength shimmered across her shoulders and tingled her spine. The way Foxhaven controlled the skittish stallion with his knees while holding her in place filled her with awe. No wonder people called him the Norfolk Nonesuch.

He chuckled, deep and low. An answering chord of excitement thrummed low in her belly, reminding her of wild rides across open fields and childish games of Knights of the Round Table. Only now her knight's armor had lost its luster.

Drat the man for enjoying her humiliation. Nothing he could say would make her forgive this night's work. She would give him a set-down the moment she got him alone. Her stomach flipped. She really didn't want to be alone with him.

The horse leveled out. She breathed a sigh of relief as the sounds from the ballroom faded behind them. Finally, a chance to talk some sense into the dissipated idiot. Maestro came to a stop, but footsteps trotted after them. She risked a peek.

One of Grantham's servants grabbed at a stirrup. "My lord, you must turn back."

"Stand aside," Foxhaven ordered. He lowered her to the ground, careful to set her well clear of the fidgety animal, then dismounted.

Run, her mind shouted. Her feet seemed to take root.

He grabbed her arm, tossed the reins to the slack-jawed lackey and snatching a lantern from the wall, pushed her inside the nearest chamber. "This will do."

She hadn't wanted this much privacy. Not with him.

The room smelled of mildew and damp. She straightened her spectacles. The faded blue bed hangings needed a good cleaning. Moths had made a feast of the tapestries on the walls, while a fine layer of dust coated the bedside table and the carved wooden armchair by the gray stone hearth. At least here there were no witnesses to her torture.

"Let him have his head and he'll be fine," Foxhaven said to the footman and slammed the door shut.

Someone pounded on the other side. "Open this damn door or Stockbridge will hear from me." Lord Grantham again.

"Good," Foxhaven shouted back, ramming the bolt home. "I'm sure my father will be delighted. He's in London."

"You numbskull," Grantham yelled. "I'm sending for the magistrate. God damn it, man, get this animal out of here." The noise of Maestro's hooves became faint along with the sound of Lord Grantham's threats.

Foxhaven placed the lantern on the stone mantel and turned to face her, legs astraddle, hands on lean buckskin-covered hips. Encased in a many-caped driving coat, his shoulders seemed to fill the room, while eyes as dark as chocolate and twice as tempting gazed at her. Unable to look away, she licked her dry lips. It had been months since she had tasted anything as luxurious as chocolate.

A slow smile dawned on his lean face, changing it from menacing to impossibly handsome, almost boyish. "Now, Miss Torrington. One good reason why we should not marry."

A year ago his resentment at being forced up to the mark by his father had been as obvious as storm clouds on a summer afternoon. He'd flung his proposal in her face and stood waiting for her answer like a man doomed to the gallows. The recollection still hurt. She backed into the soft wall covering, widening the distance between them. "My reasons are my own and the answer remains no. Now, let me go or face the consequences."

He raised a quizzical brow. "No one down there is going to care about a kitchen wench. Half the women are green with envy and most of the men are wishing they could get away with it."

"For goodness' sake, Lord Grantham is going to fetch the magistrate. Don't you see what you have done? I'll be ruined."

He flashed his too easy smile, the one he'd perfected in London, the one that spoke of knowledge and dissipation and set her pulse racing. "That's the whole point, I'm afraid," he said cheerfully. "Agree to marry me or I shall go down and announce whom I brought up here."

She desired above all things to blame him for her giving in, but she didn't believe for a moment that he would deliberately cause her harm. Not her friend and rescuer of old. In those days his smile had been honest and true.

Dark eyes mirthful, hands on hips, he stared down at her sprawled on the grassy bank of a swift flowing stream. Lucas. The sun burnished his dark hair and turned the sky behind his head a hazy blue. His gaze dropped to the bare leg she'd been rubbing. "What are you doing, Miss Torrington?"

She whisked her skirt-hem over the aching limb. "I tripped on a tuft of grass." She smiled to hide how awkward and foolish she felt and hoped her face wasn't too red. "I was picking flowers." She pointed to the scattered cornflowers she'd dropped when she fell. "I didn't hear you come along for the noise of the water." Otherwise she might have tried to jump up and hide her foolish predicament.

He strolled down the uneven bank and hunkered beside her, the full glory of his handsome features coming crisply into focus and halting her breath. "Are you injured?"

The concern in his tone soothed her bruised ego like balm, but did nothing to ease her physical pain. "I wrenched my ankle." Now she sounded pathetic. She held back the threatening tears that seemed more inclined to flow because of his sympathy. *"It is sure to feel better in a moment or two."*

"Let me see." He pushed her skirt a little way up her leg and ran a long gentle finger over the blue-tinged swelling just below her anklebone.

"That must hurt like the very devil," he said. He colored. *"I mean it must hurt a great deal."*

They must teach manners at school. He never used to be so formal.

"It is not as bad as it looks," she lied.

He pulled a handkerchief from his pocket. *"I'll bind it, and we'll see if you can walk."* He leaned over and dabbled the square of pristine white linen in the fast-running shallow water.

"You should be more careful," he chided over his shoulder. *"You might have fallen in the stream."*

"I know," she managed to reply, unable to do more than gaze at the fascinating contrast of jet hair curling over a stark white collar. Her pulse seemed to skitter.

"Perhaps this will help." He wrapped the sopping-wet square of white cotton around her foot. It felt deliciously cool on her heated skin. His knuckles brushed her calf as he knotted the fabric.

She inhaled a quick breath.

He glanced up sharply, removing his hand as if stung. *"Did that hurt?"*

She shook her head. *"It feels wonderful."* She felt heat rush from her breasts all the way up her neck to her face. *"I mean the cloth."* Oh darn it, now that sounded wrong.

His gaze dropped to her feet and a small smile played around his lips. *"You have nice ankles. You should take care* better care of them."

He thought she had nice ankles? Her blood ran cold then hot again. "I will. Look after them, I mean."

A faint color stained his lean cheeks. He glanced away and rose to his full height. My word, he'd grown tall, all broad shoulders and narrow hips, while in the eight months since he'd been away, she'd grown nothing but rounder.

She flipped her skirt over her feet.

He reached out a hand and pulled her to her feet. "I came to see if you wanted to go riding tomorrow, but it seems as if you will be confined to a couch for a while."

Just her luck.

"Can you walk?" he asked.

She took a tentative step. Pain shot up her leg. "Ouch." She would have fallen had he not caught her around the waist.

Tears blurred her vision. Suddenly, she was airborne, his heart thudding against her ear. "Lucas, no," she cried. "I'm too heavy."

"Rubbish. I could carry you all the way home." Brave words. For all that, he sounded a little breathless as he climbed over the tussocks to the roadside.

Caro clung to Lucas's neck. He had said she had nice ankles. No one ever noticed anything about her apart from her overlarge bosom.

His chestnut mare regarded them with interest as they approached. "Do you think you can climb up on Beauty with my help, and I'll walk you home?" he asked, his black eyes smiling down at her, teasing, but kind.

Much too kind to cause her any real damage. She lifted her chin. "Very well, Foxhaven, let us go downstairs and get it over with."

His amusement faded. In one long stride, he faced her toe to toe. He loomed over her, reminding her of his height and strength and width. "Devil take it, Caro. Why are you being so stubborn?"

The heat of his body encompassed her like a warm blanket. Eager trembles quaked in her chest. If only he really did want to marry her. "Please, Foxhaven, stop this farce. We are friends. Nothing more."

His hands dropped to her shoulders. Her stomach rolled over and her limbs developed the consistency of porridge cooked to perfection, not a single lump to hold her up.

One leather-gloved finger lifted her chin. She smothered a quick in-drawn breath at the sheer male beauty of his starkly modeled features. She forgot to breathe out.

His eyelids lowered a fraction. For one incredible heart-stopping moment, she thought he would kiss her.

"What would it take, Caro?" he asked.

She let go her breath. "Nothing will make me change my mind." The words scoured her throat.

It was so easy to deny his attraction when he wasn't standing right in front of her. She'd laughed at his exploits as reported by all the local gossips and congratulated herself on a narrow escape, even as she buried lost girlish dreams beneath calm good sense. Now her heart ached.

She jerked free of his grasp and stumbled the few short steps to the window.

"Bloody hell." Incredulity edged his voice. "Are you *scared* of me?"

Terrified she'd give in. He'd break her heart. Again. "Of course not."

He shook his head, sauntered to the chair and dropped into it. His long body seemed perfectly at ease, but beneath the studied indolence she sensed barely leashed tension. It crackled the air she breathed.

"You won't leave this room until I have your promise to wed." The deep timbre of his voice brushed her skin like the nap of finest velvet, seducing her will.

She clenched her arms around her waist. He didn't want to marry her. He never had. Tonight must be some sort of horrid prank, perhaps a bet with his rakish friends. She'd heard of such goings on in London, she just hadn't thought he'd try them on her. Unlike the Grantham boys when they were children, he had never stooped to ridicule. When she couldn't keep up during their marches across the fields, the triplets called her dumpling. He simply put her on guard duty. Perhaps he really had changed for the worst.

She flicked a glance at the door, measuring the distance.

"Don't think about making a run for it, my dear," he drawled. His voice dropped to a murmur and a wicked smile lifted one corner of his mouth. "You'd never make it through the door."

She gritted her teeth against his mocking tone. Not even the heir to an earldom could force her to marry. Her current spinster state proved it. She narrowed her eyes, trying to see past his cynical mask. "Why are you doing this?"

"For our families' sake?"

"Their wishes didn't seem to trouble you the last

time you asked. I would swear you were relieved when I refused you."

He grimaced. "I wasn't ready to settle down."

"Has something changed?" She managed some mockery of her own.

He slouched deeper in the chair. "My father will cut off my allowance if I can't persuade you to see reason by month's end."

She blinked. "What?"

He shook his head. "Sordid, is it not? I didn't think it mattered what he wanted, because my grandmother died and left me a tidy sum along with a property in Scotland. Somehow Father managed to convince her to change her will and tie the cash to my marrying according to his wishes." Regret filled his expression, softening his angled jaw. "It really is the very deuce."

He shifted in the chair, his gaze drifting over her shoulder as if he couldn't stand to look at her. And who would blame him, when she looked a worse fright even than usual? She just hadn't expected any of the guests to show their faces in the kitchen.

His glance flitted back to her face. He raised his right hand and tapped his lips with his forefinger. Once. Twice. He winked his right eye.

Their old signal for "come to my aid"? One of many coded messages they'd devised as children. She must be mistaken. She stared at him.

Again, two taps and a wink.

Disbelief clogged her throat. "No." She shook her head. "Lucas, you cannot play childish games about something as important as our futures"

"Caro, I've got to have that money." He sounded desperate.

Desperate enough to marry a roly-poly, bespectacled female. "Debts?" she hazarded.

"Something of the sort. Obligations."

Gambling debts, no doubt, like so many other young men loosed on the Town. The newspapers were full of them. And so were the debtor's prisons. It chilled her to think of so vibrant a man, her friend, locked inside dank stone walls.

No. She must not let him impose on her. She had her own responsibilities. "There must be hundreds of suitable females anxious to marry you."

He grimaced. "Not quite hundreds. A few perhaps."

"Then why does your father insist upon me?"

"He thinks you will act as a steadying influence, a vicar's daughter and all that." The expression on his face said she'd better not try anything of the sort. "He's ruining my life."

"Your life? What about mine?"

Head cocked to one side, he gave her a considering look. Another wild scheme being born in his razor-sharp brain, no doubt. She steeled herself for an argument.

"Why not make it a business arrangement?" he asked.

"That is what it is."

"Not the arrangement dreamed up by our fathers. Something to suit us."

It suited her to head down the backstairs before anyone caught her in here with him. She moved away from the window. "What kind of something?"

His brow lightened. "Neither of us wants to get married. Why not wed in name only?" He leaned forward, forearms on his thighs, dark gaze intent. "We will continue as friends, as always. No marital duties. You know, children and that sort of thing."

She might be the daughter of a gentleman vicar, but she had some idea of the duties he meant. Disappointment left her feeling empty, but unsurprised. She didn't have the kind of attributes to attract a man of his ilk. She shook her head. "No."

"If you won't do it for yourself, consider your sisters."

"You would do well to leave my sisters out of your machinations. It is bad enough that I am involved."

"You won't need to wash dishes for a living." He flashed a breathtaking smile, all seduction and even white teeth.

She became suitably breathless. "I'm not doing it for a living. I'm helping Lizzie."

Dark eyebrows rose in disbelief.

She let go a small sigh. "I couldn't pay her wages this month, but she wouldn't hear of getting another position. When Grantham's butler put the word out in the village for extra help this evening, she took the job with her sister. When Nell became ill I offered to take her place so Lizzie would not lose the money."

"Where is Lizzie?"

"She's helping in the ladies' withdrawing room. I agreed to wash dishes, where I *expected* no one would see me."

"Together we can make these problems go away."

"I prefer them to the sort of fraud you propose. What would your father say?"

"He won't know unless you tell him. Think about it. Neither of us will have to worry about finances again." He cast her a sly glance. "What will you do when the new vicar arrives? Where will you live?"

He'd spotted her weakness, of course. Now he would pick away at her defenses until she raised a white flag. Defeat stared her in the face. "I have ideas."

"Surely there's something you want, something you need for yourself?"

She had a whole well of unfulfilled desires, but what she wanted meant nothing if it didn't help her sisters. "A season in Town?"

His eyes widened. He seemed to have trouble replying.

Heat rushed to her face. She ran shaking fingers down her stiff bombazine skirts. Idiot. He meant he wanted to buy her something. If he took her to London, he'd have to introduce her to his friends as his wife. He'd be far too ashamed. Perhaps she'd found the perfect way to hold him at bay after all.

"Very well. If that is what you want," he said in rush as if afraid she'd change her mind.

She stared at him in wide-eyed astonishment. "You do realize I will need you to escort me to balls and routs? My sisters will need a knowledgeable chaperone when it is their turn to come out." She took a deep breath. "And they will each need a dowry."

He nodded, albeit a little stiffly. "I understand perfectly. Is it yes?"

She nibbled at her top lip. Since a married lady didn't need to attract young men to dance and flirt, she might actually enjoy herself. She'd certainly never have another chance to marry and this might well be her one opportunity to see something of the world beyond Norwich. She could visit the theater, see the Tower, and perhaps catch a glimpse of the royal wedding. The newspapers touted Princess Charlotte and Prince Leopold as a fairy tale couple. A long time ago she had believed in fairy tales and happy endings. "If we married, I could do just as I please?"

A frown creased his brow. "Within reason." His expression cleared. "We both could. You know, once my inheritance is sewn up, we could end it whenever it suits us. I would ensure you and your sisters were financially secure, of course."

Her head spun. "A divorce, you mean?"

"If we marry in Scotland it can be arranged, 'though it wouldn't be entirely free of scandal."

She frowned. Was this another of his tricks to bend her to his will? "Are you sure?"

A shadow of something akin to pain flickered in his eyes. She put it down to a trick of the uncertain torchlight when he curled his lip in sardonic amusement. "I didn't entirely waste my time at university, you know. What do you say? Is it a bargain? We certainly got on well enough before they threw this wedding nonsense in our paths."

"You did," she muttered, refusing to think about happier times.

She rubbed her chilly arms and turned to the window, vaguely aware of the torches twinkling along the crenulated courtyard wall. A bargain? He was proposing a convenient financial arrangement to end in shameful divorce. It sounded so cold and so daunting, particularly the part about the divorce. Her father would have been horrified. Her stomach roiled. A strange weight pressed down on her chest, something dark and slightly sad, like the sensation of finding a baby bird thrown from the nest by a cuckoo.

She swung around to face him full on. "Are you sure there isn't anyone else you can ask?"

He stiffened, his smile fading. "I'm sorry, I didn't realize you found my company so abhorrent." His voice sounded harsh, strained. Asking for help clearly stung his noble pride.

Guilt washed through her. "I don't, not really. I just thought you might prefer...." Someone he would not be ashamed to show off to his tonnish friends. The words remained stuck in her throat.

He shook his head in a slow regretful movement. "There is no time. I must have the money now."

He wouldn't be here if he had another option. A painful but honest confession. She chewed her top lip. He hadn't always been a careless rake. As a boy, he'd been gentle, sometimes rather too sensitive for his father's rough tongue. A true friend would try to turn him from his destructive path. Her beloved Papa would have insisted she make the attempt.

If she agreed, she'd be living under the same roof with him as a friend, pretending to be his wife to the outside world. It sounded like a cross between heaven and purgatory.

It all came back to money, or rather their lack thereof. If she went ahead with this, Lucas would pay off his debts and the girls could return to the luxury of their old life, maybe even better. Lizzie wouldn't need to find other employment and everyone's future would be secure. If she'd accepted him the first time, they might have had a chance at a real marriage, and perhaps her father would still be alive.

So much of the blame for their desperate circumstances rested squarely at her door. How could she refuse for the sake of her pride?

She stared at his darkly handsome face, at the fingers drumming on his knee, and crushed the flicker of hope that he might someday see her as more than a friend. If she did this, it would be with her eyes wide open.

With an impatient hand, he swept a lock of hair from his brow. A long black hank escaped its ribbon and fell in a glossy wave to his shoulder. It tempted her touch. If they married, she'd be tempted every day. But not if she stuck to their bargain. She drew in a steadying breath. "I'll do it."

He smiled.

She didn't trust that smile. Not any more. "I want the agreement in writing."

His jaw dropped in open-mouthed shock. "Impossible."

Two

"**W**HY IS IT IMPOSSIBLE?" SHE ASKED.

The golden tones of her skin, which had once reminded him of sunshine and carefree days, had faded to sallow. In her ugly black gown, she looked more fragile than he remembered, less well-rounded, as if she hadn't had a decent meal for months. He felt like a bully.

"This is as much for your benefit as for mine, you know," he muttered. "If anyone were to discover such an agreement, it would be construed as collusion, and a divorce would be disallowed."

She wrinkled her nose. "Oh."

The vulnerability in her huge, amber eyes caused a pang of guilt deep in a place he'd thought frozen out of existence. Vulnerable? What a jest. She'd defied the mighty Lord Stockbridge for months. No mean feat for a woman. It had taken Lucas years to pluck up the same measure of courage.

"If it is to be a business arrangement, we should have something in writing," she said.

There it was again, the intractability that seemed to run down her spine like an iron bar. Hell. Why quibble over a piece of paper if it got him what he wanted? "As you wish. But it must remain a secret."

"It will be our private agreement."

He nodded toward the bedside table. "See if that drawer has writing materials, will you? Lord Grantham will throw a fit if I go down and ask for paper and pens."

Lucas could imagine at least one lascivious use for a quill. The thought of drawing a feather over Caro's naked lush form and bringing her voluptuous flesh to a state of quivering anticipation stirred his blood, and things farther south.

The ancient bed looked strong enough to endure an energetic romp. If he captured that ripe mouth in a kiss, convinced her to part her lips and let him taste her sweetness . . . His breath shortened.

Was he mad? This was Caro, his straitlaced childhood friend and respected companion in countryside forays, not an opera dancer.

Fortunately she noticed nothing of his body's response to his wayward thoughts as she hurried to the table. She pulled out an inkstand and paper and set them on the dusty surface. "It has everything we need."

He dragged his chair over. After a moment's thought, he dipped the quill in the ink and wrote: This agreement is between Miss Carolyn Torrington and Lucas Rivers, Viscount Foxhaven, each being of sound mind and body. The parties agree to marry as a financial arrangement only. Both are free to live their lives as they see fit until one or the other decides to divorce. At that time, said Lucas Rivers will provide an annual income of one thousand pounds to Carolyn Rivers, née Torrington, until she marries another.

Signed this twentieth day of March in the year of our Lord eighteen hundred and sixteen.

He added his name with a scrawling flourish. "I think that should do it."

She shifted the paper out of his shadow and leaned close, peering over the top of her spectacles. She read it through twice.

Did she think he would trick her? The thought made his skin crawl. Once upon a time, he never doubted her trust.

"It seems fine," she said at last. She signed her name neatly beside his.

Take that, Father. Lucas wanted to grin, to shake her hand, but her air of forced resolution stifled the moment. It was as if she'd made a pact with the devil. He felt a twinge of disappointment. He might not have deserved her hero-worship from the days of their childhood, but did she have to view him in such a bad light?

No matter. He'd do his best to make their bargain work. And just let his old man try to interfere.

She folded the note, placed it in her apron pocket, and gestured toward the door. "Would you mind not making an announcement tonight?"

Now what thoughts were going on behind those honey eyes? "You can't change your mind, Caro. I have your agreement in writing. We leave for Gretna the moment I collect my carriage from Stockbridge Hall." Even as he said the words, he knew he wouldn't press her if she balked.

She glanced down at herself with a small, self-deprecating smile. "I'm not exactly dressed for a ball."

He released a breath. She had given her word, and she'd keep it. The tightness across his shoulders eased. He grinned. "No, that you are not."

"I will use the back stairs and let Lizzie know I'm leaving."

In a generous mood at the outcome of what could have ended in disaster, he nodded. "Good idea. I promise you won't regret this."

The corners of her mouth lifted a fraction. "Let us hope not. I will meet you at Rose Cottage in two hours."

"One."

She opened her mouth to speak, but then nodded and scurried from the room without a backward glance.

He flung himself into the chair. Damn his father for leaving him no option but to gull a green girl like Caro. A point of light reflected in the toe of his boot; he flexed his ankle, watching the light play on the shiny black leather. A season in London and all it entailed. The wretch had turned the tables on him quite handily. Perhaps she wasn't quite as naive as she appeared.

A vision of being led by the nose to a host of stuffy functions flashed through his mind. Hell, no! He had to take care of his lads.

He pushed up from the chair in a burst of energy.

The sooner he got this wedding out of the way and got his hands on his inheritance, the sooner he would finalize things with Lady Bestborough.

※　　※　　※　　※

"I cannot believe you are really married," Alexandra said.

The bed ropes squeaked as she settled herself more comfortably.

Caro leaned sideways to catch a glimpse of the slender, blonde, and beautiful sixteen-year-old in the dressing table mirror. "I can hardly believe it myself." Nor could she believe she was actually going through with her mad idea to go with Lucas to London.

Neat in black gown and white apron, and wielding hairpins like pitchforks, Lizzie shifted to block Caro's view.

"Be still, my lady. Havey cavey, I call it. Running off to Gretna Green with a man you hadn't a good word for a year ago."

"Lizzie, enough. What is done is done." A sense of foreboding made Caro's heart flutter. It might be undone all too quickly if Lucas found her tiresome.

Alex slid off the bed, squeezed past Lizzie, and rested her elbows amid the ribbons and tortoiseshell pins on the dressing table. Her blue eyes glowed. "Well, I think it is the most romantic thing."

Caro's stomach clenched at the thought that Alex might follow her example. "I do not recommend it, I assure you. We bounced over the worst roads in England for three days until my teeth were loose."

A furrow formed in Alex's marble brow. "But to

be married over the anvil . . ."

"It was cold. I had not eaten a hot meal for hours, not even a cup of coffee, and the blacksmith was no gentleman." She shuddered. The man who performed the ceremony would have horrified her father. "It was not the least bit romantic."

"Oh," Alex said, picking up a pink ribbon and weaving it through her fingers. "I still do not see why we cannot all go to London with you."

Caro wanted to agree. She would feel a whole lot less nervous about the adventure with her sisters in tow and under her watchful eyes.

Lucas had all but choked on his brandy in the inn after the ceremony when Caro suggested that very thing. Perhaps she should tell him she had changed her mind about going at all?

Alex held the ribbon to her throat and pressed against Caro to catch her reflection. "What do you think?"

"I don't think it goes with that nice new blue gown," Lizzie said, her sniff a punctuation mark. "Move over, do, Miss Alex."

Alex craned her neck to see the back of her blue, sprigged muslin. "I love this gown. Foxhaven is very generous."

Openhanded to the point of wild extravagance. "Yes," Caro said. "And it must have cost a fortune to rent this house so close to Norwich."

"I suppose so." At Caro's glare, Alex blushed. "It is much nicer than Rose Cottage." She glanced around. "And at least we have a bedroom each."

Lizzie grasped Alex's shoulders and shifted her aside. "How am I ever to get this hair of Lady

Foxhaven's looking decent with you standing in the way, Miss Alex? We can't have her going to London with her hair all straggly, now can we?"

Lady Foxhaven. How strange it sounded. A flutter of nerves danced in Caro's stomach, and she glanced down at her rose-colored brocade. Festooned around her neck and down the front with ribbons—it had been her father's favorite. "Do you think Foxhaven will approve of this gown?" Lucas had recommended she order a new wardrobe in London.

Lizzie glowered into the mirror. "He should be glad to see his bride when he hasn't seen you for two weeks, no matter what you have on. You are newly-weds."

Caro grew a little warm. She hated the lies that tripped off her tongue, but she could hardly announce the agreement she and Lucas had made. "Foxhaven says all the best houses in Town are snapped up early in the season. He had to go ahead to ensure us decent accommodations."

Lizzie snorted. "I've never heard the like of it, leaving a bride on her honeymoon."

She would never have a honeymoon, and there was no sense mourning the fact. Aware of Lizzie's suspicious glance, she blinked away the mistiness in her eyes.

"That last pin made my eyes run."

"Be careful, Lizzie," Alex said.

"You can't reform a rake." Lizzie's tone was dark as she fixed another wisp in place. "You said that to your poor dear papa, rest his soul. And he supported you. Why didn't you say yes at the time? Then at least Lord Stockbridge wouldn't have badgered him into an early grave."

Oppressed by the sense of guilt she'd carried since her father died, her shoulders sagged. "I don't wish to discuss it, Lizzie."

Running feet sounded on the stairs outside, followed by stifled giggles.

"Are you finished yet?" called Jacqueline on the other side of the door. "May we come in?" The younger girls had escaped the drawing room and Miss Salter, their governess, for the second time that morning.

Stepping back to admire her handiwork, Lizzie frowned. "It's the best I can do."

Caro nodded. "You have done your best, Lizzie. Thank you. No one can turn a sow's ear into a silk purse." Nor yet a sow into a fashionable gazelle.

"Caro!" Alex exclaimed crossly, and threw open the door. Lucy and Jacqueline danced over the threshold in new green muslin gowns. It was as if her parents had had two families. First her, and then seven years later, Alex, Lucy, and Jacqueline in quick succession. If only Mother had not died giving birth to the stillborn son and heir, who would have kept their home within the family, things might have turned out very differently for them all.

Lucy glued her gaze on Caro, her eyes like jade medallions, her curly red hair springing in little corkscrews around her face. "You look scrumptious."

Caro laughed. She knew she was mousy, not a glorious auburn like Lucy, nor blonde and blue-eyed like the other two. Mouse, plain and simple. With emphasis on the plain. The worst possible combination of her exotic French mother and sandy-haired father: brown hair, nondescript light-brown eyes, skin that would never be alabaster, no matter how much milk she used, and a figure like an overblown rose, when the fashion required elegant willows. But her younger sisters' youthful adoration glowed in her heart.

"You look like an iced cake," pronounced Jacqueline, dancing around her.

"A cake?" Caro said, uncomfortably aware of a surfeit of ruffles covering her overly bountiful bosom and generous hips. She darted a glance in the mirror.

"Silly," Lucy said. "She looks all grand, like a titled lady."

A small shiver ran through Caro at the thought of the title and all it should mean, but did not.

"I don't want you to go." Jacqueline's voice sounded as thick and damp as a foggy morning.

A shadow passed through the room, glowing faces dimmed, eyes clouded.

Caro forced a bright smile. "The season ends in July. I will be back before you notice I'm gone, and in a year's time, it will be Alex's turn to come-out. Then we will all go to London."

"A whole year." Alex flounced to the window.

"I don't mind waiting," Lucy announced, bouncing down on the bed and smoothing her new green skirts. "When it's my turn, you will know all the finest people and take me to all the best parties."

"I miss you already," Jacqueline said, her sapphire eyes moist.

Poor Jacqueline—she barely remembered Mama, and with Papa so remote the last few years before his death, Caro had come to feel more like a mother than a sister. Caro reached out and enfolded her in a big hug, ignoring the sniffles against her gown and the potential for wrinkles. "No you won't. You will be so busy having fun with Miss Salter here at the new house, she will have to remind you to write."

"I won't forget," Lucy said.

Caro reached around and pulled her off the bed and into her arms. "I hope not."

"Mind your dress, my lady," Lizzie said.

A forlorn expression crossed Alex's face. Over the heads of the younger two, Caro gave her the special big-sister smile she reserved for when the younger two were bothersome. Alex rushed forward and threw her arms around them all and pressed her face against Caro's shoulder.

A stomach-churning flutter in her stomach caught at Caro's breath. Perhaps she should stay here, safe within the bounds of her family. The idea sounded as tempting as the bonbons she'd tucked into her reticule to keep up her spirits on the ride to London.

Coward. This time she wouldn't be alone against the wall in a frumpy gown and spectacles; she'd be a fashionable, married lady. And although Lucas didn't feel more than friendship for her, she trusted him to keep her safe. At least, he would as long as he remembered her existence.

This trip was a longed-for adventure, and, like facing a high wall on a horse, she needed to hold her breath and fly.

She gathered her sisters closer, drawing courage from their slender bodies.

"Tsk tsk," Lizzie said, leaning against the door, wiping her eyes on her apron. "Lord Foxhaven's carriage has been outside for fifteen minutes or more. Let your sister finish getting ready."

Caro kissed each girl in turn on their soft, smooth cheeks, tasting salty tears. A hot, hard lump blocked her throat, making her laugh shaky and breathless. "Go and put on your hats and coats, and wait with Miss Salter in the drawing room. We will go out together, and you can stand on the step and wave goodbye."

"Me first," Lucy said.

"No, me." Jacqueline raced for the door.

Giggling and pushing, they squeezed through the opening.

With a sedate flick of her skirts, Alex followed. "You can't be first," she called out. "I'm the oldest."

Caro watched them go, her heart aching, and then glanced at Lizzie with a rueful smile. "I'm glad you are coming to London with me. I shall not feel quite so lonely."

"Lonely?"

Oh heavens, she had said too much. She peeked in the mirror and ran her hands down the front of her gown. "I really am three times the size of Alexandra."

"That girl eats like a horse."

"And I'm the size of one."

"Buxom, your Papa called it. You need to eat proper, or you'll get sick. I'm right glad you asked me to go along, my lady. You need someone to keep an eye on you in that there heathen city."

Rolling her eyes at Lizzie's foreboding expression, Caro followed her sisters down the stairs.

❉　　❉　　❉　　❉

Lucas's head ached abominably. He really shouldn't have allowed the Grantham triplets to drag him off to a cockfight at the George Inn, but it had been impossible to dampen their enthusiasm for a belated bachelor party. They'd mourned the end of his freedom in prime style, little knowing the joke was on them.

He stared morosely at the Torrington front door. He'd been married for three weeks, and now he had to keep his end of the bargain and take Caro to London. She'd wanted time to settle things with her sisters after the wedding, so he'd gone to London to rent a house. Now he was back, and he'd been waiting for what felt like hours.

The fresh east wind that sent gray clouds scudding across a watery blue sky whipped a strand of hair into his eyes. He hunched deeper into his greatcoat. He could go inside and wait, but the thought of a house full of young females curdled his blood. What the hell was keeping Caro, anyway?

"Shall I walk 'em, my lord?" asked Tigs, his diminutive tiger. Stretched to his full height, the wizened man held the tossing heads of the spirited team of grays, while the footman kept the reins from tangling from his perch on the box. Hitched to the back of the carriage, Maestro lifted a back hoof and gazed his reproach.

Lucas shook his head. Surely she couldn't be much longer?

Damn it. If marriage meant hanging about waiting, he already didn't like it.

The front door opened. At last!

The three younger Torringtons poured out in a swirl of warm wool cloaks and beribboned bonnets, followed by a tall, gray-haired woman, Miss Salter, their governess. He winced as their twittering chatter bounced around inside his skull.

Last to emerge, Caro lingered on the steps, hugging and kissing her sisters in turn. The tawny velvet cloak he'd sent over yesterday suited her unusual coloring much better than black. With fashionable clothes, something more flattering to her fulsome figure, and a little town bronze, she might even look striking.

Caro glanced over at him with a hesitant smile, a tiny curve of her full lips.

His wife. A strange warmth stole into his chest, something he hadn't felt for a long time. If his head wasn't aching like the inside of a kettledrum being marched up the hill by the Duke of York, he might have smiled back.

Lizzie pulled her black shawl tight, as if daring the wind to tug it loose, and marched down the path to the carriage. He scowled. He'd wanted to leave the self-opinionated maid behind.

A pain stabbed his temples.

He dragged himself to the front door, and in a blur he shook hands with the stick of a governess, bade the tearful sisters farewell, and then escorted Caro to the carriage.

"Are you ready?" he croaked through a dry throat, holding in check his mad instinct to flee.

She nodded, ran a considering gaze over him, and frowned.

That frown didn't bode well. His stomach felt

heavy, as if a lead ball had landed in its pit. "What?"

"You might have worn a decent cravat instead of that handkerchief thing."

A wedding didn't give her the right to dictate what he wore. "I never wear cravats. Not unless I absolutely have to."

Huge in her oval face, her fawn eyes stared back at him. "It is the correct attire for a gentleman, surely."

The belcher knotted around his throat tightened as if he'd made a noose and volunteered to put his neck in it. "How I choose to dress isn't really your concern."

She recoiled, pressing her lips together as if to swallow another admonition. After a moment's hesitation, she rested a hand on his proffered arm and stepped up into the carriage.

He regretted his harsh tone, if not the words. Bloody hell. He hadn't expected her to take her wifely role to heart. "Spring 'em," he growled at Tigs, and dove in after her.

"Good-bye," the girls chorused as Caro leaned forward and waved from the window.

He pressed his head against the squabs and closed his eyes against the hammers of hell. Damn his father for leaving him no choice.

❊   ❊   ❊   ❊

Rain dripped from the footman's tricorn hat onto his shoulders as he held open the carriage door for Caro to alight into a dull grey afternoon.

"Surely we haven't arrived already?" Caro said, glancing at Lizzie on the opposite seat.

Lizzie shrugged. "It's only been two hours since

we stopped for lunch."

Peering through the steady downpour, Caro made out the shape of a low building beyond the footman's shoulder. "Is this the Red Lion?"

The servant shook his head. "His lordship's orders, my lady. We were to stop at the next inn."

Unwilling to argue with a footman, Caro allowed him to help her down. A gust of wind swept across the field, driving icy rain into her face. She shivered.

Lucas had elected to follow on Maestro, rather than join Caro and Lizzie in the coach, citing his need for fresh air. He must be soaked to the skin by now.

She gazed at the empty road behind them. "Where is Lord Foxhaven?"

"The Guv'ner stopped to blab with a square-rigged cove on the toper," Tigs said, on tiptoes at the bridles.

Caro frowned. "A cove?"

"A regular chaw bacon," Tigs said.

Jumping down from the step, Lizzie fixed Tigs with a baleful stare. "Enough of your cant, you worthless lump o' lard."

Over the past two days, Caro had learned there was no respect between these two. She stifled her exasperation. "Will one of you please explain?"

"His lordship stopped to speak to a country gentleman. There's a mill he wants to see," the footman offered.

Lucas had never expressed any interest in farming. "Why would he want to see a mill?"

"'Tweren't a mill,"Tigs muttered. "'Twere a setting-to. Cocks."

"Cockfighting, my lady," Lizzie whispered in Caro's damp ear.

Her heart sank. How like Lucas to go off when something more interesting presented itself. She retrieved her spectacles from her reticule and put them on. The full impact of the shabby hostelry struck her like the sting of the rain on her face.

"The Bell and Cat?" Scorn dripped from Lizzie's tongue. "We can't stay here."

"His lordship's orders," the footman said, shutting the carriage door. "He said he would meet us at the next inn. This is it."

They certainly couldn't stand outside waiting for Lucas. With anger stiffening her spine, Caro lifted her sodden skirts clear of the puddles and horse manure dotting the courtyard and marched through the front door into a dingy, low-ceilinged room. The smell of stale ale and smoke stopped her short. A taproom. This inn didn't even boast a parlor.

The innkeeper's jaw dropped open in his gray-whiskered face as he looked up from behind the bar. "'Ere, who are you?"

If that was his usual greeting to his customers, it was no wonder the place was deserted. On the other hand, farm laborers would be unlikely to be idling the afternoon away even in such a downpour.

Caro forced a smile, despite her desire to strangle Lucas right at that moment. "I am Lady Foxhaven, and I need two rooms for the night and accommodation for my servants. And a pot of tea."

Brushing past trestle tables scattered around the room, she made her way to the hearth. She drew off her gloves and held her numb fingers to the meager warmth of the fire.

"I don't cater to overnight guests, and if I had rooms, I wouldn't let them to the likes of you," the landlord pronounced.

Speechless at his rudeness, Caro swung around to face him.

"How dare you speak to her ladyship like that," Lizzie said from the doorway. As terrifying as a full-rigged warship, she sailed toward him. "His lordship'll have your hide, he will, when he arrives."

Leaning back to avoid Lizzie's wagging finger, the landlord shook his head. "You ain't quality. Not stopping here, you ain't. And I don't got no rooms. Travelers sleep in the commons. Always has." He gestured to the room around him.

Sleep in here? Bubbles of anger simmered in Caro's blood. If she could get her hands on Lucas right now . . . She took a deep breath, willing herself to remain calm. "Do you have any private rooms?"

The landlord stared at her with weighing eyes.

"I'll pay you well," she said, knowing full well that if Lucas didn't arrive, she would be in dire straits.

"Aye," the landlord mumbled. "There's a room in the attic ye can have. It's small. I can take a cot up for your wench, there."

Lizzie bristled, but Caro sent her a quelling glance, and for once, Lizzie held her tongue.

Glancing past Caro through the grimy window, the innkeeper said, "Rest of servants has to sleep with them nags of yourn in the barn."

It was the best she could do without Lucas. "We'll eat supper in our room."

"All I got is the rest of the stew me cooking

wench made for me dinner. She's gone home now. I can heat it up."

Dinner in the country came at noon. Well, they would eat either the leftover stew or the bread and cheese they'd brought for the journey. After the chill of the carriage ride, the thought of cold food made her shiver. "That will be fine."

"This way then, your bloody highness." Mumbling under his breath, he led the way upstairs.

❈   ❈   ❈   ❈

The creak of the rickety door jolted Caro fully awake. A tattoo beat in her chest. "Who is it?"

"Caro?" The timbre of Lucas's deep voice cut through the sound of Lizzie's snores. "Why are you in here?"

He raised a candlestick. Outlined in the doorway, with his hair loose around his shoulders and his shirt open at the neck, he looked thoroughly disheveled and rakishly handsome.

A strange little pulse stirred in her stomach. She clutched the blanket they'd brought in from the carriage up to her chin. Now didn't seem the right moment for the choice words she'd rehearsed in the hours before sleep finally claimed her. "Go away."

"Why are you here?" He stumbled further into the room. "Ouch." He rubbed his shin and stared down at Lizzie on the cot beside the bed. "What is Lizzie doing in my room?"

"It is not your room, Lucas. It is mine."

He swayed and slapped one hand against the sloping ceiling for support. "The landlord said . . ."

Pent-up resentment sprang to life. "I don't care

what the landlord said. Go away."

"Where am I to sleep?"

"Right at this moment, I really don't care. Try the barn."

He rocked on his heels, pointing to the bundle of sheets and blankets on the floor in the corner. "I could use that."

Caro repressed a shudder. "If you want to wake up lousy, feel free to take them with you." The bedding in the room wasn't fit for animals, let alone humans. If they'd been able to open the window, she would have thrown it all out, including the mattress she'd stuffed under the bed.

Swaying, he gazed down at her, his glittering onyx eyes holding an expression different from anything she'd ever seen there before. Hot flames danced between them, and heat tingled from her head to her heels as he stared at her bosom. To her horror, her breasts felt fuller and larger than ever.

He raised his gaze to her face. "Your hair is very long," he mumbled as if his tongue didn't work properly. "It has streaks of gold." He cast her his familiar, lopsided smile. "I'd love to see it unbound."

The pulse in her abdomen jolted. A frisson of awareness ran down her spine. She recognized it for what it was. Attraction. If only they had more than an artificial marriage.

He leaned forward, his lips teasing, yet inviting. He was going to kiss her. Her heart beat twice as fast as normal, choked her throat, emptied her mind. An urgent desire to touch the skin at his throat, to run her fingers through his hair, overwhelmed her. She raised her face, closed her eyes on a sigh.

Brandy fumes wafted over her. She opened her eyes and stared into his blurred, reddened eyes. He was foxed. If he wasn't, he wouldn't think of coming to her room. He'd mistaken her for one of his other women.

And no matter how much she wanted to know the taste of his lips on hers, or what she felt deep inside, she would not take advantage of his error. It would be disastrous. For both of them.

She forced calm words past her thundering heart. "Do go away, Lucas, before you wake Lizzie. I'll speak to you in the morning."

"That sounds omni . . . onimus." He shook his head. "Ominous." He grinned and clutched at the beam in the ceiling as he lurched to one side.

With a gasp, she scooted back against the wall. He looked as if he might fall on her.

He shifted his weight, planting his feet firmly apart, and shoved a hand into the pocket of his coat. He pulled out a heavy-looking purse with a look of triumph on his slack features. "I won."

Tired, uncomfortable, and cold, she could no longer stem the tide of her temper. "Well, good for you." She grabbed up the book she'd tried to read when she couldn't sleep and threw it at his head.

Instead of dodging, he just stood there. It glanced off his cheek. He dropped the candle.

Caro dove to the floor, snatching it up before the room burst into flames.

As if numb, he watched her regain her feet. "Nice wife you are," he mumbled. "Can't even congratulate a chap. Just like my father." He tore the candle from her grasp and stomped off down the stairs.

Lizzie muttered and turned over. How on earth had she slept through such a commotion?

Fumbling in the dark, the echo of the candle flame dancing in the back of her eyes, Caro crept shivering across the room and closed the door. Next time, she'd make sure the door had a lock and key. Oh, please, don't let there be a next time.

❊　　❊　　❊　　❊

Marriage had ruined his untrammeled life. Lucas stared into the brown sludge the innkeeper called coffee and gagged. He pushed the cup aside and cradled his head in his hands. Encountering a straw, he pulled it from his hair and tossed it into the fire.

Damn it. Since when was it a crime to enjoy a bit of sport and a few drinks with some fellows?

Since you married Caro, he told himself.

Other chaps' wives didn't give them a bear-garden jaw for their nightly entertainments. It must be her puritanical upbringing.

His stomach rolled. If he was going to cast up his accounts, he ought to dash outside, except he didn't have the strength. He slouched lower in his seat, hoping his head would cease to spin.

He'd endured the edge of her scathing tongue upon his arrival from the stables this morning, finding her fully clothed, with her foot tapping on the bare boards. She had reminded him of his promise to establish her in society, not among the dregs of the English countryside, and had left him to ponder his sins.

Only he couldn't exactly remember what he'd done to make her so angry.

A picture flashed through his sluggish brain. Caro, bathed in the golden light of a candle, staring at him with luminous eyes.

"Anything else I can get you, your lordship?" The greasy landlord rubbed his hands together.

"The shot."

The gray beard split in a yellow-toothed grin, and the innkeeper slapped his accounting on the trestle table. "I expect that there trull was right glad to see you last night."

Trull? Lucas frowned as he counted out a handful of coins. He'd been to a brothel? "What?"

"Nice little armful up in the attic. Right cheeky she is, as plump and juicy as a piglet, and that wench of her'n. I charged you for her room, like she said."

Lucas jerked his head up and thought it might fall off. Glorious full breasts outlined by candlelight, their twin peaks pressed again fine linen—it filled his mind like a vision. Bloody hell. He'd gone to her room by mistake. He touched the tender bruise on his cheekbone. Devil take it. What had he done?

"I hope your lordship found everything up there to your liking." The innkeeper wheezed a laugh.

Lucas leaped to his feet and grabbed the smirking man by the shirtfront. His stomach heaved. "Stop your mouth or I'll stop it for you. You are speaking about my wife."

With his face turning red and his breathing labored, the landlord flapped his arms. "No offense, your worship," he gasped. "I just thought . . ."

Lucas dropped him. "Don't. You lack the where-withal."

With suddenly clear vision, Lucas took in the

filthy floor and the tables coated in grease and inhaled the lingering stench of unwashed bodies. He put a shaking hand to his eyes. He'd brought Caro, his best friend, to a hellhole and then insulted her in her bedroom. No wonder she could barely bring herself to be civil this morning.

That was the last time. No more Lucas the dissolute rake. He no longer needed the mask. His marriage would keep his father from meddling in his affairs, and besides, he needed his wits about him to get his lads comfortably settled in the country.

Three

ORE RAIN. ONLY NOW, INSTEAD OF MUDDY fields and dripping hedgerows, slick cobbles and black umbrellas in narrow streets met Caro's curious gaze.

London. A tremor of excitement mixed with trepidation ran down her spine.

"Nasty, noisy, dirty place," Lizzie muttered, staring out of the window on the other side.

The noises were indeed deafening. The sounds of horses and vehicles of every kind mingled with street criers shouting out their wares.

Peering back behind the coach, the glass cold against her cheek, Caro tried to see Lucas and Maestro, but it seemed as if a dozen vehicles blocked her view. These last two days, he'd chosen to ride, no doubt weary of Lizzie's complaints and bored with female company in general.

"This must be Mayfair. I must say I didn't expect it to be quite so crowded." Caro wrinkled her nose at the pervasive stench of offal. "Or so smelly."

Lizzie sniffed. "I'll not call it fair."

"Oh, Lizzie, you'll see. It will be fine and fair."

The carriage turned off the main thoroughfare, drawing to a halt beside a fenced garden on one side and a row of narrow townhouses on the other. According to Lucas, their rented house lay near St. James in the heart of the fashionable world. Caro pushed her spectacles up her nose. "I'll be so glad to be out of this coach."

The moment the footman let down the steps, Caro alighted into a fine drizzle. Crystal drops hung suspended from the wrought iron railings in front of the house. The wind shook the trees, and large drops pattered onto the lackey's umbrella. The smell of coal fires hung thick in the damp air.

Caro glanced up at her new house in awe and then turned to Lucas, who had halted behind them. Lucas threw his leg over Maestro with a wince and handed the reins to Tigs. He joined Caro at the path to the front door. "I told you it would be all the crack."

It certainly was grand. Caro ran her gaze up the three-storey facade. Identical to the houses on either side, it had ribbed pilasters bordering each window, and at the top of three wide steps, an imposing portico graced a central front door.

"It seems rather large," she said.

"Well, I daresay it might seem so to you. But if you want to entertain, you have to have a ballroom."

Caro raised an eyebrow. "Now you mention it, I can see how that is an absolute necessity."

He cracked his short laugh and looked more cheerful.

Caro squared her shoulders. "I suppose we must go in." The lantern beside the door had not been lit despite the gloom of the afternoon. "They are expecting us, are they not?"

"Yes, of course. My man of business wrote they would expect us on the fifteenth and—"

"And the fifteenth is tomorrow." Her stomach plunged. Not another night at an inn. "Oh, Lucas."

His mouth set in a firm line, Lucas took her arm. "Stop worrying so much. If we are a day early, they will have to cope."

Clutching Caro's valise, Lizzie trailed behind them.

The tall thin butler who opened the door had an impressive moustache and a frigid stare. He glanced at the carriage. "Welcome, Lord Foxhaven, Lady Foxhaven." He was a man with aplomb.

Lucas ushered Caro over the threshold. "You must be Beckwith."

"Yes, my lord." The butler snapped his fingers. A liveried footman hurried forward to take their outer garments. "If your lordship and Lady Foxhaven would care to step into the green drawing room, I will have some tea brought in." Beckwith glanced at Lucas, who grimaced. "And some brandy or . . ."

"Brandy," Lucas said.

"Tea would be lovely," Caro said at the same time.

"And perhaps dinner in two hours?" the butler asked. "Time for my lady to rest? I understand that the remainder of your luggage follows?"

"Yes, thank you," Lucas said.

Caro gazed around the square entrance hall lit by a candelabra hanging from the landing above. A set of sweeping marble stairs led upward. She hadn't imagined anything so grand.

"The green drawing room is on the first floor, my lady," Beckwith said. "I'll direct your maid up to your chamber."

A little overwhelmed by the grandeur, Caro hung on to Lucas's strong forearm as she climbed the stairs.

The drawing room was a pale shade of turquoise trimmed in white. Two tall windows overlooked the square. Caro felt drawn to the room the instant she crossed the threshold. Furnished by the owner with overstuffed green-striped sofas and chairs and the occasional mahogany table, it had an air of comfortable calm. She sank down on the sofa next to the fire.

Lucas set one booted foot on the hearth and leaned an elbow on the mantel. He looked so handsome, so self-assured, so right in the rich surroundings, good enough to eat in fact. Could he really be her husband?

"I think this will do, don't you?" Lucas said.

Do? She chuckled. "Oh, yes, Lucas. It will definitely do."

"Good. I hope you don't mind, but I am engaged elsewhere for dinner."

For one brief moment, her heart squeezed tight. Her husband in name only. A questioning expression crossed his face. She unscrambled her thoughts. They had agreed to this. She forced a smile. "Why would I mind? You are free to do just as you please."

He looked relieved. "Right. It won't do to be sitting in each other's pockets, you know. Besides, you can't go anywhere until you order a new wardrobe."

Was it guilt in his voice or embarrassment? She

retained her cheerful expression. "I have no interest in going anywhere this evening. I am much too tired."

He cast her a blindingly beautiful smile, and her heart hopped into her throat.

A discreet knock sounded at the door.

"Come in," Lucas said.

Beckwith entered bearing a silver salver. He set the tray at Caro's elbow. "Will that be all, my lord?"

"Yes, thank you," Lucas said. He waited for the servant's departure and then strolled over and splashed a generous amount of brandy into a glass. He raised the snifter in Caro's direction.

Her hand trembling, Caro poured her tea.

"No regrets," he toasted and took a deep swallow.

A queasy feeling rolled through her stomach at the thought of the deceit they were about to foist on the world. She raised her bone-china teacup in return.

"No regrets," she echoed, trying not to notice the hollow ring in her voice.

❊　　❊　　❊　　❊

A familiar, crackling voice drifted up from the entrance hall. About to descend from the second-floor landing, Lucas tiptoed to the balustrade. He peered down into the hallway as Beckwith bowed out a departing gaunt figure in widow's weeds.

Aunt Hermione Rivers. The old battle-axe hadn't wasted a moment before coming to inspect Caro. She must have been here at his father's behest. This marriage thing had more snares than the poacher's trail through Stockbridge woods.

After pausing long enough for the front door to close behind his aunt, Lucas made his way down to the drawing room. Unsure who else might be lurking under his roof, he eased open the door to the drawing room. At the window, Caro was holding back the drapery and peering down into the street.

Outlined against the light, her ample bosom strained her high-necked gown. Its soft blue fabric skimmed her shapely hips, hinting at the hollow of her waist. The severe bun and the spectacles perched on her nose seemed at odds with her lushness. When had she become so damn curvaceous in all the right places? And why hide such enticing swells and dips beneath yards of fabric? Probably because fashion had decided that a woman should look as if they had been stuffed into a pipe. God rot Caro Lamb and those of her ilk. The desire to explore his new wife's womanly figure in intimate sensual detail made his palms tingle. A pulsing warmth thickened his blood.

By George, was he so hardened by the dissipated lifestyle he'd embraced to enrage his father that he couldn't tell the difference between his childhood friend and London's infestation of trollops? He thrust the door back.

Caro dropped the curtain with a start and swung around to face him. Amber eyes gazed at him from beneath fair, straight brows with a wide-eyed beauty he'd never really noticed. His childhood friend had been replaced by a woman with a voluptuous body and the face of a Madonna. Something twisted inside him. Something strange and uncomfortable. He stood transfixed, trying to master his confusion.

She gave a small, breathless laugh. "Your aunt is

quite terrifying, isn't she?"

Jolted back to the recollection of their visitor, he nodded. "I'm afraid so. But her heart is in the right place, most of the time." He sauntered into the room. "What did she want? I didn't think you were at home to callers until your new gowns arrived."

As Caro glanced down at herself, a fleeting smile curved her lips. "It seems your aunt couldn't wait. She came to invite us to join her and your cousin Mr. Rivers at the theater on Friday. Apparently, this season's performance of As You Like It is not to be missed."

He sensed his father's hand in this. And it seemed Cedric had been roped in also, poor bastard. He curled his lip. "You refused, of course."

Her eyes widened. "She asked me if we were engaged on Friday, and I said no; then she issued the invitation. What could I say?"

He should have guessed how it would be. "You might have said you wished to consult me. I have other plans for Friday evening."

"Oh, dear. I accepted for us both. What will she think?"

The stubborn jaw warned him to tread with care. Confound it all. He had every intention of keeping his promise and taking her to a few select functions once the season got fully underway. He did not, however, intend to be marched around like a gelding on a bridle by his aunt. How his father would smirk. "I did not accept."

With agitated steps and dismay writ large on her face, Caro crossed to the sofa by the hearth and sank onto it. "Can you change your plans?"

He dropped into the chair opposite her. "You can't allow people to impose on me . . . on us. You have to stand up for yourself."

Her mouth dropped open. "It wasn't like that at all. She came to offer help with my introduction to the ton at your father's suggestion."

Just as he suspected.

"She was kindness itself," Caro said.

He took a deep breath, maintaining control of his growing irritation. "That is fine, but you don't need to include me."

Her fingers twisted on her lap. "Why are you being unreasonable? This is your family. She is trying to help."

The underlying expression of disappointment in her golden gaze drove a spike of guilt through his gut. He hadn't explained his distant relationship with his father, though she must surely be aware of it. "You don't understand them the way I do. First a visit to the theater, and before you know it, they will be running our lives. This is not what we agreed."

Her jaw hardened. Her chin came up and her eyes flattened to polished bronze. Their gazes clashed for a moment before she gave a small half-smile. "You might have warned me about your aversion to your aunt. In future, I will have Beckwith deny her admission."

He relaxed at her obvious attempt at a jest. "Wouldn't that set the old biddies' tongues wagging? Truth to tell, it never entered my mind that my father would ask her to take a hand in your introduction."

"Well, I for one find it a kindness." She made a small gesture of appeal with her hand. "I'm sorry—I will not let it happen again, but I cannot be so rude as to cry off now."

Bloody hell. This arrangement of his was fast turning into a nightmare of surprises. He certainly didn't need someone to serve as his conscience with regard to his father. Nor did he appreciate the distress in her expression or the hope in her gaze.

"Dash it. Yes, I'll go. In future, don't accept any invitations without speaking to me first." The watery smile that greeted his capitulation eased the tension in his neck.

"Thank you," she said. "I am sorry I made a mess of it. I'm sure I will do better next time."

Now her gratitude had him feeling like an ogre. "No harm done, I am sure."

"Your aunt promised to introduce me to all the hostesses and arrange for vouchers for Almack's. I thought it was a good idea. Is that something you prefer to do?"

The black pit of matrimony yawned at his feet. A sudden gleam of mischief danced in her eyes. Was she playing some sort of game for control? He'd beaten a far better player than she would ever be.

"No. I can't get you vouchers." He grimaced. "To be honest, I would just as soon not set foot in the place. They serve nothing but tea, and the men are required to wear knee-breeches."

Unexplainable disappointment filled him as the light faded from her face.

"Then I will accept your aunt's offer of assistance." She rose and strolled to the window, her hip-skimming skirts swaying to each step. A low pulse thrummed in his blood. Had he lost his reason along with his bachelorhood? No one could mistake Caro for anything but a vicar's daughter in her old-fashioned round gown and plainly dressed hair. The spiteful ladies of the ton would tear her to shreds if she went about looking dowdy.

"I assume Madame Charis will have something ready for you to wear to the theater on Friday?" he asked.

"If not, I'll wear the gown I wore to leave home."

"Lord, no." The words were out of his mouth before they hit his brain.

She swung around to face him, twin spots of color on her cheekbones. "My father loved that gown."

Her spark of anger always caught him by surprise. Like a skittish mare, she balked at trifles. He put up a pacifying hand. "I liked your gown, Caro, but it is not fashionable enough."

Her expression eased. "I know."

"And you really should hire a proper lady's maid to do something with your hair."

"I don't need a lady's maid. I have Lizzie."

His patience slipped from his grasp. "Do you want people to laugh at you behind your back?"

She winced and pressed her lips firmly together. He wished she'd just speak her mind. This was all so new to her, and she had no one else to advise her. Lord knew he was hardly the best candidate for the job. "Caro, if you want to be accepted by polite society, you have to look up to snuff."

A gentle sigh relaxed her shoulders. "You are right, of course, but I will do nothing to hurt Lizzie's feelings."

Caro was a tiger when it came to loyalty to those she considered her friends.

The weak spring sun cast elongated diamond patterns on Stockbridge's gleaming oak desk. The familiar friendly scent of Father's study, beeswax, leather, and old cigars filled Lucas's nose.

"Someone left the gate open between the stallion and the mares this afternoon," his father said in unusually grim accents with his dark eyes locked on Lucas's face. "I lost ten years of careful breeding in an afternoon."

At Lucas's side, Caro seemed to shrink into her riding habit. Lucas's father always had that effect on her.

"That's awful, Father." The stud had cost a fortune these past few years.

"Is that all you have to say, son?" Father asked.

For a moment, Lucas didn't quite understand the question. "You don't think we left it open?"

His father's expression chilled further. "Cedric saw the pair of you galloping across the stallion's field after I expressly forbade it." His sharp tone cut into Lucas like a whip. "Why bother to lie?"

Caro gave a little moan.

Dumbfounded by the accusation, Lucas swallowed. "I do not lie, Father, ever. The gate was properly closed." They hadn't opened it. They'd jumped the damned thing. Also against orders.

Caro straightened her shoulders. "I did it," she announced in quavering tones.

Lucas's mouth dropped open.

Father turned his frosty gaze on her. "You?"

At the risk of arousing his father's suspicions, Lucas tapped the side of his nose to remind her to follow his lead.

"The latch must not have caught when I closed it. I am sorry, my lord," Caro whispered.

Either she was in such a panic that she didn't see the signal, or she was deliberately ignoring him. Lucas shook his head at her. She lifted her chin.

"I see, young lady," Father said softly. "Then I will have to have words with your father when next we meet. Good day to you."

"Yes, my lord." Caro fled for the door.

Father's disappointed gaze returned to Lucas. He narrowed his eyes. "Have you anything to add, son?" The pain in his voice hurt Lucas more than the disbelief in his eyes.

He couldn't give Caro the lie. Father would think he had tried to hide behind her skirts. "I am very sorry we went by way of the paddock."

"As am I, Foxhaven." Father stared at him for one very long moment, looking both sad and deeply angry. "That is all."

"Yes, Father." Chilled to the bone, he bowed and hurried out.

He caught Caro up at the front door. "What the devil made you tell such a bouncer? Didn't you see my signal?"

She stared up at him, her eyes huge in her full face. "He didn't believe you."

"I would have changed his mind, eventually. He knows I do not lie." He just wished he felt more certain. "Someone must have come along after we left, someone Cedric didn't see. I wish we had never gone that way in the first place."

"Me too." She blinked behind her glasses. "Lucas . . . I'm sorry if I said the wrong thing in there."

At twelve, she was still a baby in comparison with him at fourteen. She had no idea about a man's honor. He couldn't let her shoulder the blame for something that was *his responsibility, even if neither of them had touched the gate. He heaved a sigh. "Do not worry. Father will come around."* He hoped.

She looked decidedly relieved. "Shall I see you tomorrow?"

He stuck his hands in his pockets. His careless shrug felt forced as he thought of the unpleasant interview with Father in the offing. "Not for a few days I should think. Wait for the fuss to die down." If Father thought he'd caught Lucas in a lie, the punishment would no doubt be harsh. "I will call for you later in the week."

Oh, yes, even at twelve, Caro had been unstintingly loyal to her friends—even if the loyalty was of the two-edged-sword variety that made you want to hug her and shake her. It was the reason he had trusted her enough to propose this ridiculous marriage.

"Keep Lizzie, if you wish, but please, think about employing a hairdresser."

A quick grateful smile acknowledged his defeat. "Do you know of one?"

He opened his mouth to say yes. Admitting that kind of knowledge might raise more questions than he cared to answer. "Ask Beckwith, or the housekeeper; they are sure to know someone." He grinned. "By the way, I am expecting Bascombe at any moment. We are going riding."

"I wish I could come with you." She sent him a questioning glance. "Do you think it might be possible to hire a horse for me? I should like to ride in Hyde Park."

This was something he would be delighted to take a hand in. The thought lifted his spirits. She was an excellent horsewoman. The best he'd ever met. "Of course. But not a hired hack. I will buy one at Tatt's and a carriage and pair too, if you like."

Her face lit up like the sun emerging from a cloud. Her obvious pleasure gratified him a great deal, more than he cared to admit.

"Are you sure it is not too extravagant?" she asked. "I wouldn't want your papa to think I'm bringing you to ruin."

The warmth dissipated on a cold breeze. "What we do has nothing to do with my father, and it certainly will not do for people to think I'm too nipcheese to spring for a decent mount for my wife."

My wife. The words tasted bitter on his tongue. "By the way, I won't be dining at home. There is a cockfight at the Royale tonight."

She opened her mouth.

"No. You cannot come. Ladies don't attend sporting events. Not good ton."

"Not even with their husbands?"

There it was again. Husband. A fine web of restraint tying him down. "No."

The droop of her expressive mouth made him want to offer to come home for dinner. He must be losing his mind. If he pandered to her now, she'd be running his life before season's end. "Surely, you do not mind eating alone?"

Despite the doubt in her expression, she shook her head. "No."

"Then why the sad face?"

Her smile seemed forced. "Men seem to do more interesting things than we ladies do. I wondered if the rules were more relaxed for married women."

He considered the matter. Certainly several married women of his acquaintance broke society's mores. "It all depends on who you are and how you carry it off. Lady Louisa Caradin raced a friend in along Rotten Row and got off pretty light." On the other hand, Selina Watson, the daring widow who had introduced Lucas to the delights of the flesh when he first came to Town, had entered White's dressed as a man. Since then, all the doors of the toplofty hostesses had closed firmly in her face. "You do not want to be thought fast, do you?"

Shock widened her eyes. "Heavens, no."

"A lady attending a cockfight is definitely beyond the pale." Damn it. He was beginning to feel like the strict parent of a wayward child, and judging from her out-thrust chin, she thought so too.

Staring at Lucas's grim expression, Caro wondered if she'd ever learn how to go on in London. Her first visitor and she'd made a mess of it. Now Lucas thought her foolish.

"Very well, I will cross that off my list of things to do in London," she said primly.

He chuckled and looked horrified at the same time. "You have a list?"

Returning to the sofa, she sat down with a smile. "I have an excellent guide book. Miss Salter gave it to me. It contains a list of all the most edifying sights. I will ask Lizzie to search the luggage for it."

They glanced up at a knock at the door. Beckwith announced, "Sir Charles Bascombe to see you, my lord."

"Show him in, please."

The stocky young man who strolled in had short,

neatly styled fair hair, bright blue eyes, and an open, friendly expression. Caro had met him the day after she arrived in London. He had been at Eton with Lucas, and she had liked him on sight.

Lucas derisively called him a dandy. Today, he was certainly dressed to a shade. In a brown coat of superfine, biscuit-colored breeches and a lemon waistcoat with silver embroidery, he looked a veritable pink of the ton. His shirt collar grazed his jaw, and his cravat was a wonder of complexity.

Beside the languorous Mr. Bascombe, the lean and athletic Lucas appeared careless to the extreme. Only his shiny Hessian boots showed the least attention. With his cravat tied in a simple knot and his unadorned waistcoat, he had an air of comfort, not fashion. And yet his long hair and the hint of danger lurking beneath a thin cloak of civility made him fascinatingly attractive.

Caro's blood thrummed at the illicit thought. As her gaze reached Lucas's face, she became aware of his quizzical gaze and knowing smile. Dear heaven, he must have seen her slow perusal. And from the look in his eye, it seemed he had guessed the direction of her thoughts.

Heat burned her cheeks. She glanced quickly away, focusing on the gently smiling Mr. Bascombe.

"Pleased to see you again, Lady Foxhaven," Bascombe drawled. He nodded to Lucas. "Are you ready, Luc?"

Lucas made for the door. "Almost. I'll tell them to bring Maestro around." The eagerness in the set of his broad, black-clad shoulders indicated his desire to be gone. How boring he must find her.

As Caro gestured for him to be seated, Bascombe carefully lifted the tails of his coat and took the chair vacated by Lucas. "How are you enjoying London, Lady Foxhaven?"

His friendly smile soothed her flayed nerves. She managed a chuckle. "I haven't seen much at all, apart from the inside of Madame Charis's."

He nodded wisely. "You can't do better than put yourself in the hands of the great Madame Charis." He gazed at the door.

More heat flooded her cheeks and throat. Would she ever get all this right? He wasn't here to discuss fashion. "Lucas tells me you are going to Hyde Park?"

He grinned and glanced at the clock. "That was certainly the plan."

Guilt slumped her shoulders. Her inability to handle Aunt Rivers had made Lucas late. "I'm sure he'll only be a moment."

"Good book?" he asked, nodding at the volume on the table beside the sofa.

"Miss Austen."

"Ah. My youngest sister likes her work."

"You have a sister?"

He grimaced. "Three."

A wave of longing to see the girls washed over her. "I also have three sisters."

A knowing expression lit his blue eyes. "Quite a trial, ain't it?"

"Oh, no. I . . ."

Lucas strode back into the room and propped one foot on the edge of the hearth. "Keeping Lady Foxhaven amused, Bas?"

Bascombe nodded, his gaze fixed on her novel. "Did you purchase your book in London?"

Caro nodded. "Yes, at Hatchard's."

His expression turned serious. "You did warn Lady Foxhaven not to shop on Bond Street after midday, didn't you, Luc? Nothing but a bunch of ogling beaux." His fair skin above his collar turned pink. "You will find yourself quite out of countenance."

"Actually, I didn't think of it," Lucas said, apparently horror-struck.

How like him not to remember to tell her something so important after she had informed him of her intention to shop in Bond Street. "Thank you for warning me, Mr. Bascombe. I should hate to embarrass myself."

Lucas stared at her for a moment and then pushed himself away from the hearth and sat beside her on the sofa. He glanced over at his friend. "Bas, I had actually planned to talk to you about this."

Frowning, Bascombe crossed his feet at the ankles. "Shopping in Bond Street?"

"No." Lucas shook his head. "Introducing Lady Foxhaven to the ton. She doesn't have any female relatives of her own in London and doesn't know anyone yet. My Aunt Rivers has offered to take her to Covent Garden on Friday, but well . . ."

"Bit of a she-dragon." Bascombe's tone held sympathy.

Caro sent him a quick smile. "Frightening." Somehow she felt she could be straightforward with Lucas's good friend.

"Thing is," Lucas continued, "Aunt Rivers will

provide tickets to Almack's, but I don't think Caro will like spending all her time with a pack of dowdy dowagers."

Bascombe shot him a sharp glance. "Why can't you take her?"

He curled his lip. "To Almack's? You know me. Balls, routs, and debutantes. Not my style."

"You don't have to worry about debutantes any more, you lucky dog. No need to dance with anyone except your wife."

The expression of distaste on Lucas's face remained firm. He obviously couldn't think of anything worse than dancing with his chubby unfashionable wife, Caro thought. Her heart sank.

"Caro doesn't want me hovering around, do you?" He cocked a brow in her direction.

She didn't? They'd agreed not to interfere with each other, and she'd started on the wrong foot with his aunt. A mistake she would not repeat. And if she was going to get all hot and fluttery every time she looked at him, avoiding his company might be a good idea. "Certainly not."

Bascombe looked from one to the other with a puzzled frown.

Seemingly oblivious, Lucas continued, "What Caro needs is a female around her own age who can take her under her wing until she gets established." His mouth turned down. "I just can't think of anyone suitable."

"That doesn't surprise me," Bascombe said. He pursed his lips, appearing to give the matter some thought. "Tisha," he announced.

Lucas looked blank.

"My married sister, Lady Leticia Audley. Thing is, Audley's in the foreign office, or some such. He's been assigned to the embassy in Paris and left Tisha moping in Town. Blue as a megrim. This might be just the thing to cheer her up."

Hope flittered in Caro's breast. "Do you think so?"

A doubtful expression lurked in Lucas's dark eyes. "Tisha's been on the town for years, and she certainly knows the ropes, but she's a bit on the flighty side. At least she was—"

Bascombe coughed. "Settled down quite a bit since she married Audley."

The more she heard, the more she liked the sound of Lady Audley. To have a friend who knew her way around the ton would be a boon. "If you think she'd be willing . . ."

Bascombe waved a languid hand. "My mother was only saying this morning that Tisha needs something to take her mind off Audley's absence. She's been in the doldrums ever since he left. Mother doesn't have the time; she's far too busy with the young'uns. I think she would feel a whole lot easier in her mind if Tisha had a sensible companion while Audley's away."

Sensible. He meant unattractive. Someone who was unlikely to get the spirited Lady Audley into a scrape. "Oh, I see."

Bascombe leaned back. "My mother would be most grateful, but there's no sense in denying that Tisha's a bit of a gad-about. I could well understand if you don't like the idea."

Someone as worldly as Leticia Audley sounded would surely find Caro dull. But not if she changed— the idea popped into her head from nowhere. "I do like it."

A piercing glance shot from beneath Lucas's lowered brows at his friend. "I'm not sure Caro is ready for your sister."

Bascombe grinned. "I tell you what, I promised to escort her to the theater on Friday in Audley's absence. I'll bring her to your box. You can see if you hit it off."

Perfect. They could look each other over before deciding anything. Caro nodded. "I'd love to meet her."

With the look of a thwarted man, Lucas clapped Bascombe on the shoulder. "What a dull dog you are, Bas, playing escort to your sister. Becoming quite domesticated."

The words must have struck a nerve with the drawling Mr. Bascombe. He glowered. "And I suppose you ain't. You're the one who's married."

Caro winced at Lucas's sudden blank expression.

He strode toward the door. "Come on, Bas. The horses are champing at the bit. "I'll see you tomorrow," Bascombe called over his shoulder on his way out.

Four

*C*ARO REACHED FOR THE STRAND OF PEARLS ON THE polished dressing table, her only piece of jewelry. It had been her father's wedding gift to her mother.

"Stop fidgeting, my lady," Lizzie grumbled.

"Sorry."

Lizzie finished tying off her stays, and Caro held up her arms to allow the maid to drop the gown over her head without disturbing her coiffure.

The hairdresser recommended by Beckwith turned out to be an artiste par excellence and had teased and curled until ringlets surrounded Caro's face and a waterfall of glossy tresses fell to her shoulder. Sadly, with her straight, fine hair, it likely wouldn't last the night.

Taking a deep breath, she glanced in the mirror. The oyster silk gown delivered by Madame Charis yesterday lived up to her promise of elegance. She fiddled with a festoon of pink and cream ribbons tied under the bust. For some reason, they drew attention to her bosom, despite a high neckline. Her vaguely brown eyes were still too big, more so behind her spectacles, she thought ruefully, her mouth too full and her nose too short. Her only good feature, as far as she could tell, was a long neck, and the new hairstyle made it look as if it belonged to a giraffe.

"You'll do," Lizzie said.

For all her blunt words, Lizzie's homely face held admiration, and Caro's fluttering stomach began to settle. She tried to smile. "I don't think I look like me anymore."

Lizzie chuckled. "Perhaps that's not so bad?"

A smile tugged at her lips. "Why, thank you." A little jolt of anticipation shortened her breath. "I suppose I should go down. I should not keep everyone waiting."

Mindful of the high heels on her new satin slippers, she glided out of the room.

Further along the hallway, Lucas's valet dashed for the servants' stairs. Lucas stuck his head out of his door, missing her by inches. "The white waistcoat," he called out.

An expression of ludicrous surprise crossed his face. It was as if he'd forgotten she lived there. "Caro. I'm sorry."

Fascinated and breathless, she stared at the triangle of manly chest and its sprinkle of dark curling hair in the open neck of his shirt. She ought to look away, but her gaze remained stuck on a hollow at the base of his strong column of throat. In such careless disarray, he had the look of a ravening pirate, a dashingly handsome one.

Lifting her gaze to his face, she observed the smug curve to his lips. A black eyebrow rose in question. This time, he definitely knew what she was thinking. Fire flamed in her face.

"You look stunning," he said.

A compliment? She blinked with surprise, peering into his face in search of sarcasm. Finding none, and feeling a tiny dash of confidence, she bobbed a brave curtsey and attempted a friendly smile. It felt more like the fatuous grin of a besotted schoolgirl. "Why, thank you, my lord." She dropped an arch glance to his chest. "I wish I could say the same about you."

He cursed softly and clutched at his shirtfront.

A little surge of triumph lifted her spirits. The ability to discomfort wasn't all one-sided, it seemed. "I'll meet you downstairs," she said and continued on her way.

On reaching the first floor landing, she glanced up. He stood motionless staring down at her, the chiseled lines of his face set in hard planes and shadowed valleys like some dark angel. She shivered. He caught her eye and turned away.

※　　　※　　　※　　　※

Whatever Caro had expected, the crowds on Bow Street outside Convent Garden Theater exceeded it by far as the coach drew to a halt. Jarveys, theatergoers from of all walks of life, and liveried footmen jostled for position in front of the brightly lit portico.

Mr. Rivers, Lucas's cousin, a thin, dark-haired man of some forty years with a serious demeanor, assisted his mother down, while Lucas attended to Caro. A rough-looking fellow pushed past them with a woman sporting a tawdry blue gown, a quantity of flamboyant red feathers, and the heavy scent of roses.

"Take care of Lady Foxhaven, Lucas," Mr. Rivers said. "There are cutpurses among the riffraff, I'm afraid."

"She is perfectly safe with me," Lucas replied. Nonetheless, he drew her tight to his side like some treasured object he'd hate to lose.

"Is it always like this?" she gasped, narrowly avoiding a foot-skewering from an elderly gentleman's walking stick.

"Pretty much," Lucas said, maneuvering them through the cheerful mob and up the columned staircase, closely followed by Mr. Rivers and his mother.

On the second floor, Lucas held back a red velvet curtain, and Caro entered Lord Stockbridge's rented box. She tiptoed to the front, put on her spectacles, and gasped. The fluted marble proscenium arch stretched to the high ceiling and framed a stage hidden by blue velvet curtains. A huge chandelier hung from a central rose to light the pit, and candelabras burned on the walls between each festooned box. Heat and the smell of tallow thickened the air, which throbbed with the noise of what looked like hundreds of people making their way to their seats.

Lucas joined her at the rail. "Does it meet with your approval?"

"Yes. It is enormous," she said.

The orchestra had already begun tuning their instruments in a cacophony of squeaks and groans.

"Mama tells me it's your first visit to the theater," Mr. Rivers murmured as he shepherded the doughty lady to a chair.

Caro untied the strings of her velvet cloak. "Yes, indeed. And my first real outing in London. I am thrilled." She smiled across at him.

Though his rather gaunt face remained stern, a friendly warmth glowed in Mr. Rivers's gaze. "Lucas, I must congratulate you on your choice of a bride. Her enthusiasm is refreshing."

As if he'd had some choice in the matter, Lucas smiled and bowed. "I could not agree more."

For his generosity, Caro cast him a grateful glance.

Aunt Rivers tutted softly from her corner. "I am glad you finally listened to your father, Foxhaven. It is time you took your responsibilities seriously."

Lucas's shoulders stiffened, and his smile faded.

"Now, Mother," Mr. Rivers said gently. "Foxhaven doesn't need you reminding him of his duty."

"Playing the peacemaker, cousin?" Lucas drawled. "My father would be glad to have you as his heir."

"Do you think I am waiting around to fill your shoes?" Mr. Rivers's tone sharpened a little. "I can assure you it is not my intention. I am fortunate your father recognizes my humble efforts."

"Too bad you can't use your influence with him where my affairs are concerned," Lucas said.

"Lord Stockbridge is perfectly reasonable," Mr. Rivers replied, "provided one always answers yes."

Lucas cracked a laugh. "I don't know how you tolerate his crustiness. You have my undying gratitude for relieving me of that burden."

"I aim to please."

The friendship between the two men gave Caro comfort. At least Lucas wasn't at odds with all of the members of his family. And it seemed through his cousin there might be a way for Lucas to effect a reconciliation with the autocratic Lord Stockbridge.

Adjusting her spectacles, Caro leaned forward and peered into a seething mass of gentlemen in beaver hats and ladies in bonnets adorned with feathers of every hue.

"We barely arrived in time," Aunt Rivers said with a brisk flick of her skirts as the orchestra struck up the opening bars. The deafening roar of conversation gradually subsided, and before many minutes Caro had lost herself in Shakespeare's words.

When the first act ended, she discovered that most of the patrons were staring at the first floor boxes opposite them. A ripple of applause broke out. "Who is it?" she asked.

"Wellington," Lucas said.

"Lord Wellington is here?" Caro stared across the auditorium.

"See, next to the Royal box?" Mr. Rivers said.

"I understand he is in town to consult with the Regent about the preparations for Princess Charlotte's wedding," Aunt Rivers said. "It is to be held at Carleton House."

Caro finally picked out a wiry gentleman with a sprinkling of orders on a plain blue coat. "Why, he looks just like his portraits."

Wellington threw back his head and laughed at something the diminutive black-haired lady in cherry red at his side must have said. "Who is she?"

"Lady Audley," Lucas said. "A veritable pocket

Venus, ain't she."

"So it is," Mr. Rivers said, leaning forward. "The Audleys are certainly flying high these days."

Caro's stomach plummeted. Lady Audley looked far too elegant to be bothered with the likes of a country vicar's daughter.

Another man, a tulip of fashion, entered the box. "And there's Bas," Lucas said. He stood up and waved.

Mr. Bascombe answered with a slight bow.

"He'll bring Tisha at intermission," Lucas said.

"And Lord Wellington?" Caro asked. The thought of meeting a war hero made her feel quite light-headed.

"I doubt the Duke will call on us," Aunt Rivers said repressively. "Particularly since your father isn't here, Foxhaven."

Caro stared at the modest figure. The hero of Waterloo.

"Don't look quite so besotted, child. Everyone will think you are some sort of provincial," Aunt Rivers said.

Sharp prickles ran down her spine. Wasn't that what she was?

"Let Caro look her fill," Lucas replied with a frown. "I know I did my first time in London."

Caro wanted to hug him for rushing to her defense, but she satisfied herself with a smile. All the same, she shifted her attention away from the Duke.

Lucas put one arm on the back of her chair. "Enjoying it so far, pigeon?"

As plump as a pigeon. One of the nicest phrases that had haunted her childhood. It evoked memories of swallowed tears and the cream cakes her father used to cheer her up.

"Very much," she replied, miserably aware of his proximity and the scent of his sandalwood cologne. He'd never look twice at her while there were slender ladies like Tisha Audley in the world. Why couldn't men see that there were more important attributes in a woman than an eighteen-inch waist?

"Oh, look." Aunt Rivers said. "There's Sally Jersey—she's promised you vouchers for Almack's."

There was no telling which lady among the crowded boxes Aunt Rivers meant, despite Caro's best efforts to pick her out. At that moment, an actor walked on stage, and Caro once more turned her attention to the play.

At the next intermission, she glanced over to the Audleys' box. The Duke was surrounded by a crush of admirers, and the tiny lady in red had disappeared.

"Good evening," said a drawling voice behind them.

Caro swiveled in her seat to find Mr. Bascombe with his sister on his arm.

"Bas," Lucas said. "Come in."

"Lucas, Lady Foxhaven, good evening," Mr. Bascombe said. "Lady Audley, may I present Lady Foxhaven and her companions, Mrs. Rivers and Mr. Cedric Rivers."

Mr. Rivers bowed, while Caro and Mrs. Rivers rose to give their courtesies.

"Please, do sit down," Lady Audley said, her light voice friendly and musical. "I just had to meet Foxhaven's new bride."

From the corner of her eye, Caro saw Aunt

Rivers's mouth purse and Mr. Rivers' brows meet over his nose, but she ignored them and smiled. "You are very kind."

"Please, take my seat, Lady Audley," Mr. Rivers said and moved aside. "I'm off to fetch some refreshment for the ladies."

"Nothing for me, thank you," Lady Audley said. She perched next to Caro in a rustle of silk. The diamond pin between her breasts glittered with each dainty movement.

Caro couldn't imagine wearing a gown cut so daringly low. Not unless she wanted every male in the vicinity to be unable to look her in the face while they stared at her bosom as if they expected her breasts to escape their confines like flounders jumping from a fishing net.

"Bascombe told me all about you, Lady Foxhaven," Lady Audley said, her frank smile very much like her brother's, though she was as dark as he was fair. She laughed at the dismayed sideways glance Caro shot at Lucas's aunt. "Only good things."

"What else would there be?" Aunt Rivers snapped.

"Quite." Lady Audley seemed not a wit perturbed by the stiff widow. "Are you fond of the theater, Lady Foxhaven?"

"This is my first visit," Caro acknowledged. Dash it, she sounded so gauche. "I mean in London." That didn't help. She felt heat rise to her cheeks and was glad of the shadows in the box.

"I hear there is a very good playhouse in Norwich?" Lady Audley said with an amused smile. "That is where you are from, is it not? Your home is close to the Stockbridge estate, Bascombe said."

"Yes. We've known each other all our lives."

Lady Audley nodded and arched a delicate eyebrow. "And was the play to your liking tonight?"

"I liked it enormously," Caro replied with a chuckle, beginning to feel at ease with the vivacious young woman in spite of her spate of questions.

"I am so looking forward to knowing you better," Lady Audley said, echoing Caro's own sentiments exactly. "Are you free tomorrow?"

Caro glanced at Lucas. After her faux pas about this evening, she didn't dare make a commitment. "I am not sure."

"You are supposed drive with me tomorrow afternoon, Luc," Mr. Bascombe said.

Lady Audley's face fell and then brightened. "Oh, no, Bas. Have you forgotten? You promised to attend my afternoon tea."

Mr. Bascombe groaned. "Dash it all. Luc, we will have to go another time."

"There," Lady Audley said to Caro with a triumphant little smile on her rosebud lips. "You are free. You must come to tea tomorrow afternoon at four. Foxhaven, you will also attend."

Lucas didn't look exactly thrilled, but he didn't say no.

"Here is your wine, Mother," Mr. Rivers said, squeezing around Mr. Bascombe and handing a glass to his mother. "And ratafia for you, Lady Foxhaven."

Lady Audley inclined her head. "It has been lovely meeting you all, but I really must return to my box before the iron duke sends out a search party."

"He would too," Mr. Bascombe muttered. "The

old boy makes me feel like a schoolboy when he looks down his long nose in that way of his."

Lady Audley's laugh rang out as she stood up. "Peagoose. Wellington is a perfect dear. No, please, don't get up, Mr. Rivers. Bascombe will see me out. Don't forget, Lady Foxhaven. Four o'clock tomorrow."

She swept out on her brother's arm, and it seemed to Caro as if someone had blown out a candle and turned the box into an empty cave.

"Well, really," muttered Aunt Rivers. "What a flibbertigibbet. Audley must have had brain fever when he married the chit."

"Now, Mother," Mr. Rivers said. "Lady Audley only means to be kind."

Caro hoped it was more than kindness; she hoped they could be friends. She stifled hope and stared out into the auditorium. Perhaps Lady Audley had been forced into this by her brother and would find Caro dreadfully provincial. She stiffened her spine. Just because she had been brought up in the country didn't mean she wasn't good company. Just not very exciting. Vicars' daughters were supposed to be models of decorum.

Lucas leaned forward in his seat. "By Jove." The relaxed, laughing man he had been a moment ago disappeared in an instant. His eyes narrowed. Tension radiated from his lean frame.

"What is it?" Mr. Rivers asked, following the direction of his gaze.

"Someone I need to speak to. What a piece of luck. I hope you will excuse me."

"Really, Foxhaven," Aunt Rivers said. "Can't you

be still for an hour or two?"

"Go," Mr. Rivers said with a conspiratorial wink. "I'll take care of the ladies and bring them home too, if you wish."

A pang of disappointment tightened the smile on Caro's lips. The evening had felt quite special with Lucas at her side.

Lucas, on the other hand, looked relieved, as if Mr. Rivers had rescued him. "Thanks. I've no idea how long it will take. You really are a brick, Cedric. No wonder my father places such reliance on you."

A rather resigned smile played at the corners of Mr. Rivers's thin mouth. "I'm surprised you noticed."

Lucas shot him a grin. "I'll try to get back before the last curtain." He bade them a brief farewell and strode off.

Aunt Rivers glared at his departing back. "That boy is a scoundrel. It is time someone took him in hand, my lady."

Aunt Rivers expected Caro to do something about Lucas? A feeling of panic stirred in her breast. Their agreement precluded anything of the sort.

In an attempt to divert the older lady's thoughts, Caro nodded at a box on the third floor where a blonde woman wearing a glittering necklace of emeralds hung over the rail to greet friends in the pit. "Who is that?"

"A brazen hussy," replied Aunt Rivers. The gray hairs around her pinched mouth bristled in disapproval. "Lady Louisa Caradin. One of the so-called dashing widows."

She reached across her son and tapped Caro on

the knee with her black lace fan. "Don't have anything to do with her. She's fast. Every bachelor in town is sniffing at her skirts."

"Mother." Cedric sounded almost cross. "She is not worth talking about. Look, down there in the pit. It's Lord Castlereagh. He has caught Wellington's attention. Lady Audley will have her hands full with those two once they start on politics."

The Duke had indeed risen to his feet and acknowledged the gentleman in question.

Caro's gaze drifted back to the glamorous widow's box. Near the curtain at the back, a dark-haired gentleman handed his hat to the footman.

The bottom dropped out of her stomach. Lucas.

As if he sensed her gaze on him, Lucas looked directly into their box. He nodded. The woman in diamonds and emeralds turned her head, saw him, and rushed to drape her arm around his neck.

A sharp pain sliced between Caro's ribs. It hurt so much she couldn't breathe. No regrets indeed.

With shaking hands, she removed her spectacles and returned them to her reticule. Better not to see him.

Aunt Rivers said something in low icy tones to her son. Caro caught the word "rakehell," followed by a murmured, "What did you expect?" from Mr. Rivers.

Pretending not to hear, she kept her face averted, wanting neither their pity nor their curiosity. She stared blankly at the rising curtain. To her relief, the orchestra struck up a tune, drowning out their voices.

She stared at the stage, unable to make out more

than a blur of light and the sound of the actors' voices speaking. Nothing they said made any sense. All she saw in her mind's eye was Lucas and the slender creature twined around him.

※　　※　　※　　※

Attar of Roses threatening to choke him, Lucas peeled Louisa Caradin's arm from around his neck. With his gaze unaccountably drawn to the box on the other side of the auditorium, he'd been too late to take evasive action.

Louisa placed a slender white hand on his waistcoat and twirled the top button. A ruby flashed on her gloved hand. "Foxy, darling." Her husky voice dripped sugar and arsenic. "How wonderful. I didn't realize you were back in town so soon after your wedding."

He brushed her hand off and kept his voice chilly. "Good evening, Lady Caradin."

Her wide mouth curved in a wicked smile. "La, my lord, such formality to one who knows you so intimately." She turned her creamy shoulder and cast him an inviting glance from beneath lowered lashes. "Come, do sit beside me and tell me your news."

Lucas resisted the temptation to look across the pit once more. Caro looked the best he'd ever seen her tonight, a muted dove in contrast to this strutting bird of paradise flaunting her plumage. He unhooked Louisa's fingers from his coat. "It's over, Louisa. I came to talk to Lady Bestborough."

On the other side of her box, Lady Bestborough's peacock feathers nodded as she chatted to the elderly dandy seated beside her chair. Wrinkled by time, heavy-jowled, and prone to flashy clothes and flashier jewels, the placid widow enjoyed the company of idle rakes and racy women. They gathered to her wealth like wasps to rotting fruit. On the one occasion Lucas had met her, he had liked her razor wit and the way she delivered her stinging set-downs in so mild a manner that her acolytes never caught on. She made him laugh.

Finding her at Covent Garden rather than some gambling hell was unexpected good fortune. He'd been searching her other haunts for days.

Louisa tugged on his arm, her slash of a mouth in full pout. "Why don't you want to talk to me?"

He glanced pointedly at her necklace. "I think we finished our conversation a few weeks ago." It had cost him a king's ransom to get out of her clutches— another reason he needed his inheritance.

"How cruel you are, Foxy." She narrowed her eyes. "Shouldn't you be dancing attendance on your . . . buxom bride? Take care or you'll find Cedric Rivers poaching on your manor."

The venom in her tone reminded him of another reason he had tired of the boney witch. "My cousin doesn't poach, unlike you."

Her lips twisted. They both knew he referred to the reason she'd received her congé.

"Damn you," she muttered.

At last, the elderly macaroni relinquished his seat with a bow and an alarming creak of the stays holding his portly bulk in check. Lady Bestborough raised an inviting brow at Lucas. He closed in on his quarry, tension tightening his jaw.

"If you want to talk to me, Foxhaven"—Lady

Bestborough patted the vacant seat—"you will have to sit down. I'm too old to tolerate a crick in my neck from talking to a beanpole."

Lucas laughed, kissed her outstretched, gloved hand, and dropped into the chair beside her. "I hope I find you well?"

"Don't play the gallant, Foxhaven. Say what you have to say and be done."

He grinned. "I want to make you an offer for Wooten Park."

Her eyebrows shot up. "I thought you didn't have the money?"

"I do now."

A pair of wise, dark eyes searched his face. "Setting up your nursery?"

Involuntarily, he glanced over at Caro, but she had disappeared into the shadows.

"Well?"

He started at Lady Bestborough's sharp tone. She'd asked if he was planning a family, and he hadn't even blinked. It would never happen. That would play right into his father's hands. He shook his head. "It's a private matter. Will you sell it to me?"

"Not if you can't meet my price." She'd been playing catch-as-catch-can ever since he had broached the sale with her, making out that she had no wish to sell even though it had been on the market for months.

"I am prepared to pay what is fair."

"Lucky at the tables, were you? I'm asking ten thousand."

"It needs a great deal of work. I'll give you five."

"Six."

He repressed a smile. He had been prepared to go to at least seven. This meant his lads could leave London before Stockbridge learned of their existence. "Done." He shook her papery hand.

Lady Bestborough tapped his shoulder with her fan. "You drive a hard bargain, young man." She grunted. "Just like your father."

Lucas shuddered inside. "I would never reach so high," he replied smoothly.

※　　　※　　　※　　　※

The hot chocolate scalded Caro's tongue the next morning as much as the vision of Lucas and that woman had burnt her heart.

An iota of commonsense would have told her he wouldn't change, not for her. But she'd let her hopes get in the way of good sense. She just hadn't admitted to having hopes before last night.

She sighed. She never had a scrap of sense where Lucas was concerned. How would she be able to stand seeing him with other women? Especially if they were as beautiful as that one and as thin as a fashion plate in La Belle Assemblée. Mr. Rivers must have seen her distress, as much as she had tried to hide it. He had been so kind in suggesting they leave before the end of the farce. What if she had bumped into Lucas and his inamorata on the way out of the theater? Her blood ran cold at the thought. She put the empty cup to one side and reached around the rose-colored bed hangings to ring for Lizzie. Whatever happened, no one else must know how she felt and look on her with pity.

She slipped on her dressing gown and went to the

mirror. The remains of the tangles and teasing had the look of a bird's nest after a high wind.

The door opened to admit Lizzie.

Caro did a pretty good job of smiling. "There you are. Help me with this dreadful mess. I want to go to Hookham's this morning and borrow a book."

Lizzie took the brush from her hand. "You'll wear your poor eyes out, my lady. It's not right—you sitting here day after day, reading, and his lordship gallivanting who knows where. Why, Mr. Beckwith said he didn't come home last night and—"

To hear about Lucas and his debauchery in her own bedroom hurt more than she could bear. Smoldering disappointment flared out of control. In an instant, she leaped to her feet and snatched the brush from Lizzie's hand. She pointed it at the maid's chest. "How can you repeat servants' gossip to me?"

Lizzie backed away.

Caro advanced, waggling the brush. "How could you listen to such nonsense?"

Lizzie edged around the end of the bed.

Caro followed her. "I don't want to hear another word about the Viscount Foxhaven and what he does or does not do. Do you understand?"

Out of breath, she halted. Lizzie, eyes wide, pressed flat against the wall, nodded.

"Talking about me?"

The indolent drawl sent a jab of pain to Caro's temples. She swung around to see Lucas in the doorway, his face full of laughter.

Damn him for arriving right at this moment. "Why would I be discussing you?"

His gaze ran over her in an insolent appraisal, and

she snatched her dressing gown close. "Sorry," he said, spreading his hands wide. "I thought I heard my name."

He stepped into the room dressed in last night's attire. His long hair had escaped its ribbon and fallen to his shoulders in ebony waves; his cravat hung limp around his neck. He had just arrived home after a night with that woman. He looked dissolute and dangerous. Dangerous to her peace of mind.

A hard, hot lump threatened to choke her. Her grip tightened on the brush.

His grin broadened. "Go ahead, throw it."

"Don't tempt me."

He laughed. "I'm doing my best."

She opened her eyes wide. Was he flirting?

The old urge to laugh back, to give in to his smile, softened her anger. No. One woman falling at his feet in a day was quite enough. How could that pirate smile set her pulse racing and her heart beating faster? She pulled herself up to her full height and gathered the remains of her dignity. "If you'll excuse me, my lord, I am preparing to go out. I have rather a busy schedule planned." She glanced pointedly at the door, sat down at the dressing table, and offered the brush to Lizzie.

Lucas remained in the doorway. "Caro?"

Why couldn't he just go, before she burst into tears? She shot him an impatient glance. "Yes?"

A hesitant expression crossed his face. He gazed at her for a long moment, his eyes unsure. "I just wanted to tell you how lovely you looked last night."

The words failed to register until he had closed the door quietly behind him. He thought she looked lovely? It was the second time he had said something nice about her appearance last night. Did he mean it? Or was it just a ploy to get back into her good graces? She wished she knew.

She suddenly felt as limp as week-old cabbage. She slumped back against the chair. "I'm so sorry, Lizzie," she whispered. "Please forgive me."

Lizzie, her lips pressed firmly together, attacked Caro's tumbled locks. "Aye, I'll forgive you." She drew the brush through a long strand. "There's others what don't deserve forgiveness. Never. Not nohow."

Five

CEDRIC SHIFTED HIS WEIGHT ON HIS ACHING FEET and leaned one shoulder against the jeweler's bow window frame. He stared over the heads of pedestrians and between Bond Street's steady flow of traffic. On the opposite side of the road, Bingo Bob in a gaudy blue coat touched his hat. Curbing his distaste for the fat, red-nosed, greasy member of London's underworld who had brought the news of Lady Foxhaven's unescorted foray to Bond Street, Cedric nodded his acknowledgement.

Hookham's brown-painted front door opened. A couple of somber gentlemen emerged, shook hands, and strode off in opposite directions. Cedric groaned, pulled at his fob, and checked his watch. It must have been at least two hours since she had entered the bookshop.

The door swung back again. He straightened, craning his neck around the fashionable couple who had paused to admire a display of rings.

At last. Lady Foxhaven, in a dark-green spencer trimmed with black frogs and a matching silk bonnet, hesitated on the threshold. After a brief glance around her, she tucked a book under her arm, and with her reticule swinging from her wrist, she plunged into the eddying stream of shoppers, hawkers, and sauntering dandies.

In line with his instructions, Bingo Bob lumbered into motion behind her. Cedric remained a few steps behind on his side of the street, joining the pursuit at a steady pace. All his senses heightened. Sweat cooled on his brow, one prickling drop at a time. Each indrawn breath rasped in his ears and left the acrid taste of coal smoke on his tongue. The crimson of a passing lady's spencer seemed more vivid; the accoutrements on a carriage horse flashed and dazzled. The clang of a muffin man's bell added another distinct note to the music of London. A feral power pulsed in his veins.

And all the while, the green bonnet bobbed through the forest of feathered plumes and jaunty beaver hats. His heartbeat quickened to fever pitch. His balls felt full and heavy in the confines of his tight pantaloons. Controlled and alert, he followed. A hunter on the prowl.

A group of Bond Street beaux in deep conversation blocked the footpath and Carolyn stepped off the curb. A broken-down nag missed her by inches, the carter yelling an obscenity. She leaped back, a hand to her throat. In his mind, Cedric thought he could hear her gasp.

She fumbled in her reticule, put on her spectacles, and once more picked her way through the fashionable jungle.

For a woman of generous proportions, she seemed so very vulnerable.

Bob closed in on her heels.

Cedric curled his lip. Foxhaven was so damn careless with his property. Excitement as carnal as anything he'd known with a woman made his blood run hot. He curled his fingers around his walking cane. You are mine.

He lunged across the road, reaching the curb a few feet behind Lady Foxhaven and the encroaching tub o' lard.

Bob nudged at her with his protruding belly. Her head whipped around. She hesitated and tried to dodge. Bob edged her toward the alley beside the tobacconist's shop.

Cedric sidestepped an idle rake ogling a curricle. He was too far back. Hell. He broke into a run.

"You ought to be more careful of the road, sweet," Bob's fruity voice was murmuring as Cedric caught them up. Bob slipped an arm around her waist. "Yer needs a man to take care of ye."

Panic blanched her face and widened her eyes. "Unhand me, sirrah." She twisted out of his reach.

Out of breath, Cedric leaped forward. He swung the fat man around by the shoulder. "You heard the lady. Release her."

Bob jerked back.

Relief flooded Lady Foxhaven's face. "Mr. Rivers," she gasped.

Cedric flicked the catch on the head of his walking cane with a lethal snick and slid a fraction of wicked steel from its polished-wood concealment. "How dare you importune this lady?"

Bob spread his arms wide, licking loose lips. "Didn't mean no harm, yer 'onor." He backed away and trundled off.

Cedric made to start after him but then halted. He turned back to Lady Foxhaven. The admiration in her large brown eyes sent an unexpected glow of warmth to the pit of his belly. He stilled, shocked by the unexpected pleasure pulse.

He managed a stiff bow. "Are you all right, Lady Foxhaven?"

She clasped her small gloved hands to her magnificent bosom. "Mr. Rivers, how can I thank you enough for your timely rescue?"

A pang of guilt, a sensation long forgotten, disturbed his thoughts. He brushed the weak protest aside. Too much of his future rode on this scheme to let conscience interfere. He glanced around. "Where is your footman or your maid, my lady?"

Hanging her head, she traced a crack in the pavement with the toe of her shoe. "I didn't think an escort necessary when I left home so early in the day, but time escaped me, I am afraid."

He held out his arm, and she took it. "Come, I will escort you home. Surely my cousin warned you against lingering on Bond Street?"

Shame-faced, she nodded. "He did. I know I should have been on my way home long before noon."

"The time of day has nothing to do with it, Lady Foxhaven. No lady walks alone in London. I will have to speak with Foxhaven about this." While I watch the arrogant bugger squirm.

An imploring glance peeped up from beneath the

brim of her charmingly modest bonnet and lace cap. Her eyes reminded him of the color of sherry in candlelight. "Please, Mr. Rivers, do not mention this to Lord Foxhaven. I do not want to worry him. I assure you, it will not happen again."

The appeal in her pale oval face gave him pause. Not only was she most anxious to keep this from Lucas, but the gentle creature trusted him already. How useful.

He permitted himself a small, swift smile. "As you wish, Lady Foxhaven. I shall say nothing, if you promise to walk with your maid in future."

"Believe me, Mr. Rivers, after today, nothing would persuade me to leave home without an escort. I beg you won't betray me." Golden lights danced in amber eyes and sunlight streaked into his dark world.

Struck blind, he sought the dark cave of cool detachment and crawled inside its shadowy protection to find a guarded response. "Please, call me Cedric. After all, we are now family."

She smiled, a tremulous curve of her lips. "If you will call me Carolyn. Lady Foxhaven sounds so stuffy, don't you think?"

"The Foxhaven and Stockbridge titles are old and proud ones. They came to our family through Henry the Second."

Her hand trembled and slid from his arm.

Swift to sense a distress he didn't understand, he caught her fingers and replaced them on his sleeve. He softened his tone. "Forgive my pride, cousin. When you have sons of your own, our name will mean as much to you as it does to me."

A seemingly nervous spasm tightened her fingers on his arm. "I expect you are right," she murmured.

He glanced down, but could see nothing of her expression for the cursed brim shielding her face, but his nerve endings tingled. He had been right to suspect this marriage.

"You know, cousin, it would greatly please my mother if you allowed her to help with your introduction," he said.

"She is truly kind."

Not many people recognized his mother's worth or realized the shabby treatment Stockbridge meted out to his poor relations. He bowed slightly. "She can be a little outspoken at times, but I assure you she means well."

He ran his cane along the green wrought iron railings shielding the area steps of a small townhouse. It made a pleasant musical sound. "Will Lucas bring you to Almack's on Wednesday?"

"I don't believe so." The merest hint of a sigh followed the words.

"It would be a shame not to attend after Mother went to the trouble to obtain vouchers."

"I appreciate her kindness, I do assure you."

Good. Gratitude ranked almost as high as fear in garnering cooperation. He bared his teeth in a smile. "My mother is already fond of you. She makes the offer as much for your own sake as she does out of duty to Lord Stockbridge."

Once more, the lady at his side averted her face. "How exceedingly generous."

Too vulnerable. A pang of guilt squeezed his chest. Damn. He didn't have room for weak emotions. "I see you borrowed a book?"

She held up the volume for his inspection. "A rather dreadful novel by Mrs. Radcliffe, I'm afraid." She chuckled. "My father would never have approved. I started reading it in the library and lost all track of the time." A rueful smile touched her full, soft lips.

He raised a brow. "I've done the same thing myself and caught a scolding from my mother."

She laughed. Cedric thought that distant church bells on a summer Sunday never sounded so sweet.

Lush yet modest, her air of purity called to him with unaccustomed allure. Foxhaven didn't deserve her any more than he deserved his fortune or his title. The urge to know her better, much better, stirred his blood.

He crushed the sensation and buried it beneath a mountain of disappointed hopes. Far more urgent considerations required his attention than the unruly demands of his body. He forced sincerity into his voice. "If I or my mother can ever be of assistance, you promise you will not hesitate to ask?"

Once more, her eyes shone, for him. "As you did so fortunately today. I am forever in your debt."

A genuine grin stretched his lips, a smile so broad his stiff cheeks complained of unaccustomed use. "It gives me great pleasure to be of service to you."

❖　　❖　　❖　　❖

No bloody workmen.

Lucas drew his phaeton to a halt on Wooten Hall's weed-infested drive and glowered at the Tudor mansion's crumbling façade.

Where the hell was the builder? His man of business had said work would start immediately.

"Take their heads, please, Tigs."

The tiger leaped from his perch, landed with a crunch on the uneven gravel, and rushed forward.

Lucas jumped down.

He ran a critical eye over the old place. Ivy trailed from the patterned red brick walls as if ripped aside by a mighty hand. Broken chimney pots stuck up like rotten teeth. A casement hung drunkenly on its hinge above the magnificent columned portico, and missing panes of glass gave the house a gap-toothed appearance. At least the gray slate roof kept the rain out.

The gardens also required urgent attention. Tangled and matted like a whore's hair after a night of debauchery, weeds overgrew what remained of rosebushes and shrubs. He'd have to hire a gardener from the local village.

He sighed. A place like this would quickly eat all his capital if his recent investments didn't come through. He eyed the whole thing through narrowed eyes, imagining it in its former glory. The house nestled against a hodgepodge of green fields broken by stands of oaks and beeches on the hilltops. In the valley, the spire of Wooten's village church poked into an azure sky.

Caro would like to ride here. The thought brought a smile to his lips. A picture of her as a child galloping, racing him neck-or-nothing, across the fields surrounding Stockbridge Hall flashed into his mind. What a contrast to this morning. She'd looked temptingly lush and tumbled. Mentally, he groaned at his body's instant response to the recollection. That was not something he should be thinking about—especially considering that she had seemed ready to murder him.

What on earth had he done? Appearing in a state of undress at her door, no doubt. He didn't recall her being so particular when they were children. Perhaps the strawberry roan he bought at Tatt's would turn her up sweet as well as occupy her while he kept busy here.

A projectile hurled into the back of his knees. "Whoa!" he shouted.

Small hands gripped his coattails, and a bullet head pressed against his arse.

"Milud, you gotta come an' see it."

Freeing his coattails from the bony fingers, Lucas stared into the excited, thin face of a blond youth jumping up and down under his nose.

"Steady on, lad."

Jake had filled out these past few weeks. He'd lost some of the pinched look of starvation and fear. Lucas put his hands on his hips and frowned.

Jake stilled, his face dropping. "Wot?"

Shaking his head, Lucas held out his hand.

"I never took nuffin'." Jake drooped. "Well, just a wipe." He drew Lucas's pocket-handkerchief from inside his coat and placed it in Lucas's palm.

"And," Lucas said.

"Yer ticker."

Lucas repressed a grin as the nine-year-old raga-muffin fished into the deep pocket of his thread-bare dung-colored coat and held Lucas's timepiece dangling from its gold chain.

"And," Lucas repeated.

Jake's shoulders slumped, and he handed back the sovereign Lucas always carried in his fob pocket. "Bleedin' hell, yor worship, I gotta keep me hand in, don't I?"

"No, you do not. Keep that up, and you will end your days with your neck stretched on the nubbing cheat."

The boy kicked at a stone on the drive. "They ain't never going to 'ang me. They gotta catch me first."

But they would. And what a dreadful waste of marvelous talent. The long fingers, which picked pockets with ease, worked magic when they played the violin. "I caught you."

"You're different. I lets you catch me." Jake drew his sleeve across his nose, leaving a slimy trail on the rough fabric.

With an inward shudder, Lucas held out the handkerchief. "Here, use this."

"Cor. Can I keep it?"

Lucas nodded. "It is a gift."

Jake hopped on his toes. "But you gotta come and see the pianny. It came yesterday. It's huge." Once more, his mouth turned down in sulky lines. "Fred won't let us nippers anywhere near it. He's says we'll knock it or somethin'."

Ah, Fred. Lucas's greatest treasure and biggest worry.

"Lead on, McDuff."

"I ain't McDuff. I'm Jake. We ain't got a McDuff."

Lucas laughed. The sooner this child was educated, the better it would be for all of them.

The boy sped off, his trousers skimming his sparrow's

ankles and his cuffs flapping below his hands. He looked like a miniature scarecrow. With any luck, the new clothes Lucas had ordered would arrive this week.

He ambled after the skinny legs pumping Jake toward the side door in the moderately habitable west wing. He sauntered down the narrow passage to the conservatory where the boys had temporary lodgings.

Filled with bright light from its domed skylights and the bank of windows along the south-facing wall, the conservatory had once been Wooten Hall's crowning glory. Added in the old king's reign, it epitomized Palladian architecture and provided a perfect studio for his music school for orphaned street musicians.

Doric columns supported the arching roof, elegant niches housed classic statuary, and pale gray marble graced the floors. The room should have trumpeted wealth and privilege. Only now, wooden boards filled in for panes of glass, and cots with rumpled blankets and discarded items of clothing turned one corner into a rat's nest. Boxes and trunks crowded the wall nearest the door. At the far end, fiddles and flutes lay discarded near an ancient pianoforte.

Pristine in a clear space in the center, a mahogany Broadwood grand piano basked in majestic isolation against a backdrop of fine English countryside. Three feet separated it from Jake, who, with his hands in his pockets, grinned at a lanky dark-haired lout wearing a multicolored waistcoat and the pugnacious expression of an English bulldog.

Fred.

He turned as Lucas's booted steps echoed off marble and bounced against the bare walls. The aggressive stance and balled fists disappeared. He nodded at Lucas and swaggered to lean against the nearest pillar.

Jake dashed at the piano and patted the mirror-polished surface. "See," he crowed.

"You'll scratch it," Fred said, with a growl. "An' next, you'll be carving your initials in it."

Pulling the key from his waistcoat pocket, Lucas strolled to the keyboard and unlocked the lid. Jake pushed in front of him and ran his hands over the blazing white ivory.

"There," Fred said, drawing close and peering over his tousled head. "Look at them mitts. They're filthy."

Shoving his hands back in his pockets, Jake backed up. His hatred of soap and water was a standing joke among the boys.

"What do you think?" Lucas asked Fred. At sixteen, the lad's ego was as sensitive as a girl's and his temper incendiary.

His eyes hungry and his mouth sullen, Fred stared at the instrument. "It's all right I suppose . . . milud."

Fred hated to use Lucas's title. Mr. Davis, the housemaster Lucas employed to look after the boys, would have chastised the studied insolence. Lucas let it slide. He sat down on the polished bench stool and ran his fingers over the keys. He picked out the notes of a Beethoven sonata, pleased he still remembered.

"Strike me," Jake whispered. "You're good."

"I was better at your age."

"Why ain't you a musician, then?"

The answer tasted of ashes. But to win their trust, he'd always been honest with these boys. "My father had other plans."

"I wish mine had," Fred muttered.

Lucas had found him in a public house bashing out tunes on an old piano for beer, having fled his home, wherever that was. He was no ordinary urchin. As much as he tried to hide his origins, somewhere along the line, he'd received an education, including music lessons. If he heard a tune once, he played it perfectly. Seeing Fred in that tavern had given Lucas the idea for the music school.

"Try it," Lucas encouraged, getting up.

Tossing him a lowering glance from beneath beetled brows, Fred pulled back the stool and slouched down. He hit middle C.

For all his cynical sneer, reverence shone in the lad's eyes as the note rang out clear and true to the vaulted ceiling. He caressed a chord and listened to its sweetness die away. Then, his fingers as light and delicate as a butterfly, he drew out a few notes.

Settling himself more comfortably, he banged out a rousing ditty popular in the stews of London with words to make a sailor blush.

Jake, his voice as pure as an angel's, picked up the refrain, and the story of Mother O'Reilly and what her old man did with her duck filled the room. The three other boys—Red, named after his hair; Aggie, a gangly piccolo player; and Pete, blond and blue-eyed and the finest flautist Lucas had ever heard—tumbled into the room and joined the chorus.

Fred challenged Lucas with a sly glance.

With a grin, Lucas added his tenor to the boys' heavenly trebles and slid onto the bench. He picked up the harmony, occasionally passing across Fred's hands and his fourp'ny rabbit chest.

"Oh, my word." Mrs. Green the cook, her mouth open, paused in the doorway with a tray of lemonade and biscuits.

Distracted, Fred hit a sour note, and the music died away, leaving Jake, his eyes closed and head thrown back in oblivion, to finish the fornication of the poor fowl.

"Well, really." Mrs. Green slammed the tray on the box set up to serve as a table and marched off, her nose held high.

The boys collapsed in mirth—all except Fred, who kept a wary eye on Lucas as if he expected a beating.

Although Lucas wasn't sure he would ever earn the tortured youth's acceptance, he remained determined to try.

"Bravo," he said. "But we should keep an eye out for Mrs. Green next time." He winked.

Chuckling, the boys crowded around the tray. They crammed their mouths with warm shortbread and guzzled the lemonade.

Lucas recalled his own boyhood; he was always ravenous at mealtimes as his body outgrew his clothes in a week. And he had never gone without. "Now about this piano—"

"You said I'd 'ave me own room?" Fred interrupted, the gleam in his eye militant.

"You will, when the work on the house is complete."

Fred curled a sullen lip. "I 'ad me own room at Ma

Jessop's. You said it'd be better here." He sent a disparaging glance at the cots in the corner. "All I got is a bunch of snivelin' young'uns crying for their mamas." His glance swiveled to Jake.

Jake sniffed.

Forcing a patience into his voice he didn't feel, Lucas replied, "What you had at Jessop's was a rat-infested corner in a leaky attic."

"Ma" Jessup, a man who wore a silk dressing gown most of the time and hence the sobriquet, ran the street gang to which the boy had belonged. Under Jessup's tender care, Fred had graduated from pickpocket to ken cracker after perfecting the technique for entering wealthy homes and making off with the silver.

"It was me own room. Private. Better than here."

As private as a backyard privy. "I'll find you something while we wait for the bedrooms to be finished. Give me a couple of days."

The shabby coat shifted as Fred shrugged.

Lucas made a mental note to ask Mr. Davis to keep an eye on the lad. He feared Fred might be too old to give up the lure of easy money. Anger choked him at the thought of the waste of a God-given talent—his own as well as Fred's. He stamped hard on his regrets. These boys were the important ones now.

"Back to the piano," he said. "The most important part is not the outside, but the guts." He nodded at Fred. "Open the lid."

His swagger in full evidence, Fred sauntered to the instrument and propped up the curved top. The boys and Lucas peered into the exposed workings and inhaled the scent of new pine.

"Watch," Lucas said.

The younger boys jostled around him. "Play a scale, please, Fred. Slowly, if you don't mind."

The hammers struck the strings and they vibrated with sound.

"This instrument could be covered in firewood or mahogany," Lucas said. "Dented or scratched, it would make no difference to the sounds it makes."

The boys nodded wisely. Fred snorted.

Bending beneath the lid, Lucas reached inside and slipped his calling card between a hammer and its string. "Give me a high C, Fred."

The hammer thumped dismally against the paper. "This is the part you need to care about. The case enhances, makes better, the sound, but it's just a container. This is the heart of the music."

Fred stuck his head in the gap. A lank lock of black hair fell forward. "It's kind of like people," he muttered. "It don't matter what they look like; it's what's inside them wot counts."

This lad reeked of sadness, but every time Lucas tried to get to the bottom of what troubled him, the boy retreated into his devil-may-care shell. It felt so damn familiar it hurt.

"Yes, Fred. Exactly like people."

Lucas stepped back and took in their eager faces. "Now, here's the thing. I want you all to learn to play the piano. We've got the old piano for everyone to use for lessons and whenever they feel like it. And we have this one. If you practice your scales for an hour every day, you can have another fifteen minutes on the Broadwood to try your hand at some tunes."

"'Ooray!" shouted Jake. "Me first."

Jostling and shoving, they pushed each other off the bench with bony elbows, observed by a disdainful Fred.

"Stop," Lucas shouted above the din. "To make it fair for all, Fred will organize the schedule and make sure you abide by it." He glanced at the older boy, who seemed to stand a little taller. "Is that all right with you, Fred?"

"I suppose . . . milud."

"Good. You will start tomorrow. Behave yourselves, now. I have to talk to Mr. Davis."

He headed for the door and then stopped and swung around. Four pairs of mischievous eyes and one sullen pair returned his gaze. "By the way, I think I have found you a music teacher. He's an old school friend from Eton. He arrives in London on Wednesday, and I will bring him down that evening. I think you will like him. I know I do."

"Has to be better than Davis," Fred muttered. "He don't know an A from a bleedin' bull's foot."

Whooping with laughter, the younger boys sparred and slapped each other on the back. Fred sneered.

Lucas departed, shaking his head at the impossible task he'd set himself. It seemed to be the story of his life. He'd look like some pretty kind of a fool if this project of his cost him a fortune and failed.

Damn it, he answered to no one.

He pulled out his watch. Hell. He'd be late for Tisha Audley's bloody tea if he didn't get a move on.

Six

WHERE ON EARTH WAS LUCAS? CARO GLANCED at the tall case clock beside the front door, again. Almost half past three. If he didn't arrive soon, she would have to leave without him.

Perhaps he'd met with an accident on the road. Caro's breath caught as if her corset had shrunk and her lungs were being squashed.

Beckwith hurried to open the door at the sound of a carriage outside.

Not injured then. Just late. She should have known better than to worry.

He crossed the threshold and tossed his hat to the butler. His hair tousled, his jaw dark with stubble, and his coat covered in road dust, he looked more like a gypsy than a viscount.

Her stomach gave a happy little lurch of welcome. She couldn't think why, when he looked so disreputable.

"Where have you been?" she asked "You promised

to be here at quarter past three to take me to Lady Audley's." It sounded shrewish, but with her nerves stretched to breaking, she couldn't keep silent.

A haughty expression transformed his face from cheerful to frigid in the blink of an eye. "My business took longer than expected."

The pressure on her chest increased as an image of the dazzling Lady Caradin took shape. He certainly wouldn't have rushed from that woman's side to escort Caro to tea. She failed an attempt at a smile. "I didn't want to be late and create a bad impression."

"Then we will leave immediately."

"You can't go dressed like that." The words came out impulsively with the thought.

One hand on the knob, he turned to face her and raised a brow. "Tisha won't care, I assure you."

A hot buzz of anger released the band of iron compressing her chest. "I care! No gentleman would arrive in a lady's drawing room in all his dirt."

His expression darkened. "Are you implying I'm not a gentleman?"

Oh heavens. She'd insulted him. Hot and cold chills followed each other in quick succession. "Of course not. But it's improper to make a call dressed like a . . ."

"Like a what?" His voice held danger.

Dash it—he was in the wrong, not her. She met his challenging gaze. "Like a groom." Or rather a pirate from a Minerva novel.

One shoulder against the doorframe, his lean body emanated the challenge of a cocked pistol ready to trip at a touch. An arrogant smile pulled at one corner of his mouth. "Do you want to leave now, before it's too late, or do you want me to change?"

It was an impossible choice, and he knew it.

"I want you to behave in a gentlemanly fashion." Startled by her own bravery, she eyed him askance.

He pushed upright, brushing his coat back, hands on narrow hips. "It wasn't included in our bargain, I'm afraid. You got me exactly the way I am." He swept a glance from her head to her toes. His voice lowered. "Just the way I got you."

The words delivered in deep, husky male tones sounded sensual, but their meaning was clear. Anger drained away, leaving her feeling shriveled and parched inside. For all her new clothes, she hadn't changed any more than he had. She wasn't even a proper wife. She bit her lip.

"Nor," he continued, his face set in hard lines, "did I agree to squire you about like a leashed dog. Had I known you would turn into a prosy bore, I would have left you in Norwich with your sisters. In fact, I've a good mind to send you back."

Her eyes narrowed. "You can't. My coming to London is part of our agreement." She pasted a smile on her lips and waved an airy hand. "You should have told me you didn't want to go. I am quite content to go alone, and I prefer not to be late."

Something like regret flickered across his face. He heaved a sigh. "I'll change and meet you there."

She kept her tone light. "Please don't trouble yourself."

"Dash it, Caro. I really meant to be back earlier." Genuine concern rang in his voice.

Sure that he would see right through to her heart-pounding fear at the thought of entering the fashionable Lady Audley's home alone, she kept her smile fixed in place. "It is a simple afternoon call. And it wouldn't do for people to think you are under the cat's paw."

An appreciative grin dawned on his face. "Doing it rather too brown, I think, my dear. Besides, I plan to meet Bascombe there afterward. He promised me a drive in his new phaeton. I'll join you and spend a few minutes in Tisha's drawing room before we leave."

She flipped him a teasing glance. "A true sacrifice indeed, my lord."

The tension snapped on his sudden crack of laughter. He made a dash for the stairs. Two steps up, he stopped and turned as if to speak.

Caro waited, her pulse speeding up as his dark gaze locked with hers. He frowned. "I honestly didn't intend to leave you in the lurch, you know. I am glad I haven't put you out." He didn't look the slightest bit glad. In fact, he looked thoroughly irritated, as if she'd done something wrong. Then he turned and continued on his way.

Didn't he want her to be independent? She swallowed a shaky laugh and a dry lump in her throat. This whole thing was just too confusing.

"The carriage is at the door, my lady," Beckwith announced and opened the door.

She drew in a deep breath and braced to take her first step into fashionable society.

�֍   ✖   ✖   ✖

A rumpled neckcloth joined five others on the patterned rug. Lucas cursed.

Danson's beagle eyes met Lucas's gaze in the mirror. "What's bitten you in the breeches?"

The lantern-jawed valet had worked as a footman in the Stockbridge household when Lucas wore leading strings. Lucas glared back. "Nothing."

"It's a lot of to-do for nothing," Danson muttered.

Picking up another strip of foot-wide muslin from the pile on the walnut dressing table, Lucas folded it in half lengthways.

After leaving Caro downstairs, he'd set the household on its ears with demands for a bath and a change of clothes, all to no avail. The water took ages to heat, his hair dried too slowly, and now even the damned neckcloths conspired against him.

With the starched white cloth draped around his neck, Lucas carefully creased the fabric, proceeding with the tedious task of tying a mathematical. He narrowed his eyes. Caro darn well better appreciate the effort.

He fumbled at the knot and pulled it tight. He stared at the lopsided affair in the mirror. "Devil take it. What a dog's breakfast."

Danson came around to look from the front. He shook his head. "Do you want me to try?"

"Not if I want to get to the Audleys' on time." He brushed Danson's gnarled hand aside. "There's more chance of me pissing in the Prinny's hat than you being able to tie a decent cravat."

A grim chuckle met his snarling words.

He hadn't hired Danson because he was a good valet; he'd done it to annoy his father and to get rid of the mincing Frenchman the old man had tried to foist on him. And Danson didn't fuss over nonsensical issues like the precise fit of a jacket or the shape of a calf—not that there was anything wrong with his calves, as far as he knew.

Ripping off the disaster at his throat, Lucas dropped it with the others. "I'm out of practice, that's all. Give me some room, why don't you?"

Danson wandered off to do whatever valets do, and Lucas clenched his teeth and began again.

To hell with Caro for making him feel like a recalcitrant child. He refused to answer to her or anyone else. But the disappointment in her melting honey eyes and the guilt at letting her down still stabbed his conscience.

He should not have gone to Wooten. There simply hadn't been enough time to get there and back before Tisha Audley's tea. But when his man of business had reported that the work would start today, he'd found the temptation irresistible.

Sliding the end of the cravat through the knot, he gave it a gentle tug and worked at the folds.

He'd been right to go. The house's disastrous condition and the lack of progress required his attention. If nothing happened soon, the boys would drift back to their old haunts and their old ways. It had taken Lucas too long to gather the little band together to let them slip through his fingers.

Yes. Finally, the strip of cloth bent to his will. He held out his arms, and Danson eased him into his shoulder-hugging coat.

As tightly trussed as a capon, he inspected himself in the mirror. The regulation black coat, pearl-gray waistcoat, and neatly tied, white cravat ought to satisfy the suddenly particular Caro.

He frowned. Since when did he care what other people thought?

Since I married Caro, he thought.

Lucas stilled, his throat as dry as if he'd swallowed a mouthful of feathers.

She'd presented such a pretty picture with a jaunty little blue shako perched on her shining tawny locks and her spencer clinging to her ripe curves that he'd wanted to sweep her into his arms and kiss away her frowns.

Bloody hell. Lack of female companionship these last few months had turned him into a ravening beast. His taste ran to flirtatious widows who understood the rules of amour, not modest vicar's daughters who looked shocked every time he opened his mouth.

There were plenty of other men to entertain her—men like Bascombe, who had nothing else to do but worry about the set of his coat and the cut of his hair. Men who might well turn the head of an innocent newly on the Town. A strange feeling writhed in his stomach. Unease. It had to be fear for Caro's safety and nothing to do with the fact that she was his wife.

Damn. He'd have to warn her against men who trawled the fashionable waters for a fleeting liaison. Perhaps he was mistaken in thinking he could leave her to her own devices. He'd talk to Cedric about keeping an eye on her. His stomach slowly settled.

The clock on the mantel chimed a quarter to six. His heart dipped. Arriving too late seemed worse than not arriving at all. Tisha's function ended at six. His redemption had slipped away in the sands of time.

He eyed the cravat at his throat with distaste. If he'd just worn his normal neckerchief, he would have been able to spend at least a half an hour doing the pretty with Caro. Instead, he'd tried to prove he was the dandified type of gentleman she seemed to prefer. He stared at the pile of ruined cravats. Apparently not.

Danson held out his shoes. "Sit down, your lordship, and slip these on."

"Not those. My riding boots."

"I thought you was going to a fancy tea party?"

Lucas tore the cravat from around his throat and shrugged out of his coat. "I'm going driving with Charlie Bascombe."

Danson stared at him, his mouth agape.

Lucas unclenched his jaw. "I've changed my mind, if that's all right with you." He'd have to find another way to make up to Caro for this afternoon's debacle.

This marriage of convenience entailed a deal more work and worry than he had anticipated, blast it. And it couldn't have come at a more inopportune time.

Seven

*C*ARO HAD FLOATED HOME ON A CLOUD OF confidence. Her first outing amongst the ton, and she had survived without a single faux pas. Lucas would no longer find her a troublesome burden.

With two hours remaining before dinner, she settled on the sofa in the drawing room with a cup of tea and The Mysteries of Udolpho. Thank goodness things didn't happen like that in real life.

Two chapters later, she glanced up to find Lucas watching her from the doorway. He flashed her a hesitant smile. "Nose stuck in a book as usual, I see. What are you reading?"

Her disappointment salved by this afternoon's triumph, she smiled back. "A rather dreadful novel, I'm afraid."

"Can we talk?"

"Of course." She set her book face down on the seat beside her.

He strolled into the room and leaned one elbow

on the mantel. Dressed in buckskins and only a belcher handkerchief at his throat, his attire was completely inappropriate for her drawing room, and yet her heart lifted to see him.

The light from the wall sconces on each side of the chimney gave his angled face a devilish cast. A thrill hummed through her veins. A sweet ache pulsed somewhere she didn't want to think about. It would be better if he just stayed away.

"I'm sorry I didn't make it to Audley's in time," he murmured.

She blinked. "I honestly didn't expect you." She hadn't. She wasn't in the least surprised he'd abandoned her completely after she'd scolded him. No man expected his wife to question his movements. It just wasn't done.

The shadows on his face seemed to deepen. "Did you have a good time?"

"Yes, I did. Tisha is an excellent hostess and introduced me to lots of people. I just hope I can remember their names when next we meet."

He grinned. "I'm glad you enjoyed it."

The silence stretched out. The tick of the mantel clock filled the room. She searched feverishly for something to say. "Tisha offered to accompany me to Almack's. She said I will receive lots of invitations after today—which reminds me . . ." She jumped to her feet and went to the silver tray on the console table. Unaccountably breathless, she held out the white card with black script for him to see. "We are invited to a ball by His Grace the Duke of Cardross."

The amusement in his face dulled. "That will be my father's doing. He's thick with the Duke. We will have to attend."

"Don't feel obliged to go on my account. I'm sure your cousin Cedric would be willing to escort me."

For a moment, he looked almost relieved, but then a muscle flickered in his jaw. He shook his head. "Cardross is not a man to be taken lightly. What a bore. Which night is it?"

She glanced at the card. "Friday week." She returned to her seat. "The following week, I am invited to join Lady Audley's party at Vauxhall."

He nodded. "You will enjoy that. Don't forget to order a domino." His brow furrowed. "You will need to take care. There are a lot of undesirable types at Vauxhall, cits and mushrooms. I've a good mind to join you."

She held her breath in hope.

He shoved off from the fireplace, shifted her book aside, and dropped down onto the cushion, angling his body toward her. His gaze intensified.

Her breath hitched in her throat as his face came into focus. His stark beauty never failed to tear at her heart or to remind her of her own shortcomings. "What?" Her voice sounded sharper than she intended.

"I truly want you to enjoy your season in London. I'm sorry my business calls me away so often."

The business of his mistress. An ache throbbed dully in her chest. As soon as the season was over, she would return to her sisters in Norwich and leave Lucas free to continue his untrammeled life. Unless she found a way to create a real marriage, she thought. Certainly carping would not lure him away from a woman as lovely as Louisa Caradin. She forced a bright smile. "I really don't mind."

He relaxed against the sofa back and triumph tingled in her veins. Perhaps if she made him comfortable at home, he wouldn't want to racket around Town.

"I will try to rearrange a prior engagement on Wednesday and take you to Almack's." He paused. "And Vauxhall. That, at least, would be good sport."

She crossed her fingers in the folds of her gown. "I would like it very much, but please don't change your plans on my account."

He gave her a thoughtful glance. "Bascombe thought you seemed a little overwhelmed at Tisha's."

To her chagrin, her cheeks heated under his steady stare. She shook her head. "Not at all. I am perfectly capable of making an afternoon call. I just didn't expect to find it quite so crowded."

"I neglected to say so before you left, but you certainly looked top-of-the-trees today." He ran a fingertip across the point of her shoulder. A tingle ran all the way down her back to her toes.

And she thought he hadn't noticed her new gown. "Thank you."

Afraid she would say something to spoil their accord, she stood up. "If you will excuse me, my lord, I think it is time to change for dinner."

He rose with her. He reached for her hand and brushed his lips across her knuckles. "I'm only sorry I can't join you, my lady." He raised his gaze to hers, and her heart leaped at the piratical gleam in his eyes.

She managed a shaky laugh. "There isn't any point. I'm planning an early night."

A teasing smile curved his lips. "I wouldn't mind an early night myself."

Trembles shivered her stomach, and a delicious warmth heated her skin. He was flirting again. She searched her mind for a witty response. "It might do you some good." How feeble she sounded. How green girlish.

His lids dropped a fraction. "Perhaps on another occasion?"

Utterly charming. A jolt of something hot arrowed to her core. No wonder women flocked to please him.

This practiced flirtation meant nothing. It couldn't, not with her, but if he said one more word, she'd turn into a puddle of mush.

"I'll certainly look forward to it," she managed to gasp and swept out of the door on legs seemingly made of butter.

❋   ❋   ❋   ❋

"How is that, my lady?" the hairdresser asked.

Caro stared in awe at her reflection. With her hair piled high on her head, she did look less of an apple dumpling, as the hairdresser had promised.

"Thank you, it's perfect."

"You are welcome, my lady." He packed up his pins and ribbons and brushes. "It is a pleasure to work for such a lovely lady." He bowed himself out.

Flatterer. The mirror didn't lie. She might be tricked out in finery and primped and curled, but her figure retained all its old faults, even if they were better disguised by the stylish gown. And her hair and eyes remained the latest shade of mouse. No wonder Lucas never spent time at home.

She turned to Lizzie, who stood ready to help her into her gown. "Do you prefer the straw-colored silk or the white muslin?"

"Either one will suit," Lizzie muttered, still sulking about the hairdresser.

Caro slipped her arms out of the dressing gown and stared at the two creations on the bed.

"Wear the yellow," a deep voice pronounced.

Her breath escaped in a rush. She whirled around. Lucas, bare-chested, clad only in his breeches, slouched against the doorjamb of their adjoining chambers with the grin of a satisfied cat.

She snatched up the first thing to hand, the yellow dress, and clutched it against her chest. Her flaming face promptly set light to the rest her body. "What are you doing in here?"

Lizzie's gaze flicked from one to the other.

He crossed his arms over his chest. "Lizzie, be gone."

Frozen by his shocking state of undress, Caro kept her gaze located somewhere above his right shoulder. At least, she tried to keep it fixed there and not on his sculpted arms, or the sprinkle of dark hair on his broad chest, or the ridges of muscle beneath clearly defined ribs and not an ounce of fat to be seen, curse him. "Stay, Lizzie," she choked out. "His lordship is leaving."

She groaned inwardly. Could a wife be any less welcoming?

"Out, Lizzie," Lucas said. "Lady Foxhaven will ring for you when she needs you."

Lizzie whisked herself out of the door with eyes

as round as tea plates.

Caro inhaled a shaky breath. "I haven't finished dressing. I will be late."

He stared at her hair and nodded slowly. "It looks nice." His gaze dropped to her face. "I have barely seen you all week."

Hardly her fault. He came home late every night.

She kept her tone neutral. "It seems we have both had plenty to keep us entertained."

A wistful smile curved his lips and tugged at her heart. "I wondered how you were doing."

She gave him a brilliant and patently artificial smile. "I'm doing very well, thank you."

"Good. I hope Cedric has been taking care of you in my absence. Important business, you know."

Lady Caradin? Or had some new light of love caught his wandering gaze. Pinpricks raced over her skin. "I'm sure."

He gestured at the gown clutched to her bosom. "Wear that one. You will stand out amongst all the vestal virgins."

"I think the white would be best."

He cocked his head to the side. "Why so?"

"I really don't want to stand out, and the neckline isn't quite so low."

"And besides," he said, with a grin so cheeky it drove her breath from her lungs, "you are a virgin."

A blazing furnace engulfed her. At any moment, she'd be naught but a smoldering heap of ashes on the pale blue carpet. She swallowed. "I think you should leave me to dress."

With slow steps, he moved toward her. "I can help you with your gown, if you wish."

His murmur caressed her skin as if he'd run his hands over her body. Flames turned to liquid fire and ran in her veins, setting off hot explosions in her breasts and deep between her thighs. Her heartbeat slammed against her ribs. She had wanted his attention. But now that she had it, it frightened her to death.

His gaze devoured her face and neck and slid down her body, heating each spot where it rested. "Both are lovely, Caro. It won't matter which one you wear."

She retreated a step and found the wall at her back. She had nowhere left to go and no voice to speak. Even if she had a voice, what would she say? Take me, I'm yours?

She stared into his face, lean and angled and strong. Tears and laughter hovered in her throat, and a strange feeling of power thrummed under her skin.

The gleam in his dark eyes danced. In a flash, large hands braced against the wall on each side of her head, broad forearms imprisoning her. His smoldering gaze held her pinned. The aromatic scent of sandalwood filled her every quick breath.

Do something, she thought. The gown fell in a puddle at her feet. She pressed her hands to his chest flattening the rough curls, absorbing the silken warmth beneath. Her palms tingled.

His gaze raked from her face to her breasts, and his nostrils flared as if he might inhale her. He dipped his head, dark lashes drooping to cover his eyes and long hair falling forward, skimming her face and blocking the light.

She parted her lips to taste him.

A rarified headiness numbed her thoughts and emboldened her spirit. Without thought, she brushed her lips across his mouth, tasting brandy, warmth, and velvet softness.

His mouth angled, pressing down, scorching and moist. A shiver, hot and sharp, tore into her stomach and then slid lower, deeper, in pulsing waves. Breathing became impossible as he cupped her face in his hands. His tongue traced her lips and then touched her tongue.

Lightning seared down her spine.

The heat of his hard body pressed against the hills and valleys of hers flowed through her skin like warm sun. She arched closer, felt the pressure of his thigh against her hip, his heartbeat battering her sensitized breasts. She trembled, not from cold, but from a delicious aching tension.

He lifted his head, staring at her as if seeing her for the first time. He drew in a deep shuddering breath. "My God. I must be mad."

Mad? The word slashed her with the bone-chilling force of a summer hailstorm. "W-what?"

He turned away and curled his fist around the bedpost, his knuckles white as he stared at the carving in blank disgust. "Good God. I should never have come in here. What a dreadful mistake."

Dreadful? She had thought it wonderful. Misery seeped into her soul. Mountains of flesh thrown wantonly his way had scared him off.

Cool air chilled her bare skin. She wrapped her arms around her waist. He plucked her dressing gown off the end of the bed and handed it to her without looking back. He evidently couldn't stand the sight of her. She shoved her arms in the sleeves and tied the cord.

"A mistake," she echoed. "Quite." She felt a burning prickle of tears in her eyes and forced them back with a firm blink. "How did you get in here, anyway?"

He gave her a half-ashamed smile over his sculpted shoulder, a shoulder she had felt under her hands moments before. "Through the window?"

"Very humorous. I thought the door between our rooms was locked."

"It was. From my side." He strode to the door and pulled the key from the other side. He tossed it on the bed. "I'm sorry."

So was she. That he hadn't wanted her. She felt as empty as church on Monday morning and twice as cold. "Apology accepted." What else could she say if she wanted to retain a shred of self-esteem?

He opened the door. "I promise you, it won't happen again." He closed the door behind him.

Caro flashed across the room. She needed to lock it before tears of embarrassment started to flow.

❀   ❀   ❀   ❀

The metal tumblers clicked. Lucas stared at the oak-paneled door and swore long and fluently beneath his breath.

The echo of her ripe voluptuous form beneath a mere whisper of fine lawn branded his skin. The urge to kiss the anxiety from her tawny eyes had sent him beyond reason. She tasted like wild honey or some exotic nectar, an intoxicating brew that had made him lose his mind. She'd yielded to him with such sweetness that all thoughts of honor had departed on a tide of lust. He touched his lips, seeking the essence of her mouth with his fingertips. Kisses weren't the only thing he wanted. What the hell was the matter with him? She was his friend, not some lightskirt. Did he want to prove her right not to trust him, the way he'd proved his father right all these years?

Confound it. She was an innocent. He must have scared her witless.

In the only free moment he'd had in days, he'd intended a friendly visit. If he couldn't keep himself under control, he'd be better off going to his club than going to Almack's. Damn it, he would not go back on his word and ruin their friendship. Nor would he risk getting her with child and playing into his father's hands.

No regrets? Bloody hell.

He picked up the crystal goblet from his night table and flung it at the wall. It shattered with a crash.

"Something wrong, my lord?" Danson emerged from the dressing room on the other side of the chamber.

"Nothing is wrong," Lucas said through his teeth. "Put out the black coat and silver waistcoat. I'm going out—hopefully today, if it's not too much trouble."

"I'll have no truck with your temper, lad," Danson replied. "You'll wait until I clean up this glass."

※　　　※　　　※　　　※

"I thought Luc planned to join us," Bascombe said, following Caro into the Audleys' shining black carriage when he and Tisha collected her at nine o'clock.

Caro smoothed her skirts with studied nonchalance. "No. He despises Almack's. They serve nothing but tea." She sent him a quick smile. "I thought you knew."

The coach swayed and then rumbled forward.

"They serve orgeat also," Tisha offered from her corner, her face alive with merriment. "I doubt Lucas would care for that either." The shake of her head sent the diamonds artfully wound through her raven curls winking in the lamplight.

Bascombe frowned. "He said he might rearrange something and come with us."

"He did?" Could that be why he had entered her chamber? And then something she'd done had repulsed him. A horrid little lurch in her stomach nauseated her. She hunched into her cloak, glad of the shadows in the carriage. "Lucas changes his mind with the weather."

Bascombe chuckled. "He probably received a better offer after I spoke to him this afternoon."

Or the sight of me practically naked made him ill.

"Pay it no heed," Tisha said. "There will be lots of other gentlemen to dance with, in addition to Charlie here."

A stifled groan issued from Charlie's corner. Tisha rapped his knee with her fan and then held it open for inspection with a deft turn of her wrist. "Do you like it? Audley sent it from Paris with Wellington."

"It's lovely," Caro said.

"Chicken skin," Tisha said. She held it close to the lamp. "It has scenes from Paris. Look, the Tuillieries and the Seine." She pouted and slumped back. "I wish he had delivered it himself, or better yet, sent for me, so I can see them in person."

"You know it is not safe. France is far too unsettled." Bascombe said.

"You are just siding with Audley," Tisha said. "I'd be perfectly safe in Paris with Wellington in charge of the allied army."

"You must miss your husband," Caro said.

Tisha's shoulders drooped even more. "This is the first time we have been apart since we married. He promised it will be the last time. He doesn't like it any more than I do, but it is important for his career."

A love match. How wonderful that must be.

"Don't take on so, old thing," Bascombe said, patting her hand. "He'll be back the moment Stuart can release him."

"I know," Tisha said on a wistful note. "The ambassador places great reliance on him, you know, Carolyn. Audley hopes to make the cabinet one day. In the meantime, he expects me to attend all the parties and routs and write to him about all the latest on dits. So we must make good use of our evening."

By the time the carriage arrived on King Street outside the Assembly Rooms, Caro's jangled nerves had settled into the occasional sick roll of her stomach each time she remembered Lucas's kiss. Unfortunately, that occurred with horrible frequency.

Bascombe guided them up the stairs and inside. A large number of people had already filled the grand chamber.

The moment she entered through the hallowed portals, Caro glimpsed Aunt Rivers seated near the musicians. "I must greet Lucas's aunt," she murmured to Tisha.

"Of course you must. I will go with you if you wish."

In her pink silk gown and glittering diamonds, the diminutive countess swept down the room like royalty, acknowledged by everyone she passed.

In her wake, Caro happily disappeared into insignificance.

She had almost cried off this morning after jolting awake in the middle of the night with a heart-stilling memory of her wallflower status at assemblies in Norwich. In those days, she'd disguised her chagrin by taking up residence behind a potted plant, a large one. She didn't see any suitably sized greenery in Almack's ballroom.

Upon reaching Aunt Rivers, Caro performed the introductions. Tisha's friendly manner seemed to warm the frosty widow. Cedric's face broke into one of his rare warm smiles. "I hope you will honor me with the first country dance, cousin."

His offer to dance made her glad she had stiffened her resolve to attend. "You are very kind."

With a reassuring smile, Tisha drifted away to greet other friends.

The musicians struck up a reel, and Cedric held out his arm. Knowing she was smiling far more than she should, and unable to do anything about it, Caro took his arm, and he led her into the closest set.

Across the square from her, Cedric's serious face settled into grim determination. His black tailcoat fit snug across his narrow shoulders, and his sky-blue waistcoat with silver embroidery nodded modestly to fashion. Not a dark hair out of place, his shirt points just high enough to be fashionable without being pretentious, he exuded respectability. Lucas could do worse than follow his cousin's example.

Cedric also danced with solemn care. For the first time in her life, she felt comfortable on a dance floor. Her smiled broadened. She was actually dancing at Almack's. She couldn't wait to write and tell her sisters all about it.

At their turn to go down the set, their hands met in the center, and they passed between the lines of other couples. "Someone has just arrived I know you will wish to meet," Cedric murmured, leaning his head close.

Lucas? He'd come after all. Her heart beat a little harder. "Where is he?"

"With my mother."

The gentleman beside Aunt Rivers was nothing like Lucas—she could see that from his height and the set of his shoulders, even without her spectacles. How foolish to think he might have followed them after all.

"Who is he?" she asked

"I will introduce you."

Cedric had an air of suppressed excitement. She nodded and concentrated on her steps. She had no wish to make an idiot of herself by tripping head over heels. It would take at least five of these delicate dandies to set her back on her feet. Well, maybe not five, but a couple.

At the end of the dance, they rejoined Cedric's mother, and at their approach, a gentleman in a dark brown coat with olive skin, hair the color of coffee, and a flashing white smile flourished an elegant bow.

"Lady Foxhaven, allow me to introduce the Chevalier François Valeron," Cedric said.

The room tilted and then steadied. "Valeron? That was my mother's maiden name."

A triumphant smile spread across Cedric's stern face. "François is your distant cousin. We met in Paris. He mentioned his hope of locating a relative who fled to England during the terrors. It was not until Mother mentioned your mother's maiden name that I realized the possible connection. I took the liberty of writing to the Chevalier to tell him of my suspicions."

"Mademoiselle, *enchanté*." The Chevalier Valeron tapped his forehead. "Forgive me. Now you are Lady Foxhaven, *n'est ce pas?* I am *desolé*. Your husband, he is here also?"

His accent and husky voice combined in fascinating charm.

Smiling, Caro held out her hand. "Can it be true, indeed? I understood all of my French relatives had perished."

Putting a hand on his heart, he smiled. "I hate to argue with a lady." Sadness crossed his suave features. "*Mais non*. Not all. Some were lucky, as the English say. I am doubly fortunate, now that I meet you."

He bowed low, with astonishing grace.

"I can't quite believe it," Caro said. "My mother never heard from her family. You are sure?"

"*Vraiment?* I am positive, sweet lady."

"A cousin?"

"By adoption. There is also your great aunt, Honoré, and some distant cousins who live near

Reims. But tell me about your family. Mr. Rivers told me your poor *maman* died many years ago, but there are sisters, *non?*"

"*Non*, I mean, si. I have three sisters. Both my parents passed away."

"I am so sorry. However, if your sisters are half as lovely as you, they will be *ravissant.*"

"You flatter me, Chevalier."

"No, indeed," he said, his brown eyes sincere.

Caro laughed, utterly dazzled. He was just the sort of relative one would wish for, a man of the world with elegant manners and perfect tailoring.

"Thank you, sir. My sisters are, in my eyes at least, the most beautiful girls in the world, and I miss them terribly."

"They are younger?"

"Alex—Alexandra that is—is seventeen, Lucy is sixteen, and Jacqueline is fifteen."

"Ah, Jacqueline. A French name like yours, *n'est ce pas?*"

"*Oui.*" Although she had not conversed in French for years, Caro slipped into it easily. "My mother tried to keep some of her heritage, although the French are not so very popular in England at the moment."

He shook his head. "I have received a warm welcome."

"I'm glad."

"I wonder if I might have the pleasure of dancing with you later this evening?"

"Of course." Caro glanced up at Cedric.

He raised an eyebrow and then nodded.

"Ah," François said, reverting to English. "The

cautious Mr. Rivers. Did you know he spends as much time in Paris as he does in London?"

"I had no idea," Caro said.

"Lord Stockbridge has a great many interests in France and particularly in Champagne," Cedric said. "I represent him on business."

"And I am grateful for the opportunity to be of service to Mr. Rivers," François said. "His lordship is a lucky man to have someone so careful with his investments."

Unlike Lucas, who had frittered his money away on gambling and unmentionable interests, Caro thought. She inclined her head and gave Cedric a warm smile. "Lord Stockbridge is indeed fortunate."

François kissed the tips of her gloved fingers and bowed. "Until later, cousin Carolyn." He sauntered away. He was a man of enchanting address.

The evening passed all too quickly. Tisha introduced Caro to members of her set. Caro danced with Bascombe, François and again with Cedric. To her surprise, several other young gentlemen also asked her to dance. They must have done so to oblige Tisha.

Tisha laughed when she said so. "Ah, my dear Carolyn, you are one of a kind, it seems. You will be the season's incomparable; just wait and see."

Caro giggled. "Hardly." But how sweet of her to say so.

Tisha simply arched a brow.

The whole thing would have been perfect if only Lucas had been present to witness her success, she thought sleepily on the carriage ride home at two in the morning.

A yawning footman admitted her into the house. "Good evening, my lady."

"More like good morning," she said with a stab of guilt, handing him her cloak. "Thank you for waiting up. I won't need you any more this evening. Please do go to bed."

She headed for the stairs, her legs like lead.

A door creaked open. "So there you are at last, pigeon," Glowering, he stood outlined in his study doorway.

"I wish you would not call me that," she said.

His frown deepened. "Did you have a pleasant evening?"

"How kind of you to wait up to inquire. It was very pleasant. You will never guess—"

"Oh, very pleasant." His mouth curled up in a sneer. "Enjoyed the dancing, did you?"

She stiffened. "Yes, of course."

He slouched against the doorframe and crossed his arms over his chest. "So I saw."

"You were there?"

"At the door. I arrived after eleven. Willis wouldn't let me in."

A vision of the careless Lucas in velvet knee breeches and silk stockings barred from entry drew a chuckle from her. "Too bad."

He looked as sulky as a boy refused a treat, almost as morose as the first time he had asked for her hand. "Goddamn it, Caro. It's not funny." His voice rasped and his words were not entirely crisp.

Caro blinked. With his hair falling loose, his cravat hanging free around his neck, and his waistcoat unbuttoned, he looked thoroughly dissipated. "Are you foxed?"

His broad shoulders lifted. Strange that such a small movement should have the power to hold her gaze, to fascinate. "A little warm perhaps," he slurred.

And from his expression, he wasn't particularly happy. Her exciting news would have to wait. "I hope you will excuse me. I am too tired for conversation." She picked up her skirts and started up the stairs.

His hand covered hers on the balustrade before she had taken two steps. Storms swirled in the depths of his dark eyes as he stared up at her. "I want a word with you."

"Surely, this can wait until morning?"

His warm hand clenched down like a vice. "It is important."

Prickles raced down her spine, the same kind of excitement she'd felt at his kiss. Her stomach dropped at the recollection of his distaste. She tugged at her fingers. "Do you want to wake the whole house?"

A hard smile curved his lips. "Do you?"

The thought of the servants listening stopped her dead. She shook her head.

He jerked his head toward the study. "In there."

Pulling her hand free, she swirled around and marched into the small ground-floor room where Lucas took care of his business. Whatever that was.

She sank onto the single comfortably stuffed armchair fronting the desk. "Well?"

"Well what?" he drawled and perched one hip on the corner of his desk.

She felt a flutter of disquiet. Perhaps he wanted to

discuss what had happened in the bedroom. She steeled herself. "You said you had something important to tell me."

"I wanted to warn you," he said vaguely. "You are not completely up to snuff."

"Warn me about what?"

"About the kind of men who spend their time at places like Almack's, for one thing."

"You mean men like your cousin?"

He waved a dismissive hand. "Not poor old Cedric. Men who make it their business to dance with other men's wives."

She wrinkled her nose, not sure she understood, but sensing that he placed a great deal of importance on this mysterious group of men. "Men like Mr. Walton? I danced with him. Or Mr. Bascombe?"

"Yes. Like Bascombe. Unattached men looking for the main chance," he ground out.

"The chance to dance," she hazarded, giggling at how silly it sounded.

"It is not dancing I am talking about."

This was all very confusing. "Then what?"

A groan rumbled up from his chest. "You are such an innocent. Can't you see? Almack's is not only a marriage mart; it is a place where gentlemen seek out female company."

"They could hardly dance with each other."

He blinked. "What are you talking about?"

"There is also the card room."

"At a penny a point? No self-respecting man would tolerate it unless he had an ulterior motive."

This conversation seemed to be going in circles. "Please, Lucas, what is it you wanted to say?"

"I am telling you to be careful. Take Charlie Bascombe, for example."

Caro nodded, hoping to still his growing agitation.

"He ain't interested in the parson's mousetrap. Couldn't be, if he spends all his time dancing and flirting with my wife."

She frowned. "He wasn't flirting; he was dancing and talking."

Triumph crossed his face. "There, that's just what I mean. Why is Charlie Bascombe doing the pretty with a married woman? And Walton."

"You are wrong. They all behaved like perfect gentlemen."

"Unlike me, of course."

She narrowed her eyes. She'd had just about enough of this drunken interrogation. He seemed bent on spoiling her wonderful evening for no reason at all. "Very unlike you indeed, from the way he dresses to the way he behaves with respect to his family."

She pressed a hand to her mouth, wishing the rush of words back where they came from.

"Is that right?" He stalked closer and stood over her, his eyes fathomless in an expressionless mask. His fingers encircled her upper arms and he dragged her to her feet, the smoky tang of whisky strong on his breath.

She gasped. "Stop it."

He pulled her close, capturing the back of her head in one hand, pressing his mouth savagely against hers.

Sandalwood and whisky and cigar smoke filled her senses, and she yielded to the soul-draining pressure of his hard body.

His hands ran over her shoulders and down her back, hot and heavy, pressing her into him, kneading her flesh. His harsh breathing drowned out the sound of her heartbeat.

This could only lead to trouble. He must be too drunk to know what he was doing. If only she had the strength to stop him.

But she couldn't let him go. Her body arched against him, yearning to feel him hard against her, longing for his strength, his searing kiss. Her hands slipped around his neck; her fingers raked through his silky hair. She opened her mouth to his questing tongue and quaked with passion. She had gone mad.

Their tongues intertwined. A quiver of sweet tension spiked low in her stomach.

He lifted his head and gazed into her face.

Afraid her trembling legs would give way, she clung to him.

His beautiful mouth curled in derision. "How does that compare with your perfect gentleman?"

He thought she had kissed his friend? A red mist clouded her vision. She clenched her fingers in his hair, saw his wince of pain, and felt a rush of satisfaction tinged with fear at her daring.

She dropped her hand and stepped back, her chest rising and falling in time to the angry pulse in her blood. "It bears no comparison, Lucas, because it didn't happen. Mr. Bascombe is not a despicable rake. At least he knows how to behave with honor."

He flinched.

The words hung heavy in the silent room.

He remained utterly still, his onyx eyes bleak and cold. Caro felt as if he were piercing her soul with shards of ice. Unable to bear the taut silence any longer, she ran from the room and raced up the stairs. He'd ruined a wonderful evening.

Eight

"*I* THINK LADY AUDLEY WAS RIGHT ABOUT THIS color suiting me." Caro ran her hand down the front of the rust-colored silk with its blue frog closing over the white satin slip. She glanced at Lizzie. "I would never have chosen such a strong color myself, but I think these short sleeves make the tops of my arms look bigger than they are."

Lizzie tied the matching blue cord under Caro's bosom in a neat bow. "Rubbish. It looks fine enough. But you should have let that seamstress do the neckline like the picture. All the ladies wear them lower, even out walking. There's nothing like a bit of bosom to keep a man on his toes."

Fire crept up her neck and into her face. "Perhaps a bit, but not acres."

"Lord love you, why not make the most of it?"

"Lizzie, this is hardly a suitable topic of conversation. And I know I've added at least an inch since we arrived in London."

Lizzie's homely face crumpled. "It's because you aren't happy." She shook her head. "His lordship never did you any favors asking you to marry him. Can't have, when all you wants to do is eat sweets."

"Nonsense. It has nothing to do with Foxhaven. I'm just not getting enough exercise here in Town. We never walk anywhere." Not that any amount of walking would turn her into a wraith like the wispy Louisa Caradin or the dainty Tisha Audley. Her childhood had taught her that much.

She frowned. "I suppose I should go down."

"When are you going to tell his lordship about meeting yer cousin?" Lizzie asked, holding out the spangled shawl.

Caro bit her lip while Lizzie settled the shawl around her shoulders. She hadn't set eyes on Lucas since their unpleasant encounter two days ago—the reason she'd taken to ordering cream cakes from the local confectioner. "I'm waiting for the right moment."

"Aye," Lizzie said, with a dour look. "Best tell him at dinner before you run into the fellow tonight."

Perhaps she'd tell him over dessert.

"Be off with you, my lady. And enjoy yerself."

She braced her shoulders as if preparing to face an ogre and made her way downstairs. Perhaps she would pretend that their argument had never happened.

Entering the drawing room, she found Lucas slouched on the couch, a moody cast to his mouth. He appeared to have made a special effort this evening. Even his cravat had several folds and a complex knot. His choice of a dark wine-colored coat, rather than his usual black, emphasized his dark hair and eyes and made him seem sinfully handsome.

Too handsome for a pudgy female, she thought. She could almost hear the ton whisper, "No wonder he keeps a mistress."

He rose, bowed with stiff formality, and indicated the tray of drinks set on the inlaid sideboard between the windows. "May I offer you a glass of wine, my lady?"

She forced a cool smile around the shake in her breathing. "No, thank you."

"You do not mind if I do? These types of affairs always make me nervous."

Nervous? Lucas? She couldn't imagine it. She sank onto the sofa. "Please do, if it helps."

He poured himself a drink and turned to face her. "You look charming in that color, Caro."

A swift glance at his polite expression assured her of his lack of sarcasm. "Thank you. You also look quite splendid."

The silence dragged on. Then they both spoke at the same time.

"I beg your pardon," Lucas said. "What did you say?"

"Nothing. The merest commonplace." Caro lifted her hand. "Please continue."

He strolled over to the chair opposite her and dropped into it.

A ball of wool knotted up somewhere in her hollow stomach.

"I'm sorry about the other night," he said, the words bitten out as if they cut his tongue. "According to our agreement, you have the right to dance with whomsoever you wish. I just want you to take care of your reputation. Tisha Audley is not necessarily a good role model, and Bas has a reputation as a ladies' man."

Talk about the pot slandering the kettle.

"You would do better to put yourself in Cedric's hands," he said.

For a moment, Caro longed to accede to the appeal in his dark eyes. "I like your cousin and will certainly be guided by your aunt, but Tisha and Mr. Bascombe have been nothing but kind. They are good friends."

The faint lines around his mouth seemed to deepen. "Then I will say nothing more."

Her heart stumbled, her resolve faltering as it always had when he had had that hurt puppy-dog look as a boy. It rarely appeared any more; he seemed so sure of himself these days. She drew in a breath, ready to recant.

Before she could speak, he reached into his pocket. "I noticed how little jewelry you have, and since I have not given you a bride gift, I thought you might like this." He drew forth a velvet pouch and emptied a shimmering strand of diamonds into his palm.

She gasped. "Oh, Lucas. It's beautiful, but I really cannot accept such an expensive gift."

"Why not?" His voice sounded harsh. "Because it's from me?"

"Of course not. I could never wear anything so expensive . . . so exotic."

"Nonsense. With your long neck and beautiful shoulders, it will look lovely with that gown."

Beautiful? Her. She almost melted. His eyes

gleamed as bright as the diamonds in his long fingers. Was this more of his careless flirting? "I might lose it," she murmured.

He shrugged. "Then I will buy you another. You are the future Countess of Stockbridge. How does it look if you have naught but a string of pearls to your name?" As he spoke, he came around behind her. "Hold still."

Quite enchanted by its delicacy, she let him fasten the choker around her neck. If he wanted to use this to make up for their quarrel, she ought to be gracious. She did so hate being at odds with him. She always had.

Taking her hand, he brought her to her feet and led her to the mirror beside the window. As fine as a bedewed spider's web, the necklace lay against her throat as if designed for her alone. He traced the edge of it with a fingertip. The knot in her stomach unraveled so fast her head swam.

"It is glorious," she gasped. "Thank you."

"It has been in the Rivers family for generations, but I believe it looks better on you than any of the former countesses."

"How would you know?"

"From their portraits, of course." His smile in the glass faltered. "Do you think we can call a truce tonight? It will be dashed awkward otherwise."

She'd like nothing better. They had never argued before, and it hurt. The smile on her lips trembled with effort. "Very well."

His gaze dropped to her mouth. The air between them picked up the fire of the diamonds, glittering back and forth in jagged points of heat. Her breathing shallowed to small sips of air in time with her heartbeat.

The light graze of his fingers on her throat burned a fiery trail. It drifted lower. He leaned close. He was going to kiss her again. Her heart pounded with a mixture of excited fear and terrified anticipation.

A knock sounded on the door. They jumped apart like children caught in mischief. Lucas turned away, but not before she saw what looked like disappointment on his face. A spurt of something dangerous coursed through her veins. Clearly there was more than friendship between them, now. She just wished she understood what it was.

Beckwith cleared his throat. "Dinner is served, my lord."

How could she now risk spoiling their new accord by telling him about her cousin?

❈　　❈　　❈　　❈

The line of carriages waiting to disgorge their passengers started almost two streets from the Cardross townhouse.

Lucas passed the time telling wicked gossip about the people they were likely to meet. By the time the coach drew up, he had her in fits of giggles.

"At last," he said helping her to alight. He shot her a lopsided grin. "Ready to face the beau monde? Don't worry, I'll be right behind you."

"I would prefer to be behind you. Not that it would do me much good." It would be like trying to hide an elephant behind a gazelle.

He chuckled, resting his hand gently on the small of her back, guiding, supporting, assuring her she wasn't alone.

A sense of indescribable happiness swept over her.

Things were back to normal. She wanted to throw her arms around his neck and kiss him. A strange little smile caught at her lips. That might prove risky in public if their response to each other flamed out of control, the way it had the last time they kissed.

Arm in arm, they strolled up the steps of the magnificent portico and past the waiting servants. A butler took Lucas's card at the entrance to the ballroom and bellowed, "Viscount and Lady Foxhaven."

Caro snickered.

"Behave," Lucas muttered and gave her arm a friendly squeeze. His eyes gleamed amusement. "You're not supposed to look as if you are enjoying this. Ennui is the thing."

Why couldn't it always be like this? The way they were before he left Norwich for London.

"There are Bas and Lady Audley," he said.

In an overflowing ballroom, Lucas had managed to see their friends over the heads of the crowd. He guided her through the crush of the crowd, and they joined a merry group of young people.

Some of them Caro recognized from Tisha's afternoon tea and others from Almack's. She joined the conversation as if she had known everyone all her life.

Within minutes of her arrival, several gentlemen claimed dances. Lucas had insisted on two waltzes before they left home, and Charles asked for a quadrille.

"Shall we?" Lucas asked as the orchestra struck up the first waltz.

"I would love to," Caro replied, smiling up at him. Content that she looked her best, she held her chin up as Lucas swept her onto the dance floor. He danced with ease and grace, his body flowing with the music. Instead of feeling awkward and leaden, she floated beneath his gentle guidance.

She glanced up at him.

Neatly avoiding another couple, he raised a brow. "Do my buttons meet with your approval?"

As usual, her heart tumbled over at his closeness, but she managed the cool smile of the jaded fashionable lady. "Indeed."

"You dance divinely," he murmured close to her ear.

A frisson of awareness rippled over her skin, and her unruly pulse picked up speed. "I didn't suspect you could dance," she shot back bravely. "I thought Corinthians despised such dull entertainments."

She'd watched him dance at the Norwich Assembly from behind her favorite plant. Elegant and thoroughly bored, he'd left after a row with his father because he'd danced three times with a female of suspicious morals.

It was as if he had deliberately set out to annoy his father.

"I'll tell you a secret," he whispered, drawing her far closer than regulations allowed. "I only dance with special ladies."

Caro heard emphasis on the plural. "Then, I suppose I must consider myself honored, my lord."

He swirled her around the end of the dance floor to the dying notes of the music and then escorted her back to their friends. Bascombe greeted her with a glass of champagne.

Lucas laughed when she wrinkled her nose.

"The bubbles make my face wet," she explained. She glanced around the room. "You know we really should go and greet your Aunt Rivers."

"You go." He flashed a wicked smile. "I'm promised to Tisha for this next dance."

He wasn't, but Tisha cast him a roguish smile and allowed him to lead her onto the dance floor. Pride and a small ache pulled at Caro's heart. No woman could resist Lucas when he smiled like that.

A passing footman took her empty glass and handed her a new one. Sipping it, she wove among the chatting groups of ladies and gentlemen. Glittering jewels and rich colors of silks and satins blended together in an artist's palette of swirling colors. Solid shapes jumped out from the mix as she passed through them. She pulled out her spectacles and made a concentrated search for Lucas's aunt.

Seated against a wall at the back of the room with a stiff, formal Cedric at her side, the elderly lady held out her hand. Caro took it and curtseyed. This was how she imagined an audience with the Queen, something she would have to endure later in the season.

Aunt Rivers directed a glare behind Caro. "Where is that good-for-nothing husband of yours?"

Cedric tutted.

A sudden urge to stuff her handkerchief in her blunt aunt's mouth, or to rush to Lucas's defense, parted Caro's lips.

"Close your mouth, Carolyn," Aunt Rivers rapped out. "I see him now, tripping around the dance floor with that flighty Lady Audley when he ought to be here paying his respects."

Aunt Rivers might be right, but Caro's sympathy

went out to Lucas. His aunt gave no quarter. "I'm sure he will come to see you as soon as he is able."

"Cousin Carolyn," a silky voice murmured behind her.

The arrival of François brought relief to the uncomfortable silence. Caro held out her hand, resting her fingertips on his glove as he bowed. Amusement glimmered in his brown eyes. "I hope you have saved a waltz for me as you promised?" he asked.

"I always keep my promises, sir."

"Waltzing? It is shocking," Aunt Rivers pronounced. "A peasant dance. It was not allowed in my day."

"No, indeed, Mother," Cedric said in soothing tones. He smiled at Caro. "I too would like to dance with you. A cotillion, if you please."

Caro liked the way he respected his mother's feelings. "I will be delighted."

"I do hope to be introduced to your so very fortunate husband this evening," François said. "I understand he likes the sports. How do you say it? He is a sportsman, *non*? He likes to gamble?"

"He's a rake," Aunt Rivers muttered.

Prickles danced down Caro's spine as another defense of Lucas hovered on her tongue. If only she had the courage to voice them. Only with Lucas did her words tumble forth—and always with disastrous consequences.

"You would be better to steer clear of him, young man," Aunt Rivers continued. She frowned. "No need to blush, girl. I am not saying anything that is not common knowledge."

Caro's tongue remained firmly stuck to the roof of her mouth. She hadn't missed how every woman in the room regarded Lucas with the half-fearful, half-fascinated expression of a lamb before a wolf. They must all know his reputation.

His voice kind, Cedric put a hand on his mother's shoulder. "He's young yet, still finding his way."

"Nonsense," his mother uttered with the arrogance of age. Her pointed nose rose a disdainful notch. "He's a married man and should be thinking about settling down and starting a family."

Mortification heated Caro's cheeks. They would never have children.

"Don't worry, Mother," Cedric said in soothing tones. "After all, he did purchase Lady Bestborough's house."

"A house?" Caro said.

Cedric's gaze slid away.

Aunt Rivers pursed her corrugated lips. "I, for one, am not surprised you know nothing about it. I expect he bought it for something other than setting up his nursery."

Caro's stomach plunged to the soles of her golden slippers while her mind scrabbled for some reasonable explanation for this latest surprise.

François leaned close. "I believe this is our waltz."

Blessed escape. She clung to his arm as he drew her onto the floor.

He cast her a teasing smile. "You are charming when you blush, cousin, but I must say your aunt has a tongue like an asp, *n'est ce pas?* Right now you feel like Cleopatra, *non?*"

Caro sighed. "I suppose I must learn not to pay

attention to gossip."

With gentle pressure, he twirled her around, and she relaxed. Almost as smooth in his steps as Lucas, he brought her a little closer than she thought proper. Clearly, the French danced a more risqué form of the waltz.

She sought a safer topic of conversation. "How did you meet Cousin Cedric?"

"We have mutual business acquaintances in Paris. Lord Stockbridge places more trust in him than in his son, I hear."

Caro stiffened. More brickbats tossed at Lucas.

François grimaced. "*Pardonnez moi!* Now it is I who have the tongue like the snake. Forgive me."

The sincerity beaming in his eyes diluted her anger. She inclined her head with a brief smile. "This time."

"You are *trés gentil*. I meant his lordship has investments in the Champagne district and my family— your family too, I remind you—also has business interests there. You must come and see."

"Mother always hoped to return to Paris one day. She spoke of it often when I was a child. I would love to meet the rest of my family."

"It would be my pleasure to introduce them to you."

Although he was not as tall as Lucas, or as broad in the shoulders, François's charm of manner and Mediterranean good looks blended in a devastating mix. A lock of brown hair curled on his brow, and his mouth smiled all the time. If all Frenchmen were like him, she looked forward to meeting more of them.

In a sudden rush of steps, he swirled her in a tight

circle. Her head seemed to have trouble catching up to her feet. She clung to his coat sleeve as the music died away, trying to regain her balance and feeling rather hot.

With a touch on her elbow, François indicated a door. "Would you care for some fresh air? I believe there is a balcony through those glass doors, which for some reason the English call French windows."

Breathless, Caro laughed at his quizzical expression. "I think fresh air is a good idea."

The doors opened to a balcony lit by cleverly placed lanterns and a fortuitously full moon. With her arm looped under his, he walked her to the far end.

His teeth flashed white in the dim light. "There is a garden you can view from here. I think you will find it charming."

More lanterns hung in tree branches. The garden presented intriguing glimpses of stone cherubs, elves, and winged animals among the shadows. Caro leaned over the parapet. "How pretty."

The breeze cooled her cheeks. She stared into the night, waiting for her head to stop spinning or the ground to still.

"I would so like you to meet your aunt, Carolyn." His French accent caressed her in the cool dark night. "*Tante* Honoré, she grows old. I know she desires to meet you too. Do you think you can visit soon?"

One arm resting on the wall, his body angled toward her, he seemed more interested in her profile than the view. Interested in her as a woman.

A little pulse shot through her veins. She felt deliciously wicked, but safe. "I don't know. I would dearly love my sisters to see my mother's birthplace." She turned to face him. "I'm not sure Lucas would wish to go."

"Your French is impeccable, much better than my English. Paris would adore you."

"We used to converse in French all the time when *Maman* was alive. I fear I have forgotten much."

"I would be happy to, hmmmm . . ."

Entranced by his hesitation as he searched for a word, her gaze traveled over his face. He had none of Lucas's stark angled beauty; his face was fuller, more florid, but very pleasant to look at.

"I think of teach," he said with a small frown. "But it is not right. Perhaps tutor is better?"

"*Mais oui,*" Caro replied. "Your English is excellent."

He continued speaking in French. "Forgive me for asking, my dear, but you do not seem so very happy for such a new bride." Concern and curiosity lurked in his eyes.

It was obvious then. Her chest swelled with emotion at his gentle understanding and the caring she'd missed since her father died. She shook her head, unable to speak for the sudden tightening of her throat.

The cool breeze carried his floral cologne as he moved closer. A gloved fist ran down her jaw. "Not tears in those beautiful golden eyes?" he asked in a low whisper.

Her laugh sounded shaky. "Of course not."

One finger gently tipped up her chin. "Let me see."

※   ※   ※   ※

"Who is dancing with Caro?" Lucas asked Bas.

"A Frog. Chevalier Valeron. I met him at White's the other day, with your cousin. Seems a decent enough sort for a Frenchman. Plays deep, but pays promptly."

"Valeron? The name sounds familiar. Friend of Cedric's, is he?"

Beneath the central chandelier, Caro laughed at something the Frenchman said. Tawny flames danced in her hair and eyes. The restlessness that had consumed him when she danced with Charlie returned with a vengeance.

She had never looked so gorgeous, even if the modest cut of her dress hid most of her curves, the curves he'd felt yielding under his hands last night. Unwelcome heat rushed to his loins.

Tisha rapped his forearm with her fan. "I just left Julia Fairweather. You will never guess who is here."

"No, Tisha, I never will. I do not care for guessing games." And besides, he wanted to keep an eye on Caro and the good-looking Frenchman holding her undivided attention.

Tisha plucked at his sleeve, and he glanced into her face, which was brimming with mischief. "Your father arrived a half hour ago."

Inwardly, Lucas groaned, but he wasn't surprised. Not when his father had practically ordered him to attend this damnably boring function. Bloody hell. The evening had just become a whole lot less pleasant.

"You really should pay your respects, Luc,"

Bascombe said.

To hell with that. He didn't owe his father anything. He glanced at the dance floor. The waltz had ended, and Caro had disappeared.

Bascombe coughed behind his hand. "Went out on the balcony with the Frog. Better fetch her back before anyone notices."

With a curse, Lucas strolled around the edge of the dance floor, greeting acquaintances with as much calm as he could muster in his impatience. Any sign of a hurried exit, and he would raise the scent of scandal—something the ton adored.

Once outside, he glanced along the balcony's length. The couple murmuring in the shadows seemed unaware of his presence. They were much too engrossed in each other.

"Another conquest, Caro?" Sarcasm edged his words like a knife. A knife in the Chevalier's guts would have felt more satisfactory.

Caro jumped and stepped back.

The Frog merely smiled and turned to face him. "Lord Foxhaven, I presume." He bowed with an airy flourish.

"You have the advantage of me, sir," Lucas grated out, unable to take his gaze off a flushed and lip-nibbling Caro. She had every reason to feel nervous.

"Indeed, I believe it is so," the smooth French voice uttered mildly.

Lucas absorbed the double meaning. Heat burned his face, and he curled his fingers into his palms instead of around the Frenchman's neck.

Once more, the Chevalier made a leg fit for a king. "The Chevalier François Valeron, *à votre service*, milor'. I am cousin to your so charming wife. We were catching up on some family news." Turning to Caro, he switched to French. "Is that not so, cousin?"

"Well, Chevalier," said Lucas, in equally faultless French and clipped accents, "if catching up on news requires your hands on my wife, I will find it my pleasurable duty to teach you a lesson in English manners. I trust I make myself perfectly clear, you little worm."

Caro clapped her hands to her ears. "Lucas, how could you?"

"Indeed, my lord," François said, reverting to English, "you make yourself very clear, and with . . . eloquence. Since I find myself de trop, I will bid you both good evening. I look forward to our next meeting with much anticipation." Menace seethed below the Frenchman's suave, smiling surface.

Lucas watched the Frenchman's languid departure, his jaw tight enough to break his teeth. A pistol or a sword would be a handy thing to have right now, and to hell with polite society. He turned to glare at Caro.

Rosy-cheeked and with anger glistening in her eyes, she glared back and waved her arm in a dramatic sweep toward the garden. "How dare you speak that way to my cousin?"

She'd unsheathed her claws on the wrong man. "I dare because you are my wife, Caro, and your behavior in this leaves much to be desired. I heard about your little escapade in Bond Street, and now this. Are you so careless of your reputation? Even someone as easy-going as Tisha Audley will not tolerate such conduct."

"Who told you about Bond Street?" Her belligerent tone startled him.

The urge to fold her in his arms and stem her temper with a kiss on her full soft lips roared in his blood. But by God, he'd promised her a marriage in name only, and he would not go back on his word. He shoved his hands in his coat pockets. "A friend saw you."

Her eyes narrowed. "What friend?"

Their earlier camaraderie became a distant memory. How dare she question him? He suffered enough of that from his father. Nor would he lie. "Lady Caradin, if you must know."

Caro snorted and swung her arm in a wide semicircle. "What was Lady Caradin doing in Bond Street in the afternoon, answer me that?"

Lucas backed up a step and stared at her. He'd never seen her behave so oddly or her color quite so hectic. "How many glasses of champagne have you drunk?"

She put a steadying hand on the railing. Her voice increased in volume. "What has that got to do with Bond Street?"

Hell and damnation. At any moment, more people might wander out here. He tried to sound calm. "Nothing. I'm sorry, Caro. I was worried about you. I should not have said what I did to your cousin."

She pouted. "Hmph. You shouldn't have your mistress spying on me either."

His mistress? She thought Louisa Caradin was his mistress, and she didn't give a damn? Well, hell.

He kept his voice low. "This is not the time or place for such a discussion. Let us go back inside and enjoy the rest of the evening as if nothing untoward occurred."

"Nothing untoward did occur," she muttered, her eyes suddenly glassy with unshed tears. Her expression filled with a sadness he didn't understand. It was as if he'd crushed something she treasured beneath a careless boot heel. Guilt rocked him, and there was something else, something that hurt deep in his chest. Had she fallen for this fellow she'd met only twice?

He took her hand, relieved when she didn't pull away. "Then there is no more to be said. Let us continue with our truce as we agreed."

Her full bottom lip pushed out. "You should not have said—"

"You have had more than one glass of champagne, have you not?"

"Yes, I had two." She wrinkled her nose. "Or three. What has that to do with anything?"

If he didn't feel so off balance, he might have laughed. "I think it went to your head. Come, let us go back inside before we are missed."

He glanced into her huge fawn eyes and felt himself drowning. He took a deep breath. "Caro, please try to smile before you create a scandal."

Nine

"*Y*OU ARE A DAMN FOOL." STOCKBRIDGE, HIS mouth turned down, drew on the cigar clamped between his teeth.

In the matching bottle-green wing chair across the hearth from his father, Lucas stretched out his legs and leaned back. He blew out a sigh and waited for the rest, damning his father's tendency to arrive at ungodly early hours. Lucas had been thrown out of Hell's Kitchen at six this morning, and his head ached and his tongue had enough wool on it to make a blanket.

On his way to bed when his father arrived, he'd raced down to the library clad in his dressing gown. Another mark against him, no doubt.

"I can't believe any son of mine would behave this way," Stockbridge pronounced.

Having heard those words and many others like them before, Lucas closed himself off from their condemnation. He thrust his clenched fists deep in the slippery silk of his pockets. "My wife is perfectly satisfied with our arrangement."

His father's voice increased in volume. "Are you telling me Carolyn agrees with you racketing about town, gambling and carousing and setting up a house for your mistress?"

Hell. So that's what they were saying about Wooten House. Lucas flashed a negligent smile. "Yes."

His father eyed him balefully. "It won't do, sir. You owe it to your family name to produce the next heir. You need to pay attention to your wife."

Anger boiled in his veins, threatening to spill over. He rolled his shoulders and pretended a yawn. "I don't believe we are interested in breeding."

A dark red flush traveled up his father's face into his hairline. "By God, boy. It's your duty."

The old man would have an apoplexy if he didn't take care. Lucas's gut slipped sideways. He didn't want that guilt on his head. He kept silent.

Stockbridge tossed the cigar into the fire. He rested his forearms on his knees and lowered his tone. "Now listen to me, Foxhaven. This is important."

The reasonable tone of voice and the obvious attempt at control stirred suspicion in Lucas's breast. When his father wanted something, it came with a price. "I am listening."

"What I am about to tell you must not go out of this room. Do I have your word?"

"Would you trust it if I gave it?"

The fire crackled and hissed. Stockbridge glared and pressed his lips together.

By dint of long practice, Lucas kept his expression

bland and suffered the pain of his father's low opinion in silence. He forced a calm reply. "I give my word not to speak of it."

Stockbridge flicked his cigar into the fire and leaned back with the air of a man about to impart welcome news. "Any son produced by Carolyn is heir to a large inheritance from her mother's side of the family."

Every nerve jumping to attention at first, he then slouched deeper in the chair. "Rubbish. She only married me because her father left the family destitute."

"The Valeron family chateau and estate in Champagne is hers for the taking."

"There you are wrong. There's some cousin or other floating about. I met him." And would have killed him, given half the chance. He'd hoped to run into the bastard at one of the clubs or hells the previous night. A challenge over a gaming table would have been a fitting end to the scene on the balcony. Only Caro would never forgive him. An unfamiliar tightness squeezed his lungs.

Triumph turned his father's smile into a sneer. "The so-called Chevalier, you mean? He's not a blood relative." He reached into his breast pocket, pulled out a new cigar, and lit it.

Lucas waited. Father would not be rushed.

Stockbridge blew a smoke ring. "The old matriarch, Honoré Valeron, found him abandoned and adopted him after Carolyn's mother fled France with her parents. Somehow the old woman managed to keep her head and her estate. As the last direct descendant, any son born to Carolyn will inherit everything."

"This is significant?"

"God damn you, Foxhaven. Of course it is. Such a holding in France will have tremendous importance for the future."

Power. It was the one thing his father truly valued. Power over people, over decisions, over wealth. And he expected Lucas to feel the same.

Lucas gazed at his father. The noble brow, usually smooth and impassive, creased. A slight wavering in the drift of smoke from his cigar revealed a rare tremble to his hand. These were signs of stress under strict control; there was an element of panic behind the bluster. "Not done up, are you?" Lucas asked.

A muscle jerked in his father's heavy jowl. "Don't talk nonsense. You know nothing of business or politics. Just do as you are told."

Someone had Stockbridge backed into a corner. Lucas felt it in his bones. He pushed to his feet, wanting the interview over and not sure how to end it without forcibly throwing the old man out. He leaned his elbow on the mantel, staring into the flaming coals. He tapped the horse-headed, brass fire irons hanging from their stand with his booted foot. They chinked against each other, a carillon of tawdry bells.

He kept his voice casual. "How long have you known this?"

"Before I made the marriage contract with Torrington for his dumpling of a daughter, of course."

Lucas stiffened at the slight. He wanted to push the words down his father's throat. He clamped his jaw down hard. Anything he said would be grist for his father's mill.

Uninterested in any opinion Lucas might have, as always, Stockbridge continued his monologue. "The old fool. Never could see beyond the end of his sanctimonious nose. So glad to get an advantageous match, he couldn't wait to sign her over."

And you couldn't wait to do the same to me. Bitterness and sour brandy scoured Lucas's throat.

Damn it all. By serving his own ends, he'd become a pawn in his father's machinations—something he'd sworn never to allow again. He shot a sidelong glance at his father. "Why the haste? Heir now, heir later, what is the difference?"

Stockbridge spoke slowly as if instructing a child. "Because, my dear boy, if Carolyn doesn't have an heir before Honoré dies, it all goes to the Chevalier. According to Cedric, she wants to see it settled."

Why the hell hadn't Cedric told him what was in the wind? He usually forewarned him when Father had one of his starts. He spoke with chilly indifference. "I see. I will diligently plough the Torrington furrow, produce a nice little French heir, and assure the Stockbridge family a place in an anglophile France." He nudged at the coalscuttle with his foot. "In the meantime, the Stockbridge family fortunes will be augmented by a sound business proposition."

His father flashed him an ironic smile. "Your perspicacity, for once, is outstanding, Lucas."

The use of his Christian name meant his father presumed he'd won.

"How much is it worth?" Lucas asked.

"Twenty thousand a year, maybe more."

A soft whistle escaped him. Enough to bring the joy of music to hundreds of orphan boys. "To do anything else would not make sense, I suppose. Twenty thousand pounds a year would be an incentive to bed even the most unattractive female."

Stockbridge's gaze glittered with anticipation. "At last you show sense."

Lucas gripped the edges of the white marble mantelpiece, feeling the cold under his clammy palms. The plan did not benefit Caro one iota of course. She would simply be the conduit to more wealth for the Stockbridge coffers. He felt sick to his stomach at the betrayal.

He pushed away from the mantel and dropped into his chair. "Why the hell didn't you tell me about this before?"

"What?" His father's eyes opened wide and then shuttered. "It wasn't necessary for you to know."

"Because you knew I'd tell her father the truth. Because you knew she could marry whomever she pleased." The thought chilled his hot-blooded fury to ice.

"One fortune hunter is as good as another," Stockbridge said. "And even then you made a mess of it. Frightened her off the first time."

Lucas thumped the chair arm with his fist. "She only agreed to marry me because she had no option. What is she going to think when she finds out?"

"You are married. What can she do?"

She could invoke the escape clause in their agreement. Unless he got her with child. He had barely kept his hands off her these past few days. If he lost control again, that option would be lost to her. He felt like a bear in a trap. He'd have to chew off a limb to escape.

He would not go back on his word.

"Well?" Stockbridge said.

He gave his father stare for stare. "It all seems eminently reasonable, my lord. Therefore, I must refuse."

For a moment, Stockbridge's jaw worked as if he chewed on unpalatable fury. He leaped to his feet, his fleshy throat wobbling. "You impudent puppy. Are you telling me you won't get an heir?"

"Your grasp of the English language is extraordinary, sir."

Stockbridge's chest heaved on a huge in-drawn breath, and his black eyes bored into Lucas. "Damn you." He drew himself up straight. "There is one thing I can always say about you, Foxhaven," he grated out. "You never fail to disappoint me."

Refusing to flinch from the disgust on his father's face, Lucas rose languidly from his chair and, with a curl to his lip, executed a bow as elegant as the Chevalier's. "Glad to oblige, Father."

Stockbridge shoved past him and stormed out through the open door. His heavy tread clattered down the stairs, and a few moments later, the sound of the front door banging echoed through the house.

With a long sigh, Lucas relaxed. Once again, he'd proved the old man correct in his bad opinion. Any hope of resolving their differences vanished.

He squeezed his eyes shut and willed the pounding in his head to cease. He'd have to find a reason to stay out of his wife's company if he wanted to avoid the worst case of lust he'd ever experienced.

He strolled along the hall to the breakfast room.

✖   ✖   ✖   ✖

The buttered toast tasted like blotting paper. Caro replaced it on her plate and clenched her shaking hands together on her lap, staring at the four neat squares of browned bread, one nibbled at the corner. Something to eat always settled her nerves. Her father always swore a good meal cured bad humors. Another old homily he favored pattered through her mind like well-remembered footsteps: eavesdroppers never hear well of themselves.

Twenty thousand pounds a year would be an incentive to bed even the most unattractive female.

Lord Stockbridge wanted an heir to the title, and Lucas had agreed—for a tidy sum.

Misery washed through her. Lucas had lied. She swallowed, but the hard crumb in her throat remained stuck. He'd agreed they could divorce at any time. They couldn't if they had child.

In the distance, a bang signaled Lord Stockbridge's departure.

Someone with so little to offer could expect nothing else, her mind whispered. A man like Lucas needed a bribe to suffer her as a wife. Her heart shriveled into a bloodless lump in the cavern of her chest. Hot tears pricked behind her eyelids.

She blinked furiously. Having come to London to establish herself as a fashionable lady of the ton, she would not go home a failure. Unattractive she might be, fat and plain too, but she'd stood up to Lucas before, and now that she knew the truth, she could do so again.

Composing her face into calm indifference in case

Beckwith should return to tend the buffet on the sideboard, she slathered her toast with peach preserve and took another bite of now-sweetened blotting paper.

The door swung open, and Lucas, eyes red-rimmed, unshaven, and dressed in a blue silk dressing gown over his breeches, sauntered in. He looked like a disreputable pirate ready to ravish an innocent maiden.

Excitement shimmered deep in her stomach. How mortifying that after what she'd heard, she couldn't resist him in such tempting disarray. She managed a cool smile. "Good morning."

"Good morning." He strolled to the sideboard, poured coffee, and browsed the silver dishes, selecting coddled eggs and a slice of ham.

Every movement emphasized his sculpted muscles beneath the soft folds of silk. A beautiful male, her husband, and he found her unattractive. It wasn't anything new, but hearing him say it so bluntly cut deep.

Caro forced her gaze back to her plate.

From the corner of her eye, she watched him carry his cup and plate to his usual seat around the corner from her. He rarely rose before noon, but when he did come to breakfast, she was always thrilled to see him. Today she wished him elsewhere.

"My father just left," he said. He speared a piece of ham.

"I hope he didn't think me remiss in not bidding him welcome." She'd almost walked in on their conversation, and only the sound of her name stopped her from opening the half-closed door.

Lucas grimaced. "He came on business."

The business of Lucas getting her with child. She held his gaze. "I'm sorry I missed him." She brought her coffee cup to her mouth, proud to see that it shook only a little.

He seemed at a loss for words, his eyes wary. "Did I tell you I am going out of town again tonight? I am engaged to go to Charlie's hunting box for a couple of days."

Relief washed through her. His absence would give her some needed time to plan her escape from this marriage. "I wish you a pleasant trip."

A smile lightened his expression. "Thank you. What are your plans for today?"

That smile turned him from disreputable to seductive in the blink of an eye. Once more the charming pirate caressed the innocent maid with his gaze. But this time, the maiden knew better than to fall for his sinful good looks. She hoped.

Resting her wrist on the table edge to still her trembling hand, she carefully set her cup in her saucer. "This morning, I am going to Madame Charis's. Later, I am going riding in Hyde Park."

"I will go with you. I want to take a look at that mare of yours. Tigs said she's too high strung for a lady's saddle."

"He's wrong. She is perfectly sweet tempered. She needs frequent exercise, that is all."

Not exactly sweet. Fraise had tried to unseat her in the stable yard the first day she tried out her paces, but after a brief tussle of wills, Caro had brought the spirited mare under control.

He frowned. "If she's unmanageable, I'll get you

something more suitable."

"You will not put me on some slug. You know I am too good a horsewoman for that. No, Lucas, I want to keep Fraise."

"I still wish to see for myself."

"Not today. I have an engagement."

Fires smoldered in the depths of his narrowed eyes. "Who?"

"Does it matter?"

"Who is it, Caro? I am your husband and am responsible for you."

More of him dictating to her while he did whatever he pleased. "That is not our agreement. If you really must know, it is Cedric and Tisha." And the Chevalier. She inwardly winced at her cowardly omission.

"Oh, Cedric." His mouth curled in a quick smile. "In that case, I'll look at the mare another day." He seemed amused as he picked up the newspaper Beckwith had placed beside his plate. The pages rattled as he disappeared behind them.

She rose to her feet. "As you wish."

She skirted around him, heading for the door. "I hope you will excuse me, but my riding habit needs a slight alteration, and I am hoping Madame Charis can do it while I wait. I want to wear it this afternoon."

"Order another one," he said, not looking up.

Lucas cared nothing about economy. Why should he when twenty thousand pounds awaited him?

The newspaper rustled as he turned the page. His dark gaze rose to meet hers. "About last night . . ." He grimaced.

Twenty thousand pounds a year would be an incentive to bed even the most unattractive female.

She didn't want to hear a word about last night. "Yes?"

Wooden-faced, he held her gaze. "I don't want to find you alone with another man. You'll cause a scandal you won't like. And nor will I." He sounded tired, weary of having to do his duty to his unattractive ignoramus of a wife.

"Were I alone with a man with your reputation, Lucas, I might understand your concern. But when the gentleman is my cousin François, or your cousin Cedric, or even your friend Mr. Bascombe, no one could possibly imagine anything except what it was, a conversation on the balcony."

Liar, whispered her conscience.

A shadow seemed to cross his face, turning his eyes as black as the deepest abyss, his fingers crushing the edges of the paper. "Is that what you think?"

"Yes. It is."

She swirled around and opened the door.

"I mean what I said, Caro. For your own good," he said with deliberation. "One breath of scandal, and it's back to Norwich you go."

She glanced over her shoulder. "We agreed not to interfere with each other. Are you going back on your word?"

"Damn it, you're my wife; you have to listen to me."

"No regrets, Lucas."

She swept out of the door and up the stairs.

Ten

"ARE YOU FEELING WELL, COUSIN?" FRANÇOIS murmured from the back of a prime chestnut gelding walking beside Caro's mare. Beneath his curly brimmed beaver, his handsome face mirrored the gentle concern in his accented voice.

"I thought we were going riding, not walking," Caro said as Fraise ambled between her escorts, her spirits dampened by the slow pace of their progress.

The group of fashionably attired pedestrians in front of them stopped to greet friends in a barouche traveling in the opposite direction, bringing the trio to a halt.

"The unusually mild weather has brought out the crowds," Cedric said in pacifying tones.

François's coffee-colored eyes danced with amusement. "*Vraiment* it is slow. But own to it, *mon ami*, you prefer this pace."

Poor Cedric. He sat upon the sluggish gray mare as if he had a broomstick between his knees and feared it might fly away. He had more chance of the horse dropping dead than it breaking into a trot. No wonder Lucas had abandoned the idea of coming with them so readily.

Cedric grimaced. "The afternoon promenade is not about equestrian antics. It is about engaging in conversation and meeting friends." His horse sidled. He clutched at the pommel with a nervous grunt. Caro resisted the urge to reach out and hold his reins.

A half-smile curved François's mouth. "I think one is also expected to be beautiful, non? This mount of yours, Cedric, it flees the abattoir."

The man certainly had a way with words. The urge to chuckle twitched at Caro's lips and eased the pressure on her chest. She should not be a damper on the outing. After all, her escorts were not responsible for her black mood. "La, sir. Be kind to your friend."

Cedric's mouth turned down. "Do not concern yourself, Cousin Carolyn." He stared with grim concentration between the mare's flicking ears. "This nag was all they had at the hostelry this morning." He glanced at François's chestnut. "I'm surprised you found anything better."

"Ah, my dear friend. I won this fine steed at cards last night. Sadly, I will have to sell it tomorrow. I must take my leave of you."

"You are leaving when we have only just met?" Caro said.

"The Chevalier has pressing business matters. He manages your great aunt's estate," Cedric replied, almost a little too swiftly.

A sudden feeling of loss rushed through her. "I had wished to hear all about my aunt and the estate in Champagne. Now there is no time."

His expression full of regret, François bowed, quite as elegantly on horseback as in the drawing room. "I too am sorry. I will visit you tomorrow morning and carry a letter to Aunt Honoré, if you desire. You must promise to visit her."

"I'd love to go to Paris, but Lord Audley says France is not safe."

"Pshaw," François exclaimed. "Paris is as it ever was. Drawing rooms full, people meeting, the best actors in the best theaters in the world. Your friend's husband is too cautious."

"Tempers also run high in the House of Deputies, while the Bourbons jockey for position," Cedric interjected. "Audley is wise to keep his wife at home when he is on official business. The Paris salons are one thing. The army of occupation quite another."

François stiffened. "They will leave soon."

Aiming to deflect the argument, Caro put in, "Are you sure you must depart right away?"

François flicked her a quizzical glance, but allowed the diversion. "I must. But I leave the oh-so-careful Cedric to take my place. I hope you will not miss me."

"I should rather think you want her to miss you a good deal," Cedric said with some asperity.

"I will," Caro said, setting Fraise in motion now that the people ahead had continued their stroll. "With Lady Audley's husband back in London, I don't expect to see much of her either."

Tisha had sent around a barely legible note. Regretfully, she had to cancel their engagement to ride to take full advantage of Lord Audley's short furlough in town.

"I will be here," Cedric said.

"There is also your husband?" François' eyes said he didn't believe it.

Caro felt a pang of sadness in her chest. Lucas never had time for her. She shook the thought off. She'd made a bargain, and no matter what Lucas arranged with his father, she planned to stick by it.

"He has other interests." She gave a careless little laugh. It sounded too brittle, too hard.

A gap opened up in front of them, and she urged Fraise forward at a trot.

The two men caught her up at the next hold up in the traffic.

"Really, cousin," Cedric said, his mouth a thin line. "Have a care."

"Nonsense," François retorted. "Lady Foxhaven rides like angel. I am sure she longs to race the wind."

"Hmmp," Cedric grunted. "My cousin may look well on horseback, but nonetheless, I would not like her to come to grief."

Their gallantry and squabbling soothed her bruised heart. She did not, however, want it to ruin their friendship.

"I promise to be careful," she said.

Cedric seemed mollified, and François cast her a sidelong glance and a wicked smile.

"Speak of the devil," Cedric said.

Lucas? Caro craned her neck to see. A curricle traveling in the other direction at a smart pace, wove in and out of other, more staid vehicles on the row. A lady in turquoise silk and a wide-brimmed hat waved wildly as she went by.

Unable to make out her features, Caro squinted into the blur.

"Not wearing your spectacles, cousin?" Cedric said. "I wonder you dare ride. That was Lady Audley and her husband." He stared after the carriage. "He's a hard man by all accounts, but she seems to have him wrapped around her finger."

François leaned close. "Except in regard to Paris." His breath tickled her ear, and his rather cloying perfume caught in her throat.

Fraise skittered at her jerk on the reins.

Cedric lurched forward at his mare's toss of her head. He muttered something under his breath.

François laughed, a bit unkindly, Caro thought. "And here is another acquaintance," François said, raising his crop in greeting. "The charming Mrs. Selina Watson. Do you know her, cousin?"

"I don't believe I do," Caro replied, staring at the tall woman who approached riding a showy black and wearing an equally showy riding habit à la militaire. A rakish shako perched atop the dusky curls framing her face.

François performed the introductions, and the woman wheeled her horse around to join the slow promenade.

She eyed Fraise with a discerning eye. "I do like that strawberry roan of yours, Lady Foxhaven. If you ever decide to sell her, you must let me have the first option." She raised her glance to François with a pert smile. "I like any creature with spirit."

François's smile broadened, and Cedric frowned.

How wonderful to have the nerve to flirt so unashamedly. Caro patted Fraise on the neck. "I would never sell her. I just wish I could take her for a good gallop."

"Perhaps later in the season, when the weather is warmer, we could get up a party and go out into the country?" Mrs. Watson said. "Hampstead for instance. We could test your roan against my Jet, here." She leaned forward and ran her hand down her mount's glossy neck. The ebony coat matched her shining curls.

"I will ask my husband," Caro replied.

"Foxhaven?" Mrs. Watson laughed. "Does he keep you on so tight a leash?"

A river of hot blood bathed Caro's face. She must sound like a terribly dull creature to the dashing Mrs. Watson. "I meant I would ask him to accompany us. Here, there is none of the thrill of the wind in your hair or the excitement of jumping a fence."

"You hunt, then, Lady Foxhaven?" Mrs. Watson's voice held a surprised note.

"No," Caro said. "I always feel sorry for the fox." The thought of cruel jaws snapping at their victim turned her stomach.

"If it is excitement you seek, we could race." A challenge gleamed Mrs. Watson's dark eyes, and a predatory smile curved her lips.

"Galloping in Hyde Park at the fashionable hour is not only unacceptable; it is passé," Cedric said in quelling tones. "It has been done before, and by you, Mrs. Watson. I'm sure my cousin is not looking for that kind of thrill."

She wasn't? Any distraction from the hard lump of disappointment crushing her ribs held allure. Tisha had her husband to keep her busy, and because

François would return to France tomorrow, the immediate future loomed painfully empty.

With a toss of her head, Mrs. Watson laughed. "You are too staid, Mr. Rivers. Besides, I was thinking of something more akin to what you young blades are wont to engage in."

Cedric visibly shuddered. "I can assure you, I neither consider myself a young blade, nor do I enter into the kind of behavior indulged in by a set of idle rakes."

He meant Lucas. Cedric always defended him, but he didn't approve.

A deep chuckle cut across the ensuing silence. François's horse kicked out and started forward a few steps, causing Cedric to grab his mount's saddle. Caro winced. He really was the worst horseman she had ever laid eyes on.

Still chuckling, François waited for them to catch up. "*Mon cher ami*, so staid. It is *joie de vivre* which makes them engage in such pranks. Sadly you have none."

"Not all of us have the opportunity or desire to waste our youth in foolishness." Cedric softened his tart rejoinder with a sad smile. "I gather from your remarks, Monsieur Le Chevalier, you do not find boxing the watch or losing the family fortune at cards abhorrent?"

Was that the reason Lucas needed yet more money from his father? Caro's stomach tightened. "Please, gentlemen, I do not like to see you argue."

François raised a calming hand. "Forgive me, Lady Foxhaven. My good friend misunderstands me. I do not approve of tricks that cause harm to others—but a race? A test of skill? Where is the harm in that?" The twinkle in his dark brown eyes made Cedric's stuffiness seem ridiculous.

Pointy white teeth gleaming as she smiled, Mrs. Watson leaned across her horse's withers toward Caro. "Well, Lady Foxhaven, shall we show these smug men our mettle?"

It sounded dangerous and exciting and just the sort of thing Lucas would do. "How could we do that?" Her voice came out in a breathless rush.

"There is one record I would like to best."

"Record?"

"You are new to Town, are you not? The gentlemen are always setting records, walking backward down Bond Street, racing to Brighton in a curricle, or racing the Piccadilly run on horseback. It is this last of which I speak. How well do you manage that mare of yours in traffic?"

Caro lifted her chin. "I can handle her."

Mrs. Watson's cat-grin widened. "Then try to show me a clean pair of heels. We race from the park gate to Piccadilly, passing Clarence House. Fifteen minutes to tie the record, fewer to beat it, and the winner takes all."

"Good God," Cedric exclaimed. "Lady Foxhaven would never dare anything so dangerous."

"I can ride as well as anyone," Caro challenged.

François sent her a smile of approval. "If it is to be a race, I will put one hundred guineas on my cousin and her noble Fraise."

"I will see your hundred," Mrs. Watson responded.

Three pairs of expectant eyes focused on Caro. Her heart picked up speed. After such a bold speech, she could hardly back down. "Yes, of course. One hundred."

"Cedric?" François asked slyly.

"Not me. I do not have money to lose, and I will not bet against my own cousin."

Her greatest ally thought she would lose. An unexpected flash of something hot and bold seared her veins. "I'll raise you another hundred for the record," she said. Now she was really in the soup. She didn't have one hundred guineas, let alone two. She had to win.

Mrs. Watson flourished her whip. "Done. A woman after my own heart. We need timekeepers. Mr. Rivers, you will start us off. Dear Chevalier, you must wait at the finish line."

A chuckling François compared his timepiece with Cedric's "*En avante, mes dames,*" he called out before tipping his hat and trotting off.

Caro hoped her face didn't show the panic clogging her throat as she trotted beside the jaunty Mrs. Watson toward the gate.

Cedric tried not to smirk. It wouldn't do to let Lady Foxhaven see his delight. Mrs. Watson had fared better than he could ever have anticipated. Foxhaven controlled his wife as badly as he did everything else. He followed the two women—one willowy tall and as mean as a ferret, the other as voluptuously plump as a pigeon and as innocent as a newborn lamb.

A sacrificial lamb. His heart twisted. What the devil? He slaved while Lucas frittered his future away, and he'd be damned if he'd let anything stop him now. Fortune smiled only on those who helped themselves. Perhaps he'd find a way to help himself to the fair lady too.

He felt a sneer curl his lip. The marionettes jerked their limbs to his pulling of their strings. Stockbridge, the Chevalier, and now Lady Foxhaven, all dancing to his command whether they knew it or not. The sense of his own power gave him a heady feeling. He forced himself to remain cool, in control. The next steps needed a light hand. But his dreams began to look as solid as the ground beneath this cursed animal's hooves.

At the entrance to the park, he halted his mount alongside Lady Foxhaven.

"Take the first right," Mrs. Watson was saying, pointing with her crop. "Then on to the Haymarket. The Chevalier is waiting at the top on Piccadilly. Are you clear?"

"I think so," Lady Foxhaven replied.

She didn't sound particularly sure. It would be too bad if she missed her way or lost her nerve.

"You could withdraw," Cedric muttered.

Shock opened Caro's mouth. "Wouldn't that be dishonorable, after I made a bet?"

He nodded. "Some would say so."

"Then I couldn't think of it."

Clay in his hands. He pursed his lips. "If you are unsure of the way, the best thing you can do is stay right behind her. Try to pass her on the last dash to Piccadilly. I will pay for any damage as I come through."

A startled expression crossed her face. "Surely we won't cause any harm?"

An heiress with a broken neck would not serve his purpose. "Not if you are careful."

He dismounted and checked Lady Foxhaven's girth and then went to Mrs. Watson's side and did the same.

He made a show of straightening the blanket beneath the saddle while she fiddled with her stirrup.

Her head close to his, she murmured, "Well, Rivers, does it serve, do you think?"

The malicious gleam in her eyes satisfied him more than he cared to admit. He grinned. "You are very clever, my dear. I never expected her to take such a dare. Will it pay Foxhaven back for casting you off in favor of Louisa Caradin?"

"It might, along with the money you promised."

Cedric nodded. "She doesn't know her way around Town. Make sure you don't lose her. She will pass you at the end."

Her brows arched in question.

"Don't worry, you will not be out of pocket," he said.

"Much better than that I hope," she murmured, with a sharp stare.

"Without doubt."

A ragged girl selling flowers held up a basket of violets and primroses. "Buy a posy for the lady," she called.

How apropos. He purchased one bunch of each and pinned the yellow flowers on Caro and the purple on Selina. Both women carried his mark as surely as he shaped their destiny.

He pulled out his watch.

"Well, Mr. Rivers," Mrs. Watson snapped, curbing her fidgety mount.

Caro gulped a breath of air into her tight lungs.

The hammering of her heart must surely be audible to everyone within a hundred feet.

The cool and confident Mrs. Watson seemed unaffected. She patted her restive black's neck, her lips curved in a smile of pure devilment.

Caro tightened her grip on her reins and focused her gaze on the blur of Cedric's face.

"Go," he said.

The quietly spoken word froze Caro. Mrs. Watson slapped her horse's flank with her whip, and within seconds, she had merged with the traffic on the bustling street.

If Caro lost sight of the black horse, she had no chance of winning. Caro urged Fraise forward, shortened the gap, and fell in behind her rival. Her own noisy breath and the clatter of hooves filled her ears.

Mrs. Watson pushed her horse into a canter.

It was madness to go so fast in traffic.

They passed Green Park to their right, weaving in and out of carriages. Fraise slipped on the uneven cobbles. Caro's heart lurched, yet somehow she checked the mare. A fall could be fatal to horse and rider.

A wagon and a pair of stolid oxen blocked their path. Caro reined in. Mrs. Watson mounted the footpath, scattering pedestrians. Bad sport. Caro hesitated. She shouldn't do this. Mrs. Watson glanced back and raised her whip in a triumphant gesture. Dash it. Caro wouldn't let her win because she cheated. She urged Fraise forward, her heart in her throat, led on by the darting ebony gelding.

Shouts of anger and curses rose up around them.

A coal heaver reached out to grab her bridle. Fraise, ears flattened, neatly sidestepped.

Openmouthed ladies and gentlemen stared from coach windows and high perch phaetons. Street vendors and pedestrians scattered, shouting and shaking their fists.

A horrible sinking feeling invaded her stomach. She should have listened to Cedric and refused the bet. She should stop. She imagined the scorn with which Mrs. Watson would inform everyone of her cowardice. She would be a laughing stock. Cheeks on fire, she set her teeth and kept her gaze locked on the wild figure in front.

※　　　※　　　※　　　※

"I say, what's this?" Lord Cholmondly, a goblet of ruby port in his hand and a plate of cheeses on the table in front of him, leaned forward in White's bow window.

Lucas glanced up from the Gentleman's Magazine.

"By Jove!" Cholmondly jumped to his feet. "A race."

Opposite him, Lord Linden turned and also rose. "Well, well. Selina Watson up to her old tricks." He chortled. "Stap me. Doing the St. James circle. She said she would, if she could find anyone mad enough to take her challenge. Foxhaven, unless I'm mistaken, your record is about to be broken."

"Who's the challenger?" asked one of the men crowding into the bow window.

Clearly audible catcalls and jeers rose from further down St. James. Lucas, craning his neck to see over the shorter men, could not see the face of the challenger, but the distinctive roan looked unpleasantly familiar. It couldn't be Caro. Someone must have stolen her horse.

Then he recognized the riding habit. He swore and pushed his way through the crush of leering men toward the door.

As he reached the exit, Cholmondly shouted, "It's Foxhaven's wife. Stap me! Who will take pony on Selina Watson? Lady Foxhaven will never catch her now."

"I wouldn't mind catching Carolyn Foxhaven," someone yelled out. Coarse male laughter burned Lucas's ears.

"I'd give her a ride for her money," another called.

The stupid little fool. Lucas gritted his teeth and swallowed his challenge to the multitude of ribald comments flying around the room. He couldn't fight all the men in London, nor did he have the right. Caro had earned every word. The only sane thing to do was cut her off and put a stop to it before someone got hurt. He hurtled down the stairs and out of the door without stopping for his hat and coat.

On foot, even cutting through the back alleys around St. James's Square, the busy streets made his task impossible. He wiped the sweat out of his eyes and glimpsed the riders ahead of him. When he turned onto the Haymarket, he watched Caro give the roan her head.

He groaned and increased his speed. If she fell and hurt herself, he wasn't sure what he'd do. She passed Selina Watson, barely missing a brewer's dray. He let his breath go as she drew up short at the corner of

Piccadilly. She leaped off the mare and into the waiting arms of the Chevalier.

Chest heaving, lungs desperate for air, Lucas stopped stock-still and watched the blackguard pick her up and swing her around. As the Chevalier placed her on the ground, she tipped her face and kissed his cheek.

The little traitor. What the hell was going on? Had she given her heart to the slimy Frog? If so, what else had she given him? The thought seemed to poison the air around him.

Selina Watson cantered up to the pair on her sweating black, laughing and shaking her head. "I can't believe you passed me on the hill," she called out.

With wooden boards for legs, Lucas strode toward them.

A laughing Caro pulled on the Chevalier's arm to look at his watch. "Did we beat the time?"

The Chevalier shook his head. "I regret, no. Five minutes too long."

The Chevalier glanced up and grinned at Lucas. "You will be pleased to know, my lord, your record remains."

Lucas wanted to choke the life out of him. He could scarcely see for a thick red cloud of anger.

Caro swung around. The laughter died from her face. "Lucas." She glanced over his shoulder and waved. "Cousin Cedric!" she called out. "I won."

Cedric knew about this? Lucas jerked around. "How could you let this happen?"

"A bad business." Cedric's disapproving gaze caused Lucas to remember his hatless, coatless state.

"I warned against it."

Unable to stand the curious stares of passing pedestrians a moment longer, Lucas grabbed Caro's arm and pulled her away from the Chevalier. The stiffness in his jaw and lack of breath roughened his voice. "Get back on your horse and go home."

She flinched. He ignored her wounded expression. He grasped her around the waist and flung her up on Fraise, not caring if she hung on or not. She did, of course. She was too good a horsewoman not to. "I will speak to you at home, madam. Cedric, accompany her."

Cedric pulled at his lower lip with his teeth. "Certainly."

Selina Watson tittered, and Caro turned dull red. "Lucas, what is the matter with you?" she protested from atop her hard-breathing mount. "It was only a race."

Only a race. Bile clogged his throat. "Leave, now, before I do something I will later regret."

Sullen-faced, she wheeled the mare around and rode down Piccadilly with Cedric lumping along behind.

Lucas was hot and breathing hard, and with Caro gone, all he wanted to do was murder the damned Frenchman. Ill-concealed amusement twinkled in the other man's shrewd brown eyes.

Determined to conduct himself with honor, Lucas took a deep breath. "Now, Chevalier. You have some explaining to do. Tomorrow morning in Green Park will be a perfect opportunity. Name your friends."

Dark brows shot up to meet a carefully arranged

lock of brown hair on the Chevalier's brow. The slimy bastard raised his hands, palms up. "*Mais non, mon ami.* I am but a pawn in this. The ladies asked me to oblige them. What could I say?"

"It's true, Lucas." Selina's triumphant smile carved a hole in his chest. "If the Chevalier hadn't agreed, we would have asked someone else."

"I thought it better to keep it *en famille,*" Valeron said with what Lucas could only describe as a smirk.

"In the family?" Lucas clenched his fists. He wanted to throttle him, beat him to a jelly. The red haze at the back of his eyes threatened to blind him. "Do you know the route they took?"

François shrugged. "I am not familiar with all the twists and turns of your so beautiful city. If it were Paris now . . ."

"Well, it's not Paris; it's London, and this . . . female went right down St. James Street like a common tart." In his rage, his voice turned into a growl.

A vicious smile spread across Selina's face. "And your wife followed right behind me."

Hamstrung. The bitch knew he could do nothing. If he called out Valeron, a family member, it would worsen the scandal. He forced his hands to remain at his sides to stop himself from pounding the Frenchman to a pulp. The way things stood, the news would spread through the ton like a forest fire in a high wind anyway. Caro had placed herself beyond the pale.

"Damn you both to hell." He hauled in ragged breath and stomped down the Haymarket.

He collected his hat and coat at White's and endured the banter of friend and foe alike, trying to pass it off as a foolish mistake, and then he headed home to face his resentful, reprehensible wife.

Eleven

LUCAS HAD NO RIGHT TO TREAT HER LIKE A DISobedient child. Having changed from her riding habit into a fawn-colored morning gown, Caro paced the drawing room from sofa to window and back. He'd ruined her victory. Or he would have, if visions of shocked faces and leering men grabbing at her skirts weren't already sending mortifying quivers through her abdomen.

Footsteps sounded on the stairs. Caro's heartbeat quickened. She scurried for the sofa and, picking up her book, set her face in calm unconcern. The letters on the page refused to form into any kind of order. It might help if she removed her spectacles.

Too late. The door swung open.

Grim lines carved brackets around Lucas's mouth. He surveyed her from the doorway, and her foolish heart gave its usual lurch. Accompanied by the roiling in her stomach, it made her feel quite nauseous.

With what she hoped appeared to be calm

aplomb, she laid her book face down on the table beside the sofa. "Lucas. How kind of you to find the time to join me."

His gaze dropped to her book and then rose to her face. "Kind? I ought to wring your neck."

She stiffened. After all his misdemeanors, how dare he utter a word of criticism. She arched a brow. "'Pon rep, Foxhaven, you look just like your father." It was an unkind cut that must have hit the mark, for he winced.

A rueful smile twisted his lips. "Don't think to play off your tricks on me, Caro."

He pushed the door closed with his shoulder and strolled to the hearth. He took up his usual stance, one elbow resting on the mantle. Tension vibrated in the air of her normally peaceful drawing room. A deep frown creased the space between his brows. "Lord, what a bumblebroth," he muttered.

The pity in his eyes sent a cold chill down her spine. She'd seen that look too often not to get the urge to take cover behind the nearest potted palm. She lifted her chin. "What can you mean? I won a horserace and one hundred guineas. Regretfully, your record still stands, or it would have been two hundred." There, that sounded calm, if a little defensive.

"My record has nothing to do with it. It is your reputation at stake."

Shame might be merciless in burning the back of her throat, but she would not admit it to one of London's foremost rakes. She forced a brittle laugh. "Do you mean to say there is one standard of behavior for me and another for you?"

A muscle jumped in his jaw. "You know there is. And society sets it."

She clenched her trembling hands in her lap and cast him what she hoped was a look of sophisticated nonchalance. "Surely it is not as bad as all that? It was a horserace for heaven's sake, not a murder."

He raked long fingers through his tousled hair. "You rode down St. James' ogled by every male member of the ton. They made wagers on the outcome in White's. Your name will be on the tongue of every Bond Street beau by nightfall."

A huge lump clogged her throat at the horrid picture he conjured up. "I see."

She got up and paced to the window. Long shadows from the houses opposite darkened the street. Dusk already. It might have been better if she had stayed in bed this morning. She had never felt so foolish in her life. "Mrs. Watson didn't seem care."

He made a derisive sound. "Use her as your model at your peril." His tone hardened. "And what was my cousin about letting you engage in anything so foolhardy?"

Her gaze faltered, and she stared at the rug. "He advised against it."

"Advised? Very good of him, I'm sure. Why the hell didn't he stop the whole thing?"

She glared at him. "No, Lucas, I won't hear a word against him or the Chevalier. This was all my own doing."

"Damn it all. Must I watch your every move? Surely, commonsense would tell you it went beyond everything acceptable. I certainly never imagined you would do anything so mad."

Mad described her stupid impulse quite nicely. "I thought you liked females with spirit," she tossed back, resenting the echo of Mrs. Watson's sly tones.

He fixed her with a gaze so cold, she actually felt a draft. "Did you?" His voice was deceptively soft for the undercurrent of anger. "And I suppose demonstrating your spirit means publicly throwing yourself into the Chevalier's arms."

"I did nothing of the sort."

"I saw you. And so did a hundred other gawping spectators on Piccadilly."

A blazing inferno engulfed her face as she recalled the kiss she had planted on François's cheek. "It was merely the excitement of the moment."

"Like the moment on the balcony at the ball the other night, I suppose?"

The sarcasm in his tone crawled over her skin. She seemed doomed to make one stupid mistake after another and drag François after her. "I told you. We are friends."

His lips thinned. "Just as you and I are friends?"

"Yes. I—I mean, no."

He raised a brow.

"You are deliberately confusing me," she said.

"Am I?" He sauntered toward her. "I think I'd like some of the treatment you accord your friends."

Warmth radiated from his lithe frame as he towered over her. She tried to ignore the quick-time beat of her pulse and put out a hand. "Please, Lucas."

"Happy to oblige, my dear." His voice had the consistency of deliciously thick cream. "Perhaps it is time you understood the consequences of playing the flirt."

The intense mildness caused her to step back. "I was not flirting."

"You are serious about him, then."

A pulse beat in her temple. "Stop it."

His hand lashed out and caught her elbow, dragging her toward him, his face a magnified blur.

"Let me go."

His other hand came up, and long fingers cradled her head, holding her still while his mouth came down on hers, savage and hard, his breathing short and jerky.

The instant their lips met, his touch softened and moved with gentle tenderness. A sense of sweetness flooded her. A flutter like whispering leaves caught in a breeze ran down her spine.

A practiced seducer, a rake, who tasted of sweet wine and smelled of sandalwood and sweat and musky male. Her husband.

Meaning to fend him off, she lay her hands on his shoulder. There they stayed, caressing the rough wool of his coat, slipping around his neck, twining with the silky strands of his hair, while the mindless kiss went on forever.

She parted her lips and he plunged his tongue inside her eager mouth. Familiar with the technique this time, she joined the dance with her own.

A deep groan rumbled up from his chest. He raised his head, removed her glasses, and tossed them on the nearby chair. His wonderful face came into focus.

"What are you doing to me?" he asked.

"Me?" she managed to squeak. "I'm not doing anything."

"No?"

His half-lidded gaze caressed her mouth. She parted her lips in response, aching for his touch, and he smiled. "See. That's what you do."

His murmured words made her feel soft and melting inside, like a honeycomb.

He dipped his head and captured her mouth in a hot kiss. She dissolved into him. She shouldn't do this. It wasn't part of their bargain. She couldn't think for the drumming in her blood.

His hands skimmed down her back, a trail of weighted warmth. They cupped her bottom, cradling her against his lean hard length. Captured in the cage of his arms she felt wanted, desirable.

His tongue traced the seam of her mouth. Pleasure shimmered through her, and she opened her mouth and welcomed him in with a moan. She arched her back. His thigh pressed against her hips. Delicious pulses of heat spread out from the contact. The room seemed to spin, not as if she would faint, but more like heady flight. She never wanted him to stop. If he did, she might regain her senses.

He grabbed her shoulders and set her aside, striding for the door. Cool air replaced the warmth of his body.

She froze in place. How could she have let passion carry her away? She watched him go, her chest so tight it hurt.

He turned the key in the lock. "Insurance against unwelcome visitors." His low voice sent a jolt of desire straight to her core.

She released her breath as he prowled his way back, a powerful, magnificent male sensuously sure of his welcome. She lowered her gaze to the patterned carpet. Could dreams come true?

His chuckle, low and deep, seemed to say they might, and his encircling arms confirmed it. He swept her up and carried her to the sofa as if she weighed no more than kitten. Desire, as bright and sharp as her own, shone in his eyes.

He laid her down and knelt beside her.

Today, the pirate would have his wicked way with the maiden. She relaxed in his arms. "Lucas." It had the sound of a plea, not a protest.

"Shhh, my darling," he murmured against her temple and stretched out beside her, one hard, heavy thigh resting on hers.

He never called her darling.

Languidly, she gazed at smoky fires deep in his eyes. She needed his touch, his heat, his desire. Now. She held still, afraid to break the spell.

He traced her jaw with his fingertips, turning her face toward him. He brushed a tendril of hair from her cheek with fingers as light as thistledown, brushing her skin as if she were delicate china and could shatter at a touch. She smiled at the thought. She had already splintered into a thousand pieces.

A smile softened his expression in return.

"You know," he murmured, "Selina could not hold a candle to you today, the way you sat that horse. You truly were magnificent."

"Magnificently disastrous."

"That too." He gazed into her eyes.

Had today's devilment caused him to see her differently? How often had she yearned for him to look past the plump vicar's daughter who hid behind her spectacles and potted plants, and into the woman who loved him with a passion so vast she daren't delve its depth and keep her sanity? She ought to try to keep sane.

His tongue swept her mouth, more satisfying than a dozen cream cakes. His hand ran up her arm to her throat, blazing a trail on skin so sensitive it robbed her of thought. Graceful fingers, lighter than butterfly wings, traced her collarbone. It was a sensation so arousing that tears welled in her eyes. His knee nudged between her thighs, and she let them fall open. A hot blush suffused her body.

Their limbs intertwined. His sigh, a sound of deep contentment, induced a long breath of her own. He wanted her.

The knowledge gave her power, as if she had drunk too much champagne. She arched her hips up, seeking sweet pressure.

His heart hammered against her ribs as he trailed baby kisses from one corner of her mouth to the other, teasing her jaw, lingering at her ear. Hot breath sent arrows of pleasure to her most secret place. Delightful agony and deliciously wicked.

"Oh, Caro," he whispered.

His mouth returned to hers, urgently plundering. She let the delightful sensations roll through her, until she was nothing but a bundle of tightly strung harp strings plucked to his tune.

As his lips plied their magic on her mouth, his hand fondled her breasts. Her nipples tightened inside the confines of her flimsy gown, and for once, she felt as though there was far too much fabric.

With slow, deliberate strokes, his hand moved across

her ribs and lingered at her waist before resting on her hip. Warmth seeped into her skin from his touch.

She ran her fingers through his hair. It fell around his face in silky hanks, caressing the hard cheekbones. She returned his kiss with wanton abandon, drinking him in, breathing his scent until it became part of her.

It wasn't enough. She arched against his thigh, sparking shivers so deep in her core it felt like a knot of pain laced with pleasure.

To her disappointment, he broke their kiss, his gaze following the trail of his hand down her leg. He caressed her ankle with sure, firm fingers. She glanced down to see her skirts thigh-high and her rosebud-embroidered garters in full view. But worse than that was the sight of and expanse of naked flesh above the white silk of her stocking. Her hem barely concealed what lay between her thighs.

God, what must he think of so much skin?

She swallowed and made a grab for the wayward fabric.

Lucas trapped her fingers in his, raised them to his lips in turn, and then turned her hand to press his lips to her wrist, before placing her hand on his shoulder. He bent his head to kiss the hollow at the base of her throat, the rise of her bosom at the edge of her gown, the peak of her breast. Warm moist breath permeated all the way to her nipple. It budded to life. Her breasts became full, heavy, while her heart galloped like a colt out of control.

Once more his hand slid down her leg to cup her calf. "Lift for me sweet," he murmured into her décolletage.

Lift?

The gentle pressure beneath her calf focused her scattered wits. Unable to muster an ounce of resistance even had she wanted to, she relaxed her leg, and he hooked her heel over the back of the chaise. Her skirts fell to her hips. Before the protest on her lips formed into words, his mouth covered hers, soft and wooing and infinitely delicious, while his fingers performed lazy circles on her raised calf, her knee, the shivering skin above her stocking.

Soft yet searing, his touch blazed a trail almost too delicate to bear. The sensation made her writhe and gasp as he tortured and then soothed. All thought fled as her body responded like a musical instrument, vibrating, humming, the chords growing ever tighter. The scent of him filled her senses. The driving force of need raised her hips, clenched her inner muscles, made her fight for every lung full of air. Attuned to his desire, she wanted, needed.

The firm press of the heel of his hand against her mons brought sweet relief even as it tormented. She clutched at his shoulders, urging him on. She heard the sound of ragged breathing, hers and his, and felt his chest rising and falling against her breasts.

More kisses descended on her mouth, small brushes of hot lips against hers, quick flickers of tongue that left her breathless. Eyes closed, she savored the darting, teasing pleasure.

He raised his head. His thumb grazed her lips. She tasted salt.

He pulled out of her grasp, and she opened her eyes to see his dark head lower as he eased off the sofa.

"Lucas. What . . ."

"Hush."

The pressure on her mons stopped, replaced by a draft of warm breath, a shock that sent an electric thrill to her breasts.

She whimpered her need for him to end the torturous climb to some far-off peak.

Gentle yet firm, with his other hand still at her face, he slid one finger between her soft and swollen womanly flesh. A flood of moisture met his probing touch.

"Oh, yes," he said with a groan of satisfaction.

Another finger joined the first, stretching, stroking. Wave after wave of pleasure barraged her senses.

She raised her head and opened her mouth, drawing the thumb of his other hand inside her mouth with a hard suck.

A hiss of breath told her he liked her bold move.

Pleasure spiraled out of control. She reached some place far beyond her experience. It drove her to madness. He continued without mercy.

She bit down on his thumb.

He groaned and pressed harder at the entrance to her body. Light burst in her head. She was entirely centered on that one point of pleasure-pain that had become the sum total of her existence.

"Come for me, Caro," he said.

In that moment, she would have done anything he wanted, as long as he found a way to break the tension that was wound so tight she feared the explosion when it finally broke.

An abyss opened before her, black and beckoning. "Oh God!" she cried.

She fell over the edge and was lost in wave after wave of crashing delight, to wash up on the far distant shore a shattered wreck and delightfully languid.

Bliss turned her bones to blancmange and her muscles to water. Lucas gathered her into his arms and rested his forehead against hers, breathing hard. She stared in fascination at the evidence of his arousal, a hard ridge jutting beneath the fabric of his skintight pantaloons.

She reached down to touch. He groaned.

She glanced up at his face, wondered at the agony on his features, and felt a surge of strength.

He raised his head. "Lean forward. Let me unfasten your gown."

Shocked, she stiffened.

"It's all right," he murmured. "I won't hurt you, I promise."

He meant her body, but what did he know of the pain he could inflict on her heart? She wished for the will to say no.

A hot dark gaze drifted to her neckline.

A murmur of protest formed in her throat, but a moan of pleasure replaced it as he brushed his knuckles across her breast's sensitive peaks.

He promised he wouldn't hurt her.

Raising herself on one elbow, she tucked her face in the curve of his strong neck while his fingers nimbly undid the small hooks down the center of her back and then attacked the strings of her stays. He must have had lots of practice.

Perish the thought.

He slid her gown over her shoulders and pressed her back against the cushion. Brocade scratched her bare shoulders. Cool air brushed the tops of her breasts. She closed her eyes, not wanting to see his reaction.

Silence.

She risked a peek. The expression on his face was neither shock nor astonishment. It was something she had never seen before, something far more profound, something terrifying.

"My God," he whispered.

A warm calloused hand cupped first one breast and then the other, as if testing their weight. He grazed his palm over the chemise-covered nipples. They tightened. A sweet, sharp tingle shot to her loins. She shivered with the delicious chills of desire.

His hand went to the buttons at his falls, his breathing harsh and rapid.

"Oh, Lucas," she breathed.

He stilled, looked up at her face, and stared almost without recognition. Then the haze cleared from his gaze like a chill breeze blowing mist from a fathomless pool.

"Hell," he said. "I can't do this." His voice sounded ragged. He looked as if he were being strangled.

Not enough money to bed even the most unattractive wench.

She clutched at the neckline of her gown and pulled it over the mountains of jiggling flesh.

He pulled her skirts down over her calves and turned his back to her. "Damn it to hell."

His father wanted him to consummate the marriage, and he couldn't do it. Her jaw locked to hold back a sob of humiliation.

She pulled her bodice up over her shoulders, leaving the stays loose, and fumbled with the fastenings.

"I . . ." He smoothed his hair back. "I'm sorry."

An empty numbness took over her body. "It is of no consequence."

She had all the fastenings done up except those in the middle of her back. She lowered her feet to the floor and twisted her arm behind her, feeling for the little hooks.

"Here," he said, sounding strained. "Stand up. I'll do it."

Once more, he exhibited his skill as a lady's maid. Ladies he'd wanted to make love to. She swallowed what tasted like a mouth full of burnt biscuits.

"You have to go back to Norwich right away," he muttered to her back. "You should leave tomorrow."

She whirled around. "You are sending me home because . . ." She glanced at the sofa, her face blazing. But blazing with what? Anger? Embarrassment? Probably both.

God, she thought, he really must despise her after what he'd seen. How could she have lain there exposed to his scornful gaze?

But he had seen almost as much the other night in her room. He knew what she looked like. Only then, he hadn't been under his father's orders to get her with child.

She held herself rigid. "You promised me a season. I won't be packed off home."

"You little fool. You cannot stay in London. If you don't believe me, ask Cedric. No one of any consequence will speak to you. You are ruined."

He headed for the door, turned the key, and then looked back. "I will ask Beckwith to make the necessary arrangements. I will join you as soon as I am able. I am afraid I have a prior engagement and cannot go with you."

Hunting. A hot flood of fury nearly blinded her. "I wouldn't dream of imposing on your time, my lord. However, you might want to include a trip to Scotland in your future plans."

His lips thinned. "If that is your wish. But we should discuss it first—when we are both in a more rational frame of mind."

"I think we have said all that is needed."

He bowed and snatched the door open. "Very well. We will discuss the arrangements when I join you in Norwich."

The front door slammed as he quit the house. She pressed frigid palms against burning cheeks. What had she done?

Twelve

"WHAT DO YOU MEAN, FRED HAS GONE?" Lucas asked.

The candelabra on the old piano cast a circle of light into the conservatory. Six faces met his searching gaze. The four boys—Red, with his hair gleaming like fire; Aggie, already growing out of his new clothes; the angelic Pete; and little Jake—all stared back in silence. Davis, a short, stocky Welshman with a full set of whiskers and a pair of coal black eyes sparking anger, stood next to them. James hunched his shoulders and his long scholarly face looked sadder than usual.

Davis folded his arms looking smug. "I caught him stealing my watch from my chamber, don't you know. I locked him in to await your justice, my lord, and the coward fled."

"Yer a bleedin' liar," Jake muttered, throwing a kick at the piano leg. His gaze slid to the floor.

Trouble followed Fred like a shadow, it seemed.

Damn it. The lad had seemed almost settled these last few days.

Lucas didn't need this now, not when he wanted to settle matters with Caro. How could he have let her get in such a coil? Because his attention had been taken up with these boys. Guilt grabbed at his gut, and sweat started on his brow every time he thought about his surge of unbridled lust.

He shouldered his personal problems aside. "Tell me what happened."

"I asked Mr. Davis to release the boy to rehearse for the concert tonight," James said. "He refused, even though Fred gave his word to await your judgment on the matter."

Beside Jake, lanky Aggie clenched a knobby fist. "He never stole nuffin'. He found it and were putting it back."

"Cock and bull," Davis snorted. He puffed out his burly chest. "What else would you expect from a bunch of prigs and pickpockets, I ask you? It wouldn't surprise me if they were all in it together, mark you. It is the constable we need."

The boys retreated to the far reaches of the dim light, their eyes darting wildly around the room.

"Enough. Can't you see you are scaring them?" Lucas rapped out. An intense stare from James gave him pause. He sank down on the piano stool. "Perhaps I should hear this from the beginning."

"There's not much to tell," Davis asserted, tucking his thumbs in his waistband. "I caught him entering my bedchamber. He tried to pitch me some gammon about finding my watch and intending to replace it. We had a few words, and I locked him in his room. He left through the window sometime between lunch and supper."

A vague disquiet nibbled at Lucas. The proud Fred never lied about his thieving. "Did anyone see him find the watch?"

"Are you calling me a liar, my lord?" Davis snarled.

"I am," Jake mumbled.

Lucas glared at the boy before answering Davis. "I'm asking the boys what they saw. Did you see him with it?"

Aggie, Red, and Pete shook their heads. Jake flicked a glance at them and then gave a quick shake of his head, avoiding Lucas's gaze.

Hell. It would take hours to get to the truth at this rate.

He'd only come tonight because he'd promised the lads. He wanted to get back to Caro. The drive had cleared his head. Perhaps there was a way to mitigate the damage so that she didn't have to leave London. But he could not leave Fred out there, alone and lost.

Davis curled his lip. "The little rat has gone down the nearest sewer."

"'Tain't fair," Red said. "The bleedin' Taffy's al'ays pickin' on Fred. 'E wouldn't listen when he said he found the ticker. Raised the hue and cry and locked him up. Said you'd have the Beak ship 'im off to Botany Bay."

It was a threat real enough to frighten anyone. Lucas narrowed his eyes. "Do you have your watch now, Davis?"

"Of course he does!" Jake yelled.

Davis took a threatening step in Jake's direction. Jake cowered, arm raised in feeble protection, his pallor increasing, but fear didn't stop his mouth. "Bleedin' schoolmaster. Fred was puttin' it back. I 'ates you."

"I have it all right," Davis bit out. "After I searched the little bastard. What's needed around here is more switch and less talk. We'd soon find out where the lad went."

Christ, the puritanical Welshman was just like Lucas's father. A bully. He should have seen it. A familiar sense of failure twisted his gut. He took a deep breath and flexed and relaxed his fingers. Anger wouldn't help Fred.

He sighed. "Davis, I suggest you pack and leave."

Over Aggie's head, James gave a slight nod of approval.

Wide-eyed, Davis stared at him and then drew himself up to his full five feet. "It will be my pleasure. Just be careful they don't find you murdered early one morning, my boyo." He swung around. His steps echoed as he stamped out.

"The boy will be lost." James's deep timbre held concern. "If we were in the city, I wouldn't worry as much. In the country, he's a fish out of water. We need to mount a search."

Lucas skewered Jake with a look. "Come here."

The boy hunched his thin shoulders.

"Now," Lucas said. "I want the whole story."

Like a whipped dog, the lad slunk toward him. "I don't know nuffin'."

A couple of feet from Lucas, Jake halted. Back against the piano leg, he slid to the floor. He buried his forehead on his knees. "I ain't staying, neither."

The rage and anguish in the thin voice twisted Lucas's heart. "Why did you do it?"

Lifting his head, Jake scooped up a little pile of dust missed by Mrs. Green's broom. He trickled the fine white powder on the knee of his new gray trousers.

Red opened his mouth, exchanged a dark look with Pete, and closed it again. A covenant of thieves, a common front against whatever the world might throw at them.

They trusted no one, least of all him. Lucas swept his disappointment aside. "You stole the watch, and Fred took it back. Right, Jake?" Lucas prompted. "Nothing bad will happen provided you tell the truth. That is the honorable thing to do. No one will tell the magistrate, nor will you be beaten. I swear it."

Tears welled up in Jake's gray eyes, and he dragged his sleeve across his face with a sniffle. "Davis said you'd horsewhip us after we put salt in his tea yesterday. I took the watch to serve him right for tattling. I never meant to keep it." His gaze begged for understanding. "Fred saw it under my blanket when he came to check on our cots. He said Davis'd have my gizzard if I let on it was me."

"Fred al'ays babies him," Red muttered.

Jake threw a punch at the other boy's thigh. "I ain't a baby." He pulled himself to his feet, his expression a little less hangdog.

If only Fred had stayed to face the music, had trusted that Lucas would believe the truth and help him. Just as Caro had trusted him.

"Damn!" he exclaimed.

The boys jumped.

Lucas shook his head. He couldn't think about Caro right now. "Does anyone know where he might have gone?"

The four boys and James huddled around him.

"A city lad ought to stand out like a molehill on a manicured lawn," James said.

"Right," Lucas replied. This would take no time at all.

And he would dash back and see Caro first thing in the morning. They'd face the ton together.

※　　　※　　　※　　　※

"I fear Lucas is correct," Tisha said, her peacock-blue silk bright against the green damask sofa and the jaunty oval hat tipped over one eye at variance with her sad expression. "You have to leave London."

Still reeling from the full implication of her indiscretion, Caro bit her top lip. What if she could never come back? What if her sisters were so tainted by what she had done that they would never be admitted to polite society? She felt sick.

Lucas had been right about one thing. She had ruined everything. Worse, she might have killed someone. How could she have been so rash?

A ripple of chills ran down her back. She hoped she appeared less agitated than she felt. "I truly had no idea of the consequences. Is there nothing I can do?"

Tisha glanced down at her cup. "I will do what I can to stop tongues from wagging. I never thought to warn you about Selina Watson. She has a dreadful reputation. Who would have thought she would have the effrontery to approach you after . . ." She pressed her fingertips to her mouth, her spoon rattling in its saucer.

A sinking sensation snatched Caro's breath. "What?"

Tisha gave a little moan. "Audley is like to kill me for my indiscretion one of these days. I must be the only diplomat's wife in the world who cannot keep hold of her tongue."

Hollow inside, Caro placed her cup on the pretty rosewood table in front of her, the table she had purchased last week because it reminded her of one her mother had loved. She ran a fingertip along its gilded edge. "You might as well tell me."

"It's all foolish gossip."

A knife seemed to twist in her heart. She raised her gaze to meet her friend's sorrowful one. Caro continued, "I think it would be better if I knew the full import of my folly, don't you? What does Mrs. Watson have to do with Lucas?"

Defeat crossed Tisha's face. "It is rumored they had a liaison."

Caro tried not to flinch. "I see," she whispered.

Reaching across the table to grasp Caro's hand, Tisha continued. "It was years ago, and over long before he married you, but she caused a great fuss when he finished with her. Stockbridge got to hear of it. I understand it resulted in quite an argument. She's dreadfully fast and looking for a husband."

So this was the reason Lucas and his father didn't get along. He'd abandoned the poor woman without a thought to her suffering. She must have been over-wrought to try to take revenge on his wife. And Caro had thought she might somehow win his love. He cared less for her than he had for this woman. What was worse, Caro had always known it.

She swallowed. A thread of pride finer than a strand of silk held her tears suspended.

A knock on the door startled her. Tisha jerked her hand away.

Beckwith opened the door. "The Chevalier Valeron and Mr. Cedric Rivers are inquiring if you are at home, my lady."

Caro sighed. More recriminations. But she had to face them. "Show them up please, Beckwith."

Tisha rose, her silks rustling. "I really must go. I promised poor Audley I'd be but an hour. He leaves for Paris in the morning."

Caro rose to her feet, her heart full of gratitude. "It was kind of you to spare the time."

Tisha squeezed her hands. "What else could I do? I feel as if I let you down. It would not have happened had I been with you. Go to Norwich. By next season, it will all be forgotten."

There would be no next season. Not for her. She forced a smile. "Thank you for all you have done. I'm sorry I am such a failure as a protégée."

"Nonsense. We will come about, you will see." A scent of jasmine lingered after her departure.

A pang squeezed Caro's battered heart. She would probably never see Tisha Audley again.

The deep voices of men rumbled up the stairs. Moments later, the Chevalier, immaculate in a blue coat and crisp white linen, sauntered in with a wry twist to his lips. "My lady." He swept his usual elegant bow.

Cedric, one step behind, gazed at her with a stern expression. "Cousin," he murmured over her hand, his flat black eyes never leaving her face, "I wish you had listened to me yesterday." He had the expression of a man who had lost a crown and found a shilling.

"No sense in crying over the cat licking the cream," François said in comforting tones.

Caro and Cedric stared at him.

"Spilt milk," Cedric muttered.

"Ah, *oui*. Indeed, the spilt milk." François sat next to her on the sofa. "What will you do now?"

Deflated by Tisha's words of wisdom and her own self-recriminations, Caro could only shake her head.

Cedric lowered himself into the small chair by the window, his long limbs folding like a spider settling into a web. "What does Lucas have to say to all this? I expected to find him here."

Lucas had fled rather than look at her, she thought sadly. "He went out of Town last night. A hunting trip with Mr. Bascombe, I believe."

"Hunting?" Cedric looked puzzled. "Wrong time of year."

"I don't think the birds were of the feathered variety," François said. "Not if the gossip at the clubs is the truth." He caught Caro's wide-eyed stare and raised his gaze to the ceiling. "I beg your pardon, Lady Foxhaven. Can you ever forgive me?"

A grain of anger at Lucas's cavalier attitude grew into a desert full of shifting dunes. "You mean he can do whatever he pleases, and I am shunned for nothing but a horserace?"

"Banished," Cedric uttered in hollow tones. "I never thought a family member of mine would be cut."

Put like that, it sounded worse than anything Tisha had said. Caro slumped against the couch. "Both Lucas and Lady Audley think I should go back to Norwich until the gossip blows over."

His face lit up with mischief, François snapped his fingers. "Don't go to this dreary Norwich. Come to Paris. The season is in full swing. You will be *adorée*."

She stared at him. "I couldn't."

"What difference, provided you leave London?" François said.

That was certainly true. And if Cedric approved . . . She managed a weak smile. "I couldn't possibly descend on my Aunt without warning."

"An excuse. *Tante* Honoré longs to hold you in her arms," François said, a twinkle in his brown eyes.

"My sisters. The scandal."

He waived an airy hand. "Write to them. No one in Paris cares about these silly English rules."

A chance to meet her great aunt seemed too good to be true, and this way, her sisters would not need to know of her disgrace. The thought of telling them chilled her blood.

If Tisha was right—that given enough time, the talk would die down—perhaps she could return in a month or two.

She glanced over at Cedric.

"What will Foxhaven say?" he asked gloomily.

Lucas didn't care where she went. She disgusted him. A huge ache filled her throat. Lucas never wanted this marriage. He'd cheerfully sent her packing while he continued his own pursuits. It wasn't the first time he'd abandoned her for something more interesting. The room blurred.

The croaking of happy frogs filled the warm night air. A rhythmic splash of oars brought Caro's head off her knees. The cool breeze ruffled the wisps of hair around her face. She jumped to her feet, peering into the dark at a twinkling bobbing light on the lake. "Lucas?" she yelled. "Over here!"

The splashing ceased and then picked up speed. "Pigeon?" he called back. "Is that you?"

Who else would it be? The lady of the lake? She rubbed at her chilled arms. This was the last time she'd agree to be left behind like some unwanted baggage just because the triplets decided they had precedence because they were older.

The rowboat crunched against the island's sandy shore. Lucas stood up. The boat rocked wildly, causing the lantern balanced on the bow to flicker. "You are still here."

"Where else would I be? I'm practically marooned. You promised to come back for me and the picnic basket the moment you dropped the triplets on shore." The boat wasn't big enough for all five of them.

"Father sent a groom to tell me Aunt Rivers and Cedric had arrived for tea." His voice sounded odd. The boat wobbled unsteadily beneath his feet. "I asked Matthew to row back and get you. He promised."

"He must have found something better to do. I haven't seen hide or hair of him."

"Blast. I should have guessed he'd let me down." He sounded genuinely disgusted.

She shook her head. "It was me he let down." She heaved the basket into the boat. "Well, you are here now, and I really must get home before Father finishes tomorrow's sermon and notices I'm missing. One of my sisters is bound to mention I've been gone all day if I am not there to stop them."

"Right. Climb in, and I'll row you across." He hiccupped and then giggled. In the lamplight, he looked owlish, and his grin seemed just a little too broad, as if he was cup-shot.

"Are you foxed, Lucas?"

He scratched at his ear and shook his head. The boat wobbled worse than before. "Can't be. Cedric says it takes more than a couple of pints to make a man bosky."

Cedric. She might have guessed he'd be involved. More and more, he seemed to pull Lucas away from his friends. Caro stifled her vague pang of anger at the older cousin she had never met. He was Lucas's family after all. But he wasn't the one getting in a boat with Lucas.

"Come on, then," Lucas said, waving an arm.

She grabbed hold of the gunwale and threw one leg over the top. "Where is your cousin now?"

His gaze fixed on her bare ankle. He swallowed loudly and then gestured in the direction of the far shore. "He went for a stroll with the barmaid." He giggled again. "I got tired of waiting. That's when I started wondering if Matthew had kept his promise. 'Sides, I needed some fresh air."

"Lucky for me." The boat rocked, and she lost her footing. She grabbed at the rowlock and knocked the oar into the bottom of the boat.

"Hey," Lucas said. "Be careful."

She reached out. "Don't just stand there; give me a hand."

"Sorry." He grabbed for her arm, tripped over the oar and fell backward.

Preferring the bottom of the boat to the water, Caro launched forward and sprawled on top of him.

Their chests collided. His grunt of surprise rushed past her ear, all warm and tickly. His hard thigh slid between her legs, causing a tingle down her spine. Her stomach gave a strange little lurch, and odd sensations of excitement shimmered deep inside.

"That is one way to get on board, I s'pose," he mumbled, breathing hard.

Her face buried in his neck, she felt amazingly lightheaded. She chuckled. "Idiot. Why did you fall?" Her lips accidentally brushed the warm skin below his ear.

He hissed in a breath.

She lifted herself, hands on each side of his head, and discovered unusually sweet pressure at the apex to her thighs. "Lucas? Am I hurting you?"

The lantern revealed his expression. He was staring at her, lips parted, eyes half closed. He looked so handsome, so dear, so . . . delicious. Her heart raced. Unable to resist the urge, she dropped a kiss on those full, perfect lips.

His arms went around her back, squashing her hard against him, and then he was kissing her back, with lips like velvet, his heart hammering against her ribs.

It felt as if a lightning bolt had shot through her body. She jerked away.

His head fell back with a crack. "Cripes." He struggled beneath her. "Caro, get up. You are nigh to crushing me."

It served him right. She giggled at the note of panic in his voice and untangled her limbs from his until they faced each other from opposite benches.

He picked up the oars and began rowing furiously. He looked hot and tousled and in some sort of pain.

"Are you sure you are not hurt?" she asked.

"It's nothing that a swim in the lake wouldn't fix," he muttered.

Her stomach dropped. "Is the boat going to sink? I can't swim."

"Dear heaven," he said. "You have no idea, do you?"
He half-groaned and half-laughed, his teeth a flash of white
in the lamplight. "The boat is fine. And you can't drown—
the water is only two feet deep."

One of the blades skipped on the surface of the water,
splashing them with muddy-smelling water. "Oh, Lucas.
You are drunk. Let me row. You just sit and relax."

"Sounds good to me." He handed over the oars and
leaned back on his elbows. "Row, galley slave. If you get me
to shore safely, I'll feed you grapes and sweetmeats for a
week."

The practical matter of food reminded her of the time.
Her stomach growled. "I'd sooner go home for dinner. I'm
starving."

He threw back his head and laughed.

On that occasion, he'd come back for her, but this
time, he'd gone off in a rage and left her to cope by
herself. She blinked back the hot rush of tears and
swallowed hard. She only had herself to blame.
Perhaps Tisha was right; if Caro left London now, the
scandal would die down. In the meantime, why not
make a perfectly respectable visit to her aunt in
Paris?

She didn't dare go to Paris.

Or at least, the old cautious Caro didn't dare, but
the new Caro, the Caro who raced down St. James's,
certainly might.

Caro raised her gaze to meet François enquiring
brown eyes.

"Yes," she said. "I would very much like to go to
Paris. There is no need to inform Lucas of my plans.
Not until I return to Norwich."

❊　　❊　　❊　　❊

Lucas watched the Chevalier's lips curve in a mocking smile from behind his pistol. A black circle rimmed in silver filled Lucas's vision

Consumed by fury, he couldn't breathe or move. Air, thick and heavy with stink of leaf-mould, pressed in on him, his feet seemingly held fast in the black miasma.

Lit by a shaft of sunlight through the bare trees, dressed in nothing but her shift, her hair hanging to her waist, Caro paced back and forth behind the Chevalier's elegant figure. Lucas glanced at her. It hurt that she would not look at him.

The Chevalier's finger tightened. The hammer lifted in agonizing slowness and demanded Lucas's attention.

The bullet left the muzzle in an earsplitting roar.

Lucas turned his face away from the speeding, deadly lump of gray lead. He didn't want to watch.

Exploding pain seared in his temple.

A yawning black pit swallowed him as blood flowed, warm and sticky beneath his cheek.

Dead.

A groan came from the region of his chest.

If he was dead, why the agony in his head? The smell of stale brandy choked him. He coughed.

Not dead.

He seemed to be sitting in a chair, his head on something hard. He groaned again and forced his gritty eyelids up, lifting his head a fraction, dreading what he would see.

His signet ring glinted in the narrow bar of golden

light across his desk. A puddle of clear liquid rippled beneath his shaking hand.

A nightmare. He sighed. Suddenly nauseous, he pushed himself upright in his chair. He shuddered. Four empty bottles ranged across the polished wood of his desk in front of his nose. A fifth lay beside them, a pool of amber dregs leaking from its neck.

His head pounded as if hell's blacksmith had taken up residence. Tentatively, he touched his temple. The pain eased as he kneaded a tender indentation caused by sleeping on his ring. Better than a bullet wound, he thought wryly. Or not. He scrubbed his palm across the stubble on his cheeks and chin.

His gut felt as if it hadn't been fed for a week.

Five bottles. Or at least four and a half, in . . . how long? It must be a record. Who cared?

He squinted at the clock on the wall. With the curtains pulled together all but a crack, he couldn't make out the numbers.

He leaned back in the chair, closing his eyes until the room steadied. The room stank of stale cigars, spilled brandy, and sweat. A charred and crumpled piece of paper lay before him on the smeared wood. It was the reason he sensed a huge hole where his chest used to be.

Caro had run off to France with the Chevalier.

He pressed the paper flat. It shocked him to see his fingers tremble. Leaning on his elbows, he squinted at the neat handwriting, vaguely hoping the words would say something different.

Dear Lord Foxhaven,

A nice friendly start.

My cousin François kindly offered to escort me to Paris.

Kind. What a bloody joke.

Under the circumstances, I would be obliged if you would. . .

The rest of it disappeared into the blackened edge. It didn't matter. He could still see it in his mind's eye:

. . . be so good as to arrange our divorce. Carolyn Rivers.

And she hadn't sent it until four weeks after she left.

The hole in his chest opened like the pit of hell, and he felt his life's blood drain away. He glanced down at his front to be sure it was all in his mind, and he let the paper fall to the table. He'd been such a fool. Why hadn't he believed what he saw? He'd just never expected Caro of all people to betray him.

She hadn't even waited to tell him to his face, curse her. Utter despair swamped him. He didn't want to curse her at all. He wanted to kiss her, to tell her he was sorry for what had happened. All of it.

She had every right to choose, he snarled at himself. And she'd chosen the Chevalier. Only oblivion dulled the pain.

He snatched up the last bottle and drained it dry. The liquid burned his gullet and spread warmth to his belly. His head drummed an evil tattoo in protest.

More brandy would ease the pain in his chest. It had to.

He eyed the bell-pull on the wall by the fireplace. If he could reach it, he could ring for Beckwith.

A knock at the door made him turn his head. He groaned at the crushing ache, peering at Beckwith in the doorway. Good man that. He knew when he was needed.

"Brandy," Lucas croaked.

"Yes, my lord. Mr. Bascombe is asking to see you."

For a moment, the words failed to register. Lucas blinked through the blur filling the gap between him and the butler.

"Mr. Bascombe," Beckwith repeated through stiff lips.

So he'd annoyed the stuffy old bugger, had he? Lucas would have laughed, if he could remember how. "Not home," he managed instead.

"'S'blood, Luc," Bascombe said, pushing past Beckwith. "You look like the very devil."

Lucas kept his gaze fixed on Beckwith. "Brandy. Now." His roar came out a raspy whisper.

Beckwith left with what Lucas was sure was a sniff.

"Go 'way, Charlie."

Bascombe sauntered in and hitched a hip onto the corner of the desk. Lucas palmed Caro's letter and slipped it into his desk drawer.

Bascombe cocked a brow. "Not like you to shoot the cat." His voice held sympathy.

Lucas didn't want his damn sympathy. He wanted a mind-numbing drink. "Piss off."

"M'sister sent me." He spoke as if that answered why he didn't move.

"Bugger her."

The blue eyes hardened. "Damn you, Foxhaven."

Lucas rested his elbows on the desk and carefully placed his head in his hands. It felt safer that way. "Told you. Go 'way." God, it hurt to talk.

"Lady Foxhaven is in Paris," Bascombe announced.

Bloody hell. Did everyone know his business? He surged to his feet. The room swirled, sucking him into its vortex. Bile rose in his throat.

Oh, Christ. He was going to cast up his accounts. Groaning, he dropped back into the chair. "Leg it, Charlie." He closed his eyes and waited for the room to steady.

Beckwith entered with a silver tray, a bottle of brandy, and two glasses. He set it on the desk. Lucas watched him depart and then lunged for the bottle. He pulled the stopper out with his teeth.

Bascombe placed a restraining hand on his wrist.

Lucas cursed and jerked away.

"Didn't you hear what I said?" Charlie asked. "Audley says your wife is in Paris. She's using the name Torrington."

She assumed the divorce was a *fait accompli*. Sadness swamped him.

He picked up a glass. The decanter's rattle against the rim exploded in his head like gunfire. He lifted his eyes from the amber liquid and glared at Bascombe. "Leave me alone, Goddamn it."

Charlie recoiled, his expression a mix of comical fear and genuine concern. "No need to shoot the messenger, you idiot."

Lucas breathed through his nose, around the burning sensation in the back of his throat. "I know she's in Paris. Tell me something I don't know."

"She's staying with a Madame Valeron in the Faubourg Saint-Germain. Been there a few weeks, apparently. She's the latest rage, and the on dit is that she is to marry the Chevalier and bring him some sort of fortune. Sounds like a hum to me."

Lucas swallowed. The inside of his mouth tasted of old leather boot. "I said tell me something I don't know. Bugger off, Charlie."

"Tisha's doing her best to stop the tongues wagging here, but it will all be for naught once news of her dashing off alone to France gets out. Good thing you did dive into a hole these past few weeks. You have to sort this out. She's your wife."

Not for much longer.

His stomach roiled. He was duty-bound to honor the agreement he'd made with her. By rights, he should have posted off to Scotland the moment he got her note, almost a week ago.

He hadn't wanted to be married in the first place, and now he didn't want a divorce. Curse it all, she was his wife, but she despised him as a rake. She'd told him so to his face. She didn't know anything about him. No one did. Except maybe the lads at Wooten Hall. But whose fault was that?

Curse Fred for running off. If he hadn't got himself lost for five days, Lucas might have been in time to stop her. He had thought she was in Norwich and had very nearly posted up to see her a couple of times, but his lads' upcoming debut at King's Theater had kept him fully occupied.

Then her note arrived, and he'd been imagining her with the slimy frog ever since.

Hell. This was all his fault. He should never have married her in the first place. He liked her too well. But since he had, then he should have made sure she was up to snuff. How could he have guessed she'd fall into such a coil? She'd seemed perfectly fine with Cedric and Tisha to guide her.

Guilt twisted like a knife in his gut. He'd been too busy with his own affairs to make sure. "It's too late, Charlie."

"Rivers is there too."

Lucas snapped his head up and groaned. "Cedric? That's all right, then. He'll keep an eye on her."

"Tisha thinks there's more to this than meets the eye."

His head pounded with the effort to understand. "What do you mean?"

"Why didn't Cedric put a stop to this damn race? He was there."

"He tried."

"Are you sure?"

He wasn't sure of anything. His wife had left him, and no doubt everyone would think he deserved it after his past mistress had led her into such fast behavior. "I wasn't there. If I had been, it wouldn't have happened."

Charlie nodded. "Right. It's high time you were there."

"Blast you, Charlie. And blast Tisha. She doesn't know what she's talking about." He'd made a mess of the whole marriage thing from the beginning. He wasn't cut out for it.

Charlie gave him a discerning look. "Get to Paris, man."

Perhaps he ought to make sure she really did want a divorce. And why hadn't Cedric informed him where Caro had gone?

Lucas nodded slowly, careful not to set the room spinning again. "I'll think about it."

Charlie slapped him on the shoulder. "Good man.

By the way, that investment you put me in the way of came up trumps. Thanks. I doubled my blunt."

Lucas nodded dully. Then he must also have made a fortune. His father, who had instructed him to sell on Cedric's advice, must have lost a huge sum. A brief pang of sorrow surprised him.

None of that mattered. He had to decide what to do about Caro. He wanted his wife back, he realized. And to win her back, he needed to show her he was every bit as good as some smarmy Frenchman. He rose unsteadily to his feet.

And if he couldn't have her back, he needed to set things to rights.

Thirteen

$\mathcal{C}$ARO'S AUNT, MADAME HONORÉ VALERON, A SEP-
tuagenarian of generous proportions who clung
to the powdered wigs and hooped skirts of her youth,
presided over her usual Wednesday afternoon salon
reclined on a chaise by the hearth. Caro glanced
around the baroque drawing room. As on the previous
five occasions, the room burst at the seams with elegant Paris society, and the conversation ebbed and
flowed on the fascinating topic of French politics.

Seated on a gilt chair at the foot of her aunt's
chaise, Caro leaned forward to catch the words of the
Marquis du Bouvoir over the buzz of conversation
and clink of coffee cups. Attired in the glittering blue
uniform of the Guarde Royale, he was one of the
many officers who made up the company.

"But how can I hold up my head, if I do not
secure one dance with the incomparable
Mademoiselle l'Anglaise?" the marquis asked with a
flash of white smile beneath his dark moustache.

Caro frowned at the handsome olive-skinned noble and shook her head in mock disapproval. "You make me sound like a dessert."

He waggled his brows. "A exceedingly delicious one."

"Enough of your flattery, sir. I will grant you the last waltz of the evening."

Aunt Honoré flicked her ostrich fan in their direction. "Monsieur, take your argument and my niece elsewhere. How can I hear the Prince de Tallyrand above your nonsense?"

The pale elderly man murmuring in her aunt's ear raised his piercing gaze, and Caro suppressed a wriggle. She wasn't sure what was worse, the way he seemed to see right through her skimpy gown or the knowledge that he had played an influential role in every French government since the Revolution. Her aunt seemed to dote on him.

Glad of the excuse to escape Talleyrand's unnerving observation, Caro relinquished her coffee cup to a lackey. The marquis led her through the press of fashionable ladies and gentlemen and the colorful uniforms of every army in Europe to the window overlooking the rue de Lille.

"You are an incorrigible tease, and I adore you," the marquis said, his hazel eyes gazing into hers.

She laughed. "You, monsieur le marquis, are an outrageous flirt."

He grinned as if she had paid him a compliment. "What else am I to do, since your Chevalier has stolen a march on the rest of us poor mortals?"

Unwelcome warmth washed over her. "We are cousins, nothing more."

"Come now, mademoiselle, your aunt makes no secret of his intentions."

"And that is why you feel free to practice your wiles on me," she flashed back.

He gave her a knowing glance. "Methinks the lady doth protest too much. And how prettily she blushes."

Her color had nothing to do with her relationship with François. She should never have agreed to hide her married state from her aunt, even if it did mean admitting she had left London in disgrace.

Being caught in the web of lies concocted by Cedric after he learned of her arrangement with Lucas weighed far more heavily on her conscience than the truth. Cedric meant well, but it left her with the uneasy sensation that her skin didn't quite fit her new persona.

The marquis lifted his quizzing glass and inspected the room. "Speaking of your admirer, where are the elegant Chevalier and his so—very-English friend?"

She didn't want to think about where François had gone. "They have gone out of town on business, I believe."

"Ah, *oui*, champagne." He kissed his fingertips. "The nectar of the gods, and the best of it comes from Chateau Valeron."

He glanced idly around the room, his quizzing glass dangling from his fingers. "And here Lord Audley brings yet another Englishman to our salons. Paris becomes more British than London."

She raised a brow. "In the face of such disapproval, perhaps I should depart immediately."

A droll expression of horror crossed his face.

"Pardon me. It is not the so charming ladies of whom I speak, *je vous assure.*" He swept a languid hand to the room in general. "It is the foreign soldiers billeted in our homes and the businessmen from every country in Europe, the vultures in black suits, to whom I object. The city is under siege, and French treasures flood across the Channel like blood from a wound."

She'd heard the complaints before. The British ambassador purchased vast quantities of priceless books and furniture, Wellington collected Boulle cabinets and empire tables, and Sir Charles Long harvested paintings for the Prince Regent to hang in Carleton House. She had no consolation to offer.

He narrowed his eyes. "This one looks like a nobleman."

She turned to observe the object of his displeasure.

A strange little jolt in her heart stopped her breath and quickened her pulse. The dark-haired man with his back to her topped the stern Lord Audley by half a head, and they were the tallest men in the room. Could it be Lucas?

She peered through her usual blur. A wave of disappointment emptied her chest. The man's carefully ordered black hair barely brushed his collar. She turned away.

"Why the sad expression, mademoiselle?" the marquis asked. "Were you expecting someone?"

When would it stop? Each time she glimpsed a dark-haired man of above-average height, her heart took flight like a bird, only to crash to earth when she realized he wasn't Lucas. Why her heart hoped to see him in Paris when she had sent him to Scotland, she couldn't imagine.

She forced a smile. "How could I possibly look for someone else, when I am in your company?" She raised a brow. "Provided we do not discuss politics."

"*Touché*, mademoiselle."

"Mademoiselle Torrington, du Bouvoir." Audley's distinctive gravelly voice came from behind her.

Thank goodness Tisha had not introduced them when he last visited London. She turned to greet him. "Lord Audley, how pleasant to see you again." They had met at a British Embassy soirée the previous week.

The marquis bowed. "You ruin our *tête-a-tête*, milor' Audley. Don't follow in your Lord Stuart's footsteps, if you please. Leave the single ladies to us bachelors."

Audley bowed, his expression impassive, despite the overt reference to the British ambassador's penchant for Parisian courtesans. "With pleasure, monsieur le marquis."

Du Bouvoir lifted his quizzing glass. "And whom do you bring with you today? Another of King George's parliamentarians to advise us how to run our Chamber of Deputies?"

The imposing figure beside Audley swam into focus. Lucas?

The room receded, leaving only his face in her vision. It was as if her thoughts had conjured him up, and something had gone wrong with the spell. In a black superfine coat, pearl-gray waistcoat, and intricate starched white cravat, he looked wickedly elegant and utterly different—sterner, more formal.

And he'd cut his beautiful hair.

A patter of nerves skipped through her stomach, her lungs straining for air in the overheated room. Had he come here to find her? Would he now expose her for a fraud? She flashed hot and then cold.

"Allow me to present Lord Foxhaven," Lord Audley said.

She managed a smile through stiff lips. "Lord Foxhaven, welcome to Paris." Her voice sounded hoarse.

He executed a swift, graceful bow and a bone-melting smile. "*Enchanté*, Mademoiselle Torrington."

"Mademoiselle Torrington came to us from London, Foxhaven," Audley said calmly. "Had you not stayed in the country in pursuit of other matters, you might have met her in London."

"An omission I deeply regret," Lucas murmured. His gaze fell to the neckline of her gown and lingered for a moment.

Warmth unfurled deep in her stomach as her body recalled the delight of his touch, the feel of his hands and his lips on the décolletage now daringly bared to the world.

Instead, she plied her fan with vigor, aware of the silence, of eyes watching her, unable to utter a word for the turmoil in her head.

"Are you well, mademoiselle?" the marquis asked, all gentle concern.

"It does seem a trifle warm in here," she managed.

"Allow me to let in some air." He strode to the window and wrestled with the casement.

"Excuse me," Audley said. "I see Monsieur

Jeunesse. I have been trying to reach him for days."
He sauntered away.

Caro resisted the urge to call him back, to use him
as a shield against whatever Lucas might throw at
her. She braced herself for the onslaught.

With an eye to the marquis, Lucas drew closer.
The scent of his sandalwood cologne touched her
senses with a painful familiarity. A slow, lazy smile
curved his lips, and his raking glance flared with
what looked like appreciation. "You look beautiful,
Caro. Stunning."

She suppressed a gasp as her toes curled inside her
satin slippers. Beautiful? Did he mean it? And the
heat in his gaze. He never looked at her that way in
company.

Hiding her face with her fan and wishing it were
large enough to cover her bosom, she whispered,
"Why are you here?"

He grimaced a little, whether because of her lack
of response to what he had said or because of impatience, she couldn't be sure. "I heard from Audley
you were here and using your maiden name."

"Impossible. He doesn't know who I am."

"Apparently, Tisha pointed you out in Hyde
Park."

On the day of her disgrace. He didn't say the
words, but they hung awkwardly in the air between
them.

Caro darted a glance at the granite-faced attaché
talking to the Monsieur Jeunesse along with his wife
and their willowy daughter, Belle. Audley had
disguised his knowledge well.

Belle Jeunesse shot Lucas an avid glance. Caro

turned, expecting to find him ogling the dusky maiden's undeniable charms. Instead, he seemed not to have noticed. "Why did you come?" she asked.

"Does it matter why?"

Having thrown open the casement, the marquis rejoined them. He glanced from one to the other, his imposing moustache stiff with suspicion. "What is the question?"

Her mind went blank. She couldn't think for the tension sparking the air.

"I asked Mademoiselle Torrington if she would do me the honor of driving out with me tomorrow," Lucas drawled, arrogance in every word.

The thought of being alone with him made her heart beat faster.

The marquis visibly bristled. "I had intended to ask the lady to drive with me in the morning." He fingered the hilt of his dress sword. "You are forward, milor', on so short an acquaintance."

A muscle flickered in Lucas's jaw, and his lips thinned.

Caro's heart drummed a warning. Although tall for a Frenchman, the marquis was no match for the towering Lucas. She steeled herself to step between them.

Lucas inclined his head and waved a languid hand. "Indeed, monsieur le marquis, I concede to your earlier claim. Perhaps Mademoiselle Torrington will join me another day?"

The marquis's jaw and corded neck visibly eased, and Caro let her breath go. How unlike Lucas to play the diplomat. She smiled her approval.

The marquis narrowed his eyes. "Now I see how

it is." He bowed. "Mademoiselle, if it pleases you to drive with your countryman, who am I to stand in the way of your pleasure?"

Had it been that obvious? She opened her mouth to protest.

The marquis gave his moustache a twirl. "After all, *mon ange*, it is I who have secured your last waltz tonight." He bowed and sauntered away.

"What a pleasant fellow," Lucas said, surprising her. "He is a lucky man to win a waltz. If it is truly your last one, I am *desolé*." His smile was so sweet, she tasted sugar.

She swallowed. She'd never been a recipient of his famous charm, and her heart raced at double time. No wonder ladies fell like ripe plums at his feet. "I didn't know you were in Paris." It sounded like an accusation.

He cocked his eyebrow at her, and his voice contained lazy amusement. "If you had, would you have saved me a waltz?"

Was he really flirting with her? Replying to the marquis's nonsense had been easy. Now her mind and her tongue felt clumsy. "Well, I didn't know, so the answer is moot."

"Indeed." His dark eyes warmed with gentle laughter. She had an overwhelming desire to rest her head on his shoulder and ask him to take her home.

His lingering gaze swept her length. Her skin shimmered as if his glance had substance. "I meant what I said, just now. You look wonderful," he purred. "Paris suits you."

The sincerity in his voice and expression pulled at her heartstrings. This was not the Lucas she knew, her friend or her absentee husband. This was the gallant knight of her dreams. If only he meant it. "You look different also," she said, hating how breathless she sounded. "You cut your hair. I almost didn't recognize you."

His gaze dropped to her neckline. "I would recognize you anywhere."

Heat raced to her cheeks, again. Her stomach flopped over. Did he have to remind her so obviously of the last time they met?

Dash it all, she wouldn't let him put her out of countenance. She'd learned the art of repartee from the best Paris had to offer. She arched a brow. "Your eyesight always was better than mine."

"You will drive with me tomorrow, won't you, Caro?" he asked in an intimate growl.

A pulse of excitement fluttered deep in her core. Only Lucas ever sparked such a visceral response. And that was the problem. Clearly, the sooner they resolved things between them, the better. "I will drive with you, if my aunt grants permission."

He gaze flicked to the chaise. "Of course. Audley introduced me when we came in. I will speak to her immediately."

His apparent eagerness sent a tiny thrill through her, cracking her hard-won armor. Would she never learn? If he was here because of her, then it was because he wanted something.

She schooled her face into a cool smile. "Please do."

His practiced smile changed to a boyish grin. "Until tomorrow, then, mademoiselle."

He didn't have the slightest doubt about his powers of persuasion, and with her as an example, why would he?

"I will count the moments," he said, with a bow so elegant that she feared she had to escape his presence before she lost what little remained of her defenses.

She inclined her head. "If my aunt agrees, then yes, until tomorrow." She strolled away to the sound of her pounding heart and joined a group of intense young ladies and a brown-coated Prussian officer discussing the future of France.

From the corner of her eye, she watched Lucas stride purposefully to her aunt's chaise. The old lady smiled. She liked handsome young men who took the trouble to charm her. And Lucas would certainly manage that. Caro breathed a sigh of relief as her aunt nodded.

Inwardly, she wagged a finger at herself much as Lizzie would. This meeting was to discover Lucas's intentions in coming to Paris. Nothing more.

❈　　❈　　❈　　❈

"How do I look?" Lady Foxhaven said.

Lizzie glowered at the laces running down the back of the green muslin walking gown. Not Lady Foxhaven. Miss Caro Torrington again. She couldn't keep up with it all. "Stop fidgeting." She tied a bow. "You're as nervous as a hearth-cat with a singed tail."

"I want to look my best, that is all."

The brittle smile in the mirror didn't match her mistress's brave words, nor did the twisting fingers.

Lizzie frowned. "You look as if you barely slept a wink, and that gown could do with a bit more fabric." She handed over the chip straw hat.

Her mistress popped the hat on her head as if it hadn't taken an hour for her aunt's dresser to arrange her hair. She tied the green ribbon below her left ear. "Do you really think it's too revealing? I am almost falling out of it."

Faced with the anxious stare, Lizzie eyed the bosom emerging from the straw-colored silk. The golden skin had not a blemish in sight, but the snug fit and the plunging neckline revealed far more than anything her mistress had ever worn before. Her father would never have approved. Best not to mention that. "It's not as bad as that there ball gown what arrived yesterday." She nodded toward the dressing room. "Why not wear that nice lemon cashmere shawl you bought the other day?"

Caro tugged up on the neck of the gown to no avail. "It is rather low." She bit her lip. "I must have been mad to let my aunt talk me into a gown like this, or the others. I swear there's more of me than ever."

Caro sighed, and it cut Lizzie's heart to ribbons.

Lizzie tipped the tiny hat forward. "Not an inch have I had to let out of your gowns. But if they are a smidgen tight here or there, eating all this strange food has done it. Too rich by half."

Caro's glance darted to the mirror and she pressed her palms against her hips. "Mademoiselle Jeunesse eats it, and I could swear I'm twice the size of her."

Lizzie snorted. "She's a Frog. She's used to it. What you need is some good plain English food. A nice jam pudding or a steak and kidney pie." Her mouth watered at the thought of apples in steamed suet.

"That's the kind of food the vicar liked. Your ma never ate all this French rubbish neither, even though she came from here."

Caro's lips pursed as if she had sucked a lemon. "I know you don't like France, Lizzie. Why not go back to Norwich? The girls would love to see you."

The hairs on the back of Lizzie's neck stirred. It wasn't the first time she'd heard those words since they'd got on that dreadful boat across the channel. "And leave you with this bag of Captain Sharps? And not one of them speaking the King's good English? No, my lady, not while there's breath in my body."

"Then please don't complain."

There was hurt in the soft voice, an underlying anguish Lizzie couldn't fathom. Something had happened before they left England to wound her mistress, something like when she'd turned his lordship down the first time. She'd sobbed in her pillow then too. Bloomin' rakehell. Who would have thought that angelic little boy she used to see in church would turn out so bad.

Still, it wasn't her place to pry. She lay the cashmere shawl over Caro's stiff shoulders with a pat. "Keep that 'round you. The wind can be sharp this time of year."

Her ladyship swung around, a hectic color in her cheeks and gold sparks in her eyes. "Lord Foxhaven is taking me driving this morning." The words seemed to burst out of her.

"Land's sake. So that's what this is about." Lizzie put her hands on her hips. "Has he come to fetch you home?"

"I am not sure. I don't think so." With one last

glance in the mirror, Caro snatched up her parasol and whisked out of the door.

Lizzie picked up the dressing gown from the floor and draped it over the foot of the bed.

Whatever next?

❋　　❋　　❋　　❋

Half way down the stairs, Caro caught sight of Lucas waiting in the entrance hall. On time for once. Her heart swelled out of all proportion to the event. Would she never learn?

Hands holding his hat and gloves behind his back, he stared at a Valeron family portrait. Darkly handsome in a navy driving coat with several capes and his buff unmentionables tucked into shining black Hessians, he seemed completely engrossed. The fanlight cast his face into the strong planes and angles of a marble statue—except that mere stone could not capture his restrained vitality or raw masculinity.

She missed her step and clutched at the balustrade with a gasp.

He swung around, and his gaze swept over her with barely concealed heat that seemed to coil around her and steal the air from her lungs. As usual, he was using his devastating charm to get what he wanted. If only she knew exactly what that was.

She retreated behind a polite smile and continued on down with outward aplomb and a racing pulse. "Good morning, my lord."

"Mademoiselle." Lucas briefly took her hand as she reached the bottom. "You look *enchantée*."

Aware of the tingle in her fingers, she nodded. "Thank you."

The dour Valeron butler appeared from nowhere, a saucy, red-haired woman in tow.

Lucas raised an eyebrow.

"Cecelia, Aunt Honoré's maid, is to accompany us," Caro explained.

His dark brows drew together.

Her heart sank. He wouldn't accept the insinuation of his lack of honor, and Aunt Honoré would not let her go without a suitable chaperone. She should have known better than to get her hopes up about this outing. "I'm sorry, Lucas." Heat rushed to her cheeks. "I mean, Lord Foxhaven."

The butler sniffed.

Caro glared at him. His steadfast refusal to speak English made Lizzie's life miserable below stairs, but he clearly understood it well enough.

He gave a stiff bow and marched back to his kingly domain.

Lucas's expression cleared. "I understand perfectly." He held out his arm. "Let us depart before the horses become restless or your aunt decides we should also take her pug."

"She hasn't got a pug,"

"Thanks be to providence."

She laughed, delighted by his humorous acceptance of the situation. She placed her hand on his sleeve.

In short order, Caro sat crushed between Lucas and the bony Cecilia in Lord Audley's midnight blue and gold phaeton with a pair of matched grays in the traces. After turning out of the portes cochères at the entrance to her Aunt's hôtel, they left the Faubourg Saint- Germain behind and rumbled over the River

Seine at Ponte Louis XVI.

"Where are we going?" Caro asked.

A smile curved his sensual mouth. "You'll see." His voice had the texture of treacle, sweet and rich with undertones of something dark. A shiver of pure pleasure raced down her spine. She'd missed the sound of his voice.

A long, lean thigh pressed against her soft one, and warmth slowly infused her. The sky suddenly seemed bluer and the streets of Paris more alive.

The wide, tree-lined Boulevard des Italiens bustled with carriages, most of them English. A couple of hussars in busbies and jaunty blue fur-edged pelisses, strolled arm-in-arm with a pair of scantily dressed females. A Parisian country gentleman glared and shook his fist at being forced to wait while a company of Austrian soldiers dazzling in white marched across the road in front of them.

"How do you think they stay clean in battle?" Caro said. "And all that embroidery—it would be such a shame to spoil it."

"They probably wait in the rear until it's all over," Lucas said.

She laughed.

Pedestrians sauntered slowly along the wide sunlit street and mingled in outdoor cafés. Between the buildings, narrow dreary alleys writhed into the depths of ancient city. Filth coursed down their central kennels, overflowing into the boulevard and bringing the fetid stench of poverty into the open. For all Napoleon's improvements, it was easy to imagine a desperate mob pouring from the depths of such squalor to murder their aristocratic oppressors.

She shivered. London had its poverty and its riots, but somehow England had avoided anything as vicious as the guillotine.

As they drew up, she cast off her morbid reflections. "Tortoni's. I love their ices."

"You have been here before?" he asked.

"I have, with my cousin. It is one of my favorite places."

He looked a trifle disappointed, but replied cheerfully enough. "Mine too. I thought we could spend a pleasant hour here while Cecelia goes shopping. Then I will show you my surprise."

An avaricious little smile lit the maid's face. "The milor' has money?"

Lucas grinned. "He does."

A strange little jolt hit Caro's stomach. So he'd thought of a way for them to be alone. No wonder he had taken Cecelia's presence in such good part.

He threw a sous to a loitering street urchin. "Take care of the horses?" he asked. "There will be another when we return."

The boy nodded.

Lucas handed Cecelia a fistful of coins. "Be back in one hour." The moment her feet touched the cobbles, Cecelia trotted off without a backward glance.

Lucas reached up and caught Caro by the waist. She grasped his shoulders for support. Sinews moved beneath her fingers, and his strong hands filled the hollow beneath her ribs and scorched through her gown. Sandalwood and heat swirled around her as he held her close. She slid down his length, his coat buttons grazing her breasts, until her eyes were on a level with the diamond in his cravat. Awareness shimmered across her skin in delicious waves.

"Lucas," she gasped.

He raised a brow. "What?"

She swallowed. "Put me down."

A laugh rumbled through his chest. "I'm sorry. I didn't realize your feet weren't on the ground." He lowered her to the cobbles.

Of course he knew, and his knowing quickened her heartbeat. "Thank you." The tremor in her voice annoyed her, and she straightened her spine.

He bowed. She tucked her spectacles in her reticule and placed her hand on his outstretched arm, and together they sauntered into the fashionable establishment.

Signore Tortini, a black-haired jolly Neapolitan brought to France by Bonaparte, greeted them with a flourish and led them to a round table in the corner by the window. The bright suite of rooms burst with the haute-monde talking and laughing to the musical chink of spoons on glass dishes.

A waiter in a pristine white apron arrived instantly to take their order. Caro requested a lemon water ice, and Lucas asked for ice cream.

While they waited, fashionable ladies at the nearby tables glanced sideways at them. Well, really at Lucas. They probably wondered how she had managed to attract the attention of such a handsome man.

She felt a little spurt of pride. He was hers. But not for much longer. Was that sorrow she felt in the pit of her stomach, or the need for food? As usual, anxiety sharpened her appetite.

The treats arrived accompanied by wafers and an ice-lined carafe of water.

Caro spooned up a mouthful. A small pain stabbed her forehead. "Ooh. Cold."

He grinned in sympathy and scooped up his ice cream. He turned his spoon the wrong way round and licked it, his eyes cast heavenward. "Food for the gods."

Caro giggled and savored the tart burst of lemon on her tongue. "Ambrosia. I didn't realize you knew Paris so well."

"I come here occasionally on business. The French stock market is a profitable proposition at the moment."

Business. A shadow seemed to dim the room. A horrid rushy breath filled her throat, and she forced her words past it. "Is that why you are here?"

He nodded. "There are matters which require my attention, certainly."

No doubt she was one of those matters. Enough to bed the most unattractive female. She stirred the watery yellow remains with her spoon, her ice melting along with her hopes.

He reached out to capture her hand, his large and warm and hers chilled from the dessert. She tried to pull back, but he held it fast.

"I had another, more important reason," he said.

The intensity in his eyes held her transfixed. They weren't black, but shades of dark brown all swirled together like hot chocolate and cream. He brought her hand to his mouth. At the last moment, he turned it and brushed his lips against the inside of her wrist.

Treacherous desire blossomed low in her stomach. Memories of what those wonderful hands could do to her body jolted her femininity to pulsing life. She glowed.

"Come back to London, Caro," he said.

Yes, her heart said. "Why?"

For a moment, he appeared to be stunned, but then he raised a questioning brow. "I thought we had an agreement?"

The pain she'd felt all those weeks ago in London came back raw and fresh. She tugged her hand free. "You made a new agreement with your father. You agreed to get me with child to inherit my aunt's money."

Guilt and embarrassment flashed across his face. "Damn it, Caro, where did you get such an idea?" Several heads turned their way. He glared back, and their glances dropped away. "Who told you such a thing?"

"I heard you talking in the library."

His eyes narrowed, and his head tilted to one side, considering. More deceit hatching in his fertile brain, no doubt. "I admit to the conversation. But not to agreeing."

"Then your coming here is not about getting me with child to get your hands on my aunt's money?"

Horror filled his expression. "Absolutely not."

Heat flamed in her face. "You couldn't do it, could you? After the race." He couldn't bring himself to bed his dumpling of a wife.

His gaze lowered to her bosom for a second, and color stained his cheekbones. "I made a mistake. I apologized then, and I apologize now. I promise it won't happen again."

That was supposed to make her feel better? A tiny

seed of hope shriveled and died, leaving a lump in her throat. She traced her spoon around the edge of the little glass dish. "There won't be another opportunity."

A strained expression passed over his face. "You mean you won't give me a chance to make things right?"

"Cedric says our marriage is a fraud."

"You told Cedric? How could you? It's private. Between us."

"He said you wasted your grandmother's money to buy a house in the country. A house I've never even seen." A house for your mistress. The thought sent a river of ice through her blood.

His voice lowered to a growl. "Is the whole world a party to my affairs?"

He was acting as if it was all her fault. How dare he try to make her feel guilty? She retorted, "You made me look like some kind of fool, and I discovered I didn't like it. Then one of your bits-of-muslin decided to use me for revenge."

He cracked a laugh. His lip curled in disdain. "One of my bits-of-muslin? Such language from a vicar's daughter. What do you take me for?"

"A rake and libertine." She sat back in her chair waiting for him to deny it, wanting with every fiber in her being for him to say it wasn't true.

He stared at her, silent, his eyes hard and bright and totally unreadable.

His hand clenched on his spoon, the haft began to bend. He dropped it as if it was hot. "All right. I admit it was all my fault. I should have made sure you knew the rules."

He brushed the spoon away with a careless flick of his hand. It struck the glass dish with a loud chink. "As for the house, it isn't important. I'll get rid of it. Believe me when I say I never meant anything to harm you. Nothing like that will happen again."

She stared at him, biting her lip. He seemed genuinely sorry, and she desperately wanted to believe.

"Caro, I swear I will stand by our agreement." He shook his head, hesitating as if he would say more.

She didn't want their old agreement. She wanted more.

"You really mean you will give up your other . . . pursuits?"

Disappointment reflected in his eyes and the set of his sensual mouth. It was too great a sacrifice, she realized. But he squared his shoulders. "Yes."

Her mouth dropped open. "How can I know you will keep your word?" She wanted to bite out her tongue as bleakness filled his gaze. "I should not have asked that."

He held up his hand and shook his head. "I made a mess of things. Give me some time to live up to my side of the bargain. Give me a month. If you aren't satisfied then, I'll arrange the divorce and no arguments."

She didn't have a month. "Cedric is due back in two days. He went to Bordeaux to see a protestant bishop about an annulment."

A muscle jumped in his jaw. "Do you have any idea what kind of scandal that will create?"

"I'm ruined already. What difference would it make?"

He shook his head. "Not so. Tisha has all but the

highest of sticklers convinced you made a genuine mistake. If you had stayed, the whole thing would have blown over."

A rush of tears misted her vision. If they hadn't had that dreadful argument after the race, then he wouldn't have kissed her to such utter distraction that she allowed him the liberty of her person. Perhaps then she could have retained her stupid dream that one day he might grow to love her. "It's too bad you didn't think of that before you packed me off to Norwich."

The lines around his mouth deepened. "I'm sorry. What more can I say?"

He caught her hand across the table, and for once, she saw more than a charming rake in his gaze. She saw hope, shadowed by something else. Fear. Yearning. She couldn't be sure.

It would never work. She could never keep him at her side with so many other more beautiful women waiting to catch his roving eye. It all seemed so hopeless. And yet she longed to try. "You have two days, before Cedric comes back."

He blinded her with a lopsided smile. "Two days it is. You won't regret it, I promise."

Her laugh shook. "I think I've heard that somewhere before."

He raised a brow. "This time it's true. You will see. Now, let's find that maid. I have a surprise."

Fourteen

*L*UCAS TURNED DOWN THE RUE VIVIENNE TOWARD the Palais Royale.

Although Caro had never approached the center of Paris life from this direction, its risqué reputation and wonderful shops and restaurants were legendary. Everyone visited the Palais Royale. She frowned when he brought the carriage to a stop outside a bow-fronted shop.

He grinned.

"What is this?" she asked.

"You'll see." The deep timbre of his voice sounded smug as he handed her down.

An excited buzz hummed through her veins. Lucas had never thought to surprise her before. A waiting lackey took charge of his horses. They left Cecelia in the carriage with a smile on her face and a large package clutched between her knees.

A bell tinkled as the doorman bowed them in.

A bookshop.

Entranced, Caro dragged out her spectacles and perched them on her nose.

English newspapers lay over a stand by the counter. Shelves with English titles lined the walls and ran down the center of the narrow room. An English bookshop in Paris. Why had no one told her?

"Lucas," she squeaked.

He shot her a warning glance.

A smile tugged at her lips at his concern about appearances. "I mean, Lord Foxhaven."

A gangly, monkey-faced proprietor came forward to greet them. "Welcome to my establishment. I am Monsieur Galignani." He bowed.

"Oh," Caro said. "Someone gave me a copy of Galignani's Paris Guide. Is it yours? It is so very informative."

The Frenchman's thin chest swelled, and the creases in his face organized themselves into a smile. "Mine indeed. Do you seek anything in particular today?"

A banquet could not have produced more confusion in a starving peasant than that which whirled in her brain. She shook her head.

"Browse around," Lucas drawled, settling into a leather sofa with its back to the bow window. "However, if you want to get back to your aunt's house at a reasonable hour, you ought to get busy." He picked up a newspaper from the table and disappeared behind it.

A rush of tenderness swelled her heart and cut off her breath. He looked so handsome, his long legs stretched out in front of him, the hard planes of his face softened by the spring sunlight shining through the square windowpanes. Did she dare believe his intentions were honorable?

She stared around the shop. This gift demonstrated a sensitivity she never suspected. It meant more than diamonds. And yet he offered only friendship, someone on whom she could rely. She wanted so much more. But the ache in her heart had nothing to do with the blur in her eyes. Bookshops always attracted dust. Determined not to spoil the moment, she smiled and turned her attention to the feast laid out for her delectation.

A half hour later, Lucas folded the English Messenger published by Monsieur Galagnini for the Englishman in Europe and tossed it on the table. News from home paled beside Caro's eager investigations, and after all this time, she seemed no closer to selecting a book than when they had arrived.

An adoring captive in her wake, the wizened proprietor pulled out books, pointed to volumes, and climbed the ladder each time she expressed the faintest interest in something high on a shelf. He gathered books under his spidery arm as they went.

Lucas could watch her lush form and delighted expression all day long. Knowing he had put the smile on her face gave him a rare sense of contentment. If only life were this simple.

As if to thwart his pleasure, she made her final selection, and Monsieur Galignani took it to the counter to wrap.

Eyes glowing, she returned to the sitting area. Lucas rose from his chair. He gazed into her lovely oval face with its enchanting smile on rose-colored lips. All he wanted to do was kiss them. He wanted to cup her golden cheeks flushed with pleasure in his palms, to lose himself in her honeyed sweetness. He let her see some of his consuming heat and delighted in the parting of her lips and shortened breath. "Promise me something?" he said.

A hint of suspicion clouded her brandy-colored eyes. "What?"

The bitter taste of disappointment dried his mouth. He had so little time to win back her trust. He kept his smile in place. "Promise you will shop for books only with me?"

She tipped her chin as she considered his request, and an overwhelming urge to pull her close fired his blood. He needed to feel her dissolve against him, into him, the way he knew she would if he kissed her. If she so much as brushed against him, he'd lose all control. He didn't dare risk all for fleeting pleasure.

"Very well," she said.

"What?" He shook his head to clear his mind. She meant shopping for books. "I mean, that's good." He paid for the purchase. "Are you ready?"

Bidding farewell to Monsieur Galagnini, Lucas ushered her out. Her perfume enveloped him as she swept past. He inhaled vanilla and roses, fresh and sweet. He'd missed her perfume these past few weeks, missed her voice, missed her like the very devil. He wanted her back where she belonged.

The thought shook him to the core. If he revealed this weakness she evoked in him, she'd try to run his life the way his father had. He would not give up control in exchange for passion.

He handed her up into the phaeton. Cecelia squeezed hard against the edge to make room. Lucas vaulted up beside Caro. "What book did you buy?" he asked, easing into the traffic.

She ducked her head as if ashamed. "Byron."

"Ah, romance."

"Foolish, I know," she said. A breathy sigh escaped her. His groin tightened at the memory of that sigh against his skin. Involuntarily, he tightened his grip on the reins. His leader faltered, and the carriage lurched.

Caro gasped as Cecelia squeaked.

Hell, Lucas thought. "I beg your pardon, ladies." Anyone would think he was a cow-handed farmer, not a nonesuch. "There is nothing foolish about Lord Byron. He is an accomplished writer."

"Are you teasing me?"

The questioning sideways glance from beneath her lashes revealed an unexpected warmth and laughter in the depths of her eyes.

He grinned. "I admit Lord Byron is not my favorite author, but I can appreciate his talent." He certainly knew women. "If I wrote only half as well, I might have the right to criticize his work."

A curve to her full luscious mouth rewarded his words. The warmth of her approval seemed to penetrate his chest. Burgeoning hope welled up inside him. He seemed to have won this hand, but would two days be enough time to press home his advantage?

※　　※　　※　　※

"It seems Lord Foxhaven is on everyone's guest list." Seated to Caro's right, the Marquis du Bouvoir sounded far from pleased as he leaned forward to inspect the new arrivals in Madame Mougeon's pretty blue drawing room.

Across the aisle, Lord Audley directed his party, consisting of Lucas and the two Jeunesse ladies, to their gilded chairs. Caro again felt in her stomach the sensation of a flock of starlings taking wing. When Lucas sat down next to Belle, the starlings landed with a bump. Clearly, another beautiful and petite female had captured his roving glance. So much for new beginnings.

She shifted her gaze to the front of the room where a vivacious dark-haired Italian soprano and her violin accompanist waited for the guests to settle.

"Did you drive out with the viscount yesterday?" the marquis asked.

Fortunately for Caro, the violinist tapped the side of his instrument with his bow for silence and precluded the necessity of an answer.

The singer poured her heart into an aria from Rossini's L'Italiana in Algeri. Caro tried to ignore Lucas's presence, but she sensed his gaze on her face as surely as if his fingers were touching her skin. Couldn't he be satisfied with the woman at his side?

At the intermission, the marquis offered to fetch coffee from an adjoining salon, and while Aunt Honoré gossiped with a widowed friend, Caro wandered the perimeter of the room, inspecting the portraits and country scenes hung tastefully on the walls.

"How are you enjoying it so far?" Lucas's deep voice asked.

Caro started. She hadn't heard him approach. "Do you have to sneak up on me like that?"

"I'm sorry. I didn't mean to surprise you." He

gestured to the portrait of a Mougeon ancestor in a Roman toga. "It seems you are interested in all the arts." His breath stirred the curls on her cheek.

She darted a glance at Mademoiselle Jeunesse, who was talking to their hostess by the piano set in the window. "I might say the same about you."

His expression turned serious. "I only have two days, Caro, and since you were already engaged to come here with the marquis, I needed an invitation. I persuaded Audley to add me to his party. I'd far rather take you shopping for books."

A wicked flick of his brow sent a shimmer of awareness over her skin. She returned her gaze to the portrait. "Perhaps some other time." There, that sounded calm enough.

"Your profile is enchanting, but I prefer to see both your beautiful eyes."

The words turned her insides to porridge. She fought for control. "Do not practice your wiles on me, sir. It will not wash." Or so she hoped. She searched for a neutral topic. "The opera singer has talent, does she not?"

"She is as good as everything I have heard about her. I'm going to invite her to perform at King's Theater."

Caro blinked.

"I thought you knew—I am one of their patrons."

"It seems there are many things I do not know about you."

"As yet," he murmured.

The lascivious undertones sent trickles of heat coursing through her blood. She inhaled a steadying breath and tried to look calm.

The marquis joined them and handed Caro her coffee. "Lord Foxhaven, we meet again. What a coincidence."

Lucas's easy manner of moments ago sharpened to a dangerous edge. "Isn't it?" Although his face held nothing but friendly politeness, his words might have been sword blades. He must have sensed her her growing anxiety, because the moment she opened her mouth to say something to ease the tension between the two men, he offered a reluctant smile. "If you will excuse me, I must return to my friends."

The marquis nodded. " And I must return you to your aunt, my dear Mademoiselle Torrington."

No matter how hard she tried, Caro could not prevent her gaze following Lucas's progress through the crowded room. Mademoiselle Jeunesse welcomed him to her side with a dazzling smile. If only the poor girl knew the truth about his married state. It was most unfair of him to encourage her to hope.

"Be seated everyone, please," the lady of the house announced, shooing them back to their seats. "We have many more delights for you this afternoon." She bustled to the front of the room. "Our dear Mademoiselle Jeunesse has agreed to play a piece from Beethoven's Pathétique.

She held out a welcoming hand.

Blushing, the slim beauty in a gown seemingly made of gossamer made her way to the piano. She played the complex piece with verve and undeniable talent. Applause as loud as that for the singer greeted the end of her performance, and she curtseyed with obvious pleasure.

On her way back to her seat, she stopped to

whisper in Madame Mougeon's ear, all the while looking at Caro with a sly little smile. A tingle lifted the hairs on Caro's nape. She looked away. She must be imagining things.

Madame Mougeon returned to the front of the room. "I understand we have another talented young lady in our midst." She stretched out a hand. "Mademoiselle Torrington, will you play for us?"

Caro felt the blood drain from her face before rushing back in a hot tide. She shook her head. "No indeed. I don't have any music, and my skill is mediocre, I assure you."

Twenty pairs of eyes stared at her, and the sight faded into the red haze of her embarrassment.

"I brought another piece," Mademoiselle Jeunesse said with a simper and cold eyes. She held out a sheaf of paper.

"There you go, mademoiselle," the marquis said, passing the sheets to Caro with a flourish. "I would adore to hear you."

Caro stared at the paper, her fingers trembling. Semi-quavers and treble clefs skipped from bar to bar like raindrops on a roof.

"I can't," she gasped. This was a nightmare. Everyone was staring. She glanced around wildly, saw Lucas frowning, and tapped her finger to her lips twice and winked. It had worked for him. Now it was his turn to help.

"Really, I insist," Madame Mougeon was saying, tugging at her arm.

Long, elegant fingers plucked the music from Caro's hand. "Miss Torrington," Lucas said, his smile the most charming she had ever seen. "I will play, if you will sing. As I recall, you have a lovely voice."

That was not what she had in mind when she requested his help, but his confidence gave her the courage to nod in acquiescence. Warm and large and strong, his hand closed around her cold one and pulled her from the fog into the light.

He placed her hand on a forearm that was rock steady under her shaking fingers and led her to the piano. He flashed her a grin, flicked his tails out from under him, and sat down on the bench. He arranged the music on the stand and ran his fingers over the keys in a soft chord.

Caro took a deep breath. She could do this. She removed her spectacles. Better to see the music than all those curious faces.

"Can you read enough of the music to turn the sheets at the right time?" he murmured under his breath.

She smiled. "I think I might actually be able to tell from the words."

"*Touché,*" he said with a small grin.

She leaned closer and whispered, "I forgot you played."

"It's been a long while. I am relying on you to hide my mistakes."

He drew forth a chord and began the opening bars.

Liquid notes wafted across the Stockbridge formal gardens. Caro crept through the shrubbery to huddle beneath the music room's open window in the crisp morning air. She loved listening to Lucas play. When his mother was alive, she used to sit beside her on the sofa and listen. He had hardly touched the keyboard since his mother died and since his father sent the teacher away.

Somewhere inside the house, a door banged.

Caro winced, but Lucas must not have heard because the thrilling melody continued uninterrupted.

All she could see through the window was his beautiful profile, his expression one of total absorption, as if his spirit existed in fingertips producing sounds so sweet they were heartbreaking.

The door on the far side of the room swung back. Before she ducked out of sight, Caro glimpsed Lord Stockbridge, his face red and full of disgust.

"No longer will you waste your time on this namby-pamby nonsense, Foxhaven!" Stockbridge yelled.

"But Father," Lucas said. "I—"

Something must have struck the keyboard very hard because a harsh chord rang out, followed by the bang of the piano lid closing.

"I'm going to burn the damned thing," Stockbridge said.

"It was Mother's," Lucas said. "She wanted me to practice."

"And it's your mother's fault you turned out so badly." Stockbridge's voice grew louder and deeper. He appeared at the window and stretched up to grasp the sash.

"Mother said I have a talent," Lucas pleaded.

"You, my boy, have a talent for trouble, and this time, I have had enough." He slammed the window shut.

The sound of a falling chair issued from inside the room.

Caro recoiled. What on earth was wrong with Lord Stockbridge? Poor Lucas. He loved his music. Perhaps she should go and comfort him. She backed away and tiptoed around the front of the house. In the drive stood a carriage.

Mrs. Rivers and perhaps Cedric must have called in. She pressed her lips together. If Lord Stockbridge had visitors, it might be better to talk to Lucas tomorrow, when tempers were cool. Feeling a little cowardly, she turned for home.

She had never heard Lucas play again until today.

Faultlessly, smoothly, he finished the introduction and Caro joined in at his nod. She liked to sing. Lucas must have remembered.

At first, she kept her gaze on the music, but after a shaky beginning, the melody took hold, and she managed a glance or two at the misty audience. The expressions of her aunt and the marquis were full of pride, and did much to settle her nerves. Her voice did not have the depth or range of the opera singer, but she managed well enough.

The warm applause as the notes died away lapped over her. She curtseyed to Lucas and smiled her thanks, shaking her head at the kind calls for more. Back in her seat, she resisted the urge to stick out her tongue at a rather sulky-faced Mademoiselle Jeunesse. Caro had survived the worst form of torture without ridicule because Lucas had rescued her, just as he had when they were children.

"And now Lord Foxhaven will read his sonnet," Madame Mougeon announced.

A sonnet? Lucas? Caro felt her mouth drop open and snapped it shut.

"Bravo," called out the marquis. He leaned close to Caro. "It's a brave man who would write poetry for such a critical crowd—let alone read it."

Athletically graceful, Lucas sauntered to the piano, leaned one hip against the gleaming mahogany, and withdrew a sheet of paper from his breast pocket. Light from the window warmed his handsome face to bronze and glossed his black hair. He looked so easy, so elegant, that Caro drew a quick breath.

This was not the devil-may-care Lucas who avoided boring social events like Almack's and refused to wear a cravat. Perhaps he really had changed. Or was it all a ploy, a charming act to get what he wanted? A pang of longing in her chest betrayed her hope that he was sincere. She tried to ignore it.

"My humble offering is titled 'To Her Amber Eyes,'" he announced with a soulful expression.

A ripple of interest stirred through the room. Ladies peered into each other's eyes. The black-eyed Mademoiselle Jeunesse pouted. The marquis straightened in his seat and glanced at Caro, as did several others.

She held herself rigid. Lucas must mean someone else. Or he meant to tease her. Her stomach dropped at the mortifying thought.

"Phoebus' rays in their honey'd deep,

Secrets kept from all who seek,

to know,"

A swift glance at his face told her he was perfectly serious. Not even the glimmer of a smile lit his eyes. She'd know if he was laughing at her; she always did. She gripped her hands in her lap as if the pressure might calm her skipping pulse.

The words came to her in snatches of his deep, smooth-as-cream voice.

"What warms those luminescent jewels so rare?"

The marquis leaned over. "Good, isn't he?"

She wanted to say "Hush," but she nodded and tried not to beam like an idiot. Lucas had actually written a poem for her.

From the front of the room, he caught and held her gaze until she thought her heart would melt into a puddle at her feet. Perhaps he really did care for her in some corner of his heart. It might be enough. As long as she believed it, she could survive.

"How pale the dawn in eastern skies,
Compared to her beloved amber eyes."

Silence filled the room. And then came the applause.

"Who is the lucky lady?" a gentleman called out.

Lucas smiled. "I believe she knows who she is." He bowed and, with one brief glance in her direction, returned to his chair.

A tug of joy pulled at her heart.

❖   ❖   ❖   ❖

Lucas prowled the salons of the Hôtel Richard. Decorated in the Egyptian style, it recalled the halcyon days when Bonaparte straddled the world like a colossus. The bulky furnishings matched the heaviness in his chest.

Failing to find Caro in the ballroom, he sauntered into the card room and took a seat carved with crocodile scales and claws for feet alongside Madame Valeron, who was engrossed in a game of piquet.

"Good evening, madame."

"Lord Foxhaven," she acknowledged. "I assume you are seeking my niece."

A discerning woman. He smiled. "I wished to greet you, madame, but thought to ask Mademoiselle

Torrington to dance."

Madame Valeron picked up her cards from the green baize. "She is not here. She is unwell."

Anxiety surged through him. "Nothing serious, I hope?"

She shrugged. "A minor malady. A headache."

In all the years he'd known Caro, he'd never heard her complain of a headache. "I am sorry to hear it. Please give her my best wishes for a speedy recovery."

She discarded a deuce. "I will pass on your wishes, along with a hundred others, milor'."

A headache. He didn't like the sound of it. Unease crawled over his skin.

In a welter of impatience, yet not wishing to damage Caro's reputation, he forced his attention on the game. He must not appear too anxious. Madame Valeron played her cards well and took the trick. As she gathered up her winnings, he departed with a brief farewell and a bow. He strolled out to the foyer and requested a lackey to bring his hat.

Mademoiselle Jeunesse, a vision in white silk and diamonds, floated toward him on her way back from the ladies' withdrawing room. Her full red lips turned down at the sight of him. "Leaving already, milor'? I suppose you have discovered Mademoiselle Torrington is not present this evening."

This young lady had thrown far too many lures in his direction for propriety. He kept his voice cool. "Regretfully, I have an engagement elsewhere, mademoiselle."

She glanced around and drew closer. "She won't have you."

"I beg your pardon?"

She placed a slender white hand on his arm. "Mademoiselle Torrington. She is going to marry her cousin. Her aunt has her heart set on it." She pouted. "Before the Chevalier left for Champagne, they were as close as turtledoves. She merely amuses herself with you in his absence."

Fighting anger and doubt, Lucas kept his expression blank. "You seem very aware of their affairs."

"Ah, but you see, milor', I am in the same position as you. Before she came along, François was at my feet." Her expression hardened. "He adored me. Now it is all the English mademoiselle. He does not move from her side. You will see when he returns."

She cast him an arch look and a seductive smile. "Perhaps you and I should show them we do not care." Her fingers crept up his sleeve and drew a circle on his shoulder.

Oh no. He was no fool to be caught by such an obvious ploy. He stepped back out of reach. "Sadly, I leave France in a day or so, but meeting you, Mademoiselle Jeunesse, will remain among the memorable experiences of my visit to Paris."

The lackey returned.

"Bah!" she said, and whirled away in a rustle of silk and a strong aroma of violets.

Lucas clapped on his hat. With only one day left to convince Caro of the seriousness of his intentions, it worried him that she had cried off tonight. Either she was ill, or something else was afoot. He particularly didn't like the hints dropped by Mademoiselle Jeunesse.

He needed to see Caro tonight.

❈   ❈   ❈   ❈

The words wavered on the page. Caro snapped her book shut with a sigh and swung her feet down off the drawing room sofa. Rarely did her woman's courses affect her, but on the occasions they did, she felt as dragged out as a half-drowned cat.

After the excitement at the musicale this afternoon, the thought of making polite conversation with a room full of people seemed to have aggravated the cramps in her abdomen. Dressed and ready to go, she must have looked a fright because Aunt Honoré shook her head and suggested a tisane and a cold compress for her forehead. After a brief argument, she had agreed to stay home.

She rose to ring the bell for Lizzie.

Who was she fooling? The pains in her stomach were all about Lucas and an afternoon spent bolstering the courage to agree to return to England as his wife. They had an agreement. No regrets.

Only a hundred.

He'd never offered her love. And she'd accepted his terms. She just hadn't expected him to change the rules and ply her with his rakish charm half of the time and ignore her the rest. And those plundering kisses. They drove her to distraction until she lost all control.

Here in Paris, he seemed so sincere, so changed, so determined to behave the gentleman. If he continued this way, their long-standing friendship would allow them a comfortable existence. Friends and companions for life. The thought settled on her heart like a cold rock.

No matter how charming his smile, how sweet his touch on her skin, he deserved better than a forced marriage to a chubby woman derided by his friends. Even a rake deserved true love.

The room disappeared in a blurry fog. She wished she hadn't hoped for more. It wouldn't hurt so much.

She dashed her hand across her eyes and yanked on the bell pull.

And another thing. She should never have come to Paris with Cedric and François. It had been wonderful meeting her aunt, and she hoped the friends she had made would continue to think kindly of her after she left, but her flight to Paris now seemed utter madness.

Apart from her own feelings, she ought to consider her sisters. A divorce or an annulment would have scandalous repercussions.

The door opened, and François hesitated on the threshold.

She stared. "François." Her stomach plummeted to the floor. She didn't want to talk to him now. Not until she had seen Lucas and given him her decision.

A quizzical smile lit his handsome face as he sauntered into the room. "I understand you are unwell?"

"A headache." It wasn't a lie. Her head started to thump the moment she saw him. She pressed her fingers against her temple. "It is nothing a night's rest will not cure."

He took her hand and kissed it, lingering just a little too long. She resisted the urge to snatch it away. He must have felt her tension because he glanced up and regarded her intently. "Your appearance concerns me. Beautiful as always, but you are far too pale."

"You flatter me. I wish you would not."

"Please, sit down. May I ring for some brandy?"

"No, thank you. I am on my way to bed."

He emanated palpable tension. "I have news."

A premonition shivered down her spine. She wished for a way to hold back his words, but nothing came to mind. "Oh?"

He grinned. "Do not look so afraid. It is good news, ma chére. The Bishop of Bordeaux is a distant relative and has agreed to annul your marriage, provided your husband does not contest the validity of your claim. Your word along with the agreement will suffice."

She had been wrong to show Cedric the agreement. He had insisted it was his duty to inform François, her closest male relative, and between them, they had decided to take a hand in the matter before she had time to think it through. She couldn't entirely blame them. At the time, she'd been furious with Lucas and wanted nothing more than to make an end of the farce.

"Carolyn, is something wrong?"

She stared at the floor, at the toe of her gold satin slipper. She couldn't keep François dangling on a string. It was wrong and cruel. She lifted her gaze to his intent brown eyes. "I have changed my mind. I have decided to return to my husband."

His expression hardened, eyes flattening to the color of dead leaves. "You think he will take you back?"

With his icy tones, a chill blanketed the room. She shivered. "He is here, in Paris. He asked me to go home with him."

Lines deepened around his mouth.

"I am sorry, François. I was wrong to leave for Paris without discussing it with him first."

Red stained his cheeks. Muscles in his jaw worked on words unspoken as his gaze slid away, and he stared over her shoulder. "*Ma pauvre petite.* You will have to share him with every female who crosses his path."

Even her cousin, who seemed to admire her, agreed she wasn't attractive enough for a man like Lucas. She hid her hurt with a shrug. "We understand each other." Her voice tremored, and she took a deep breath.

"Bah." His hand clenched into a fist. Anger held under tight control swirled in his eyes. "It pains my heart to hear you throw your life away on a man who does not appreciate you."

She'd wounded him. "Please, François, I am sorry."

He slammed his fist into his palm. "I thought . . . I was going to ask you . . ."

Although she understood her aunt's wishes, she had made no promise to François. He had no right to press a married woman. She stood up and paced to the window. The flambeaux at the arched entrances to the mansions along the street pierced the darkness.

Guilt choked her throat. Although she had said nothing to make him believe she had feelings for him, she had lived in his pocket since her arrival here, had relied on him to ease her way into Paris society. In return, she had wounded him—if not his heart, then his pride. Sadly, she understood how he felt only too well and would not compound her crime by lying to him. "François, I like you very well as a cousin. That is all."

He crossed the room to her side. He tipped her chin with a knuckle and gazed into her face, his voice thick with emotion. "He will never deserve you, *ma chère*."

Hot tears escaped and rolled down her cheek. "Please don't hate me. I don't want to lose you again."

His expression softened. He pulled a handkerchief from his pocket and dabbed at her cheeks. "I cannot hate any member of my adopted family. Without them, where would I be?"

Overcome with relief at his generosity when she had been nothing but foolish, she leaned against his shoulder. "Thank you."

He encircled her in comforting arms.

"Very touching." Lucas's biting words jolted through her.

She pulled away from François.

With an expression bordering on murderous, Lucas glowered at her from the open doorway. "Your aunt said you were ill."

Fire licked at her cheeks. "Lucas. I—"

François stepped forward. "Sir, this is my house. You are interrupting a private conversation."

Caro gasped. He was making things worse. "François, please."

Lucas stiffened, his gaze flicking from Caro to the Chevalier. "Both private and intimate, I see." He narrowed his dark, blazing eyes. "Apparently, on this occasion, I am *de trop*." He bowed with infinite politeness. "I must beg both of your pardons." He turned and left.

Caro stared at the empty space in the doorway and then whirled on François. A satisfied smirk curved his lips. Something hot and unreasonable buzzed in her head. "You had no right to speak as you did. This is my aunt's house too."

He recoiled. Anger rolled off him in waves before he let out a long ragged breath. "Excuse me, cousin. I did not like his tone. He was not polite."

"No, he was not. But you gave me no chance to explain."

Something flashed in his eyes. Something akin to triumph. But it was gone in a moment, and she decided she must have been mistaken when he gave her a rueful grin. "I'm sorry. Would you like me to go after him and set matters straight?"

Damping down her anger, she gave a terse shake of her head. "I don't think it would help." Slow to ignite, Lucas's temper burned hot and long. Anything said now, especially by François, would only fan the flames. "I will speak to him in the morning."

He nodded. "As you wish. If I cannot be of service, then I will take my leave."

She forced a smile. "I am truly sorry things turned out this way."

His eyes clouded. "As am I. No matter what happens, I hope you will understand I have only your best interests at heart."

She accepted his farewell salutation with a breath of relief.

What she really wanted was a nice warming pan in the middle of her bed to ease her aching back and a cool damp cloth on her forehead.

She would straighten it all out with Lucas tomorrow.

Fifteen

LIZZIE FROWNED AT THE SHADOWS BENEATH HER mistress's eyes. "How tired you look this morning, my lady."

The wan smile Lizzie received in the mirror gave her a sinking sensation. It wasn't like Caro to be out of sorts.

"Not still feeling poorly, are you?" she asked. "How about a nice cup of tea and a nap? Not that the fancy chef down below would know a good cup of tea if he had it poured over his head."

Caro sighed. "I have to see Lord Foxhaven this morning."

An odd flutter caught at Lizzie's throat when Caro avoided her gaze. There was something going on. Lizzie threaded a blue ribbon through her mistress's fine hair. "Monsooer this, mamselle that, chevron the other, 'tis no wonder you look so peaky. Your father would turn in his grave."

Her ladyship's back stiffened, and Lizzie wished

she'd bitten her tongue.

"That's quite enough, Lizzie. These are my mother's family. I know you don't like it here, and quite honestly, I am hoping Lord Foxhaven will take us back to England, but there is no need for rudeness."

A rush of joy filled Lizzie's heart until she thought her stays would burst. Her grin stretched so wide she could swear her ears were waggin'. "We're going home?"

"Perhaps."

"Heaven be praised. I've had enough of these Frogs. Not one of them can understand a word I say, 'cept young 'Enri."

A small smile curved Lady Foxhaven's lips. "Did it never occur to you that you should speak French in France?"

"Lawks, my lady, me, learn that gabble? Not on my best bonnet. So, we're really going back to Norwich?"

"Don't get too hopeful." She heaved a sigh. "Lord Foxhaven was none too pleased to find the Chevalier alone with me last night."

Lizzie stared at her young mistress. "So that's the cause of the megrims this morning." She put her hands on her hips and narrowed her eyes. "Mark my words, his lordship ain't one to reckon with no rival, I'll bet a pound. Dead jealous, he'd be of that there chevron." She nodded her head. "All gentlemen are like that. Why, I remember a time with young Ned . . ."

A rush of warmth heated Lizzie's cheeks as the rest of the saucy story popped into her head. "Never mind that. You tell him you're ready to go back with him, and he will be as happy as a grig."

Lady Foxhaven turned in her seat, open-mouthed. "Jealous? Lucas?" Her laugh crackled like tissue paper.

Lizzie resisted the temptation to rap her stubborn mistress over the knuckles with the silver-backed hairbrush. "Lord love you. What else would it be?"

The shrug Lady Foxhaven gave as a reply seemed unsure. "Whatever it was, it is imperative I speak to him as soon as possible, so please hand me my bonnet and spencer."

❄   ❄   ❄   ❄

Having sent a lackey to find her aunt's butler, Caro buttered one of the delicious sweet rolls served each morning in the small breakfast room on the second floor. Aunt Honoré never arose much before midday, and Caro quite often broke her fast alone. This morning she felt particularly in need of sustenance—something to fortify her for her coming meeting with Lucas.

Cedric, in his usual somber black, strolled in. "Cousin Carolyn. You arose early today."

She smiled and held out her hand. "I did not expect to see you back so soon. Did you return with the Chevalier?"

"No, indeed. He and I had business in different directions. He has returned, then?"

"Last night." She smiled. "I hope your business prospered?"

A wry grimace twisted his thin lips. "It was satisfactory."

He wandered over to the buffet. "May I pour you a cup of coffee?"

"Yes, please."

The butler entered with a brief knock and a stiff bow. "You wanted me, mademoiselle."

"Yes, Philippe. I would like the carriage brought around at once. I have an errand to run."

The butler's eyebrows rose to crumple his usually bland forehead. "Now, mademoiselle?"

A flicker of anger rose in her breast. "Yes, now." This man treated Lizzie in a very ill manner, Caro gathered from the little Lizzie had let drop about life below stairs.

"I regret, it is not possible, mademoiselle. Madame Valeron never goes out before noon. Nothing is prepared."

"My carriage is at the door," Cedric announced. "I would be honored to take you to your destination."

"As always, you come to my rescue. What would I do without you?" She smiled. "If it is not too much trouble, I need to visit Lord Audley's residence."

Cedric nodded. "I am pleased to be of service." He poured coffee into two cups. "I hear Foxhaven is in Paris staying with Audley," he said over his shoulder.

"Yes," Caro said, aware of her heart's little leap at the sound of Lucas's name.

He handed her a cup and turned to the waiting butler. "That will be all."

"Yes, monsieur." The butler bowed himself out.

She sipped the coffee and made a face. Even with all the sugar and cream Cedric had added, it tasted burnt. She would never get used to the strength of French coffee.

"Is it your plan to return to London, Caro?" Cedric asked.

"I am not sure. At least, I think so. But I must speak with Lucas at once."

"I see. Well, drink your coffee, and then we can leave."

"I'm not sure I want it."

"Nonsense. I insist you drink it before we leave. It will put heart into you."

※　　※　　※　　※

"Toot sweet," the stuck-up French butler said and snapped his fingers.

"What does the old goat want now?" Lizzie grumbled at Henri, the under-footman perched on a stool in the corner while he hunched over his daily task of cleaning the silver. The fair-haired, tall, young man was the only servant in the household who admitted to speaking English, and even he had trouble understanding her.

"Goat?"

"Philippe. The mater dee."

Henri huffed on the coffeepot clenched between his knees and gave it a hard rub. "He says the Chevalier demands your presence immediately."

"Demands?"

"He said demands, immediately."

After shooting him a sharp glance, Lizzie sniffed. Henri had a wicked sense of humor underneath a humble demeanor, but he never lied.

She rose to her feet and flicked her skirts straight. "Demands, does he? We'll see about demands when I'm having my first cup of tea of the morning." She followed the stiff-backed butler out of the kitchen.

The Chevalier met her in the entrance hall. "Ah, the good Lizzie, is it not?"

Lizzie bobbed a curtsey. "Yes, sir."

"Mademoiselle Torrington is leaving for London, and she asks you to pack her things."

They were going home. Her spirits soared. "Right away, Chevron Valeron."

"*Bon.* Philippe, send a footman up for mademoiselle's trunks in half an hour." He turned his gaze on Lizzie. "You will have them ready by then?"

His cold-eyed stare sent a shiver down her spine. Something about him always made her nervous. "Not a minute longer, your honor."

"*Tiens,* it is good. In one half hour, I shall return with the carriage."

Lizzie rubbed her hands together and whisked up the stairs. It was the best news she'd heard in weeks.

Before the half hour was up, Henri appeared to carry down the trunk, his mouth turned down in his pale, fine-boned face. "You leave us, Mademoiselle Lizzie?"

She swept a glance around the room. Nothing left behind. She nodded. "We're going 'ome, young 'Enri. 'Ome to civilization."

"I will miss you."

The wistful note in his voice dampened her joy. An orphaned noble without proof of his birth or any relatives to speak for him, he'd formed an alliance with her against the formidable butler these past few weeks.

She softened her tone. "Ah, love, you'll do fine. You'll get a position worthy of you one day."

He straightened his thin shoulders. "You are right. I do not lose hope." He hefted the trunk and staggered off.

With a light heart, Lizzie picked up the remaining portmanteau, closed the door behind her with a snap, and followed him down the stairs and out the front door.

Beside the shiny black carriage hitched to four impatient brown horses, the Chevalier watched the loading. He stepped between her and the carriage. "But no, Lizzie. You misunderstand. You are not going."

Her heart picked up speed. "Of course I am going."

"*Mais non.* There is not enough room."

Anger and fear churned in her belly. She understood the word *non*, right enough. "Now you listen here, Chevron Charmin', I go where my lady goes and no mistake about that."

He smiled, all nice and friendly like to a babe. "Just go inside, and I will explain."

She shook her head. "Explain it out here."

A frown darkened his face. "You are impertinent. Do as you are told."

Something wasn't right. She lunged for the carriage door.

His eyes turned hard, and his mouth thinned. He shot out a hand and grabbed her wrist. Pain shot up her arm. "If I say you are staying, that is what you will do. Understand?"

"No."

His hand whipped out with a slap to her cheek, and her head snapped back. She cried out. Henri's shout of horror rang in her ears.

She kicked the Chevalier on the shins. He loosened his grip. She made another dive for the door. He grabbed her shoulder and swung her around, his fist raised.

She dodged. Too slow.

His fist slammed into her jaw. She sprawled on her rump, the jolt jarring up her spine and pinpricks of light flashing in her eyes. Daylight faded to black.

The sensation of being carried made her feel sick. She heard a moan. Hers. She blinked to clear her sight. Henri had a hold of her feet, and the coachman was holding her under the arms. Puffing and blowing, they lugged her down the basement stairs.

She lashed out with feet and hands. "Get off me, you great lummoxes."

"Lie still, mademoiselle," Henri said in agonized tones. "The master will punish you more if you do not be good."

Tears welled up in her eyes. "Please 'Enri, she can't mean for me to stay here."

The other man said something in Frog, and Henri's face flushed dull red.

"What did he say?"

Henri turned his face, away biting his lip.

"'Enri?"

He shrugged.

A scream ripped from her throat. Something bad was happening, and the only person she trusted in this dreadful place now refused to speak to her.

※　　※　　※　　※

What the hell did Audley want in such a damnable hurry? Lucas wondered. The note had been vague to the point of silent, a demand he come to the embassy right away.

He strode along the rue du Faubourg St. Honoré until he reached number thirty-nine. Built for the guillotined Duc de Charost, and once home to Bonaparte's sister, Princess Josephine, the magnificent eighteenth-century Hôtel de Charost had been commandeered by Wellington for the British.

Lucas acknowledged the red-coated infantryman at the embassy side door with a nod. He'd been here several times on business, and the guard let him in without question.

His long stride carried him through the back hall and up a dingy set of stairs to the second floor where Audley had his office.

He rapped once and pushed open the door to the paneled room. The sight of Audley offering tea to a bedraggled Lizzie slumped in the armchair in front of the fireplace halted him in his tracks. The liveried servant standing behind Lizzie shuffled his feet.

"What the . . ." Lucas stopped before he uttered the oath on his lips.

Audley glanced up, a rather relieved expression on his face. "Thank you for coming so quickly, Foxhaven."

Lizzie swiped at her eyes with a crumpled handkerchief and gazed up at him. She had dirt on her face and a livid bruise on her jaw.

Lucas drew in a sharp breath. A vision of Caro injured flashed through his mind. "Good God. Has there been an accident? Is Lady Foxhaven all right?"

"Oh, my lord," Lizzie moaned. "Her cousin took her to Champagne this morning."

A kick in the kidneys would not have winded him as much. Today Caro was to give him her answer.

Hell. He'd felt so sure of her after their last two encounters that he'd deliberately left her and the Chevalier alone together, left Caro free to make her decision. A lump of ice formed in his chest. It slowed the beat of his heart. She'd chosen her cousin. "I see."

He stared blindly at the plain white door. It wobbled out of focus. He wasn't sure he could actually walk through it, his legs felt so strange. But he wouldn't stay here and make a fool of himself.

He started to turn to leave.

"We was going home," Lizzie said.

"What?" He blinked and stared down at her. His mind recorded her dishevelment, the stringy strands of brown hair straggling from beneath her cap, and the dirt on her tear-streaked face. "Why didn't you go with her ladyship?"

Her lower lip trembled. "That there Chevron fellow hit me, then locked me up. He said Miss Caro would have French servants to care for her." Her lower lip quivered.

A creeping chilly fog of fear filled his gut. Caro would never let anyone harm Lizzie. On the other hand, the maid could be a handful. "You say he locked you up?"

Lizzie nodded. "Wait till I gets my hands 'round his neck. He hit me, he did. 'Enri got me out through the cellar window."

"A cellar?" Lucas echoed.

"Smart fellow, that Henri," Audley interjected.

The lad standing behind Lizzie colored up and fixed his attention on his buckled shoes. It dawned on Lucas that the man was not an embassy servant, but wore the Valeron livery.

A fog seemed to have filtered into his brain. He didn't understand any of this—except that Caro had left. The empty sensation in his chest that had all but disappeared returned with a vengeance. She hadn't even had the decency to tell him no.

The walnut desk in the corner offered refuge from the three pairs of staring eyes. He slung himself into the leather wing chair behind it and leaned back, careful to keep his expression impassive. He shoved a cut glass inkpot from the center of the polished surface to one side. "If Caro wants to visit her cousin's estate, that is her prerogative."

The words cut a swathe through his heart that he refused to acknowledge.

Lizzie sniffed and then blew her nose on the grubby handkerchief.

Audley handed her a clean one from his pocket.

"My lady didn't say anything about it," Lizzie mumbled. "She went off with Mr. Rivers first thing this morning."

"Cedric? I thought you said she went with the Chevalier?"

"She said Mr. Rivers was driving her to your house." Lizzie glanced at Henri. "'Enri said the Chevron told the coachman they were to meet Mr. Rivers on the road to Reims."

The skin of Lucas's scalp tightened and prickled. Cedric had been behaving rather oddly these past few weeks. But surely he wouldn't be involved in anything underhanded. "You are sure Lady Foxhaven was on her way to see me?"

Tears streaked Lizzie's dirty cheeks again. "Yes."

Perhaps she'd been coming to tell him she had chosen the Chevalier. The hurt intensified. He stabbed a new quill on the inkstand into the pool of black ink with a vicious twist and wished it was Valeron's guts.

"Perhaps you mistake the matter, Lizzie," Audley said.

"No." Lizzie shook her head so hard her cap slipped to one side. "Then, 'cause I didn't know where you lived, 'Enri brought me here. He said the embassy would know where to find you."

"Clever lad," Audley said.

Cedric would have made an attempt to convince her to return to London, surely? Doubt filtered through the black fog of bitter disappointment. "I should make sure this is what she wants."

"Be careful, Foxhaven," Audley said, his face stern. "The Valerons are an important family. France may be occupied, but our government is determined to tread lightly. We want the Bourbons' good will. Business must not suffer because an irate husband chasing an errant wife turns into an international incident. Do I make myself plain?"

Lucas tamped down his surging impatience. "Very."

Obviously not fooled, Audley stared at him hard. "If you get into any sort of trouble, I cannot help."

"I'm simply going to talk to her. She owes me that." He wanted to hear her decision from her mouth, see it in her eyes.

Lizzie jumped to her feet. "I'm going with you."

"Me too," Henri announced, then promptly turning the color of a house brick.

Lucas rose and shook his head. "I'm sorry, Lizzie. I will travel faster alone."

"Ho, no," Lizzie huffed. "I'm going even if I has to hire me own coach."

No wonder the Chevalier popped her on the jaw. Lucas cast his glance up at the embossed ceiling and felt sympathy for the poor fellow as he opened his mouth to explain why she and the Valeron servant could not possibly accompany him.

Sixteen

ESTERDAY'S ROAD DUST SEEMED TO COAT Caro's tongue. She swallowed what felt like a shovel full of grit and opened her eyes. Blue hangings on a white poster bed and curved white walls cocooned her.

A tower. She remembered François speaking of a tower as he helped her in from the carriage.

Light streamed through a tall window behind her head. White muslin drapes fluttered on a country-fresh breeze. Beside the bed, her spectacles lay on a night table next to a goblet of water. She sat up and put them on. The water appeared innocent enough, but after yesterday's coffee and a second dose of laudanum from François' silver flask last night, how could she be sure?

Water. It looked so inviting. She lifted the glass and sniffed. No smell. The stuff she drank yesterday had a definite smell and a bitter taste. Her heart pounding too hard for comfort, she touched her tongue to the liquid. No taste.

She took a wary mouthful and swallowed, and her throat eased. The rest went down in cool, greedy gulps.

Feeling more the thing, she pulled back the sheets and swung her bare feet to the floor. She vaguely remembered a pert dark-eyed maid helping her make ready for bed after François had dragged her up here last night.

She frowned. She'd left Paris with Cedric. He'd tricked her, the traitor, and somehow she'd arrived at the Chateau Valeron with François.

She cast her mind back to the foggy events of the day before. At least, she presumed it was yesterday. They had arrived in the late afternoon. The sandstone had glowed candle-flame yellow, and the chateau had seemed to float in shimmering heat like a fairy-castle.

"This is your new home," François had said, guiding her faltering steps to the front door.

Thickheaded and her tongue clumsy, she'd answered him boldly. "I am going home to England with Lucas."

His skin had looked sallow, his expression careworn. "In three days you will marry me. This will be your home."

A flutter of panic beat in her sluggish blood. "I'm married to Lucas." She spoke slowly to avoid jumbling the words together.

François shook his head. "Cedric is taking care of that little detail."

"Lucas is coming here?"

François raised a brow. "No."

"I need to tell Lucas I don't want an annulment."

François chuckled low in his chest. "I'm afraid it is too late." Then he had pressed his lips together and had refused to answer any more of her questions.

What on earth did he mean, too late?

She staggered to the window. The air cooled her cheeks and helped clear her wool-stuffed head. Pulling the casement wide, she stepped out onto a small balcony, the tile cold beneath her bare soles. If she could think, she might be able to figure out what to do next.

A golden sun peeped over the horizon, casting long shadows from the low wall across a dewy lawn. No one seemed to be about. It must be very early.

Beyond the wall, a phalanx of vines in green and purple uniforms followed the contours of the land into the distance. A silver ribbon of mist hung in the valley, winding through the hills. The scent of ripening fruit wafted on soft air.

François had spoken with deep pride about this estate. Seeing it from this vantage point, Caro understood his devotion.

If he married her, this was his, with or without a child. Tante Honoré had said it often enough. A bitter taste filled her mouth. Another man who wanted her only for what she brought to the wedding. At least Lucas had been honest about it. Her heart stumbled. Lucas would think she had left with François because she intended to go through with the annulment. He would depart for England and leave her behind.

She had to get back to Paris, now, today.

She ran back into the bedroom and flung open

the wardrobe beside the chamber door. Inside, she found all of her clothes. Someone had brought them from Paris.

A sinking sensation stilled her. In some hopeful corner of her mind, she had wanted to give Cedric and François the benefit of the doubt. It was a misunderstanding—an impulse. But this proved otherwise. They had planned her abduction.

Haste turned her fingers to sticks as she clambered into the most practical thing she owned, her green riding habit and boots. The wide skirt allowed for freedom of movement. Now if she could find a horse, she would show François a clean pair of heels before he awoke.

While she dressed, she tried to remember her geography. Which direction did Reims lay from Paris? She shook her head in impatience. Don't worry about such trivialities. Ask for directions on the road.

To her great relief, the chamber door opened when she tried the handle, and she found herself on a narrow landing. A spiral staircase led down. The pounding of her heart drowned out all sounds as she stepped onto the first step. She took a deep breath. Don't panic.

One damp palm on the cold granite pillar, she wound her way down. She peered around each curve, ready to run at the slightest noise.

The stairs gradually widened and then opened into a passageway at the bottom. Left or right? With the night before a barely remembered nightmare, she chose right and ran along the hallway on tiptoes. An archway at the end of the long passage revealed the grand entrance hall. She released her breath and edged her way to the double mahogany doors and freedom.

The door refused to budge at her frantic pull. Dash it all—she was trapped. She spotted a large iron key hanging on the wall and grabbed it. It turned in the lock. With one hard tug, the door swung back.

She peeped outside. Now where to go?

In front of her, a long drive swept away and ended up at wrought iron gates flanked by a gatehouse. The gates were closed and probably guarded.

She slipped out of the door. The carriage she had arrived in had continued around to the back of the house after she and François had alighted. She went that way, and the acrid smell of manure guided her to the stables on the far side of a cobbled courtyard.

On silent feet, she glided through the barn's double doors. Even if the master of the chateau slept in, the servants were bound to be about their chores.

A faint light filtered through a high window at the barn's gable end. From the stalls came the odd stamp of a horse's hoof and the occasional snuffle. Her nose filled with the smell of horse and leather and liberty. She forced herself to breathe. A few more minutes, and she'd be on her way to Paris.

The first stall held a fearsome bay stallion—not her first choice for a mount. Nor did she fancy the four carriage horses stabled next to him. Almost ready to turn back to the stallion, she discovered a white mare in the last stall. A little fat and out of condition, but calm enough.

Caro located a lady's saddle in the tack room at the end of the barn and heaved it off its shelf. A soft noise behind her caused her to swing around, the saddled clutched against her chest. She peered into the gloom. Nothing.

The sound came again. Then she saw it. A large wolf-like dog, its fangs bared, crouched and ready to spring.

"Good dog," she whispered. "I'm just going for a ride."

It growled low in its chest.

"Go on," she said. Perhaps it only knew French. "*Allez-vous!*"

The dog stared at her with red eyes.

She moved toward it. It crept closer to her and growled.

She backed up. It moved closer and raised its top lip.

It only stopped encroaching when she remained perfectly still. She glanced around. The pitchfork hanging on the wall behind the dog offered no help, and the saddle was far too heavy for her to throw. Her arms began to ache. She wanted to scream.

Very slowly, she put her burden down. When the dog didn't move, she perched on the saddle with a sigh. "Nice doggy," she said.

The dog flattened to the ground and snarled, its hackles stiff.

Perhaps she could wait him out. He might get hungry or find some other prey more interesting.

Fool. Idiot. Why hadn't she just ridden the mare bareback? At any moment, she could be discovered.

As if on cue, a lanky groom whistling cheerfully strolled between the stalls. His mouth dropped open at the sight of her. Before she could say a word, he turned tail and ran out of the barn.

Hot tears welled up and spilled down her cheeks. "Damn you," she said to the dog. It thumped its tail, and dust flew up behind it.

She wiped her eyes. "Now you want to be friendly?"

It lifted its lip to reveal long yellow fangs.

She didn't have long to wait. François, his shirt undone, his hair tousled from sleep, entered the barn. He gazed at her, one arm across his chest, supporting his elbow, while his chin rested in his other hand. "Good morning." He offered her his usual oily smile. "Going somewhere?"

She glared at him. "Out for a ride."

François snapped his fingers. The dog wagged its tail and wandered off. "Come." He signaled her to follow him. "I will not ask you to put the saddle back."

With feet of lead, she stomped after him. Damn the dog. And damn herself for not expecting it.

Outside in the morning sunshine, François strolled ahead. She glanced from his rigid back across the lawn to a small stand of trees abutting a forest on the other side of the wall. If she got a good head start, she might just make it. The trees would offer a hiding place.

She veered off, keeping an eye on François. He didn't seem to notice. Her pulse raced.

She lifted her skirts and ran as fast and as quietly as possible on the soft grass.

François shouted, "*Arrêt!*"

Oh, no. She wasn't stopping for anyone. She tucked her head down and pumped her free arm, running for all she was worth.

Heavy footsteps behind told her he was gaining ground. The trees came within spitting distance. She pushed herself harder. Her breath rasped in her ears, obliterating the footfalls of her pursuer.

A piercing whistle rang out.

The dog. He'd called the dog. Her heart thundered in her chest. She gasped for air. She felt hot breath on the back of her neck. Dear God. Not the dog?

No. Imagination. Just run.

Something hard banged against her ankles. A booted foot. She fell flat on her face on the green grass. Her palms stung, her knees ached, and her breath rattled in her chest. She rolled on her back. "Get away from me, you coward."

François, his chest heaving, loomed over her with clenched fists. His eyes glittered as he spoke through gritted teeth. "Are you trying to make me look a fool in front of my people?"

Fear closed her throat. She swallowed. "I just want to go home."

Anger flushed his cheeks. "No." His voice pitched up. "What you will do is get on your knees and beg my forgiveness."

Frightened out of her wits, she shuddered at the awful change in him. It was like facing a rabid animal. She'd far sooner face the dog. Her teeth chattered together. She took a deep breath. "It is you who should be begging my forgiveness."

He stood as if turned to stone. "On your knees, Carolyn. Now. Or I will beat you. Then they will see and know I am still master here."

He wouldn't dare. She glanced at the group of

curious servants gathered at the edge of the lawn. "You are positively medieval."

"Yes."

She folded her arms across her chest. "No."

He rapped out a word over his shoulder. One of the grooms hurried forward with a riding crop. François snatched it of his hand with a curse. The groom backed away. Cold fury filled François's expression. He meant every word. This man she had trusted would whip her without compunction.

Thoughts bounded through her mind. What good would it do to defy him? She would be no further ahead. In fact, she might be worse off after a beating. Shaken by trembles of rage mixed with a healthy dose of trepidation, she rose to her knees. To do anything else would be a hollow victory. Her face heated. She had never felt so humiliated in her life. She ground her teeth together and forced out the words he demanded. "Forgive me, François."

"*En français*, madame," he snarled. His eyes blazed so horribly that for one moment, Caro had the distinct impression he was disappointed she had given in.

Forcing her pride down, she uttered the words he demanded. "*Pardonnez-moi*, milord." And may you be damned, she thought to herself.

He flung the whip down and hauled her to her feet. His fingers dug into her arms as he marched her into the house and up the stairs.

There was no point in struggling. She would have to find another way to escape this madman.

He kicked open her chamber door and flung her on the bed. "Now I will put a guard on you night and day. If you try to leave again, they will die, and I will punish you. Do you understand?" He bared his teeth in his so-charming smile.

She thought she might throw up. "Yes," she whispered. "But I won't marry you."

"We will see." He stormed out and turned the key in the lock on the other side.

Caro sank back on the bed. How could she have been so taken in? How could this be the same man she had liked so much in London and Paris? And Cedric too? They must think her a gullible fool. Her limbs trembled. She had to escape. But how? Hopelessness clutched at her heart.

She turned over and buried her face in the pillow and wept.

Less than fifteen minutes later, the door opened. When she raised her head, a calm and smug François was leering at her, the little maid peering out from behind him. He held up his silver flask and flashed Caro a smirk. "Now you will do exactly as I say."

In control, he was his old debonair self, but his eyes were as cold and hard as bare trees in winter. The hardness had always been there. She just hadn't allowed herself to notice.

❋ ❋ ❋ ❋

Lucas paced the wall beneath the trees at the perimeter of the chateau grounds. "He should have been back before now," he growled. He struck his fist into his palm. "I should have gone with him."

"You can trust 'Enri, my lord," Lizzie said. "He's as sharp as he can stare."

Lucas had to agree that the lad had proved his

worth and his intelligence over the past couple of days. "I hate the thought of Caro trapped in there."

Lizzie shot him a darkling look. "And there's that Chevron fellow."

"Chevalier," he muttered.

"Whatever he is," she muttered. "I hates him."

He loathed the bastard as well. Anxiety that he didn't want Lizzie to see sent him pacing again.

A soft whistle halted his stride. He and Lizzie ducked into the shadows of the wall.

With a wide grin, Henri strode to their hiding place. "What do you think?" He lifted his hands from his sides and turned a slow circle.

"You look like a damn popinjay," Lucas said with a snort of derision as he took in the black and gold livery on the lad's lanky frame.

"All that lovely braid," Lizzie said. "As fine as fivepence."

"Thank you, Miss Lizzie," Henri said with a mischievous grin at Lucas. "They offered me a job on the spot. Apparently, a big wedding takes place the day after tomorrow."

A chill crept into Lucas's soul. She was going ahead with it, then. He cursed. Perhaps he should just go home and forget all about her.

"Did you see my lady?" Lizzie asked with fear in her voice.

Henri shook his head. "Mais non. No one sees her, except for one morning when she tried to go riding without permission. She is locked up, guarded day and night. No one but the master or her maid goes near her."

"I'm her flippin' maid," Lizzie muttered.

Lucas gazed at Henri's serious face. "A prisoner in fact." Perhaps Caro wasn't quite so willing. He stared across the wall. "The place is huge. It will be almost impossible to find her."

"I know where she is."

The impatience he'd been holding in check for the past hour finally got the better of him. "For God's sake, man. Why did you not say so right away? Let's go."

Henri shook his head. "It is not so easy." He leaned on the top of the wall and pointed. "See the tower there, in the corner. She is in a room at the top, where the balcony is. There is a man guarding the stairs, day and night."

Lucas stared at the tower's rounded walls. "There has to be another way in."

"No. I am sorry, my lord."

"They haven't hurt her, have they?" Lizzie asked.

Henri hesitated a second too long, and Lucas's gut clenched. He glowered at Henri. "Well?"

"No." Henri said. "I do not believe they have hurt her."

Not yet was what he meant. Lucas heard it in his tone. His stomach roiled with anger and with shame that he had caused all this. He had to get her out of there. "When are you required to return?"

"Later this afternoon."

"Good. That costume of yours might just come in handy."

Henry grinned. "That's what I thought."

Lucas slapped him on the back. He was developing a great liking for this young Frenchman. "Come on, then. We've work to do."

❊　　❊　　❊　　❊

At any other time, Lucas might have enjoyed the sight of an elegant chateau bathed in moonlight. Tonight, he would have preferred utter darkness. He and Lizzie had crept through the gate while Henri had engaged the gatekeeper in conversation. They now took shelter within the small forest on the chateau side of the wall.

He stared across the expanse of lawn. The ladder Henri had placed against the tower earlier this evening could not have been more obvious or more out of place.

"Let me come with you, my lord," Henri pleaded in a whisper.

"No," Lucas said. "I need you here with the horses. There is no sense in all of us getting caught. If anything happens to me, go to Audley for help. Tell him Caro is a prisoner."

"Perhaps we should go for Lord Audley now," Lizzie whispered. "He could bring soldiers."

Lucas shook his head. Not an option. He would not leave Caro here a moment longer than necessary. He picked up the rope they had procured earlier in the day and coiled it over his shoulder. His heartbeat kicked up a notch. He rechecked the iron bar and the pistol in his belt. "I will whistle when I want the horses."

"I understand," Henri whispered.

Seeing no one, Lucas sauntered across the moon-lit lawn, while every nerve strained with the urge to run. He reached the gravel of the courtyard with a sigh of relief. Careful not to make a sound on the loose stones, he made his way to the foot of the ladder behind the shrubbery at the tower's base. Once more, he paused to listen. Midnight and all seemed quiet. Taking a deep breath, he began the ascent.

Henri had assured him that no one inhabited the rooms with windows on the first and second floors below Caro, but he took no chances and ran past them swiftly. Because the ladder did not reach all the way to the balcony, he was forced to stretch up and grab the base of the balcony's wrought iron railing.

He let his feet swing off the ladder and pulled himself up. A sound of carriage wheels on gravel shattered the silence.

Bloody hell. Caught like a spider on a web. He hung still and silent, sure every person in France could see him outlined against the light-colored walls.

The carriage pulled up. He peered over his shoulder at the sound of voices. It seemed that Cedric and François had been off celebrating. Cedric supported a swaying François, and they laughed as they staggered toward the front door.

The muscles in his arms screamed for relief. Sweat trickled down his face and dripped off his chin.

Hurry up, damn it. See me, or bugger off.

Seventeen

His arms trembled. He couldn't hold on much longer.

Their voices murmured endlessly. Stretched on the rack of his body's weight, the burn in his shoulders became agony. He had to let go.

Damn it. Hold on.

The voices finally faded. A door slammed. All became silent except his labored breathing. Pulling himself over the railing seemed beyond all hope. He inhaled deeply a couple of times, swung one leg up, and thrust his boot between the railings. Sweet relief.

He gave his arms a moment of blessed ease and then heaved himself up and over the railing onto the narrow balcony. Lungs grabbing air in greedy gasps, he rested his forearms on the balustrade and waited for his thundering heart to quiet. Across the lawn, Henri and the horses were dense shadows beneath the trees.

He tied his rope to one of the wrought iron

uprights and threw the end to the ground. With a roll of his shoulders, he turned to the window. Now for Caro.

The window frame proved no match for his iron bar. The wood splintered with the sound of a pistol shot. He listened for signs he'd been heard. Nothing. He slipped into dark silence.

Revealed in filtered moonlight, a sleeping Caro lay on a canopied bed. A long plait followed the curve of her breast and one hand cupped her cheek. The quilt rose and fell with each slow and gentle breath. Almost too gentle.

He pressed one hand over her parted lips and shook her shoulder. She stirred, her hand falling from her cheek to lay palm up on the pillow. He tickled her palm. No reaction.

Agonizingly aware of the guard beyond the door, he put his lips close to her ear and kept his voice low. "Caro, wake up. It's me—Lucas."

Her eyelids drifted up. A slow smile dawned. "Lucas?"

He put a finger to his lips. "Shh."

"Kiss me."

"What?"

She pouted. "I like your kisses. Why don't you like kissing me?"

Startled, he stared at her. "Of course I like kissing you."

She beamed. "You do?" She curled her hand around the back of his neck, pulled herself up and planted a kiss full on his mouth. A sultry, seductive kiss. Instant heat flared in his veins. Rational thought went up in smoke as he deepened the kiss. He drew her close, her pillowy breasts pressing into his body, the scent of aroused woman filling his nostrils. Heaven come down to earth. Her hands caressed his shoulders. Even through his clothes, her heart pounded against his chest. She wanted him, not her bloody cousin.

Sanity returned in an icy rush. He dragged himself free. There wasn't time for this.

He stared into her face, all soft and hazy and confused, and at her full, moist lips offered with abandon. "I have to get you out of here."

She nodded and smiled, open and unreserved, her skin glowing in the moonbeam spilling across the bed. "I have something important to tell you."

"Not now."

She frowned. "I mustn't tell, because I have to marry François."

The words tore at his vitals. "To my knowledge, you are still married to me."

Her gaze seemed vague, uncomprehending. "Ummm. Cedric is going to . . . He's supposed to take care of that lillum . . . little detail." She shook her head. "Don' like your cousin any more; he gave me nasty stuff to drink." She blinked and wrinkled her nose. "So did François."

Drugged. That accounted for her strangely affectionate behavior. He ignored the flood of disappointment.

"Kiss me again," she demanded.

"Not now. Where are your clothes?"

Her brow furrowed, and her lips pouted. "It's my dream. You are supposed to do what I want."

"Later, Caro." He propped her against the

headboard. "Right now we need to get you back to Paris."

A breathy sigh left her lips. "I like Paris." Her eyelids drooped, and her head lolled to one side.

He crossed the room to the wardrobe and peered inside. Empty. The Chevalier was afraid she'd try riding again, no doubt. Henri had given him the full story out of Lizzie's hearing. His blood chilled. He hadn't wanted to believe Henri, but the drugs and the lack of clothes confirmed it. Damn the pair of them, his cousin and the Chevalier.

He had to get her to safety. He strode back to the bed, whipped the sheet aside, and revealed the swells and hollows of a womanly body designed for love. Desire flooded his groin, his tight buckskins barely yielding to his instant arousal. How could he have made such a stupid bargain? He swallowed a groan mixed with a curse as he fought for control. Wrong time, wrong place, as usual.

He picked her up. She lay in his arms like an innocent child, soft and yielding. A fierce desire to protect her tightened his grip when she sighed and snuggled against his chest. No time to savor the moment. He carried her out onto the balcony and set her down on her feet, supporting her under the arms. "Caro. Wake up."

Her eyelids fluttered up, and she peeped through her lashes at him.

"Listen. Remember how we got you down from the apple tree?"

She grinned. "Of course, I 'member. You nearly dropped me."

"I didn't."

"Yes, you did. Don' you 'member? You swore. Bad boy." She giggled. "And then you said I was a stupid girl 'cause I screamed. Didn't mean to be stupid." She sighed. "I just was."

They'd never get anywhere like this. "You're not stupid. Relax and don't wriggle."

He bent and tucked his shoulder beneath her ribs. He stood up, her head hanging down his back.

"Oof," she said.

He put one leg over the rail and grabbed the rope.

At that moment, she chose to push herself upright, her hands scrabbling for purchase on his back. He wobbled and clutched the rail. Heat scorched through him followed in an instant by icy chills. Sweat started on his brow. "God damn it, hold still. Do you want to kill us both?"

"There. You swore again. I need to tell you something."

Damn the drugs. He tapped her sweet, softly rounded bottom. "Be silent and keep still for God's sake, or we'll both fall."

She flopped over his back and patted his arse in return. "It's a secret."

"Yes, I know," he murmured. "And you should never tell secrets when you are drunk or drugged." He lowered himself over the balcony and felt with his feet for the ladder.

"I think it's a nice secret," she murmured. "But Lucas might not like it."

"Hush." The rungs seemed farther apart than on the way up. About halfway down, her body went limp as if she'd fallen asleep. Thank God. Better than her trying to hold a conversation. His feet hit solid ground, and he released his breath. They'd made it.

He inched out of the bushes and pursed his lips to whistle to Henri.

"Going somewhere, cousin?" The words were spoken in Cedric's unmistakable gentle tones. He stepped out of the shadows at the base of the tower.

Lucas's gut rolled over as he stared at a silver pistol pointed at his head.

"What the hell are you doing, Cedric?"

"Stopping you from ruining my plans."

"Your plans?"

"Why, of course. You don't think the Chevalier could think this through on his own, do you?"

His stomach churned. He had always thought of Cedric as a friend. "You can't mean that. Look at her—she's drugged, out of her mind, and still she knows she doesn't want to marry Valeron."

"She will catch cold if we don't take her back inside and continue our discussion."

Rage at his cousin's betrayal bubbled up. "Stand aside. I'm taking her home."

Cedric smiled apologetically. "My dear boy, this is her home now."

"Like hell it is," Lucas bit out, weighing his options.

If he signaled to Henri, they might get away, or he might get them all killed. He groped for the pistol in his belt, silently cursing the hampering fabric of Caro's nightgown.

The weapon in Cedric's hand glinted dully as he adjusted his aim. "Put her down and raise your hands."

"You don't dare shoot with Caro in the way."

Cedric's gentle but menacing smile widened. "Are you willing to take the risk? Whether she's dead or alive, I get what I want."

A chill ran down Lucas's back. He could not take a chance with Caro's life. Gritting his teeth, he eased her gently to the ground, all the while measuring the distance to Cedric's pistol. He straightened. "You won't get away with this."

The smile on his cousin's face transformed into a sneer. "Oh? And who is going to stop me? You? It is most obliging of you to come here. I thought I'd have to dispose of you in England."

Tensed, ready to spring, Lucas curled his lip in disdain. "You are a lily-livered coward."

Cedric cursed. The pistol wavered. Lucas snatched at it.

An explosion rang in his ears, and a bullet buzzed past his head. The echo bounced off the chateau walls. Shock rolled through him. Cedric really did intend to kill him. He flung himself at his cousin's throat.

The pistol slammed into Lucas's jaw. His head snapped back, and fog rolled in. Shaking his vision clear, he staggered back and yanked out his own weapon.

Shouts and yells came from all around him. Half a dozen servants ran from the back of the house. A beefy thug, pistol in hand, stormed down the front steps.

"Give it up, Lucas," Cedric said, his chest heaving. "Or I'll have my man shoot Caro as a reminder of you for the rest of her life. In a knee perhaps, or an elbow."

The servants closed in on them.

The thought of Caro crippled froze Lucas rigid. He fought a sudden burst of nausea as he realized that a man he thought he could trust with his life would carry out such a dastardly threat. "You miserable cur," he ground out. "What has she ever done to you?"

Cedric's lips drew back in a feral snarl. "She married you."

"Dear God, you mean it." Lucas flung the pistol aside and held his hands out at the sides. Henri, stay the hell where you are, he thought. "Leave her be if it's me you want."

"I want it all," Cedric muttered. He reversed his weapon. "Turn around."

Jaw clenched, Lucas obeyed. "Let her go, Cedric."

A sharp pain at the back of his head, a flash of light, and black descended.

❋　　❋　　❋　　❋

A sour taste flowed into Cedric's gullet. He stared at his handsome, quixotic, honorable cousin slumped in a heap beside Caro's ample, enticing form, every curve revealed by her flimsy gown.

He narrowed his eyes. Lucas always took everything Cedric wanted. The beast Cedric kept locked away in the deep dark place inside him slipped its chain.

He lashed out a kick. The crunch of boot leather on ribs felt satisfying. He kicked again, aiming for the gut, reveling in the soft thud and the heat in his blood, the burgeoning excitement. But vicious blows wouldn't satiate unless his victim squirmed and cringed.

He bent down, dragged the inert Lucas up by the shirtfront, and shook him. "Wake up, you dog."

Beside him, Caro stirred. He flicked her a glance. Her eyes remained closed.

Suspended by Cedric's fist, Lucas's head lolled back, his eyes closed. "You lose, Lucas," Cedric whispered.

No response. Damn him. Cedric smashed his fist into the handsome face and let Lucas's head crash to the stones. He shook his hand to ease the pain of the blow.

With a furtive glance at Caro, he reeled in his anger. He didn't want her to see him like this. Not yet.

"Take him to the cellar," he said to Caro's guard. "If he gives you any trouble, you can teach him a lesson. But don't kill him. He's mine."

The bully's brutal face split in a grin of anticipation. "Yes, sir." He hoisted Lucas across his shoulders.

Cedric lifted the unconscious Caro. Her lovely face in repose called to him as no other woman's face ever had. Brushing a strand of fine fair hair off her cheek, he ran a fingertip over her soft skin. "My little one," he crooned. "I promise you will forget him." A thrill of anticipation trembled deep in his chest.

He carried her into the house.

※　　※　　※　　※

"Mademoiselle looks lovely," the little maid said, pinning Caro's veil to her hair.

Only once had Caro tried to gain the servant's aid. The girl had reported her to François.

Caro bit her lip. The misty image in the mirror

looked beautiful, but wavered in and out of focus. It must be the effects of the laudanum François had given her last night. She pressed her fingers to her head. This morning, he'd promised not to give her any more, provided she behaved.

Behave? She had wanted to slap him. She didn't have the strength.

She stared at the cream lace bodice decorated with seed pearls and the bronze silk skirt over a cream satin slip. Bronze slippers peeped out below the hem festooned with silk yellow roses. The gown she had worn at Gretna to marry Lucas had been her Sunday-best green muslin.

Lucas. He had stood so straight and tall at her side that foggy Scottish morning. And last night, he had haunted her dreams. She had struggled to tell him that she wanted to go back to London with him, that she had made up her mind to honor their agreement even if he could never love her as she loved him. But he hadn't listened.

She'd kissed him. Heat suffused her skin at the memory of the warm, moist touch of his lips on hers. The events of today seemed less real than that kiss.

Today she would marry François.

Hot tears burned her throat. How would she ever explain that to Lucas? She lifted her glasses and dabbed at her eyes.

"Do not cry, mademoiselle. It is unlucky," the maid said.

"Are you ready, my beautiful bride?"

She whirled around.

One hand on his lean hip, François lounged in the doorway.

She hated the way he appeared from nowhere on silent feet, and she hated his smile. She clenched her gloved hands. "I won't agree to an annulment, and I won't marry you."

He glared at the maid. "Leave us."

The maid bobbed and pattered out.

His scowl turned on Caro, his expression implacable. "Once more, you shame me before a servant."

He closed the gap and brushed the veil off her shoulder. She shrank from his touch. He grimaced. "We've been through all of this. We must marry. You have been living at my house without a female companion, and you no longer have a husband."

Panic shut down her ability to think beyond the painful thunder of her heart. She had to get away. "Aunt Honoré would not want me to marry against my will."

"Her dearest wish is for you to marry me, you know that. Would you disappoint her? I will not."

"What if Lucas contests the annulment?"

His face turned to granite. "He won't."

Sadly, she feared he was right. Financial exigencies had forced her and Lucas to wed. Now that those were gone, he didn't need her any longer. Nevertheless, she refused to lose hope. "I have no feelings for you, other than as a cousin. What kind of marriage would it be?"

"It is not about feelings. I will not let it all go to your English husband."

"Lucas doesn't need your money."

"Be realistic. The Valeron estate is the only reason he married you."

Desperate denial sprang to her lips, but she couldn't

speak the lie. "It is your reason also."

"Think about your sisters."

A bitter laugh almost choked her. She wasn't fool enough to fall for that a second time. And besides, deep in her heart, she had wanted to marry Lucas. She did not want to marry François. She thought of him as family. She had trusted his protection. Anger surged through her. "I am thinking about them." Her voice rose. "Do you think they will be helped by the scandal of an annulment?"

He shrugged. "No one in Paris will care. Look around you, Carolyn. All this will be yours and mine. How can you refuse?"

He sounded so reasonable, so calm, that she almost spat in his face. "I won't do it."

"You will." He pulled out his silver flask. "I will give you just enough to make you the muddled, happy bride who imbibed too much of our fine champagne before the ceremony. And you will do just as I say."

Her throat dried. His flat eyes said he meant every word. She backed away. "That stuff makes me feel ill."

He shrugged and advanced on her. "It is entirely your decision."

Decision? She felt like a rag doll being torn apart by ravenous beasts. But she didn't want her wits numbed by laudanum. She allowed her shoulders to slump. "Very well."

"I don't trust you," he said and unstoppered the flask.

She lowered her gaze, maintaining an air of defeat. "I give you my word."

He stared at her long and hard before corking the flask and dropping it in his pocket.

She tried not to let her elation show in her eyes. "Thank you."

His gaze drifted to the window. "You haven't yet seen anything of our wonderful estate."

Unsure what had caused this sudden change of topic, she followed his glance. "No, I haven't." Out there lay freedom.

"I have something special to show you." The sincere tone she'd once found so charming set her teeth on edge. She remained silent.

"I will return one half hour before we leave for the church, and we will take a tour. After that, we will see how you feel about the wedding." He gave her a hard glare. "In the meantime, you will not leave this room." He patted his pocket. "Any trouble, and I will not hesitate to ensure your cooperation."

Her chest tightened, her lungs compressed by the weight of some unnamable fear. If only she had listened to Lucas on the day of her race and gone home to her sisters.

✷   ✷   ✷   ✷

Every bone, every muscle protested as Lucas raised his head. A groan forced its way through his lips and echoed around him. He attempted to put a hand to his pounding head and discovered he couldn't move a finger, let alone his arm.

He opened his eyes. Nothing. It was as black as a coal cellar in winter. Cold damp air stirred against his cheek. The musty smell of overripe fruit mixed with acid tainted each breath. Where the hell was he? It seemed he was tied to a chair in some sort of cave. Or a tunnel? Not a glimmer of light pierced the fathomless dark, like a grave. Buried alive. He swallowed a rush of heart-pounding fear.

Caro needed him. He strained against his bonds. They cut into his wrists and ankles. A knife-edged pain sliced through his chest. Chest pains? How had that happened? Breath hissed through his teeth, and he almost succumbed to the swirling gray fog in his brain. He clawed his way back to consciousness.

If he could see, he might find something to cut through his bonds. Where the hell was he?

He cursed. Another minute or two, and he would have got Caro clean away. What the deuce had happened to Cedric? His gut clenched at the thought of Caro in the hands of the lunatic he'd glimpsed last night. Damn, he had to get free.

If he tipped the chair over, he might be able to slide the ropes over the legs. Or the chair might break. Ignoring the pain in his chest, he rocked back and forth. The chair creaked.

Slow, methodical footsteps broke the silence. The echoes came at him from every side. He stilled. Whoever it was, it wouldn't be a friend. Nor could he risk crashing the chair over and drawing attention to his only plan. Outwardly, he relaxed, waiting, hoping for his chance.

The glow of a lantern appeared around a corner a few feet away. Before he could get any sense of his surroundings, the light shone full in his face. He blinked into the dazzle.

"So you're awake, are you?" Cedric's disembodied voice came from behind the light.

Lucas squeezed his eyes shut and then reopened them. Shadows danced across ghostly white walls that glistened with strange pinpricks of light. A chalk cave? Barrels lined the walls. Of course. The wine cellars below the chateau. He turned his face up to stare at Cedric standing over him and blinked again. "Blast you, Cedric. Untie me."

Cedric's chuckle boomed off the ceiling. "Not yet."

He set his lantern on a wooden table to Lucas's right and pulled a chair out from beneath it. He sat and hooked his left ankle over his right knee. "That's quite a shiner you have there."

A black eye. Well, that accounted for his difficulty focusing. He kept his expression blank. If he was going to help Caro, he had to get to the bottom of Cedric's plot.

The ropes around his chest and arms foiled his attempt at a shrug. "What is going on?"

The shadowy light turned Cedric's grinning face into a death's head. "I thought you might like to know why you are going to die."

Chills ran over Lucas's skin. "What the hell do you mean?"

Cedric chuckled. "I didn't think you were such a slow-top." From the table, he picked up a long stick marked at intervals with black lines. He thwacked it against his palm. "Do you think I enjoy playing the faithful family retainer, like a humble lackey?"

Lucas imagined the stick striking his head or his back. "I had not thought about it."

Thwack. "Why would you? You are the heir. But after you, I am next in line."

A wary eye on the measuring stick, Lucas managed a smile. "The old man will live to be a hundred just to spite us both."

The stick ceased to swish. Cedric pointed it at Lucas and jabbed it under his chin, forcing his head back. "Oh, it will be much sooner than that."

Something in the gloating tone turned the air noxious. Father. Lucas jerked his chin away. "What the deuce makes you think so?"

Cedric placed the end of the stick against Lucas's eye, the slow pressure building a ghastly pain. Any movement, even a little more pressure, and he'd lose the eye. His heart thundered in his ears. He held still.

The stick withdrew. "You are a quick study, Foxhaven. Did you know your father trusts me with all his investments?"

The conversational tone, like idle chatter in a drawing room, almost drove Lucas mad. He forced out a calm reply. "I knew you handled most of his business affairs."

"All of them. And what do you think he will do when he finds out his son is dead, and he is ruined?"

Lucas curled his lip in disgust. "He will know you swindled him."

Chuckles reverberated off the walls, and the stick went back to a steady slap against Cedric's palm.

Lucas tamped down his building anger.

Cedric leaned back. "Wrong. I will let him think you stole his money," he murmured. "I will salvage enough to make him grateful. I will remind him of the honor and the duty due to our family name. I might even leave one of your silver dueling pistols on his desk when I leave him alone. A fitting end to such an arrogant bastard, don't you think?"

Christ. Why hadn't he seen it before? Or suspected it? He would have trusted Cedric with his life. The sense of betrayal pained him more than his physical injuries. Muscles bulged and strained in his neck and arms as he fought the ropes. Pain tore at his chest. "Face me like a man instead of a sniveling coward," he shouted with the furor of an injured beast. The echoes battered his ears.

Cedric smiled. "I will enjoy watching you beg and plead as your life slips away inch by inch."

"You perverted bastard. You are unnatural."

"I'm no more a bastard than you are, Lucas. But you are not entirely wrong about my pleasures—which reminds me, I look forward to educating your wife."

His heart shrank at the thought of Caro in this madman's hands. Pain no longer registered as he struggled. Reason slipped into unthinking rage.

Cedric eyed him with wry amusement.

Lucas took a slow deep breath and stilled. This got him nowhere. He needed to find his cousin's weakness. "Why, Cedric?" he bit out. "My father loves you like a son. What more could you want?"

God, the truth of those words hurt.

Cedric poked him in the ribs with the stick. Lucas swallowed his groan of pain.

Cedric pressed harder, and Lucas sucked in a hiss of breath.

"It is all wasted on a rakehell like you," Cedric said. "Even your father agrees you don't deserve it. I should have been the heir. Now I will be."

"Then Caro has nothing to do with this."

With a sly smile, Cedric leaned so close Lucas could smell the wine on his breath. "I needed her. I had to convince François to play along. He had no reason to help me until he thought you and your father would take the chateau. Once he marries Carolyn, he has nothing to fear. And for that to happen, we have to get rid of you." He shrugged. "Very simple, really. All I needed was everyone's trust."

So the bastard liked to feel clever. Lucas responded, "It was a brilliant move on your part to convince Caro you had annulled our marriage."

"I know." He frowned, no longer quite so self-satisfied. "I thought she'd be pleased. But she's proving stubborn."

A growl escaped Lucas. "Then let her go."

Cedric got up and grinned down at him. "You like her more than I suspected. Good. The best part is, once Valeron is assured of the estate, he won't need her. Then she becomes mine."

Horror clogged Lucas's throat. He forced himself to remain unmoved. "Why would he give up a beautiful wife?"

"I congratulate you on your discernment, but once more, you can't see what is in front of your nose. The Chevalier doesn't want to marry Carolyn."

"You lie. He paid court to Caro from the day he arrived in London."

Cedric rapped the stick on Lucas's shin. A wave of agonizing pain shot up his leg. He gasped.

"Pay attention, Lucas. For some reason, the grasping Mademoiselle Belle Jeunesse, a rather crass young lady in my opinion, holds the good Chevalier's heart and his balls in her hot little hand. She will make him delightfully miserable for the rest of his life. But only if he has this estate. She won't have him without it. And he can only be sure of it if he marries Carolyn first. In a year or so, I will arrange for his wife's disappearance. Actually, it is too bad both you and Valeron had to wed her first, or I could have made her my countess. On the other hand, she will make a delightful mistress."

It all sounded insanely logical. A raging inferno of hell seemed to open a fiery maw to welcome Lucas in. Lucas cursed long and loud and fluently.

"Impressive. You really must stop mixing with the lower orders, dear boy. You have become quite vulgar in your speech."

"Bugger off."

"Speaking of that, she's still a virgin, isn't she?"

Sickened, Lucas fought for a semblance of calm. "I'll give you anything you want, if you leave Caro out of this."

An unholy light reflected in Cedric's eyes. "I want Carolyn. Beneath that demure outside, she is surprisingly spirited. And my God, that bosom. You never deserved her, Lucas." He licked his lips, and his eyes gazed into the distance. "In time, I am sure I will convince her that I am the better man."

"I'll do anything you want, Cedric. Just leave her alone. I'll give you my grandmother's estate."

Cedric shook his head. "Why would I need it? I'll have the title and Carolyn."

Bile filled Lucas's throat, nausea combined with black dread. He bowed his head in defeat. "I have money—a fortune in investments. Take it all. If it is me you hate, don't make Caro suffer."

"It is not that I particularly hate you, Lucas. I hate being your father's errand boy. I deserved so much more."

"In a pig's ear," Lucas growled.

Cedric grinned. "My mother always said you would come to a bad end. And so you will. What a joke."

He circled around to stand behind Lucas. "I thought I'd solved the problem of you before, you know." His musing tones were worse than his ranting. "I thought your father might actually kill you when you refused to own up to getting that wench pregnant."

The beating hadn't hurt as much as his father's disbelief in his claims of innocence. "She lied. I never touched her." A ghastly thought tightened Lucas's throat. "It was you, wasn't it? Somehow, you bribed her to point the finger at me."

Cedric chuckled and sauntered around to stand in front of him. "You guessed. How clever. Unfortunately, your father is as weak as you are. He couldn't bring himself to be rid of you, no matter how many opportunities I gave him or how much he despised you."

"Damn you. You were my friend. All those times you interceded with him on my behalf—"

A loud guffaw filled the gloomy chamber as Cedric threw back his head. "Oh, Lord Stockbridge, Lucas is in a fix again," he mimicked. "Debt up to his ears, another woman demanding money from the estate. Your own flesh and blood is bleeding you dry. I wish I could help."

He deepened his voice to the tones of Lucas's

father. "You are such a good boy, Cedric. I wish you were my son."

He winked. "Now I will be."

This felt like some bad Covent Garden play, and Lucas didn't like the script. What fools he and his father had been to trust this man. "Audley knows you took Caro against her will and knows I'm here. He'll investigate."

"Try again. The British government won't make waves. This country is in turmoil, rife with beggars and murderers at every crossroads. Your disappearance will be forgotten in a month, and to all eyes, Carolyn will be happily married to a Valeron."

The bastard had thought of everything. "Kill me. I don't give a damn," he challenged, "but leave Caro and my father out of it."

"No." Cedric pulled his handkerchief out of his pocket. "By the way, there is one scene left to play. You don't have any lines, but your role is important. Open your mouth, if you please."

Like hell. Lucas clenched his jaw and turned his face away. Cedric jabbed him in the gut with the stick. Agony tore through bone and muscle. He groaned and sucked in a breath.

Cedric stuffed the handkerchief in his mouth. "Most obliging."

Lucas breathed frantically through his nose, blackness curling in around him as his lungs ached for air.

Cedric lit candles, filling the cavern with dancing light. "Don't go anywhere," he called as he strolled into the darkness. A low laugh wafted back.

Like giants ready to spring, barrels crouched beyond the glowing circle of light. Hopelessness weighed on Lucas's chest, making breathing yet more difficult.

Henri and Lizzie knew of his and Caro's where-abouts, but what could a footman and a lady's maid do against the powerful Valerons? They could go for Audley. And Audley would do nothing.

God, he wished he didn't believe Cedric. Despair threatened to swallow him like a bog. He had wasted so much time on revenge against his father. And now that he finally knew what he really wanted, he'd let it slip through his fingers. Worse, he'd put Caro in terrible danger. The ache of his injuries was nothing compared to the pain of regret. If he hadn't married Caro for money, none of this would have happened. He had to get out of here. He had to put things right.

Think, damn it. He stared around the cellar. He struggled. A spider couldn't have bound its prey more tightly.

A candle sputtered and flickered. If he could get to the table, he might be able to burn the ropes off, if he didn't set light to himself first.

He leaned back and then jerked forward. The chair crept forward a fraction. Pain stabbed his ribs. If he pierced a lung, Caro would be on her own. He took a slow breath. This was his only chance. He clenched his jaw and established a rhythm—rock, jerk, creep. Rock, jerk, creep. Sweat poured down his face and back. It chilled instantly, leaving him shivering.

Voices sounded in the distance, followed by foot-steps.

He peered into the dark. Who the hell now?

Eighteen

"LIQUID GOLD, CAROLYN." THE REVERENT words echoed off the low cellar ceilings. François gestured to row upon row of bottles in wooden racks lining the snow-white walls. His lantern swung, casting eerie shadows on the pale walls.

The cool musty air chilled her skin, but François's air of triumph froze her to the bone. It took all her will not to shiver. "I thought it was wine?"

"Not wine. Champagne. The best in the world."

The only time she had drunk champagne, she had almost kissed this gloating beast. Shame burned her face. She aimed for indifference. "You certainly have a lot of it down here."

"This is only a fraction of our cellars. One day, I will show you everything."

If she never saw the place again, it would be too soon, but she daren't voice her opinion, not when he seemed to be relaxing his guard. "Some other time perhaps. It is such a lovely day—I thought we might look around the vineyards?" Now that she knew the lay of the land, it might be possible to slip away.

His voice hardened. "You have not the slightest interest in all this, do you?"

She rubbed her bare arms above her long gloves. "I am a little cold, that is all."

He set the lantern on the floor with a sigh. "Then we must move quickly to the real purpose of our visit."

The vague threat quickened her pulse. Did he intend to incarcerate her down here? "Purpose?"

He nodded. "Unfortunately, we have an uninvited guest. Your previous husband decided to . . . drop in, you might say."

A leap of her heart drove her breath out in a rush. Last night hadn't been a dream. Joy lightened her spirits, gave her hope. "Lucas is here? Why didn't you say so?"

François grabbed her wrist and pulled her close to his side. "I am afraid he is in grave danger."

The excited flutter in her chest slowed to a torturous drum. "What danger?"

"He forced his way in. He has some strange idea you don't want our marriage."

"I wonder why?" Tugging her arm away did nothing to free it from his grasp. She stared around her. "Where is he?" She opened her mouth to call out. François clamped his hand over her lips and nose.

She couldn't breathe. Blood pounded in her ears. She tore desperately at in his fingers.

"Hold still." His hot breath fanned her cheek. "His well-being depends on you. Make one sound, and he will suffer the consequences, understand?"

Sick fear rolled through her. This man would stop at nothing. She understood that well enough. She nodded.

He released her, and she sucked in a gulp of air, pressing her fingers to her tender lips with a deep sense of foreboding. What had he done to Lucas?

"Listen carefully," he whispered. "Foxhaven will leave here the moment we are wed, provided you convince him that you desire our marriage. If not, he will never leave us in peace."

He was right. Lucas would never knowingly let down a friend. He'd always been especially protective of her. In return, she'd covered up his scrapes, just as she had agreed to marry him. "What must I do?"

The lines around François's mouth eased. "Come around the next corner with me and make him believe you love me, and then prove it in church."

Blackmail. Once more, she was a pawn in a man's game of power. She wanted to weep with frustration. Instead she glared into his patently false sorrowful expression. "And you will set him free?"

"It will be my greatest pleasure never to see him again."

"You promise?"

"I give you my word."

What choice did she have? She tried to ignore the chill spreading through her body. "I'll agree to whatever you want."

"You must kiss me and pledge your love in front of him."

A fierceness she didn't know she possessed blocked her vision in a blood red wave. She would convince the devil of her saintliness, provided it saved Lucas's life. If only she trusted François enough to believe he would play by the rules. But until she saw Lucas, she could only agree to François's demands. "Very well."

He took her hand and led her around the corner.

In a flickering glow at the far end of the next cavern, she made out the blur of a seated figure. He raised his dark head.

She paused. François placed his hand in the small of her back. "Remember why you are doing this," he whispered and pushed her forward into the light.

Head high, she sauntered along the cavern. The tightness in her chest stifled her lungs. Dear Lord. He was bound to a chair and gagged. One eye glared from beneath a puffy lid. Blood smeared his swollen upper lip, and a scrape marred his stubbled cheek. Her heart wrenched. She longed to go to him, ease his cuts and bruises, apologize for all the trouble she'd caused. She glanced at François for her cue.

François flashed his charming, lying smile. She wanted to rake her nails down his cheek and wipe the smile from his lips. Instead, she mirrored it.

"See, it is just as I told you, Carolyn," François said. "Lord Foxhaven came in the night to steal you away."

It wasn't a dream. He had been there in her room. Her heart danced as the memory of his kiss brushed her lips. She recalled his haste, his refusal to talk. The drugs had clouded her mind, made her useless. But what happened after that? How had he ended up here?

No matter. He had tried to rescue her, and now it was up to her to make sure François set him free.

She fixed a mocking smile to her lips. "How strange. He certainly didn't want me when we were married." The fragile flower of their new understanding seemed to wither at her harsh words. Her heart ached with loss even as anger sparked in Lucas's eyes. He shook his head and winced.

"His only purpose in wedding you was to rob me of my inheritance," François sneered.

Lucas glared and strained against the ropes around his chest, his neck corded.

"Perhaps his father forced him?" she suggested softly.

François's fingers crushed her upper arm. "You don't believe that."

The belief that Lucas would never intentionally harm her strengthened, but she forced a sigh. "I heard them talking." The hurt she'd tried to dampen with logic sharpened. "His father told him that if he wanted the Valeron estate, he had to get me with child." Her voice broke as guilt flickered across Lucas's expression along with something remarkably like regret. Tears filled her throat.

She forced them down and spoke around them in a hoarse whisper. "He said that twenty thousand pounds might be enough to induce him to bed even me." This was her interpretation of his words, but it was true nonetheless. The laugh she tossed out sounded as brittle and sharp as broken glass. "It was not."

Lucas flinched and shook his head, staring at her with an intensity that seemed to sear her soul.

François's smile broadened. "He is despicable. He doesn't deserve you, cherie."

"No. But then he never wanted me." She dared

not ask for his help—it was too dangerous—but Lucas would know that whatever he heard or saw next was a lie by her signal. She tapped the side of her nose slowly with her gloved index finger, once, twice, and then tugged at her earlobe.

Would François notice? Did Lucas's eyes widen a fraction in acknowledgement? Or did her hope to lessen the impact of her words just make her believe so? If only the light were better so that she could see.

François grabbed her arm, swung her around to face him, and pressed his mouth hard against hers. Nausea tangled with tears. For a moment, she resisted the dry, hot pressure of his lips. Her limbs trembled until she thought she would fall. She must do this. Lucas's life depended on it. She brought her hands up and around François's neck and tried not to suffocate on the floral scent of betrayal.

He pulled back and gazed into her face, triumph flaring in his eyes. "I love you, my darling." He raised an expectant brow.

"As I love you," she said with barely a quaver.

A low growl issued from deep in Lucas's chest. His eyes blazed fury.

Her knees buckled.

François caught her around the shoulders, cradled her against him, and guided her back the way they had come like a lover.

"You did well, my sweet," he whispered in her ear.

Numbness enveloped her. If Lucas did not recognize her signal, if he believed the kiss and her words, he would hate her forever.

The corner and the welcoming dark seemed so terribly far away. She wondered if her legs would collapse before ever she reached it.

Lucas watched her swaying form depart, the train of her gown shimmering in candlelight. A voluptuous Venus deeply in love with another.

If he believed her words.

Had he really said those dreadful things? Judging from her anger and the underlying hurt, he must have. He shook his head. They were words taken out of context, spoken in heat. His heart twisted, a sharp pain nothing like the dull ache in his ribs. He deserved every excruciating moment.

She'd tapped her nose twice. That meant follow my lead, but she'd also tugged her ear. What the hell was that? Nerves? It had to be one of the other signs she and Matthew Grantham had created for their game of spies one summer, the summer when he began to feel too old to play with the younger set.

"I don't see why I have to be the French spy and be captured," Caro said, her round face serious. A ray of sunshine streamed between the old Folly's Romanesque pillars and flashed off the spectacles perched on the end of her nose.

"That's the game," Lucas said. He probably shouldn't have agreed to join them. He was getting too old for such things, according to Cedric. But it had felt just like old times.

He turned back to the task of laying the ropes straight across the round rickety wicker table next to the rusty seventeenth-century sword he'd borrowed from the attic. *"Besides, you are French."*

"Half French," she snapped as usual.

He tried not to smile. *"I wouldn't mind,"* he said, only a little surprised to discover he meant it, *"but the triplets would never allow a girl to win."*

A shout came from outside. Caro pushed her spectacles up her nose and ran to look out. "Here they come on the barge now."

"Hurry up," Lucas said. "Sit down and I'll tie you."

She dashed to the table and snatched up one of the ropes. She gave him one of those funny teasing smiles that these days always made him feel too hot under the collar. "The French spy captures the English nobleman, but then gives him the secret code so that he can escape. Come on, Lucas. Let me rescue you. It is only fair."

The appeal in her golden eyes shook his resolve. He fought the desire to make her happy. The triplets would be furious and would probably want to fight him for real. And he wasn't allowed to hit them back because they were younger. "Why would a French spy turn against her country?" he asked, settling on logic as a diversion.

Her eyes turned smoky. "They could fall in love. Perhaps he kisses her and changes her mind about the revolution."

The vision she invoked gave him a stirring pleasurable sensation in the pit of his stomach. He remembered their bungled kiss in the boat the week before and felt his face go red and his yard swell and harden. He couldn't charge out and meet the triplets in that state. They'd never let him or Caro forget it. God knows they'd snickered about her overlarge bosom often enough this summer. Perhaps the erection would go away in a minute or two. It usually did, if he didn't let his imagination wander.

"All right," he said. "But no kissing. I'll just convince you that revolution is wrong."

He plunked into the garden chair.

Rope in hand, she knelt at his feet. The sight of her

nape, bare all but a few tendrils of brown hair, while her hands fumbled with the knots at his ankles, made his mouth dry. He reached out and touched the soft golden skin with a fingertip.

She shivered and glanced up, with lips parted and pink cheeks.

In the gap between her dress and her throat, he glimpsed a full creamy rise of flesh. Was it as soft and smooth to the touch as it looked? He swallowed.

Something must have shown on his face because she tilted her head in question. "Is the rope too tight?"

"No," he said, his voice raspy.

She nodded and rose to her feet and bound his wrists in front.

All he had to do was loop his hands over her head, pull her onto his lap, and feel her soft rounded bottom against his very ready dick. He almost groaned out loud.

She raised her gaze to his face, looking like one of those angels in a religious picture, all chubby cheeks and huge-eyed innocence—a cherub or a seraph or something.

"Are you sure you don't want me to kiss you?" She smiled a far-too-knowing smile for his peace of mind. The twin spots of color in her cheeks made him think she guessed at more than she should, in which case, she was nothing but a little flirt. His cock gave a happy little pulse of hope.

Oh, yes, he wanted a lot more than a kiss.

Hell's teeth. This was Caro Torrington, his friend and an innocent, despite her burgeoning curves. He grabbed a breath of air and tried to distract his thoughts. "Are they almost here?"

She blinked as if she'd forgotten about their game, but then dashed to the window. "They are right outside. Now you have to convince me to set you free."

What he had to do was get out of here, before he did something they'd both regret. "Tell me the secret code, French spy."

"No, Lucas, not like that. You have to be more . . . heroic."
She blushed again.

He tested the ropes, struggled against their bite, and felt them loosen. Just as he expected, she'd tied granny knots, and they slithered undone. He lunged for the sword hilt and waved it in her direction. "Tell me the code—now, or you will breathe your last, wench."

She looked so forlorn his chest hurt. "A tug on your earlobe," she muttered.

"Good girl." He gave her an encouraging pat on the shoulder. "Follow me, and I'll get you to England, safe from the mob outside."

The hero-worship rekindled in her eyes as she realized he was going along with her idea. Suddenly, he felt taller, more of a man, as if he could take on the world. With her close on his heels, he charged down the steps.

A tug on the earlobe was the password to freedom, his freedom no doubt. It would be just like her to sacrifice herself to save him. Bile rose in his throat. Cedric clearly had no intention of letting that happen, but Lucas would not let Cedric win, not with Caro at risk. Somehow he had to put a stop to that wedding.

He returned to his slow torturous rocking.

Ah, hell. More footsteps heading his way. Had all his luck disappeared? He rocked faster, racing the oncoming sounds. He had to get to the table and the candle flame. The chair teetered on its back legs, and his heart lurched. He leaned forward, halting the dangerous tilt. Careful. No! Too far. The chair crashed to the floor. Cold stone slammed against his cheek. Every bone in his body vibrated. His ribs hurt like the devil. He was done for. Once more, he'd failed Caro.

The heavy steps broke into a run.

Damn. Damn. Damn.

Lucas shook his head clear and gazed at the toes of a pair of scuffed brown boots inches from his nose. He squinted up a pair of sturdy legs in nankeen trousers to a broad chest topped by a brutal face. It was the beefy fellow who had charged out of the chateau last night.

"'Ad a bit of a haccident, did you, yer lordship?" He was an Englishman.

Lucas concentrated on breathing through his nose.

Beefy cut him loose from the chair, and he fell on his chest with a groan. Slowly, he flexed his hands and then pushed painfully to his knees. His ribs screamed agony.

The guard knocked him flat on his back with a swift knee to the gut and then tied his wrists. This cur certainly knew his business. Was this his executioner? He wasn't ready to die. Not with Father and Caro facing very real danger.

The brute dragged him through a series of cavernous chambers to a door beneath a set of wide stone steps.

"In yer go," Beefy muttered and pitched Lucas to his knees into a small square room with stone walls and floor.

More dizzying pain. Lucas took an easy breath. He couldn't breathe too deep, or it hurt too much. No execution yet, then. Just new quarters. He rolled on his back.

Beefy tugged the handkerchief out of his mouth and tossed it to one side.

"These too," Lucas said, holding out his wrists.

"Sorry, mate, those yer gotta keep." He went out and slammed the door behind him. The lock clicked loudly.

Lucas took stock of his prison. A smudge of daylight entered through a dirty window near the ceiling, an opening far too small for his shoulders. The plank door had solid iron hinges set in the stone wall. His situation suddenly seemed worse. He no longer had a plan.

He struggled to his feet, fighting waves of pain and nausea. Devil take it, but he hurt everywhere. It didn't matter. To have any chance of escape, he had to get his limbs moving. He paced the perimeter of his cell, flexing his bound hands, inspecting every nook and cranny and crack.

Hopeless.

The door crashed open. Accompanied by a delicious aroma of stew, Beefy marched in.

Lucas leaned one shoulder against the wall and raised an eyebrow at the sight of a tray and a chamber pot. "How considerate."

Beefy grunted. "Every prisoner is entitled to his vittles and a piss."

"It sounds as if you speak from experience?"

"Never you mind." He placed his burden on the floor and pointed to the steaming dish and hunk of bread. "With all the servants busy for the wedding, that's likely all you'll get for a while. Make the most of it."

"When is it?"

"What?"

"When is the wedding?"

"Couple of hours from now."

Two hours. He'd never get out in time. "I'll pay you to set me free. Name your price."

The man paused, his beady eyes glinting, and then shook his head. "I wouldn't cross Mr. Rivers, not fer nothin'." He left.

It would take a brave man to cross this new incarnation of Cedric. Why had he never seen what lay behind those gentle expressions of sympathy? "You are probably right, my friend."

The lock clicked into place.

Lucas's stomach growled. He strolled to the tray and slid down the wall beside it. The food looked dismally appetizing. At least he would meet his maker well fed. How bloody ironic.

With nothing else to do, he fell to with a will, tearing at the bread as best he could with bound hands and dunking it in the gravy. The lack of cutlery made it decidedly inelegant, but the food assuaged the gnawing in his belly. It did nothing to ease his fears for Caro.

He pushed the tray to one side and, offering silent thanks to Beefy, made use of the chamber pot. He tucked it under the tray.

Less than two hours. He returned to his pacing. No inspiration struck him from the blue. Caro's bitter words echoed around his brain, diverting his thoughts. If she wanted a divorce, he'd happily oblige. But he would not allow Cedric a free hand with her or his father, not now that he knew the truth. He could not let others suffer because he had been a fool.

Damn it. There had to be some way out. He slammed his fists against the wall as if by some miracle it would crumble.

Perhaps he could pick the door lock. Hampered by his bindings, he fumbled through his pockets. Any self-respecting dandy would have a quizzing glass or a nail file. He didn't even have a hoof pick, confound it.

Steps sounded in the hallway outside. More trouble. Think, he said to himself. It was too early for Cedric. It must be Beefy coming back for the tray. This might be his only fighting chance.

He flattened himself against the wall behind the door and raised his clenched fists, gasping at the stab of pain. One blow was all he asked. A bitter smile curved his lips. This was going to hurt him as much as it hurt his jailor.

The key turned. The door swung open.

Steady. Wait for it.

"Milor'?" a soft voice whispered.

Lucas's mouth dropped open. "Henri?"

A grinning face popped around the edge of the door.

"By God, man, you are a welcome sight," Lucas said, releasing his breath. He drew his sleeve across his sweating brow.

"I followed the man with the tray from the kitchen. I took the key and his weapons when he passed me on the way back.

Henri pulled Beefy's knife from his belt and sawed through Lucas's ropes. "You are hurt?"

"Never mind me. Where's the man who brought the tray?"

"On the stairs. He won't wake up soon."

"You are a bloody wonder, my lad. Can you get him in here? We can't risk him raising the hue and cry."

Moments later, he helped Henri drag Beefy's limp form over the threshold.

"With a bit of luck, they won't discover him before tonight," Lucas said, breathing harder than he cared to acknowledge. "You have my undying gratitude, my friend."

Henri grimaced. "I had no choice, milor'. Miss Lizzie said she will cut out my heart if I come back without you."

His morose tone forced a painful chuckle out of Lucas. "Quick then. We have a wedding to attend."

※　　　※　　　※　　　※

"Try to look happy, Carolyn. After all, it is your wedding day," Cedric murmured in her ear. Just a whisper of his breath on her skin sent shudders down her spine. Of the two of them, he scared her most. The avariciousness in his gaze sucked the strength from her bones.

Having agreed to their demands, why should she to pretend to like it? Because she'd given her word. For Lucas's sake.

A pang of sorrow pierced the numbness she'd drawn around her. He'd never forgive her. Or perhaps he'd be only too happy to wish her well.

She forced a halfhearted smile and almost choked on a breath of incense-perfumed air. She'd get through today, but she never wanted to set eyes on either one of them again.

Heavenly music soared to the rafters, and the congregation, a sea of faces and waving feathers, rose in unison.

"Walk," Cedric muttered.

"I can't see without my spectacles." They'd taken them in case she tried to run away again.

"Just follow my lead, and all will be well." He hooked his arm in hers and started walking

By all, he meant Lucas. She clung to that hope, but niggling doubt slid around in the pit of her stomach. She didn't trust them an inch, but nor could she think of any other course of action. Smiling faces emerged from the mist on both sides as they traveled down the aisle. She didn't recognize a single soul, not one person she could ask for aid. A figure in front of the altar moved forward to greet her.

She squinted. François, her groom, with a gargoyle grin. Had she really thought him handsome and charming? More proof she should have stayed in Norwich. She bit her lip to still its tremble and curled her fingers around her bouquet. She must do this right, or Lucas would suffer.

The organ crashed out a crescendo loud enough to shake the roof, and absolute silence followed. The sound of her own rushing blood filled her head.

The priest flowed down from the altar in a white surplice. She knelt beside François on the cassock, and Cedric hovered at her back. The priest spoke in

Latin. She tried to follow his words, waiting for her turn to answer. Vibrant colors from the stained-glass rose splashed across his pristine robe. It reminded her of Ashbourne village church and long-ago Sundays listening to her father's sermons.

The priest asked a question. She opened her mouth. François shook his head. Of course. The impediment question. With the faintest of hopes, she glanced over her shoulder.

Cedric glowered. She flinched and faced forward.

"I know a reason." Lucas's deep tones rang out from the shadows. "This woman is my legally wedded wife."

A sharp gasp escaped François. The priest's jaw dropped. Caro swung around. Somehow Lucas had set himself free! Relief flooded through her. She didn't have to go through with this. She smiled a welcome.

A little scream issued from Tante Honoré. Her tall feathers bobbed dismay on their snowy mountain of hair.

Cedric muttered an oath. "Ignore him. He is mad."

Lucas fixed his gaze on the wedding party bathed in light, on Caro's welcoming smile. Aware of shocked stares and not giving a damn, he strode out of the shadows and down the center aisle. "I'm mad—I'm furious," he called out. "There isn't an annulment, is there, Valeron?"

"Continue," Cedric shouted at the priest.

"Monsieur, I cannot," the priest intoned. "God's law demands that I hear him."

An usher grabbed Lucas's arm.

People pressed forward, preventing his progress. A

finger wagged in his face.

He dodged around them. More crowded in, clucking like hens. "Blast you, get out of the way." He scattered them with a thrust of his arm. Just a few more feet, and he would put a stop to this nonsense.

Cedric grabbed Caro around the waist.

She shoved him aside. "It is Lucas."

Lucas fixed his gaze on her face. At least she sounded pleased to see him.

Cedric staggered back but recovered, pulling a pistol from his pocket.

Lucas's heart thudded, sick and slow. No more was it a simple matter of stopping a wedding; this looked damned dangerous. "Cedric, give up. It is all over," he yelled and lunged forward.

A hellish expression twisted Cedric's face. He cocked his weapon. "You cannot stop me. Not now."

Caro grabbed his arm.

Panic stirred in Lucas's chest. What the hell did she think she was doing? "Caro, stay back!" he shouted, pulling his pistol from his pocket.

She planted herself in front of Cedric, hands on hips. "I will not let you shoot him."

He pushed her.

A thunderous roar filled the church. A woman screamed.

Time slowed to a crawl. Scarlet bloomed on Caro's shoulder, a flower of blood on cream fabric, spilling down her back in a gory river. Her knees buckled.

"No!" The word ripped Lucas's throat raw. He threw himself forward sliding on his knees, catching her to his chest before she hit the floor.

"Someone get a doctor!" he yelled. He thought he yelled, but his throat seemed too dry to utter a sound.

Shiny black shoes trampled Caro's gown at the corner of his vision.

"Get away from her," Cedric said through his teeth.

Hands shaking, his chest as tight as a noose, Lucas pulled his handkerchief from his coat pocket. "Don't be an idiot. Get a doctor."

The noise from the congregation broke over them in disjointed waves. Shouts. Conversation. People trying to see.

Lucas glared around. "Give her air."

Her amber eyes huge, she gazed up at him. "Cedric hit me." She glanced down and frowned. "Oh."

"Don't look," Lucas said. "It's nothing." God, he hoped so.

Cedric crouched beside him and picked up Lucas's discarded weapon. He pointed it at Lucas's head. "Step back. The wedding goes on. François, get the damn priest over here."

"It's too late," François said in a strangled voice. "The gendarmes will come."

"And he's the one they'll blame," Cedric said. "Don't be a sniveling coward."

Blood oozed dark and sticky through Lucas's fingers. He pressed the gaping wound harder. "Valeron, fetch a doctor. If she loses much more blood . . ." He choked on the words as her eyes widened with fear. He swallowed a groan. "You are going to be fine." The words were as much for him as for her.

She placed her hand over his. "Lucas."

"Hush. Everything will be all right. Cedric, give me your handkerchief and your neckcloth."

"Lucas, please," she whispered. "Take care of my sisters."

"Damn it, Caro. Don't." His hands shook. He tried to smile. "You'll be seeing them yourself soon enough."

Cedric dropped the requested items at Lucas's side.

Sweating, with short breaths tearing at his chest, Lucas wadded the handkerchief up and jammed it into the bloody rent in Caro's gown.

She gasped and bit her lip.

"I'm sorry. This is going to hurt some more. Scream all you want." Her smile shattered his soul.

He raised her. She moaned and then closed her eyes. Her body went limp. She'd fainted, thank God.

He bound the neckcloth tight around her chest. His heart pumped hard, and blood roared in his ears. Too much time was passing. "Where the hell is the doctor?" he yelled.

Her eyes fluttered open. Her fingers plucked at his sleeve. "Lucas, listen," she whispered, so low he had to lean close to hear. "I want you to make amends with your father. Families are important."

Not relatives like Cedric and his father.

"Promise me," she urged.

He gazed into her eyes and saw pain and worry—worry for him when he'd almost got her killed, when she needed all her strength just to survive. Oh, God, what if she didn't make it?

"Please, Lucas."

"Of course, pigeon. How can I refuse when you ask so sweetly?"

Her eyes drifted closed.

He looked up. A circle of horrified faces stared back at him. "Will no one get a doctor?" Damn them all. He'd find one himself.

"Get back," he growled and stood up with her in his arms. He staggered at the surge of pain from his ribs. He shook his head to clear it of dizziness.

Cedric blocked his path, his face a mask of rage, the pistol pointed at Caro.

"Haven't you done enough?" Lucas roared. "Let me pass."

"She's mine," Cedric said. "I will not let you have her."

Devil take it. They weren't fighting over some trifle the way they had as boys. A life was at stake. "Please, Cedric," he whispered, so he wouldn't scream like a banshee. "Not now." He glanced into Caro's blanched face. "Let me get help."

"Yes." Cedric licked his lips. "We will leave here, but you will obey me. I will not let you snatch her from under my nose."

Winning didn't matter. "Get Caro to a doctor; then we will talk."

Cedric scowled over Lucas's shoulder. "Valeron, make sure no one follows."

Swinging his pistol in a threatening arc, Cedric glared around him. The onlookers gasped and muttered.

"Get out of the way," Lucas roared.

The guests shuffled back, muttering and cursing. If only one of them would jump Cedric from behind.

"Her English lover," someone muttered in French, and Lucas realized he'd been speaking English. Their faces turned ugly. They blamed him for this. As well they might.

Lifeblood, warm and sticky, oozed between Lucas's fingers against Caro's back, while Cedric, with the eyes of a trapped and desperate animal, backed slowly toward the church door. One wrong move, and he'd send them all to hell.

In Lucas's arms, Caro lay far too still. His heart twisted until it was squeezed so hard it hurt to breathe. She must live. He stared at her throat, at the fluttering pulse there beneath her skin. How much longer could she survive without help? Faster, he wanted to urge, but he kept his steps steady and smooth. A jolt might be fatal. His was the blame if she died. He would not let it happen.

He increased his pace a fraction, pushing Cedric as hard as he dared.

Nervous steps trotted behind him. Valeron, no doubt. To his right, in a parallel aisle, the shadowy figure of Henri kept pace with the strange procession.

Cedric glanced around, his finger tightening on the trigger.

"Easy, Cedric," Lucas murmured. "We are almost there."

At last they reached the iron-studded doors. Lucas shifted his grip, cradling her cheek against his shoulder. "Hang on," he murmured in her ear. "We will find a doctor. We must."

François scuttled around them and pulled open

the great door.

Cedric backed into brilliant sunlight. He jerked his chin. "Put her in my carriage."

Lucas blinked and squinted into the dazzle. A sharp breath filled his lungs. He clamped his jaw to prevent its escape.

The sound of fifteen muskets cocked in unison by a troop of England's finest broke the silence.

Cedric spun around.

"Drop your weapon," the infantry officer rapped out.

Cedric's shoulders tensed. He swung back to face Lucas, his lips drawn back in a death's head grimace, his pupils blazing hatred. Lucas turned, curling his body around Caro, shoulders braced in anticipation of a bullet. He would not let Cedric hurt her again.

A shot sundered the air.

Lucas felt nothing.

Cedric crumpled at his feet in a puff of dust, a neat hole in his temple.

"Captain MacKay at your service, sir. Lord Audley thought you might need a hand," the officer said. He glanced up at the roof of a nearby house and back at Cedric's body. "Sharp-shooter. He should have dropped the pistol."

"Thank you."

One of the soldiers pointed a musket at François, who dropped his weapon and raised his hands.

Even as Lucas's mind registered relief, his heart faltered. Caro's lips were blue. It might be too late.

"She needs a physician," he croaked and fell to his knees, laying her on the cobbles. He ripped off his coat and placed it under her head and pressed against the bloody bandage. Nothing seemed to staunch the horrid flow.

The officer turned away. "Is there a doctor present?" he bawled.

The soldiers formed a ring around Lucas and Caro, a red barrier against the resentful muttering crowd emerging from the church into the square. A small man in a black coat shouldered his way through the burly hussars.

"Doctor," he said at Lucas's scowl.

Unable to utter a word for the painful lump in his throat, Lucas nodded permission. He sat back on his heels, sweating and shaking like a horse ridden too hard.

The doctor moved with swift assurance, checking the wound, rebandaging. He glanced up at Lucas. "She has lost a good deal of blood. The bullet, it goes through. It hits nothing vital, but she does not look good."

"What the hell do you mean, not good? You're a doctor—do something." Lucas couldn't contain his snarl.

"I know my business, monsieur. We need to get her to bed."

"We'll take her to the Valeron chateau," Lucas said.

"Milor', Milor'!" The cry came from a group of liveried men being loaded into a carriage by some of the soldiers.

Henri. Lucas signaled to the captain. "A friend."

"Yes, sir." The captain turned smartly to his sergeant. "Have that man released."

By the time Lucas turned back, the doctor was pointing to a nearby carriage and attempting to direct two privates to lift Caro. The men stared blankly. Common English soldiers didn't speak much French.

Lucas waved them off. He knelt at her side, drawing her unresisting body into his arms. Too still. The acid of fear burned his gullet. Didn't she know women weren't supposed to go around tackling murderers—or galloping horses down St. James? He choked on a laugh that turned into something hot and moist behind his eyes. Damn it. He'd been such a fool, and her life was too high a price to pay.

He plodded to the carriage. "I'm sorry, Caro," he said. Her lashes formed stark crescents against her dead white skin. He touched the pad of his thumb to her bloodless bottom lip and sensed as much as felt a faint breath. "Hang on."

His voice caught, his eyes burned, and he dragged his next words from the depths of his soul.

"I swear, when you get well, I will make this up to you."

Nineteen

LUCAS THRUST HIS HAT AT THE HOVERING LACKEY in the entrance to the chateau and turned to greet Madame Valeron. A tributary of wrinkles criss-crossed her pallid, sunken cheeks. She appeared to have aged twenty years. Another of Cedric's victims. Regret dampened his simmering anger, and a deeper emotion, one he did not care to examine, crushed in on him. He preferred anger.

He sketched a cool bow. "Good afternoon, madame."

"My lord Foxhaven," she murmured while curt-seying, her purple gown and plumed turban a pathetic brave show in the harsh light from the high windows.

"Madame Valeron, let us not stand on ceremony. How is Lady Foxhaven?"

A weary smile hovered on the old lady's rouged lips. "She has great resilience. She recovers, my lord."

He bit back his impatience. "The doctor sent daily

reports, but I am glad to have them confirmed. I must thank you for your care."

"It is no more than anyone would do," the old lady murmured. Her eyes brightened a little. "When she heard of your visit, she insisted on coming downstairs to the drawing room. Please, come this way."

The ton weight on his chest lightened an ounce. At least she hadn't refused to see him. "Thank you."

He followed the drooping feathers down the cool lofty passage. At the drawing room door, he halted her with a touch, the question burning his tongue. "How are her spirits?"

"She is quiet. The doctor calls it English phlegm." Her expression tensed. "I hesitate to ask, my lord, but do you bring us news from Paris?"

Damn, he'd forgotten the letter. All he could think of was Caro and what she might say at how he'd bungled things, getting her shot and her beloved cousin sent to prison.

He withdrew the note from his inside coat pocket. "From the Chevalier, madame." He handed it to her. "I am not privy to the details, but I understand he has made a full confession to the authorities. Now the matter rests in their hands."

She clutched the paper to her bosom. "I must express my gratitude at your forbearance, my lord. I understand you spoke for him. You saved his life."

He forced civility into his tone. "Your nephew was not the only one duped by Cedric Rivers. It would do none of us any good to have more scandal in the family."

Her old head inclined graciously. "Your generosity

does you credit, my lord. Come, we must not keep our patient waiting any longer."

He squared his shoulders, ready to meet his fate, holding fast to the thought that Caro had been on her way to find him when Cedric spirited her away.

Madame Valeron preceded him through the door.

Caro reclined on a chaise lounge angled toward an open bank of French windows. A light breeze stirred the air. The late afternoon sun gilded her creamy skin and glittered in her tawny curls.

"Look who is here, *cherie*," Madame Valeron crooned in the hearty tones always demanded by a sickroom.

Caro turned her head. Bandages swathed her shoulder beneath her loose robe. Lilac shadows painted half-moons below the large amber eyes in her pallid oval face. His heart bumped erratically. He had never felt this uncertain.

Madame Valeron surged forward and straightened the embroidered rug over Caro's lap. "His lordship brought a letter from François." She waved the paper.

"That is wonderful news, Aunt," Caro said.

It seemed he'd done something right, even though it left a bitter taste.

"I will leave you to talk," Madame Valeron said. "I will be outside if you need me." She drifted through the balcony door.

Caro gestured toward the gilt chair beside her couch. He gave thanks for the delicate tinge of color in her cheeks. Surely a good sign? A small smile curved her lush lips. "Welcome, my lord. Please, be seated."

My lord. It was to be formal, then.

"How do you do?" He took her hand and raised it to his lips.

A faint wince flickered across her expressive features.

Clumsy fool. "Forgive me. I did not intend to hurt you."

"No, no. It is nothing." He saw the lie in her eyes.

"You look wonderfully well." He lowered himself into the chair and hoped she didn't see the truth in his.

"Indeed. I am much improved."

"I'm sorry I couldn't stay." He glanced over at the open French doors and lowered his voice. "It was such a mess. The officer in charge insisted I return to Paris with François under guard the moment the doctor said you would recover. Audley needed me to explain the presence of troops in the Champagne to the Ambassador and the French authorities. I never expected to be gone so long, but with a British subject dead and a Frenchman arrested for abduction and fraud, it turned into a bureaucratic nightmare."

"I'm glad you went," she said. "Without your intervention, my cousin might have faced more than a few months in prison." She shuddered. Unshed tears turned her eyes to liquid honey. "I have to thank you, Lucas. I don't think I could have borne it if François had been . . ."

His chest constricted. He'd been wrong about her signal. Until now, he had hoped she'd been forced to say the words of love she'd spoken in the cellar to Valeron, another man, then, who had used and abused her.

Hell, he should have killed the blackguard on that

nightmare carriage ride to Paris. Mad with worry about Caro, he didn't know why he hadn't choked the slimy bastard with his bare hands. Except Caro would not have been pleased.

"It was my duty," he said.

"Thank you." She smiled at him.

His heart seemed to fill his throat at the sheer beauty of that curve to her lips. He'd bring her the Chevalier garlanded in flowers for the favor of such a smile.

"What are your plans?" he asked.

"My plans?"

"Yes. When you are well?" Did she intend to stay here with Valeron?

"I would like to go home to Norwich."

He let go a breath. He liked this plan.

She smiled sadly. "It has been a long time since I last saw my sisters. Their letters are full of worry. And you?"

"I am needed in London." Dear God, could he be more blunt?

Her translucent fingers entwined in strands of blanket fringe. Her arm had lost its pretty dimples. Had she been so ill?

"Your business affairs call you home, I expect," she said, her voice barely audible.

"My father fell into a decline at the news of Cedric's death. His man of business wrote to say there seems to be some misappropriation of funds. Things are in pretty serious case, I believe. I must leave as soon as you are well enough to travel."

She glanced up, her expression instantly sympathetic. "Your poor father. He set such store by

Cedric. And his mother. Poor Aunt Rivers. The loss must be devastating. You must go to them at once."

His stomach dropped. She couldn't wait to be rid of him. "I cannot let you travel alone." His voice sounded harsher than he intended.

"I insist. Your father needs you."

And she didn't. Had he really expected she would ask him to stay? Not expected. Hoped. He thought he might shatter if he said a word, so he nodded.

"You promised to heal the breech with your father. Families are all we really have."

The concern in her voice sparked to life a smidgen of hope that she cared about him after all. But he could not lie. "I'm not sure it is possible after what has happened." He saw her chin lift and managed a shaky laugh. "I will do my best."

"That is all anyone can ask."

He wanted her to ask for so much more, but he didn't have the right. "I will post up to Norwich at the first possible moment. Your sisters will want a firsthand account of how you do." Hell, now he was using a hearty sickroom voice.

"It is good of you to think of them," she murmured. Her chest rose and fell on a sigh.

He forced himself not to look at the tempting curves beneath her flimsy gown, even as her body called to his basest nature, the desire to brand her as his own, to claim her as his wife in truth. The instinct was so basic, so visceral, he shook with the effort to hold it in check. Only his admiration for her courage and loyalty gave him the strength to resist.

"If only I had listened to your advice after that dreadful race and gone home to Norwich," she said.

"None of this would have occurred."

"Not so. I left you to face the scandal alone. I was wrong. And besides, you always wanted to meet your French relatives." Not to mention Valeron's promises of an annulment. His stomach hit bottom. "It is over and done. We need to discuss the future."

She stared down at her fingers and released them from the knotted threads as if she had only just noticed them. "Yes. We must."

Why did she have to remain so quiet, so still? He wanted her to fight him as she had in Paris, to tell him what she wanted. He had sworn not to influence her decision in any way—not to beg, or make a case for remaining married, or use his charm.

The choice had to be hers.

God, he wanted her to choose him.

"We can continue our arrangement, if you wish," he said casually, too casually. He winced. "Remain married, I mean. It would forestall any unpleasantness. I promise not to trouble you." At least not without permission, maybe a hint of permission.

"I don't think that is such a good idea, do you?"

The words knifed deep. He squeezed his eyes shut briefly. He hadn't expected to feel so much pain as his hopes drained away. Nothing mattered except her happiness. "Probably not. I can only say, I am sorry I forced you into marriage. You didn't even need my money. You were an heiress in your own right." He swallowed a bitter laugh.

She stared out of the window. All he could see was her beautiful profile, the elegant line of her neck, the swell of her magnificent bosom. He longed to press his lips against the tiny pulse beneath her ear.

"Did you know? When you asked me, I mean?" she asked.

"No." The word exploded from him. He softened his tone. "I swear I knew nothing of your fortune until after we were married."

She turned her face toward him. Her eyes were like gold medallions, flat and shiny and for once completely unreadable. Her lips curved in a wry little smile. "If I recall, you made no secret that you were not terribly keen on the idea of marriage."

He couldn't open his mouth. He shifted his gaze to the vines on the distant chalky hills, to the fingers of afternoon shadow stretching out to clutch the meandering valleys. He felt trapped in the bottom of one of those dark crevasses, fighting to reach the light with nothing to guide him.

Long ago, he'd changed his mind. If she hadn't seen it in Paris, then it probably wasn't enough to make a difference. "You are right. I was not, then."

"You needed money," she said, her voice far away, as if she was remembering. A faint smile tugged at her lips. "I suspected you had gambling debts, but it turned out you wanted to buy a house."

The house. The boys. She'd like them, if she ever got a chance to meet them. He'd scarcely given them a thought these past few weeks.

"I can explain."

"Please don't," she said. "It really doesn't matter. If I had refused you that night, would you actually have taken me downstairs and ruined me?"

What did that have to do with anything? He had somehow lost himself in the deepest abyss. "No," he said cautiously.

She nodded as if it meant a good deal.

He awaited an explanation. The silence dragged on.

Damn. He'd rehearsed this scene over and over on the drive here, played it out the way he wanted it. Not like this.

He gripped his knees until his knuckles hurt. He welcomed the pain. "What I want to say is . . ." He cleared his dry throat. "I blackmailed you into this, and if you desire a divorce, I will arrange it."

She didn't seem to be breathing. Perhaps she didn't understand.

"Caro. I'm offering you the way out I promised you, if that is your choice."

She lowered her gaze. "I think it would be best."

The words hammered into his skull. Breath rushed from his lungs, and his heart stilled.

When it really mattered, he counted for nothing in the eyes of those for whom he cared most. It was as if he had no substance, was merely air and water, not blood and bone and heartache.

He forced a lazy smile, got up, and strolled to the window. The manicured lawn looked far too green and fresh when everything inside him had shriveled to dust. He spoke over his shoulder, not trusting himself to hold steady in the face of her decision. "If that is what you want, I will arrange it as soon as you get back to England."

He hesitated. "You understand there will be a scandal? One from which your reputation may never recover, even though I will assume all of the blame?"

"I imagined it might be so."

So she'd made her decision before he arrived. His chest tightened. He wasn't sure a breath would fit in the resultant small space.

He curved his mouth into a sardonic smile and turned to face her. "Well, that's settled."

She nodded. "Yes. It is." Her voice was as clear and chill as a mountain waterfall. Her skin looked like marble, the outside all warm luminescence where the sun touched it but deeply cold within. He had no idea how to reach her.

He must accept her wishes as he had promised. He had only himself to blame. Hot moisture pricked his eyes. What sort of idiot had he become? He clenched his jaw, breathed hard through his nose, and struggled for control. He forced hoarse words past the hard lump in his throat. "I will wait on you in Norwich at the first opportunity. I must leave at once if I am to catch the next packet to Dover."

She nodded.

As sore as if his body had been beaten with the flat of a sword, he sauntered to her side, the arrogant careless noble who cared for naught but his own pleasure, a role he played to perfection. Inside, he was nothing, an empty shell.

She smiled politely. "Thank you for taking time out of your journey to come and see me."

He bowed. "Au revoir, Caro."

"Good-bye, Lucas." Her gaze returned to the view.

For one almost irresistible moment, he imagined throwing himself at her feet, begging her to let him prove himself worthy to be her husband, to be someone other than himself, the kind of man she wanted. A long time ago, he'd sought his father's approval by giving up his dreams and control over his destiny. It had earned him nothing but scorn. He wouldn't do it again. Caro had made her decision.

No matter what his father said, Lucas always kept his word and always took his punishment like a man.

❋   ❋   ❋   ❋

NORWICH, MARCH 1817

When a small square of notepaper franked by Lord Grantham arrived addressed to Lady Foxhaven, an uncomfortable flutter stirred in Caro's stomach. She didn't think anyone besides Lucas and her sisters had been informed of her return.

"Who is it from?" Alex asked, looking up from the book she was reading aloud while Caro plied her needle.

Caro opened it. "It is an invitation from the Granthams to a musical evening two days from now." The Granthams had no idea of her impending divorce, or they never would have sent an invitation.

"Oh goody. Can I go too?"

"I'm not going."

"Why ever not? You always used to go."

"I have no wish to attend." She glanced at the clock. "It is time for my walk." She hadn't informed her sisters of her impending divorce either. Eventually, she would have to tell them, but not yet, not until it was a fait accompli, much like her disastrous marriage.

"Can I come with you?"

"Don't you have a map of India to finish?"

She permitted Alex to do some of her studies in the drawing room, leaving the younger girls in the schoolroom under the strict eye of Miss Salter.

Alex groaned and flicked a golden braid over her shoulder. She pulled out her schoolbook and went to work on the table by the window.

Focusing on the buttons of her coat and the ribbons on her bonnet, Caro kept her mind empty of everything except the simple task of dressing.

Regular exercise had toned her limbs after months of bed rest, and she had resented the rain of these past few days. The shoulder wound had healed well, but the fever that had beset her after Lucas's visit to the chateau had slowed her recovery. The doctor advised walking every day to regain her strength.

From the front door, she strolled along the lane and took the footpath up onto the common.

A week or two ago, the walk up the small rise from the style had left her panting, but now she climbed it with ease, reveling in the pull on her muscles and the cool breeze tugging at her hair and skirts. This daily respite from her chattering charges provided a chance to set her thoughts in order, an opportunity to plan for the future.

She sighed. What a bumble broth she'd got herself into because of her desire to help an old friend. They could never be friends again. It was far too painful to contemplate.

At the top, she stared over the valley and absorbed the surrounding peace. New leaves sprouted on hawthorns full of twittering sparrows, and the fields in the distance showed a hint of green fuzz. The air smelled of damp earth and new beginnings.

She took a deep determined breath. As soon as she returned home, she would send a polite refusal to the Granthams' invitation. Caro was not so gauche as to inflict herself on people before her next disgrace became public knowledge. In a similar vein, she and Miss Salter had already discussed plans to find someone else to chaperone Alex's first season in London.

No regrets? She couldn't regret a loveless marriage, but she did miss Lucas's friendship, and it was that particular loss that caused the hollow ache in her chest. Nothing else. And she would bear it.

The thought firmly in place, she marched down the hill to the copse at the bottom. The pale yellow face of a primrose peeped from beneath a fallen log. She removed her glove and picked it. More were nestled in the grassy hollows. Ignoring the mud caking her shoes and soiling the hem of her gown, she wandered from clump to clump until she had a small bouquet. A sunny promise of summer to take indoors.

She plucked a few velvet green leaves to frame her posy and strolled out from the woods.

"Good day, Caro."

The deep, rich voice caused her heart to forget to beat.

Lucas and Maestro. Magnificent together, they towered over her. He stared at her, his gaze dark and piercing. Her mind went blank. Her heart jolted to life, the blood roaring through her body so fast that she felt dizzy. "Lucas. What are you doing here?"

His eyebrows drew together. "Riding." He nodded at her flowers. "Primroses already?" He swung down, his greatcoat swirling around his athletic form. "Remember how we used to pick them on my father's land as children?"

She remembered everything they had done together. She buried her nose in the fragrant petals, hiding her shortness of breath and flushed cheeks. "Mmmm." It sounded suitably noncommittal.

"You look well," he said. "You are fully recovered?"

His stiff tone and unsmiling expression curled around her heart like cold fingers. She inclined her head in assent. "The doctor, my aunt, and Lizzie took good care of me. I had no choice but to get well."

"I'm glad." He drew Maestro's reins through his gloved fist. "Speaking of Lizzie, would you tell her that Henri is working for Audley and doing very well by all accounts?"

Lizzie had told her all about Henri. "She will be happy to hear it."

"Yes." He lapsed into silence, and they walked side by side up the hill.

Any moment, he would mention the trip to Scotland. Strain tightened every nerve in her body; her legs felt wooden. She nibbled her bottom lip, trying to think of some commonplace remark. "How is your father?"

"Not well." A shadow passed over his face, and his jaw softened. "I returned home to discover he had suffered an apoplexy. The business with Cedric hit him hard. Not just his death—Cedric embezzled most of his money." Lucas stopped and turned to face her, his eyes haunted. "He is walking a little now, and his speech has improved, but his spirit is low."

The thought of the awesome Lord Stockbridge as an invalid filled her with pity. "I'm sorry. I had no idea he had been quite so ill."

Maestro reared and snorted his impatience. Lucas forced him back. "Steady, boy. It is the reason I haven't been back before now. We've been keeping the worst of it quiet. Thanks to you, we cleared the air between us."

A purposefulness she'd never sensed before emanated from him. His cheeks had hollowed, hardening his lean features and giving him a careworn expression. Deep lines etched his sensuous mouth. He'd let his hair grow again, and dark silky strands curled over his collar.

She pushed her spectacles up her nose and walked faster. "I'm glad he came around."

"It wasn't all his fault." Lucas put his hand on her arm.

A frisson of awareness trickled across her flesh; heat radiated up her arm. She pulled free.

His eyes flashed the pain of a creature in torment and then dulled to disinterest.

Maestro's nose intruded over his shoulder. He rubbed it gently. A cynical smile curved his lips. "Father's old friends walked away when they heard he was ruined."

"How awful. I'm so sorry."

He gave her a sharp sideways glance. "Me too. He's tired of my company already. Would you call on him?"

If meeting Lucas unexpectedly tied her tongue, it would be doubly bad under formal circumstances,

with his father looking on. She glanced around frantically. A nearby rabbit hole looked inviting. "I don't
know when I would have time."

A muscle flickered in his jaw, and diffidence edged
his tone. "Forgive me. I do not mean to impose."

Guilt knotted her stomach. Papa would not have
approved of such callousness, nor did she. "Perhaps
when he feels better . . ."

"Come tomorrow."

The primroses were beginning to wilt. She eased
her grip on the delicate stalks. "I believe I have
another engagement."

As if seeking divine intervention, he cast his gaze
heavenward. "I won't be there, Caro. I have business
in Norwich that requires my attention. I don't like
leaving him alone."

Put like that, what could she say? "Tomorrow,
then."

His jaw relaxed, and a shadow of his old lopsided
smile warmed his expression. "Join him for tea, why
don't you? I'll have the carriage sent at half past two."

She caught a glint of triumph in his eyes and
knew she'd been manipulated.

Why didn't she mind?

Twenty

"HOW LONG WILL YOU BE STAYING HERE IN the country?" Caro asked across the tea table set out in the oak-paneled drawing room.

On the other side of the hearth, Lord Stockbridge's blue-veined hand clawed around the head of his silver-headed cane. "Indefinitely."

The fire threw red lights into his shock of recently whitened hair as he shook his head. "Lucas thinks it is better for me here. Away from the talk." His face looked far older than his fifty years. "The ton so loves to gossip." He sighed. "But of course, you know that."

Sorrow for a man whose influence and power had been unquestioned only a few short months ago washed through her. "Still," she said in heartening tones, "I gather Lucas plans to stay with you?"

"Aye, as much as he is able. He's a good boy. Damn it." He coughed. "Excuse me, please. I lost so many years thinking the worst of him because of that scoundrel Cedric, and he's everything a man could want in a son. He's salvaged a great deal, you know, but he never stops working."

Caro settled her teacup back on the tray. She really didn't want to discuss Lucas. "I'm glad he is a comfort to you."

"Carolyn?"

The hesitant quaver in his voice caught her attention. She smiled across the teacups. "Yes, my lord?"

"I don't suppose . . . no, of course not."

Caro regarded him curiously. "I beg your pardon?"

He shook his head. "I don't suppose you would care to see my latest acquisition?"

That was not the question he had planned to ask. She let it pass. "Of course, and then I really must go."

With one hand on his chair-arm and the other on the head of his walking cane, he pushed slowly to his feet. He swayed, his chest heaving.

Caro raced around the table to his side to steady him.

Danson, Lucas's valet and one of the few servants in the house, appeared as if from nowhere and hastened to assist. "What are you doing, my lord?"

"I wish you wouldn't lurk outside the door," Stockbridge said. "We are going up to the long gallery."

"His lordship instructed you were not to leave this room until he returns," Danson said.

"Nonsense. He worries too much."

This was more like the irascible Lord Stockbridge Caro remembered from her youth. Danson glowered, but appeared to be just as much in awe of him as she was.

"Perhaps another time," she suggested gently, mindful of his pride.

"You can't go back on your word, young lady. Not this time."

Caro stiffened at the bitter undertone, and a flash of heat tore over her skin. Why had she let Lucas bully her into coming here? The fire's crackle and Lord Stockbridge's heavy breathing filled the uncomfortable silence.

After a short, irritable exhalation, Stockbridge tapped his stick on the floor. "Forgive me. I promised Lucas I would say nothing of the past. I beg you will pay no attention to an old man. Just come upstairs for a moment."

Faced with such an apology and his pleading expression, Caro could do no more than nod. "For a moment or two."

She took his arm, and head held high, he staggered out into the hallway. Danson hovered behind.

The stairs proved a nightmare. Danson fussed and tutted, and Lord Stockbridge's grip dug into her shoulder as he fought his way up each step. She feared Lucas might come home to find his father at the bottom of the stairs.

Slightly hysterical, she pictured the scene. Lord Stockbridge on top of Danson and herself, a tangled wreckage of snapped limbs, and Lucas rigid with fury.

A sigh escaped her as they gained the landing. Danson smartly pushed a chair behind his lordship. Stockbridge flopped down with a grunt and mopped his brow. He slanted her a wicked smile. "First time I've been upstairs since we got back."

Not funny. She glared at him. "Really, my lord. I do think you might have warned me. Now Lord Foxhaven will be furious."

"Never mind the lad. He'll just scold like always. His bark is worse than his bite."

"Like yours." Caro clapped a hand over her mouth.

Danson smirked and turned away.

Stockbridge wheezed a laughed. "Always said there was more to you than met the eye, my lady." A regretful look passed over his craggy features. "Well, enough of that. Come on, we've almost arrived."

Danson bore his shuffling weight this time. Caro followed them across the landing and partway along the gallery running the length of the west wing.

"There," Stockbridge said, pointing with obvious satisfaction. "What d'you think of Lawrence's work? He's the Regent's man, y'know."

It was Lucas in sartorial splendor. Dressed for court, elegant, proud, and noble, his expression stern, without his usual insouciance or gleam of devilry.

She quelled a shiver. "It is magnificent."

She gazed at the portraits on either side. She recognized the one to the right as a young Stockbridge, painted here at Stockbridge Hall with a pack of hounds milling at his feet. The man in the other portrait bore a strong resemblance to Lucas. He wore a full-bottomed wig, and lace dripped from his sleeves and his throat.

"My father," Stockbridge said. "A bad man. Would fight a duel at the least slight. Had more mistresses than King Charles."

"You didn't approve of your father?"

"No. Dashed loose screw, pardon the expression. I thought Lucas had turned out just like him." He glowered for a moment and then thumped his cane on the wooden floor. "It was Cedric, after all." Stockbridge's voice dropped to a whisper. "D'ye know he raped a girl from the village, beat her, and then paid her to say it was my Lucas? When Lucas denied it, I called him a liar and a coward. Took Cedric's word over his." He put his hand over his eyes.

Cold filled Caro's veins. Lucas had adored his father as a boy. This explained their estrangement. "Oh, dear."

"You look sick about it. Imagine how I felt when I learned the truth." His hand dropped to her shoulder, but it was the weight of his misery that pressed her down. "He acted the rake all those years to live up to my expectations, he was so angry. Do you know what else he was doing?"

Acting the rake? What on earth did he mean? Her brain whirling, she shook her head.

"He was rescuing boys, street musicians." His voice sounded proud and pleased. "Setting up a music school. That's what he did with his grandmother's blunt, you know. Bought a house and turned it into a conservatory for boys."

Caro gasped. Cedric had lied about the house. Or perhaps even he did not know why Lucas had bought it. It wasn't for his mistress. A flutter of hope stirred in her heart.

Lord Stockbridge's mouth turned down in a bitter line. "When he was a boy, I refused to allow him piano lessons. He agreed to study the law to please me, and then I turned against him."

He glared at the portraits. "Stockbridges. Bunch of stiff-necked fools, the whole lot of 'em."

"Father. What the deuce do you mean by coming up here?"

A thunderous-faced Lucas came stomping along the gallery.

Stockbridge's lined face lit up. "See what I mean? Didn't hear you come in, my boy."

"No one did." Lucas glanced pointedly at Danson.

"Sorry, my lord. I told his lordship not to come up, but he wouldn't listen," Danson said.

Lucas's gaze rested on Caro, and her heart vibrated with silent song. How handsome he looked in the hallway among his ancestors' portraits.

"Caro, I am glad you are still here." He bowed and reached out.

Without thinking, she placed her hand in his. He brought her fingers slowly to his lips, brushing the back of her gloves, his breath moist and warm on her skin through the lacy fabric.

Her heart tumbled over, and her stomach flip-flopped. She said the first thing that came into her head—"Lord Foxhaven, I did not expect to see you this afternoon"—and then wished she hadn't, when his expression lost its warmth.

He dropped her hand. "My business took less time than I expected. I apologize if my early return displeases you."

"I mean, I am surprised to see you here." Surprised to see him in his own home? Really.

He looked at her quizzically, one eyebrow cocked. Nothing she could say would help. "Lord

Stockbridge brought me to see your portrait before I left."

He glanced up at the portrait with a grimace. "Fierce, isn't it? Have you seen the others?"

"It's a damn fine portrait," Stockbridge said.

"The likeness is very good," Caro agreed.

"If you'll wait just a moment," Lucas said, "I will help Father downstairs, and we can continue to discuss Lawrence's skill if you like." Hope and hesitancy colored his voice.

"Humor him, my lady," Stockbridge said. "Luc doesn't get much amusement with only me to keep him company."

Caro felt a strong desire to make it clear that she had no intention of amusing Lucas or anyone else. He had promised not to be here. But a glance at Lord Stockbridge's anxious face prevented her from speaking her mind. She took a breath. "I can wait a few moments."

With a firm but gentle grasp on his father's arm, Lucas guided him to the stairs.

She stared up at the portrait. Lucas had definitely changed. Although still handsome, he looked older. Worry about money and the losses Cedric had inflicted must have wrought the changes.

"Now tell me what you really think."

Startled, she gasped and whirled around. "I didn't hear you return."

"Too busy admiring me. It is awful, isn't it?"

He stood so close his heat warmed her skin. She could see each long eyelash framing his dark impenetrable eyes. Her body hummed with pleasure at his closeness.

She turned to gaze at the portrait. "You look like your grandfather."

He moved closer, his breath stirring the hairs on her nape. "You certainly know how to insult a fellow."

She couldn't think straight with him almost touching her back, couldn't breathe. "What?"

"Everyone said Cedric was the image of the old earl."

"Oh."

His hand brushed her neck, and his fingers twined in a loose strand of hair.

She leaned forward. "What are you doing?"

"Remembering." His tone was low, seductive, full of lascivious meaning. "Remembering how soft your skin is, the silky feel of your hair." She heard him inhale and then felt the warm rush of moist air in her ear. "Remembering your perfume." He breathed in. "Vanilla and roses."

She stepped aside and backed away, her heart thudding loudly, painfully. "Lucas, please. Don't do this."

He rested one elbow on the paneled wall and leaned his forehead against his forearm, his face full of regret. He traced her hairline with the tips of his fingers. "You would deny me even this small thing." A small bitter smile crossed his face. "You really do despise me, don't you?" He half turned away.

She caught at his sleeve. "How can you say that?"

"It is why you went to Paris."

She shook her head, her fingers holding fast to the dark blue fabric. "That is not true, and you know it."

His lip curled. "You prefer to wed a man like

Valeron than stay married to me."

She frowned. "Who said anything about marrying François?"

"Caro, don't play with me." His dark eyes held a warning. "Lizzie was as mad as a hornet when she told my housekeeper that you and your sisters are going to France in the summer."

She let her hand fall and looked at the floor. "I am taking them to meet Tante Honoré." She lifted her head and gazed into his eyes. "It is just a visit, Lucas. François is to marry Mademoiselle Jeunesse."

His long fingers found her chin and held her face still, staring at her intently. "I don't believe you."

"Whether you believe it or not, it is the truth." She pushed his hand away.

"I'm so sorry, Caro," he whispered.

"There's nothing to be sorry about." She headed for the stairs.

He caught her hand and swung her around. A deep frown creased his forehead. His eyes searched hers as if seeking answers. He brushed a stray wisp of hair back from her face, and Caro instinctively reached up to touch his cheek, to caress the face that filled her dreams and forced its way into her unwary mind during her empty days.

It was a mistake. That one small touch reminded her of everything she had longed for since she was first aware of her womanhood. She had been able to use her anger at his licentious behavior to keep her yearnings at bay. There was no anger left. None. Nothing but a bittersweet longing for something that had slipped from her grasp and shattered in a million pieces before she ever truly held it.

"God, Caro. I miss you."

The words pierced her heart, the pain so sudden she drew in a sharp breath. She missed him too. She would never tell him how much.

He pulled her close.

She watched his beautiful mouth slowly descend. She closed her eyes. Just one kiss. Just one drugging, mindless, wonderful kiss, and then she would leave.

The scent of sandalwood and cigar smoke and musky male filled her nostrils. She parted her lips, and she heard him groan as his mouth covered hers. Gentle, tiny, soft warm kisses rained on her lips, her cheek, her jaw, her neck. Then back to her mouth. This time hard and hungry, fiercely possessive.

She gave herself up to them. This was what she had longed for all these months since she left London. This would be her memory to keep for the rest of her life. She slid her hands around the back of his neck and leaned closer. Her heart pounded in her ears. She wanted to know the joy of fulfillment he had promised.

Need heated her skin, flittered deep inside her, tightened her breasts. She arched against his hard body, wanting him close.

He pulled away.

She slowly opened her eyes, regretful.

Dark eyes captured her gaze.

"I want you, Caro," he said, his voice thick and husky.

A jolt of desire flooded moisture to the apex of her thighs. She gasped at the shimmer of pleasure.

He slammed her tight against him with a soft groan. His tongue filled her mouth, one hand cupped her bottom, and his hips flexed against her abdomen.

He lifted his mouth a fraction, his lips grazing hers as he spoke. "You must tell me to stop right now, if that is your wish. If you wait a moment longer, it will be too late."

Lucas didn't want to stop. He wasn't entirely sure he could. But honor forced the words from his lips. He never wanted to let her go again, but if she insisted, he would. He could not force her to want him, the way he needed her.

He searched the depths of her golden eyes for permission and found rampant desire.

He picked her up and reveled in the weight of her full, ripe body. "God, you are gorgeous."

She laughed, all smiles and air and rustling silk, her form fitting perfectly in the curve of his arms. "Flatterer."

It seemed he'd said the right thing for a change.

How lucky could he get in one day? First, she was still here, when he was sure she would have gone long ago. And now she was but four short steps from his bedchamber.

She clung to him as he freed one hand to fling open the door. He kicked it closed, locking his mouth with hers before her feet touched the floor. He would not give her a moment to change her mind.

He pressed her close, tasting and kissing and melding against her enchanting softness until he wasn't sure where he ended and she began.

Feverishly seeking the fastenings of her gown, his fingers felt stiff and awkward as if he'd not done this a hundred times, not that he'd had any practice since he got married.

His blood thickened at the feel of her hips pressing against his thigh and her fingers twined in his hair. And he couldn't get the damn gown undone.

Finally, the last button succumbed. He paused a moment to savor the feel of her mouth against his, to plumb the honeyed depths, to absorb the tiny welcoming purrs from the back of her throat. Her sounds of pleasure soothed his torn and bleeding heart. How long he had yearned to make her his own. He pushed the gown over her shoulders and slid it down to her waist. It dropped to the floor with a whisper.

He stood back, holding her shoulders, devouring the sight of her magnificent bosom rising in creamy swells above her shift and stays. The dull gray light from the window beyond outlined her lush form, the curve of her waist and the curve of womanly hips.

As if suddenly conscious of her nakedness, she wrapped her arms across her body, hiding, the way she hid behind shawls and ruffles. Now she would tell him to stop. His cock pulsed a protest.

"Caro, do not do that." His voice sounded hoarse.

A startled expression crossed her face, her breasts rising and falling with each ragged breath. "What?"

A broken laugh erupted from his chest. "You are spoiling my view. Let me see you."

Scarlet cheeked, she averted her face, but let her hands drop.

His heart soared at her boldness as he drank in the view of her voluptuously firm breasts veiled by the sheerest of linen chemises above her stays and the enticing dark triangle set in smooth rounded hips.

Caro took courage from the admiration in his eyes and dared to reach up and run her hand across his brow, sweeping a dark lock off his forehead. She wanted to feel him against her, warm and vibrant, the husband she would give up. Just once, she wanted him to belong to her.

She ran a tentative hand down his back, feeling the strength of his torso, hard muscles rippling under her touch, hot through the fabric of his fine lawn shirt. She yanked it free of his waistband, and he pulled it off over his head and tossed it aside with a hiss of in-drawn breath.

Then he smiled, lopsided and wicked, teasing and promising, his dark eyes alight with a fire she had kindled. It made her feel hot and shaky. She smiled back.

"Turn around," he growled. She complied. Swift fingers tore at the strings of her stays. Her heart thumped in her chest. Would he turn away like before?

As she turned with deep trepidation to face him, he captured her face in his hands and kissed her hard and deep. She poured her soul into returning the favor.

Gentle and tender, he picked her up and deposited her on his bed. She stretched out, leaving herself open, vulnerable to his gaze and his touch, flushed, but daring his scorn for this one chance to be loved. Risking ridicule.

She forced herself not to grab for the covers.

His mouth began a long slow seduction of her body, a kiss at her collarbone, light licks between her breasts, a swirling tongue around her fabric-covered nipples. They sprang to attention, demanding his notice.

Liquid fire ran through her limbs, leaving them boneless. Trembling, her hands slid down the length of his warm, silken back, caressing and gliding over muscles of steel.

He raised his dark head with a mischievous smile and ran one finger under the edge of her chemise. A cocked eyebrow asked for permission. She managed a nod of assent.

First he grabbed the tie in his teeth and tugged the bow undone with a growl.

She laughed, and he grinned. He eased the straps over each shoulder, one at a time, and down over each breast. She watched his expression as he cupped her flesh in his hands, weighing and measuring. A strained look filled his face. "Perfect," he breathed.

"Perfectly enormous," she quipped, suddenly fearful.

"Perfectly, gloriously gorgeous," he murmured, his eyes filled with awe. "A gift from the gods. Do you not understand that the sight of such beauty leaves me speechless?"

Beauty. She read truth in his beloved face.

Although it seemed to please her, Lucas thought the word far too weak to describe her lush figure. A gift from the gods indeed.

The creamy flesh of her bountiful breasts was softer than a feather pillow, smoother than the finest silk. They overflowed his palms. His cock hardened at the sight. He nuzzled into the valley between them, losing his mind at the feel of her firm, warm flesh against his cheeks. How long had he wanted to be here, reveling in the glory of a body made for love?

He nibbled and licked his way to one dark budded peak, groaning as it furled tighter at a touch from his tongue. He kissed and suckled and drew as much as he could into his mouth and there was still more to knead and to worship with his hands.

He glanced up at her mewl of pleasure, saw the liquid heat in her gaze, felt her hands grip his shoulders convulsively in a silent plea for more. He almost lost control. The desire to lose himself deep inside her, to sink into her softness, to greedily suck at her nipples until she screamed for release beat hard in his blood.

But he had waited too long for this moment. And to rush headlong to the culmination of pleasure would be the worst kind of betrayal. If he could not say the words that would lay his soul bare, he could try to show her with his mouth and his hands, his adoration of a body that had tormented his dreams and his love for a wife whose loss had left his days feeling empty and his nights cold.

They had always been friends, but this was his chance to demonstrate his desire and want and, if he dare, his deep-seated need.

He rose over her, bending to meld his mouth with hers. She parted her lips to his kiss with such sweetness it made his heart ache. He deepened the kiss with a thrust of his tongue, his joy darkened by longing.

His heart leaped as she responded to him with a need of her own, her hands clenching in his hair, dragging at his scalp. The pain tightened the pull at his loins.

He ran his palm over her distended nipples, rolled them in thumb and forefinger, heard her sigh of pleasure, and filled his hand with her ample, delicious flesh before trailing into the dip of waist beneath her ribs and over the curve of her sweetly rounded belly, beneath the sheer fabric of her chemise. He rubbed gently, caressing the soft yielding flesh before dipping one finger into the deep crevasse of her naval.

Erotic.

Lust jolted his control. He had to see all of her. "Caro," he breathed. "This has to go."

His thigh, hot, heavy, and rough with hair, lay heavy on Caro's. His sculpted chest pressed against her breasts. She buried her face in the curve of his neck. But shyness could not stop her need, and she dared to peek.

Fascinated and trembling, she watched his long elegant hands torturously slide her chemise up to her hips. He bent to trail his hot lips in its wake.

Unable to bear the slow torture any longer, she found the strength to wrest the fabric free and pull it over her head. Too long she had dreamed of this moment. She would not be denied. She made a grab for the buttons on his breeches.

With a groan mixed with a laugh, he came up on his knees and then sat on the side of the bed. "If the lady is impatient . . . it is my duty to oblige." He stripped off his boots and breeches.

The sight of his erection, dark with blood and as proud as any stallion, held her attention. Something low in Caro's belly drew in tight, painfully, pleasurably. She licked suddenly dry lips. "Lucas."

His warm hands ran over her sensitized flesh,

caressing and teasing, sending desire straight to the place between her thighs in rippling, throbbing, pleasure-filled waves.

Once more, he dipped his head and suckled at one puckered nipple while he teased the other.

A shivering sensation drove straight to her core. She gasped.

Half-lidded and sultry, his gaze rose to her face. She smiled when his triumphant glance tangled with hers.

"You are the most gorgeous woman in the world," he murmured.

And in that magical moment, she believed him.

He moved over her.

She swallowed her maidenly fear.

He spread her legs and settled between them, his dark gaze tender, his delicate touch in her inner thighs reverent. His rampant male arousal pressed against her mons.

"Please, Lucas," she begged.

He reached between them, his fingers gently probing, fluttering inside her. The sensation was so unbearably wonderful she raised her hips seeking more. She knew there was so much more.

He made circles with his thumb, and agonizing pleasure arrowed outward. She shrieked his name.

"Mmmmm," he murmured. "It feels good, doesn't it?

"Yes," she gasped.

"And this?" He moved a finger inside her and sent a wild burst of pleasure streaking through every nerve.

"Yes," she cried, not quite sure the word covered

what she felt.

Rising up on hands planted each side of her head, his dark gaze locked with hers. He teased her entrance with gentle probes of his erection. "And this?"

It felt so amazing she couldn't breathe; her limbs melted with pleasure. "Yes."

Hard and hot, he slid slowly inside. Her body stretched to accommodate his length and width. The muscles inside her clenched.

"Sweet Lord," he muttered, his breathing ragged. "Hold still. I don't want to hurt you."

He eased forward, and sweet torment built to unbridled lust. "Lucas." His name rang in her ears.

Need wracked her body. Her hips thrust up to meet him. There was a pinch of pain and then mind-numbing pleasure with each plundering thrust into her body. Nothing mattered but reaching for some far-off land. An ocean of pleasure swirled her in giddy circles.

The maelstrom crashed over her, a boiling tide of surf and spray. And then the tide subsided, leaving eddies of bliss and heat. Glorious. She surfaced to find herself in his arms, as he caressed, praised, and gently kissed her lips and the hollow of her neck. His chest rose and fell with hard breaths.

She closed her eyes and drifted.

Later, much later, eyes closed against the real world, cradled in Lucas's embrace, she lay sated. The scent of cologne and their lovemaking filled her nostrils. The warm weight of his arm draped over her ribs filled her with a sense of protection.

She wanted to stay here forever. She opened her

eyes. The daylight had faded, and she realized she must return to reality. She slid from beneath the sheet he must have pulled over her while she slept and began to dress.

Almost done, she stood up and fumbled with the fastenings down the back of her gown.

"Where are you going?"

She jumped and swung around. Lucas lay on his side, his head propped on one hand watching her.

"I'm going home. The girls will be waiting for dinner."

"I hoped you might stay and have dinner with me."

The sensual timbre in his voice tightened her breasts and started a fire in her blood. She hadn't expected desire to return so swiftly. She had thought once would be enough to satisfy her needs. Apparently, desire was fathomless. "That would be a mistake."

He recoiled. "The hell it would be."

She turned away. "I mean, it is perfectly all right because we are married. But soon we will not be. It must not happen again."

"You mean to go through with the divorce?"

Aware of his gaze on her back, she shrugged. "Why not? There is nothing to keep us together. We both have all the money we need."

"And this, today? What was that?" His voice sounded tight.

"An error of judgment," she said. Or thought she said. Her head felt so unpleasantly light.

"I see." He leaned over the side of the bed and grabbed his breeches. He turned his back to put them on. She turned hers and watched him in the mirror from beneath her lashes, the rippling muscles on his broad back, the fabric sliding up to cover his firm flanks. He was built like a racehorse, all muscle and sinew and power, while she looked like a blancmange.

It could never work.

The gentlemen in Paris hadn't seemed to mind her larger proportions, her mind whispered. Quite the opposite. And Lucas had called her gorgeous. But only in the heat of passion.

He glanced up and caught her gaze in the mirror. He shook his head.

She looked away and closed two more buttons. This strange attraction of opposites had to be lust that only appeared when they were close. Today should end it. Then why did the thought of saying good-bye leave her feeling as empty as a casket of wine after a wedding?

He hadn't once tried to change her mind, and he'd never spoken of love. She'd made her decision. She could not afford regrets.

He came up behind her, brushed her hand aside. As he closed the last fastening he skimmed his lips against her nape, a touch so fleeting and light she would have believed she imagined it without the chill of cold air in its wake.

"Come down when you are ready," he said. "I will have the carriage brought around."

Only when the door closed behind him did she permit her tears to flow in silence. One single sound, one sob, would shatter her into a thousand shards.

❄   ❄   ❄   ❄

At the rear of the Granthams' sprawling redbrick Tudor mansion, Lucas handed off Maestro's reins to a groom. Beneath the stone archway, the door to the kitchen lay open. He sucked in a breath, fighting an oppressive tightness in his chest. Had it really been more than a year since he rode beneath that arch and carried her off? What a selfish fool he'd been.

He recalled her initial disbelief and laughter when he lifted her up. Then he'd blackmailed her into a marriage. A deal with the devil. He wouldn't let it fall apart. He'd staked his claim on his woman, but this might be his only chance to win her heart and soul.

Striding through the kitchen and into the baronial hall, he avoided a pair of footmen lugging a table across the floor. Neither bright banners nor medieval tapestries made the place anything less of a mausoleum—his mausoleum, if things didn't work out. At the far end, beneath the oriole, James waved a baton while the boys rehearsed their music. Lucas hoped to God they'd get a chance to play.

A small figure leaped up from his seat and hurtled at Lucas. Lucas grabbed a pair of bony shoulders before the lad set him on his arse. "Whoa, young Jake."

At least he'd won these fellows' trust. Satisfaction tinged with sadness caught him off guard. He tousled the lad's shock of blond hair. "Back you go. You need to practice."

James strolled over to collect his pupil.

Jake dodged him. "Is your missus here, then?"

Lucas's moment of pleasure died. He clamped his

jaw and shook his head. "Later," he bit out. Maybe.

The boy winced, and Lucas cursed himself. He softened his tone. "Go and rehearse, lad. You want to be perfect, don't you?"

On the dais, Fred lifted a hand in greeting, before fixing his surly gaze on Jake. "Bloody well get over here, you young varmint." Fred looked quite the gentleman in his new suit. If he learned to control what came out of his mouth, he'd go a long way.

With a grin, Jake shot back to his companions.

Lucas glanced into James's gentle brown eyes. "Are they ready?"

"They were a bit unruly on the journey. Excited, you know," James said, his smile rueful. "Two days cramped up in a coach and a night at an inn has been an interesting experience."

The boys had the kind of high spirits Lucas's father used to hate. Tension gripped his shoulders, and he rubbed the back of his neck. "I'm sure they will be fine."

"And Lady Foxhaven?"

Lucas had unburdened some of his anxiety to the calm and wise James before he came north. "I'm not sure. I've had to change my plan. If this fails, I am scuppered."

James glanced around the room, which was filling with furniture and flowers. "It'll be a mite embarrassing if she doesna'—"

"Embarrassment is the least of my concerns. Have you see Lady Audley?"

"Aye. She were here earlier. Verra complimentary about the boys' playing, she was."

Something for which to be grateful.

❀ ❀ ❀ ❀

Alex heaved her third sigh in a row. Caro jabbed her needle into her thumb. "Ouch! For goodness sake, Alex, if you are bored, go help Lizzie put Jacqueline and Lucy to bed."

Alex lifted her head from the paper flower picture she was creating. "I still don't see why we couldn't go to the Granthams' musical evening tonight."

Alex seemed determined to be annoying. "Because I said not." Caro pulled out the lazy daisy stitch. It had turned into a knot.

"My word," Miss Salter said from the other side of the hearth, "it is past eight o'clock. It is time you were in bed, Miss Alex." She folded her tapestry and tucked it into the workbasket beside her chair.

A knock echoed through the house. Alex leaned forward to peer out of the window. "There's a horse at the front door." She put a hand over her mouth and dashed out of the room and up the stairs.

"Now what has got into her?" Caro said. She got up to look out of the window.

The knock came again, louder and sharper. The heavy tread of their footman trundled up the passage. Caro pulled back the drapery.

Good heavens. Whoever it was had brought his horse up the front path. Maestro. Her stomach pitched. Then the visitor must be Lucas. She ignored her pounding pulse. After yesterday, surely there was nothing more to say. Or was there?

"Lord Foxhaven," the footman announced.

Lucas, his black greatcoat buttoned to his chin, filled the doorway. He smiled calmly enough, but deep in his eyes swirled a dark glint of excitement. "Good evening, ladies."

Caro raised a brow and moved away from the window. "What an unexpected pleasure, my lord."

He bowed. "The pleasure is all mine."

Miss Salter got to her feet and edged toward the door. She didn't look terribly surprised. Caro gestured for her to stay. "I am afraid we are not prepared for visitors this evening. You find us en famille."

"I am hardly a visitor, Caro," he said, a faint edge of bitterness in his voice. "It is my house."

Her heartbeat quickened. The wretch. She would not engage in a duel of words. "This is not the hour for calls."

His gaze flicked to Miss Salter.

"I will just see if the girls are all right," she said and scooted past him and out of the door.

Traitor, Caro thought.

A lopsided grin lit Lucas's face. Suddenly, he seemed extraordinarily smug about Miss Salter's retreat. Suspicion unfurled in Caro's mind along with a strange sensation in her belly, anxiety mixed with a flutter of anticipation, the kind she'd felt in his arms and in his bed.

"Why are you here?" she said, aiming for calm and failing.

He cocked a brow. "Why aren't you at the Granthams'?"

"I declined the invitation."

A couple of thumps and a shriek came from above their heads. The children were playing games again, or fighting.

He took a step closer. "I came to change your mind."

"What?" Her stomach tumbled over. Fool. He meant

the party. "Do you want a worse scandal when the news of our divorce becomes common knowledge? We cannot impose on people we have known all our lives."

"Do you care so much about what other people think?"

"I care about my sisters and their reputations."

"If you really cared about them, you'd do everything in your power to avoid the scandal of a divorce." His tone softened. "You still have a choice."

Hadn't she done her best to make their marriage work in London, only to be rejected for his other affairs? The fact that his other affairs had been a music school made it easier to bear, but only a little. He had pushed her away at every opportunity—especially when their mutual lust flared out of control. Yesterday was hers to treasure.

She folded her arms across her chest. "I have made my choice."

"I claim the right of a husband to try to change your mind, not for your sisters' sake, but for yours and for mine."

She stared at him, at his face, waiting for the charming smile to cajole her, his hot glance to fire her blood. She cloaked herself in chilly resentment. Not this time.

He strode to face her and then catching her beneath her knees and around her shoulders, he swept her up into his arms. She gasped. "What are you doing?"

"What I should have done the first time."

He stormed into the hallway where Lizzie stood holding the front door open, Caro's cloak in her hand. "It's a wee bit nippy tonight." She threw the cloak over her.

"Lizzie!" Caro squeaked.

Before she could say more, Lucas pushed out of the door. "Hold tight, Caro," he warned with a frowning glance. He grabbed Maestro's reins and lifted his foot to the stirrup. "If I have to tie you up, you will come with me."

How like Lucas. A laugh bubbled in her chest despite her resolve. She tamped it down, before he sensed his advantage. "You are mad. Where are we going?"

He heaved them both into the saddle and settled her across his lap, pulling her cloak around her, tucking it between them.

"You'll see." He wheeled the horse around and out into the lane. They galloped across the common and over the hill. Maestro's hooves beat out a steady rhythm, his breath harsh in the still night air. They were headed for the Granthams'.

She bit her lip. It would be so easy to give in. If only he loved her.

Short of jumping off the horse and breaking her neck, there was little to be done until they reached their destination. She relaxed into his strong one-handed embrace, feeling the warmth of his chest against her back, inhaling sandalwood cologne and crisp night air. The wind whipped her hair in her face and his. She relaxed. If there was anything she could trust, it was his horsemanship.

It was no surprise when they rode up the curved beech-lined avenue to Grantham Hall. Flambeaux lit the courtyard, and lackeys stood at the ready, but no carriages lined the gravel drive.

"Where is everyone?" she asked.

"Perhaps they all declined," Lucas muttered. He sounded odd, uncertain, yet still full of repressed tension. The flickering torches cast light over his lean face, his eyes hidden in shadow. He was truly a darkly handsome man.

And she was still a dumpling. She didn't care, she realized. He had said she was gorgeous in his eyes. He never lied.

The door flew open as if they were expected. Tigs, looking smart in brand new livery, waved them in with a grin that seemed to reach his ears. Lucas kneed his mount forward.

The horrible truth hit her. "No, Lucas. Not inside. Not again."

Maestro shifted beneath them, his great hindquarters bunching, and then they leaped the front steps and clattered into the empty hall. The guests had indeed not yet arrived. Caro breathed a sigh of relief. Torches lit the walls, and candles and flowers carpeted the tables. Rows of chairs faced the dais, where a group of musicians practiced a rousing tune. Lady Audley floated toward them.

Tisha? Caro glanced up at Lucas; his mouth had flattened to a thin line, and his eyes had darkened to onyx. His expression seemed grim.

"Enough of this, Lucas," Caro said. "You will only anger Lord Grantham again."

"If that was my only problem, I'd be a happy man," Lucas said, his voice a low growl in her ear. He brought Maestro to a prancing halt.

Tisha's eyes twinkled with mirth. She seemed hard put not to laugh. Heat flared in Caro's cheeks. He was making a fool of her. He'd cooked up some kind of scheme with Tisha, just the way he had with the Grantham boys when they were children. "I want to go home."

"Lord Foxhaven," Tisha said, "there are perfectly good stables at the back of the house."

"I need to borrow a bedroom," Lucas said.

Caro had played this scene before and didn't like it any more now than she had then. She opened her mouth to protest.

"This way," Tisha said. She giggled and raced up the stairs ahead of them.

The world had gone completely mad. Caro's mind whirled around the possibility that she was dreaming. She clung to the only solid thing available: Lucas. Her hands clutched his lean waist. She stared at his strong throat and a jaw already shadowed with stubble. An almost irresistible urge to kiss that hard jaw quickened her pulse and tightened a throat aching with tears.

Yesterday's taste of the pleasure had been a fatal mistake, a breach of her carefully constructed resistance to his blatant allure.

Tisha flung open the door of the chamber where they had made their ridiculous agreement more than a year ago.

Lucas lowered Caro from Maestro's back, capturing her wrist the moment he dismounted. Did he think she would run away? This time, she would call his bluff.

"If you will excuse me," Tisha said. "I have a wedding to plan?" With a face as red as a peony, Tisha grabbed Maestro's bridle and trotted him down the hall.

Caro stared after her. "A wedding? I thought it was a musicale?"

"We'll discuss it inside," Lucas said and gestured for her to enter. The room seemed brighter, cleaner, less shabby—almost as though they were expected. He kicked the door shut with his heel and let Caro's wrist drop.

"Now," he said in an ominous voice.

She swung around to face him, putting distance between them. "What is this all about?"

His body lacked its usual grace, wide shoulders taut, back stiff, jaw hard. "I brought you here so we could start anew."

They were back to their agreement. She shook her head. "It won't work." She loved him far too much to be a wife in name only.

He planted himself in front of her and gripped her shoulders painfully. She gasped. His dark eyes blazed. "Would it make any difference if I told you I love you, that I want to spend the rest of my life trying to convince you to love me?"

The words came at her with such fury that for a moment, she didn't believe her hearing. "You love me?" She couldn't help the disbelief she heard in her voice.

"After yesterday, can you doubt it?"

She wrapped her arms around her waist. "Why are you saying this now?"

He fell to one knee, pulled her hand free, and pressed his lips to each finger, one at a time. Warmth trickled into her stomach; her inner muscles tightened and pulsed.

Transfixed by his dark serious gaze, she felt her

heart beat a slow tattoo of cautious joy, while her mind warned her to take care.

"Caro, my love. I love your courage and your loyalty to your family, and to me, when I never deserved it, but most of all I love you. I'm just sorry it took me so long to dare to say the words."

She opened her mouth to deny the possibility.

"Let me finish. Please."

She nodded.

"I tied myself in knots seeking my father's love, gave up my music, and followed the path he chose for me, and yet in the end, it just wasn't good enough. I wasn't good enough. I swore I would never let anyone control me like that again. My desire to please you scared me as much as your dissatisfaction with what I had let myself become." He uttered a little laugh. "Not that I am nearly as bad as I am purported to be."

"I know," she whispered. "You are good and kind. And you are just doing this to save me from scandal."

"Damn it, Caro. Can't you see? I am doing this for me . . . for us. I cannot live without you, and I will not let you leave me if I have to lock you in this room forever." He grinned. "Naked, if need be."

A shimmer of visceral pleasure pulsed low in her abdomen at the naughty image.

He sighed. "No, I won't do that. But I won't let you go, until I am absolutely sure you could never return my love. After yesterday, I won't believe you feel nothing at all. But I won't force you."

Her heart felt so light, she thought she might float away if he were not holding her fast to the ground. "You never forced me." Her words caught on a laugh. "I knew you wouldn't ruin me. I took advantage of your need for money. I thought I could change you back into the boy I remembered."

His smile died. "He's gone."

"Not entirely. He's grown up and knows pain and hurt, but he's still there, rescuing maidens in distress. But you deserve someone far more beautiful than me, someone elegant and worldly."

"There you go again, belittling yourself. Don't you realize how lovely you are to me? Didn't you see how those damn Frenchmen couldn't take their eyes from you because they thought you were unmarried? You drove me mad with jealousy. It must be your choice this time, but believe me when I say I love you. Marry me."

She blinked. "I thought we were married?"

His eyes danced. "I mean a proper marriage, not a secret agreement and a drunken blacksmith in Gretna Green. A wedding with our family and friends around us. A marriage built on trust and respect and love. There's a special license in my pocket and a vicar downstairs."

Her mouth dropped open. She closed it with a snap. "The party?"

"It's our wedding, Caro. Yours and mine. I even brought my own musicians from London."

"Your orphans?"

He nodded. "Yes. I'm afraid you are marrying into a ready-made family. They live at the house you thought I purchased for my mistress. I didn't want anyone to know what I was doing in case it didn't work."

"I know. Your father told me."

He smiled up at her, love and dread shining in his eyes. "Please, Caro, say yes. My knee will never be the same again if I don't get up soon."

She gazed into his wonderful, handsome face and laughed. "After climbing up the outside of a tower and then snatching me from a church, surely you can stand a few moments of pain."

"Not this kind. You know I hate to wait." Anxiety swirled with the laughter in his voice.

She suddenly felt shy. "Yes, Lucas, I would like that very much."

He leaped to his feet, hauled her into his arms, and kissed her soundly and deeply. The world spun away. There was only her and him.

A knock sounded at the door. Caro jumped.

"Come in," Lucas called.

Alex and Lucy and Jacqueline poured in, followed by Lizzie carrying a gown and Miss Salter with a bouquet and a floral headdress.

"Out you go, your lordship," Lizzie said. "Lady Audley said I have ten minutes to prepare my lady, and I need every single one."

"Eight minutes," Lucas said, with a laugh. "If she is not down there in eight minutes, Maestro and I will be back to carry her off."

Eight minutes later, Lucas watched his bride walk down the stone stairs. The stars in her glorious amber eyes outshone the diamonds at her throat.

He would make damn sure he was worthy of the love shining in her face. He poured his heart into his gaze and smiled his promise.

No more regrets.

ACKNOWLEDGMENTS

I would like to thank my agent, Scott Eagan, for his belief in my work and my editor, Deb Werksman, for her suggestions and effort in making the book the best it could be. I also want to thank my wonderful critique partners, Molly, Mary, Mareen, Sinead, Susan, and Teresa, for their advice, encouragement, and perseverance.

ABOUT THE AUTHOR

Born and educated in England, Michèle Ann Young loved history growing up, and as a voracious reader of historical novels, she became fascinated with the Regency era. With all the glamour and glitz of high society, the age is modern enough to be familiar some two hundred years later. She loves bringing the time period to life with her stories of women facing the same issues that women face today.

From England she moved to Canada, where she now lives and writes in Richmond Hill, Ontario, with her husband and two beautiful daughters and their adopted Maltese terrier, Teaser. Each summer, Michèle returns to England to visit family and to research her next novel.

Michèle loves to hear from readers. Visit her at her website at http://www.micheleannyoung.com, or drop by her Regency Ramble blog at http://www.micheleannyoung.blogspot.com, where, in addition to the odd bit of writing gossip, she shares the sights and sounds of Regency England from her annual travels.

www.micheleyoung.sourcebooksromance.com